Praise for *Averted Vision*

"Ever been in a tornado? McPherson describes what it's like with the precision of one who's been there! Her descriptions throughout are so good, you can smell the scenery through the pages. This is a thrill ride for sure."

"I loved it"

"Exciting book, hard to put down. Only downside, I didn't get anything else done once I picked it up."

"An absolute page turner"

"So vividly written-I feel like I know Cassie and Dale and the other characters"

"The best book I've read in ages"

"Complete with lakes, cabins, tornadoes and a body thrown into the mix, there is always a twist or turn to navigate."

"The author has a wonderful sense of humor."

"Great book. Highly recommend."

Also By Danith McPherson

AVERTED VISION

A CASSIE WINDOM MYSTERY

DANITH MCPHERSON

Wayward Serpent

This is a work of fiction. Names, characters, places, events, and dialogue are either the products of the author's imagination or used in a fictitious manner. Any resemblance to actual people, living or dead, or to actual places, events or dialogue is purely coincidental.

AVERTED VISION

Printed in the United States of America

Wayward Serpent first edition, March 2022

ISBN 978-1-950506-12-5 (print paperback)

ISBN 978-1-950506-13-2 (ebook)

Library of Congress Control Number: 2022932748

Cover design by MiblArt

Photo Credit for Ring Nebula behind title: Robert Gendler

Published by Wayward Serpent, Farwell

Up to no good but means well

For Mrs. Page, the first librarian in my life

(Yes, that's her real name.)

Chapter One

Cassie Windom had forgotten the feral panic that wrenches your gut when the sky turns puke green and you hear wind rushing toward you like a demon. Knowing she was working in the wrong order, she stashed her three most important possessions in the basement then grabbed the emergency items that should have been her first priorities.

Five feet ten, she ducked under the stairs into the wedge-shaped cubby that smelled of unfinished wood. Feeling folded up like origami, she sat on a plastic bin filled with unopened letters. This was not how she'd planned on spending a sticky Tuesday afternoon in July. Her legs straddled the eight-inch Schmidt-Cassegrain telescope, resting on a rug between her feet like a fat rocket. There wasn't room for the tripod. With so little warning, she probably couldn't have wrestled the heavy, awkward thing down the stairs in time to save it anyway.

An angry wind roared and tossed who-knew-what at the cedar siding. Debris pelted the high, slit windows, sounding like chattering teeth. She wanted to cover her ears, but she needed to hear the news bulletins on the battery-powered radio.

"*. . . We have an unconfirmed tornado sighting in central Granite County . . .*"

The announcer seemed polished and trustworthy but more than a little stressed.

"*. . . Take cover on the lowest level of the building . . .*"

She tried texting her sisters Holly, Ashley and Kayla to remind them how much fun it was to live in Minnesota. *Damn.* Cell service was nil.

The bare bulbs mounted in the rough ceiling of the open basement winked twice then were gone, leaving an unsettling, false dusk. The electricity wasn't likely to snap back on soon. A heavy-duty flashlight squatted like a yellow frog on the concrete floor beside the bin, but she didn't switch it on. The buttery beacon would only provide thin psychological comfort. Better save the batteries.

In contrast to the calamity outside, the basement air hung still. Her new puppy Jupiter leaned, fluffy-warm and trembling, against her leg. Brindle fur marbled red and black, he would be a handsome, intimidating creature someday. It seemed fitting to name him after the streaked and swirling giant planet with the Great Red Spot, even if at the moment he was an uncoordinated, floppy-eared fuzz ball.

Sweat clung to her, despite her being dressed for the season in a knit shirt over a comfy sports bra, khaki shorts and sandals. She pushed short bangs off her forehead. The deep brown, almost black strands immediately flopped back against her moist skin. The retro, flapper-style bob had proved to be a mistake. Too childish for a self-employed twenty-eight-year-old who needed to project a professional image, it constantly reminded her she'd made too many changes in her life too quickly. She gazed longingly at the electric fan on the shelving across the room. It stared back at her with a sad, round face, as if understanding its uselessness.

The beast roared and pounded on the house. Every muscle in her body clenched. "At least it's not an earthquake," she chanted to herself like a mantra. "At least it's not an earthquake."

Back in Los Angeles the volume of things she would have felt compelled to save wouldn't have fit into the tiny space under the stairs. Everything had seemed equally important and irreplaceable then. Digital files on various storage devices. Sketches and mockups and drawings and paintings for her current and past projects at the advertising agency. Books she was always borrowing from Vicky. A snow globe from the weekend she and Chad spent in San Francisco. The raincoat with sleeves that actually reached the wrists of her long arms, and she would never find another that fit her as well again.

But a bare nook in the basement—if you had one, which you didn't because it was California—couldn't save you from shifting tectonic plates anyway. Nothing could.

And "natural" wasn't the only kind of disaster in the world.

When the unbearable happened, blasting a fissure through Cassie's emotional foundation, it hadn't been a shaking of the earth but a horrifically unnatural act. She suddenly understood there were degrees of irreplaceableness. And so began her retrograde back home, swapping the congested, somewhat smoggy city for a rented cabin on the east shore of a Minnesota lake.

Letting go of her former life wasn't as simple as it had seemed from the distance of developing a plan. Escape was not as easy as changing geography. Surprisingly, she didn't miss Chad at all. Crushingly, she missed Vicky every day.

The radio announcer's voice grew more intense. He really was having a bad day.

". . . The National Weather Service has confirmed a tornado on the ground southwest of Glacier Falls moving in a northeasterly direction. Repeat, a tornado is on the ground in the Glacier Falls area. If you are in that vicinity, take cover immediately . . ."

The wind whooshed like the rush of an oncoming train, the tell-tale sound of an approaching twister.

It wasn't her first tornado. As a child, she'd resented having to rush for cover when she'd really wanted to stand out in the yard and watch clouds roil like crazy gray animals tumbling across the sky. Reality had chipped away her fearlessness.

At least it's not an earthquake.

The monster bellowed and ranted. Engulfing the cabin, it clawed the shingles and threatened to lift the structure from its foundation.

Cassie jumped at a deafening crack. Creaking, like the swing of a giant rusty gate, came from above. Something heavy crashed against the roof. The walls shuddered and groaned with the impact. Sawdust rained down on her from the rough boards of the stair's skeleton. She imagined a gaping hole in the roof with branches sticking through the ceiling into her bedroom.

Jupiter yipped and snuggled tightly against her, eyes wide in his dark face. The moist basement air weighed heavy and oppressively calm. She lifted the whimpering Akita into her lap. Her life was down to three things: a telescope; a puppy; and a box of fat envelopes, holding unread pages.

The cacophony rumbled away. An odd quiet reigned, as if a pause button had placed the world in stasis. Cassie stretched her legs and climbed out of the cubby. The kitchen still formed a solid ceiling over the basement. She set Jupiter on the concrete floor and went upstairs, not knowing what she would find.

Chapter Two

T here's always a friend waiting at SunnieChat!

Cass I get a weird message when I try to call. I hope this text gets delivered. Are you okay? Any damage to the cabin? Have the roof examined for missing shingles. If there still is a roof. Do you have the name of the insurance company? Text back asap

What happened? You know I don't get much US news here. Send pics

Cass just checking if a house has fallen on my sister. In case I'm in line to inherit shoes

Chapter Three

I t was your usual alien-shark invasion flick. The aliens and the sharks started out curious and semi-hostile toward one another. Then they got zapped by a red beam from a secret government weapon and did a merge thing. Arms and fins and teeth—lots of teeth—stuck out at odd angles from new creatures with understandably pissed off attitudes.

Dale Steinhaus sprawled on the couch, sort of watching and sort of texting his best friend Richie. He'd seen this one before and plenty of others like it, but he still groaned when his dad made him switch to a channel out of Minneapolis. That's what sixteen-year-olds did, pushed back against parental control and all that. Rebel without a clue. Some stereotypes were worth perpetuating.

A crawl across the bottom of the boring talk show listed severe weather warnings and watches. Threat of lightning, hail, tornado. The usual. Dale knew all of that. It was why he and his dad were in the house instead of outside doing chores.

The familiar shape of Minnesota was scrunched into a corner of the screen. A cluster of west-central counties, including Granite, flashed yellow. For the dummies who couldn't find themselves on the map, the names of towns in the danger zone paraded under it.

Of course, you could always just look out a window. The sky was frosted with more sickly grays than you'd think could exist. Clouds bumped and fought and merged into deformed monsters, like conjoined aliens and sharks. Something nasty was coming. It was only a matter of how soon.

The weather sure had his dad excited. Irv Steinhaus kept an eye on the flashing alerts while he paced and shouted into his phone. "Sherman," he said on the side to his son, "grab my stuff."

"Yeah, I know." Dale went to the closet and pulled his dad's Sparks jacket—official attire of the Glacier Falls all-volunteer fire department—off a hanger. He snatched a lumpy backpack from the floor. Unofficial but useful, it held packages of sugary and salty snacks. He grabbed a couple of cans of pop from the fridge, gave them a good shake and tossed them onto the Doritos. A small revenge for his dad calling him by his first name. He carried the bundles to the living room and shoved them at his father.

They were close to evenly matched since Dale's last growth spurt. Both were six-foot-three, broad-shouldered, and lean from farm work. Irv still seemed shocked his son could look him square in the eye. Juggling phone, jacket and backpack, the big man rushed out, like a little kid heading for his own birthday party.

Dale watched the dusty GMC Sierra pickup tear down the driveway. Tornado hunting made his dad happy.

Dale's mom was at her job at the drugstore in town, so he was on his own. He shouldn't leave the house. He shouldn't. He knew that. He really did. But he suddenly had a big chunk of time all to himself. He couldn't pass up a chance to read a chapter or two of *Kidnapped* undisturbed. The book was stashed in his not-so-secret hiding place in the deer stand on Red Hawk Hill. A kids' book really, but he'd found it at a garage sale for a dime and thought it looked pirate-y and all that.

He made sure the barn and sheds were closed tight. Then he grabbed a beer and drove the four-wheeled, all-terrain vehicle along the edge of the field, across the paved county road, and onto the rutted trail his dad and Uncle Hugh had cleared through buckthorn and sumac. He stopped where his route crossed another swath barely wide enough for a car.

Maybe once it had been a run for deer, fox and other critters. A hundred years ago maybe, someone had decided to make it a dirt strip winding from the county pavement to the lake. Weeds and grasses that mistakenly thought this would be a good place to grow were flattened or torn short, a sure sign someone was driving through here pretty regular.

Dale didn't have time right now to be angry about the intrusion. He continued on to where the trail ended at the base of Red Hawk. He cut the motor and swung off the ATV.

No thunder and lightning, no rain, no hail broke overhead as he climbed the slope on foot. Still, Dale swore at himself for being stupid. The air was heavier now, harder to pull into his lungs. The sky mutated from grays to an up-chuck green, turning the afternoon dark enough to be sunset.

Shit is coming down for sure.

At the top of the hill the wooden deer stand towered twelve feet off the ground. Dale's dad and Uncle Hugh built it when they were boys. It was only used for hunting a couple of weekends a year. The rest of the time it was Dale's elevated man cave. Repairs had been passed down to the next generation and were his responsibility now.

He hauled himself up the ladder, which only wobbled a little, and climbed through what served as a doorway in the south side. The space was mostly bare. Large rectangular openings in the other walls gave views to three compass points.

This time of year foliage obstructed the framed scenes. In

the fall, wind whisked away the oak and birch leaves, opening up the landscape. Dale had seen a lot of deer from here. He'd shot a few to keep the freezer stocked with venison, but mostly he just liked to watch them move silently among the trees.

Essentials were stashed in an old metal and foam cooler with a hard-turning latch. Raccoons hadn't managed to break into it yet. They would eventually. From its depths he pulled out *Kidnapped,* his favorite Twins cap, and the Leupold binoculars. He closed the lid, settled onto it and snapped open the beer. Might as well go through the ritual since he was here. Seemed the primitive part of his brain was in control anyway.

To the southwest, the Glacier Falls water tower looked like it belonged beside a toy train. Due west through the breaks in the branches, the reflection of a swirling pea-soup sky slimed the surface of Beauty Lake. As far as he could tell, no vehicles marred the shoreline.

The Swenson house sat north across the ravine. The cream-colored-stone McMansion, almost a castle, was barely visible through a thick line of pine trees. No matter how he shifted—left, right, up, down—he couldn't get a clear view past the dense branches and perpetual needles. He could only tell that lights were on in some of the rooms angled toward him.

He'd been in love with Crystal Swenson since forever, even though he knew it was hopeless. His family had a farm that kept dragging them deeper and deeper into a debt bog, while the Swensons were rich by local standards. Crystal's dad Raymond was a pharmacist at the drugstore where Dale's mom worked as a lowly cashier.

Crystal's mother Debbie acted like she came from old money, but she was only a generation away from tilling fields. The family used to own acres of wheat and soy beans in the southern part of the state. Debbie's dad and aunts and uncles turned the land into a pricey housing development just as the local hospital expanded and a Target opened. The family's sudden fortune allowed Debbie to attend a fancy college and competed in beauty pageants. She'd been crowned a bunch of things. Dale didn't know what the titles were. The state loved to promote the glories of winter through gorgeous women.

Princess Frost Bite. Queen Wind Chill. Miss Minnesota Dead Car Battery.

Crystal inherited all those beautiful genes. And she was brainy smart, destined for more than Glacier Falls. Which Dale wasn't.

Yeah, it was more than hopeless.

Dale sipped at the rapidly warming beer, wishing the evergreens would suddenly disappear so he could see into Crystal's world. There was weird stuff going on there. Stuff that had him wondering what the crap was happening in the Kingdom of Swenson. Mostly he worried about Crystal's safety. Was that really why he'd iced common sense, ignored flashing banners along the bottom of the TV screen, and climbed about the tenth highest hill in the county?

Shit. Yeah.

The too calm air made Dale's skin itch. He rubbed the sweating beer can against his t-shirt, wiping away beads of condensation. A whoosh started from far away. He froze and listened as a huge winged monster took flight.

Fuck.

A warning wail blared from the distant water tower. Dale slammed his beer onto the rough floor. He stowed the binoculars in the cooler, and stuffed the book into his back pocket.

The deer stand moaned as the wind arrived, pressing against it with a fury. It rushed through the wide openings, tugging at Dale's shirt and cap. The structure creaked and leaned. Boards tilted under his feet. He staggered to regain balance. The cooler slid past. He grabbed for the Budweiser. It tipped away from him and rolled after the container, leaving a wet trail.

Through the skewed windows, branches flatten into horizontal lines. Leaves and twigs ripped free, as if invisible fingers combed the oaks bare. Birch trunks snapped, splitting like melons as they soared away.

Dale dropped to his knees on the quaking floor. Through the filter of pine needles, he saw lights blink out at the sandstone castle as electricity failed. Above the water tower a giant, spinning beast plunged from the sky. Ribbons of gray and black twisted about it like tentacles. It howled triumphantly and whirled in a frenzy straight toward Dale.

You brain-dead screw-up. Thinking you're too smart to get yourself into serious shit then ending up there anyway.

If the storm didn't kill him, his dad would for taking the ATV out in this.

The stand shuddered and swayed. Dale scrambled to the ladder. Useless, it rattled completely loose on one side. He eased himself over the edge and hung from the lip of the floor. The ferocious wind pushed him sideways, negating the advantage of his tall frame. The Twins cap ripped from his head. He dropped, smacking his side against the ground.

He couldn't push himself up against the force. He crawled through flattened grass. Too slow. Desperate for shelter, he rolled across the carpet of long blades into the trees. A bad place to be. He knew that. But there wasn't a good place.

He smacked against a gnarled root arching out of the ground at the base of a scrub oak. With stubby fingernails, he clawed soil from under it, scraping a hole to the other side. He shoved his arm through the gap, hooking it under the root, and clutched his wrist with his other hand. Stinging debris forced his eyes shut. His heart tried to pound out of his chest.

A tornado can do crazy things. It might skip right over him. It might. More likely it would rip him from the earth, sending him flying, tree and all.

Crystal!

How could he have forgotten her, even for a moment. The

cream-colored castle, its suburban glory so out of place in the backwoods setting, begged to be smashed flat.

Dale wanted to leap across the ravine to save her, but he wasn't sure he could save himself. He sent her a desperate mental message.

Get your angel ass into the basement.

Chapter Four

The sky boiled with overlapping shades of ash. Cassie ventured out to investigate the aftermath of the storm, Jupiter trotting at her heels. The air smelled surprisingly fresh. Leaves, twigs and large branches shed by battered, mutilated trees lay everywhere. In the back toward the road a gigantic limb had split from the ancient oak that dominated the yard. It now sprawled across the roof like a gnarled snake. Cassie couldn't tell how much damage it had done.

How was she going to tell her cousin Laurel, who was handling the rental property for Aunt Renee?

Sorry, Laur, I broke the cabin.

Fortunately, Laurel was the easiest of her cousins to deal with, much more of a fixer than Rob, Cliff or Katie. At least the roof appeared to be holding up against the weight.

She walked around to the front where the lawn sloped down to a narrow ribbon of sand at the water line. The tornado had torn across the lake from southwest to northeast. A tan strip cut through the metal-blue water, showing where the twister had sucked away weeds and churned up silt from the lakebed.

A foreign rowboat had been lifted up the hill to the yard.

The distorted hull sat embedded in what was left of her aunt's redwood picnic table, which hadn't budged an inch from its original spot.

The empty boat troubled Cassie. Had a person been out in the little craft when the storm hit? That was ridiculous. Except she knew some fisherman weren't exactly sane. When she was young, she'd watched an angler hunched against a drenching rain with his line in the water. In an aluminum skiff. With lightning cracking the sky. Crazy comes in a lot of flavors.

The boat's owner might be in the water clinging to an oar. She felt compelled to check. Binoculars wouldn't give her the magnification she needed. She hauled the tripod from the detached garage then brought her telescope up from the basement and mounted it in the dovetail grooves. Usually she restricted her viewing to stellar displays. The scope wasn't designed for earth-bound observing, but she could make do.

Where to begin her search? Beauty Lake was on the small side by Minnesota standards, but that was still a lot of water. Dense woods bordered it to Cassie's immediate left. It scalloped into a bay that curved around the populated southern rim. Greenery blocked some of the view in that direction. To her right, the lake ran for a few hundred feet then bowed out of sight behind a point of land. When it became visible again, the waterline was obscured by waving reeds that increased in thickness along the northern end.

The largest open expanse in her view was directly across the lake to the west. Small cottages hugged the shore. A few larger places sat back in the trees. New bare patches in the wooded land looked as if a giant had dropped his bowling ball —several times—smashing the greenery.

Cassie needed something more specific than open water as a starting point. She aimed at the opposite shore, using the finder. A simple monocular fixed to the telescope, it was used to zero in on an object. It had a lower magnification and a wider field of view than the scope. Inexpensive and compact, it produced an upside down and reversed image. She picked out a jumble of chrome patched with blue and centered it in the finder's cross hairs. Then she looked through the telescope's eyepiece. A crumpled boat lift and canopy magically appeared in the circular frame.

The telescope's increased magnification showed greater detail than the little finder could manage, but it was not a true image. The fat Schmidt-Cassegrain design was all about mirrors. She'd purchased it "as is" from the widow of the original owner. Unlike the finder, it corrected the image so it was right-side up, but it didn't alter the horizontal flip. She was still training herself to mentally make the adjustment. The left-right reversal added a challenge to terrestrial gazing but made no difference when looking at the spiral galaxy Andromeda. She didn't feel the need to make the investment in a clever gizmo that reversed the reversal.

The telescope's altered view aside, the scene across the lake was surreal. The twisted metal she'd used as her starting point was only one of many abstract sculptures. She did a slow scan. Beams wrapped with tattered canvases tilted at odd angles. The speedboats and jet skis they usually cradled were trapped in the scaffolding or scattered across the beach like toys. A pontoon sat nestled against the deck of a log cabin like a marooned whale, still moored to a dock that was now lodged in the picture window.

A roof was gone. Make that two roofs. The walls stood like open boxes. These were older places close to the shoreline. They'd been constructed before building codes required a deeper setback from the water. They had no basements and provided little shelter from the fury of a tornado.

Cassie took several deep breaths. She had a below-ground shelter while those people had only main-floor bathrooms to huddle in. Were they now trapped under wreckage too heavy to push aside? She checked around the devastation. Figures in bright summer colors moved about. They seemed to be okay and able to help others.

Relieved, she lifted her head from the eyepiece. With the naked eye, she spotted pockets of floating debris. She leaned down to the telescope and trained it on a patch, hoping she would not find the fool who'd been out in the smashed rowboat.

A deflated red air mattress wrinkled and stretched in the waves. She scanned a fully inflated yellow air mattress. Then she focused on a dark blob of roundness and bumps that might be a partially inflated olive-green raft. Several smaller things she couldn't identify drifted beside it. A multi-colored beach ball rolling through her field of vision, light as a bubble.

She sympathized with whoever had lost their playthings. She'd spent many summers here relaxing and splashing about on one kind of floaty or another. She especially loved their cheerful summer colors, like the brightly dressed people across the lake. Scarlets, sky blues, vivid yellows, and neon greens.

Never drab, depressing olive.

Hmm. She swung back to the bumpy blob. The mottled dark green mass splotched with brown, tan and bleached accents seemed more cloth than vinyl toy. The dull colors clung together, undulating like a single creature rather than clumps of dredged up seaweed. The pattern seemed familiar, like the couch of someone with really bad taste. It reminded Cassie of the camouflage hunters and little boys were fond of wearing.

Awkwardly, she tracked its movement by hand. The tripod had a motor for making adjustments, but the heavy battery was still in the garage. She didn't want to take the time to get it and hook it up. She fiddled with the focus. The blob resolved itself into a central trunk and appendages, like arms and legs. She could scarcely accept what she saw.

A body marred the surface of Beauty Lake. Was it floating

face up? Was she seeing exposed skin, chalk white in the silvery ripples?

Cassie was a good swimmer but out of shape. People drowned trying to save others. The danger of attempting a rescue without a flotation aid had been drummed into her. She had no life vest to strap on, no foam cushion, no boogie board. Her mind riffled through other options. The closest boat was the twisted one in the front yard. Her uncle's was in storage at the farm. Damn. She couldn't do it herself. She needed help.

She raced into the house, leaving the door open to flies and mosquitoes. She snatched her cell from the kitchen counter. It still declared No Service. The tiny words seemed too small to convey such an enormously important message.

She grabbed the wall phone. No dial tone. Listening to the silence, she continued to clutch the plastic handset, unable to put it down. The repetitive pattern of birds and flowers surrounding the pine cabinets was almost hypnotic. She made a mental note to speak to Laurel about new wallpaper. Or maybe paint. Definitely paint. She'd create a mural.

She was doing it again. When stressed, her brain ran a bulldozer marathon through anything in its path. It became incapable of sorting, prioritizing, filtering out the mundane. All thoughts were equal.

The reaction had been especially bad after Vicky died. Cassie had suddenly noticed cobwebs in the corner of her living room. By the day of the funeral, her apartment was immaculate, her book shelves were arranged by size, and her finished canvasses were framed.

During the investigation and Jordan's trial, she'd labeled all her files and organized her email. She'd produced amazing art, impressing her bosses. When she left the agency, she'd been a breath away from a golden promotion.

Cassie dropped the phone. She rushed back out of the

cabin and down the slope. Carried by the waves, the camo bulk swelled and rolled.

Was the person alive but unconscious, unable to move, water clogging weary lungs? Or had the person suffocated in the lake's depths then risen like a discarded sacrifice?

The yellow air mattress rippled in between Cassie and the blob.

Better than the beach ball.

She kicked off her sandals and slogged in until the water reached her waist.

If the figure was alive, then Cassie had to do this.

If not, well, it wasn't her first dead body.

She started swimming.

Chapter Five

The roar of the rushing tornado-creature went on, as if it would last forever. Dale felt destined to hug that gnarled root for the rest of his life.

Suddenly, the monster vaulted back into the murky sky and soared away, leaving a strange silence. Dale's whole body shook. He couldn't make his muscles relax. He pressed his forehead against the root's rough bark and panted as if he'd just finished an uphill 10k.

Nausea welled up from the pit of his stomach as he imagined Crystal crushed and bleeding under the wreckage of her castle. He had to rescue her. And he would, as soon as he could force himself to move.

He blinked away grit then slowly raised his head. Painfully, he eased his grip on his wrist and flexed aching fingers. He slid his arm out from under the root and gave it a shake. Carefully, he pushed himself onto wobbly legs. Head down, he braced himself to view the destruction, wondering how much he'd be able to see through the trees.

He looked up, closed his eyes at what he saw, then opened them wide. Every pine from the crown of Red Hawk to its base lay flattened. Every single one.

A solitary sunbeam pierced the rolling gray clouds, illuminating the buff-tinted palace, untouched on the crest of the gentle hill that sloped to the lake.

Dale stared in awe at the perfect, unobstructed scene he'd longed for. He'd gotten his wish.

Lights flitted across the basement windows like crazed fireflies. Dale wondered if Crystal had dashed downstairs because of the telepathic message he'd sent her. Perhaps he'd saved her life. Tragically for him, she would never know he was her guardian, her protector.

Hell. Message or no message, it was unlikely he could take the credit. She knew what to do in a tornado the same as he did.

Dale took a look around at his own location during the twister and laughed. Knowing what you should do was sometimes a long stretch of broken road away from doing it.

The deer stand leaned forty-five degrees. He walked over to it and gave an exploratory poke. The structure bellowed like a sick cow at his touch, slowly lowered itself to the ground, and collapsed into scrap. He was too worn out to be surprised.

Toward town the sky turned a nice, comfortable, dusty pearl. The water tower still proudly stood sentry. He hoped the drugstore was okay. It had a solid below-ground storage area suitable for hunkering down in during a storm, so he wasn't too concerned about his mom.

He wondered where his dad was. Although he thought it pointless, he pulled out his phone to check for messages. As expected, at the moment the device was only suitable for playing non-network video games.

No worries. His dad was with his firehouse bros, probably checking damaged buildings for people who needed help. Dale hoped that while out in the truck tornado spotting, his dad had opened one of the shaken pop cans and sent sugary spray shooting across the inside of the cab.

Averted Vision

In no hurry to go home, Dale looked back toward the lake at the carpet of fallen pine trees stretched out before him. The sandstone house sparkled in the sliver of sunlight.

An ancient power had descended from the sky to test him. He'd survived the trial and been granted a reward. It felt penultimate epic, like in the best myth ever.

He was the luckiest guy alive.

And he was invincible.

Chapter Six

The cheerful yellow air mattress bubbled with a leak, growing softer and less supportive with each stroke. Cassie stretched across the width of the plastic rectangle with it tucked under her chest. Her arms paddled on one side and her legs kicked on the other with noisy splashes. It was just like when she was a kid, except this time she pushed a large bulk in front of her.

She forced herself to look at the bloated, fish-nibbled face. The camo-cloaked thing was absolutely dead. Ghostly white skin contrasted with the darkly mottled clothing adorned with stinky seaweed. A fragment of frayed rope snaked about an ankle. The storm wasn't to blame for its condition. It appeared to have spent a long time soaking in Beauty Lake. The tornado must have dredged it up from the water's cold depths.

Male? Probably. She refused to look again to try to figure out the gender. Forcing it through the waves toward shore, she preferred not to think of what it was, or what it had been.

Cassie's feet touched the sandy lakebed. She trudged through shallow water toward the beach with her floating burden. Her poor excuse for a life preserver had shriveled to little more than a limp bag. But it had served its purpose, and she was grateful for it.

A man rushed down the hill toward her. Close to six feet tall and lean as a birch, he wore a red shirt and matching baseball cap. "You okay?" Pale, slightly ragged hair stuck out from under the cap. She thought his sunburned face very linear, with a straight nose and thin mouth.

Cassie took a long inhale. "I'm fine. But this guy—I think it's a guy—is, uhm—"

"Beyond CPR," the man suggested.

"Yeah." She appreciated his tact.

He waded in and took control of the mass covered in green-brown camouflage. Jupiter crouched at the water line, making little puppy growls at both intruders.

Adrenaline spent, Cassie slowly shuffled to dry land. "I didn't know that when I—. I thought he might be from the boat." She pointed up the hill at the wreck embedded in the picnic table. "I tried to call 9-1-1 but both of my phones are —" She couldn't bring herself to say dead. "They're not working."

The man hefted the bundle onto the grass. The logo on his shirt and cap identified him as a Glacier Falls volunteer firefighter, a member of the Sparks. Cassie guessed he had experience with water rescues. He glanced at the parchment-white face, as she had. He looked away, took a breath, then gave the distorted features a longer examination.

Cassie's heart clenched as she realized what he was doing. He had to find out if this was someone he knew. Someone. A real person. Not a mass or a thing, as she'd classified it in her own thoughts. Not a bulk or a bundle. A person he might have played poker with or nodded to at the post office. A neighbor, maybe even a friend. She wanted to say something but felt it would be an intrusion in a private moment.

His jaw jutted out and his complexion under the sunburn blanched. He cringed and glanced at the sky. Then he seemed to remember she was there. He pointed to the plastic hanging from her hand. "When I saw you out in the water trying to make a rescue with that flimsy thing, I radioed it in. I should let them know it's no longer an emergency." He started up the slope toward the house.

"Shouldn't we stay with—" *Damn.* She was having a terrible time completing sentences. The man was talking, but not to her. She dropped the depleted air mattress, slipped back into her sandals, and followed him. The dead body wasn't going anywhere.

He finished consulting with an anonymous, staticky voice and clipped the radio onto his belt. "They'll be coming to get the body. It might be a while. Things are kind of crazy. Sorry, but I'll have to hang around until they show up."

Cassie squeezed a river from the hem of her shirt. The quick-drying fabric of her shorts was doing its best. She pointed in the direction of the damage across the lake. "It's pretty bad over there, but I can't tell if anyone's injured." It had probably already been reported, but she wanted to make sure. She led him to the telescope.

He swiveled the brim of his cap to the back. "That's an impressive set up." The tripod was set to accommodate Cassie's height. He bent to get his right eye in position.

"Cover your left eye with your hand, so you don't have to squeeze it shut," she said.

He looked silently for a long time then straightened. He pulled out his radio and relayed what he'd seen. A female voice quickly replied. To Cassie, it sounded like the muffled speaker at Burger King. "What was that?"

He translated. "Rhonda says there's one serious injury. Not life-threatening. Ambulance is on its way."

It was a small thing, but it made her feel better.

They walked over to the stairs leading to the lake-side deck. "Looks like I no longer have outdoor furniture." She hoped the plastic chairs and table were intact in someone else's yard, and that the new owner would appreciate them.

"No problem." His jeans were dripping wet from the knees down. He sat on a stair and pulled off his work boots.

Jupiter grabbed a chew toy and settled in the shade where he could keep an eye on the new guy. Cassie went inside and made a quick change into dry clothes. She dragged a comb through her tousled hair. It stuck out at odd angles, refusing to obey. When wrestled into complying, it framed her gray-blue eyes and high cheekbones, as the stylist said it would. But the sleek young man had pitched it as a carefree cut. Instead it had a temper-tantrum mind of its own.

Should she go through the pain of letting it grow out? Or should she force it to behave? Or should she just get used to it the way it was? She'd consult with her opinionated sisters, as soon as she got up the nerve to send them a photo of the mess.

Change it. Take charge of it. Live with it. It seemed those were always the choices. She grabbed a clean towel, went back out and offered it to the stranger on her stairs.

"That's okay. I'll air dry." He draped his soaked socks over the railing. "You're cousin Cassie, aren't you? Not my cousin. I didn't mean that." He gave an embarrassed smile that was just short of charming. "You probably don't remember me. Denny Zunker."

That explained "Denny" embroidered on his shirt.

"I hung around with Cliff and Rob—when we were kids mostly and then some in high school. You and your sisters visited during the summer and at Christmas once or twice."

Cassie remembered a boy with hair that bleached to white in the summer sun, but she couldn't picture the high school version. "As I recall, you and my male cousins referred to Laurel, Katie, my sisters and me as babies and did your best to avoid us."

Denny took on a look of mock seriousness. "Well, we had important guy stuff to do."

Cassie couldn't see the driveway from this angle. She was certain no car had been parked in it when she'd climbed the hill from the lake. "Do you always go out walking in storms?"

"My truck sort of ended up in the field across the road." He blushed. "I was tornado spotting. For the fire department. Usually don't end up this close to one. I was trying to radio it in so Edgar would turn on the sirens. You know Edgar. Tvrdik's Goods and Groceries. His daughter Linda was in Cliff's class."

Yes, Cassie remembered both father and daughter.

"Well, I was trying to get away from the funnel cloud at the same time. That didn't work out so well. You know, distracted driving. Went right off the road. I think I busted an axel."

A wail came from across the lake. "That'll be the ambulance from Leaf River," Denny said. "We had to get help from all over the county." The Burger King speaker went off again. He snatched the radio from his belt and joined the conversation.

Cassie got up and moved her telescope into the garage beside her sunflower-colored Mini Cooper where it would be out of the way. Just in time. Three pickups swung off the road and squeezed into the driveway. A flat-bottomed boat strapped into the cargo bed of the last one stuck out beyond the length of the truck. A red bandana fluttered from the end. Men wearing Sparks caps piled out as if the vehicles were clown cars. A few wore red shirts like Denny's with names embroidered on them.

Jupiter barked his objection. Cassie tucked him into the house, hoping he wouldn't take out his displeasure on the furniture. She came back out, startled by the quantity of strangers suddenly on her lawn, clustered around Denny.

"So we don't need the boat," Denny said, finishing what

must have been a quick explanation to the sea of red hats. The men muttered to one another, as if genuinely disappointed by the absence of an actively drowning victim to rescue. They broke the unified formation and shifted into small groups.

Cassie headed toward Denny, who seemed like a safe harbor. His soggy socks and boots were back on, as if he'd be embarrassed by having naked feet. She halted when she saw him huddle with Raymond Swenson. She hadn't met the man, but she knew he was the local pharmacist, the closest thing on Cassie's lawn to a doctor. In what looked like a serious conversation, the two strode away from the crowd and disappeared down the hill to the lake. To the body.

A gaunt, wrinkled-faced man of at least seventy was suddenly in front of Cassie. "Sorry we couldn't get here sooner," he said. "The sheriff department's only boat is over at Eagle Lake rescuing campers on the island, where they shouldn't be in the first place. I'm Boomer Danowski." He stuck a thumb at his t-shirt, which advertised the Danowski Family Polka Band. "I'll introduce you around."

He steered her into a group, disrupting a discussion of the tornado of 1966. "This here's Greg Ergen, and Junior Rasset, and I'm sure you already know Charlie." He pointed them out. "This is Cassie. She's Renee and Steve's niece."

"We had a heck of a time getting a boat," Junior said. He was a grown man yet the nickname fit him, and he seemed comfortable with it.

"We were going to use Ryan Miller's," Boomer said. "There he is over there. Give us a wave, Ryan!" Ryan was with another group. He turned around and raised a hand as if he knew the answer but didn't want to be called on in class, then he went back to his own conversation.

"But it's a big speed boat," Boomer said, "and when we got to the public access it was blocked by this huge shed."

"You wouldn't believe it," Junior said. "The storm picked it up from somewhere—"

"Knutsen's," Greg said. "It looks like Owen Knutsen's." He had thick hair that flopped boyishly to the side in a way that seemed familiar to Cassie.

"Yeah, could be," Junior continued. "The tornado picked it up, carried it ten miles or better—"

"If it's Owen Knutsen's, more like twelve miles," Charlie said. He sat on his three-wheeler. He'd driven it right up into her yard. Cassie already knew him from his daily trips along the road. Health problems made it hard for him to walk, but he was a demon on his ATV. He patrolled the cabins with dedication, checking for broken windows, cars he didn't recognize, and woodchucks.

"Yeah, I'd say twelve," Boomer agreed. "Set the whole thing down right on the boat ramp, just like it had been built there."

Greg glanced toward the red-flagged bow sticking out from the last pickup in her driveway. "Plan B, we got Irv's duck boat."

"Irv is Irv Steinhaus," Boomer said. "That's him, right over there." He pointed. "Give us a wave, Irv!"

Cassie was relieved her guide required nothing from her beyond being a convenient audience for his antics. She kept a generic, interested expression on her face. His energy amazed her. She followed the direction of his gesture.

Irv stood next to Ryan. It seemed the boat guys hung out together. He tugged on the brim of his Sparks hat and gave a little nod. He was even taller than Denny and didn't have to do much to be seen.

"Irv lives down the road," Charlie said. "So, he's real close."

Cassie was certain the local sentry knew where everyone in the county lived.

"A couple of guys can carry a duck boat easy," Junior said.

"You can launch it anywhere. Don't need a ramp. We got the radio call the body was already on shore, but we brought it along just in case."

Cassie wasn't sure what "just in case" meant. Another body in the water? She was glad no one had been bobbing about, trying to stay afloat while all that was going on.

Boomer maneuvered her to the boat-groupies so she could meet Ryan and Irv in person. "And this is Harry Ziegler. He used to be a lawyer. When you're in town, you have to watch out for his dog."

The man stood hunched over, as if worn out. Bags hung below his eyes. She guessed he wasn't as old as he appeared. Cassie imagined a vicious animal that mild-looking Harry was powerless to control.

"Chewy," Harry said. "After Chewbacca. The kids named him. They're out on their own and I'm left with the beast." He straightened his shoulders. "And I'm retired but still a lawyer."

"Sorry about your uncle's passing," Ryan said. Premature gray streaked his dark hair. She remembered him now. The only certified public accountant in town, he'd helped Aunt Renee with financial paperwork for the farm.

"Yeah." Irv fidgeted. "Real sorry."

"Yeah." Harry looked at the ground. "A real shame. He was a good man."

"Thank you." Cassie was used to people not knowing what to say when someone close to you died.

"I see Laurel sometimes," Harry said. "She says Renee is doing better."

Cassie nodded. "She's in good spirits now that she's back playing cribbage." For her aunt, anything involving cards was a blood sport.

The Sparks trampling her grass spoke to her as if they accepted her into the fold without reservation. She knew it wasn't that easy. Even with her family connection and childhood visits it would take at least ten years before they considered her anything but a transient.

They weren't wrong. With a huge tree limb smashed into the roof and a bloated body in the yard, the one-year lease on Aunt Renee's cabin felt like an eternity. This was a temporary haven, not a place to live the rest of her life.

She worried they'd grill her about why she was back in Minnesota, specifically in Glacier Falls, after building a career in Los Angeles. They must be curious, especially with the rumor circuit buzzing with speculation. Fortunately, even Boomer was too polite to ask anything personal at a first meeting.

Denny and Raymond came back up the slope, looking grim after inspecting the body.

"Do you know him?" someone asked.

That was the important question, Cassie thought, *the one everyone has been afraid of. Was this a neighbor or a stranger?*

"I don't recognize him," Raymond said. "It's hard to be absolutely sure. He's been in the water a long time."

"Couldn't be local then, could he?" Greg said, voicing a murmur that ran through the crowd.

"We'd know if someone was missing," Henry said. Everyone nodded.

Yes, they would know, Cassie thought.

"Any ID on him?" Boomer asked.

"That's for the sheriff to check," Raymond said.

Boomer's face sagged. "Hell, we've all been sworn in as deputies at one time or another. Any of us could go through his pockets." But no one rushed down the hill, especially not Boomer.

A long, somber vehicle arrived. The truck owners moved their pickups to the side of the road, allowing the hearse to park in the driveway. Discussions of tornadoes past and present softened almost to whispers as the attendants retrieved the body, slid it out of sight and closed the tailgate door on it with a soft click.

As if a low-hanging cloud parted, the mood lightened. Denny good-naturedly took a ribbing for having bounced his pickup truck through a ditch, over a nasty rock pile, and into a field to get out of the path of the twister, leaving his prized ride stuck between corn rows. "Irv and I can tow it into the repair shop for you," Junior told him.

"Good thing about the truck," Boomer said to Cassie. "Well, bad for the truck but good where it happened. So Denny could help you out and radio us right away. He's not married or engaged or anything. In case you're wondering."

"I just dragged a dead guy out of the lake, so no, I wasn't." Cassie immediately wished she'd said something more diplomatic—and less harsh. Denny seemed nice enough. Maybe she was wondering, just a little bit.

A county patrol car pulled up and settled at the side of the road behind the duck boat's flapping flag. Sheriff Justin "Justice" Wells eased out. He strolled into the yard like he was taking charge, although there wasn't much to take charge of. A hand shorter than Cassie, he looked as if he'd investigated a lot of six-packs over the years. Nut-brown hair sprinkled with gray surrounded a large bald spot on the top of his head. His molasses eyes seemed to slide over things instead of focusing on them.

Denny swept Cassie away from Boomer and introduced her to the sheriff. "She's Steve and Renee's niece." That didn't seem to impress Wells one way or the other.

"Sheriff." Cassie shoved out her hand, forcing him to give it a shake, but she couldn't get him to look her in the eye.

"She swam out and got the drowning victim," Denny said.

"You saved us some trouble then," the sheriff said, but he still seemed unimpressed. He sauntered past her to the middle of the yard. "You all need to hear this. The tornado did some damage in town. Not much. Mostly. But the sheriff's department took a big hit. It tore part of the roof off the old section. The new addition to the jail, with all its cozy, up-dated, camera-surveilled cells we so needed and were glad to get, is sheered right off at ground level. Fortunately, we haven't had a crime spree in a while so there were no detainees. The only one in the building was Rhonda. I put a double scotch in her hand and that perked her up. She's already got an agreement with the VFW to let us use some of their space. We'll be needing help from you Sparks to get equipment moved over."

"Even a tornado knows better than to mess with Rhonda," one of the Sparks remarked.

"Some good news that I know is important to all of you," Wells said. "The Dairy Queen is untouched and the drive through is open."

Cassie reconsidered his girth. Maybe it wasn't due to beer. Maybe it was because of a close, personal relationship with Dilly Bars.

The sheriff reported on snapped power lines, missing pigs, and a Buick bent around a fence post. The only death was the one right here at Beauty Lake.

Finished with the update, Sheriff Wells poked his head into the back of the hearse to make sure the corpse hadn't escaped. "We'll have to see what the boys at the state lab say about the Floater here."

The Floater. The body didn't have an identity, but now he had a nickname.

"Maybe not an accident?" someone asked quietly.

"You thinkin' murder?" someone else said loudly, as if it were a joke. "That kind of thing doesn't happen here."

Murder happened anywhere, Cassie knew. To people who deserved it and, unfortunately, to those who didn't. To people you've never met, and to your best friend in the entire world.

The hearse left quietly. The Sparks stood around as if bored and disappointed there hadn't been more for them to do. Spontaneously they gathered up the downed twigs and branches in Cassie's yard and stacked them to the side where the mowed lawn met wild prairie grass. The row boat and picnic table ended up preserved beside the pile, a monument to human arrogance against natural forces.

Ladders appeared. Charlie, the ATV-patrolling sentinel, directed removal of the gigantic limb crowning the cabin. A couple of guys who worked construction declared the roof sound. The Sparks proclaimed the state of the lawn "good enough for now," and jostled back into the clown-car trucks.

Boomer waved good-bye to Cassie as if he'd been to her place a dozen times before. She felt obligated to return the gesture. Minnesotans were wavers. She'd have to get used to that again.

Denny tried to be the last one, but Irv honked the horn at him. Junior shouted from the cab window. "Your truck isn't going to get itself out of that corn field."

"Yeah, okay," Denny yelled back. He gave Cassie an awkward grin. "Sorry this is how we met."

For a moment Cassie thought he was going to say something personal, not meant for the crowd that was finally leaving. Something just between the two of them. After all, they'd pulled a dead man out of the lake together. She'd seen his feet naked.

Denny backed away toward Irv's truck. "You need anything, call the Sparks."

Cassie nodded. Not the intimate farewell the situation deserved.

She stared at the large chunk of tree that twisted across the grass like a lawn ornament, not watching the last vehicle pull away. Now that the place was quiet again, she wanted to let herself be upset, to turn off her brain and allow her emotions to catch up with the events. But she couldn't uncork a bottle of wine just yet. She had to find a way to let her parents know she was okay.

In truth, only one of her parents would be obsessively worried. Her dad was probably swearing at the bland, automated voice explaining all lines were busy and he would have to try the number again later. His next step would be to jump in the car and drive to her place.

Cassie could count on her mom to hide the car keys and to deliver the usual lecture. *We have a smart daughter who can take care of herself. As a wise and loving father, you should let her.* Her mother wouldn't think to mention that Cassie was an adult. Age was not a factor in her parents' minds. Even to her mother, who was proud of having raised four independent beings, the sisters were, and always would be, children.

If Cassie spent more than a day with her parents, she slipped into the old habits of home. She saw it in Holly, Ashley and Kayla, too. Leaving a glass by the sink instead of putting it straight into the dishwasher. Not filling up the gas tank after borrowing the car. It was one of the many reasons why she hadn't gotten a place in Irving River. She couldn't live in her hometown again. She couldn't be Connie and Pat Windom's third daughter.

You know, the one who can draw. You remember her. She designed the homecoming button her senior year.

Going back meant going backward. She couldn't do it anymore than her sisters could. They *were* smart women who could take care of themselves.

Mostly.

Not always.

Seriously, not always. But their parents didn't have to know that. Some things were better kept within the circle of sisters.

Cassie practiced explaining today's happenings to her mother and father. Every attempt sounded like, well, a disaster. But she couldn't pretend it had just been a bit of wind and that the waves had delivered a body to her shore without any effort on her part.

She had to give them the story before they found out through other means. Which they would. Soon. Her mom was a news junkie with a police scanner app and a wide social media reach. It might already be too late to provide a calm, reassuring version.

It wasn't the worse thing she'd had to tell her parents. There'd been no way to soften the narrative of Vicky's death. She'd had to explain she was the one who discovered the murder. She was the one who'd called 9-1-1. She'd waited for the police to arrive, identified the lifeless body of her friend, sat numb on the sofa she'd helped Vicky pick out while the quiet-voiced officer asked her questions.

The gory, salacious details were broadcasted, posted and tweeted twenty-four/seven for over a year. Reporters and journalists—some professionals, most not—clogged Cassie's life, sticking mics, cameras and smartphones in her face. Crime-scene fanboys pounced on every bit of minutia—mashing, grinding and pummeling each grain into easily spooned up click bait.

Some of them still stalked her online when there were no shinier objects to play with. If this new body made national news, it would put her in their cross-hairs again.

Jordan was even more persistent in keeping track of her than the newsy predators. She blocked his attempts at contacting her through online routes, and she never answered the phone unless she recognized the caller ID.

But she couldn't stop the envelopes from Jordan that kept appearing in her physical mailbox. Tossing them, unopened, into the plastic bin was her best defense.

As she let a grateful Jupiter out of the basement, where the box of letters dwelled under the stairs like a childhood nightmare, she sternly told herself that this new death, the death of a stranger, had nothing to do with her. She wouldn't let it.

She grabbed essentials, rushed to the garage, and climbed

into her yellow Mini Cooper. She put the phone on the passenger seat beside her and drove, hoping to find a cell signal before she reached her parents' house. Normal traffic whizzed by, as if nothing unusual had happened. She watched for her dad's Subaru coming from the other direction.

Finally, cheerful chirps exploded from her phone, announcing the return of civilization and the arrival of multiple messages. Probably from her sisters.

She slowed for the next town. They were all small out here, but every one of them had greenspace sponsored by a local organization. She pulled over at the Lions Club Park.

The sun sat low in the west. Cassie leaned her forehead against the steering wheel, gathering the courage to call her parents. Her phone boomed out the theme from *The Good, the Bad and the Ugly*.

She picked it up and punched the icon. "Hi, Dad."

Chapter Seven

Make your day bright with SunnieChat!

CASSIE

Dad wants me to move in. Just for a few days

HOLLY

He says days. He means years

KAYLA

What's that song. Hotel California

ASHLEY

You'll have to go shawshank to escape

CASSIE

I told him a thousand times I'm okay, the cabin's okay

HOLLY

Did you tell him about the missing lawn furniture and the picnic table?

CASSIE

Yeah I did. Oops. Tactical error

ASHLEY

Seating for twenty coming up

KAYLA

Dad loves his power tools

CASSIE

I met Denny Zunker. Anyone remember him?

Friend of Rob and Cliff

HOLLY

More a friend of Rob than Cliff

KAYLA

Skinny. Taller than R and C

ASHLEY

Standard Minnesota Scandinavian bland

CASSIE

Is that bland or blond?

ASHLEY

Both

HOLLY

Father of five on his second marriage?

CASSIE

Currently unattached. Don't know about past marriages or kids. I remember him when he was little but not when he was in high school

HOLLY

He wasn't always around. Worked on grandparents' farm by Marshall

KAYLA

Shy. Followed R and C's lead. Holly had a crush on him one summer

Averted Vision

HOLLY

Not me. That was Ash. I was going to marry
Justin T

ASHLEY

Boring summer. Not much to choose from

CASSIE

Still not much to choose from

Chapter Eight

Sitting in the dark on an old blanket near the rubble that had been the deer stand, enjoying the fresh view from Red Hawk, it occurred to Dale to watch out for the trick buried in his good fortune. When a guy is granted a wish—not the world-peace or ending-poverty kind, but the selfish, iWish kind—there's always an evil twist.

You get a superpower, just like you always wanted, so people will call you awesome and give you stuff. You should be on your way to universal hero/celeb fame. But your new ability ends up being limp, like instantly knowing if a chunk of plastic is #2 or #5. The only place you'll wow anyone is at the recycling center.

Or you can prevent the Arctic ice pack from melting and flooding Florida, but only if you live alone in a yurt in northern Greenland for the rest of your life.

Yeah, he would suffer for wanting to see Crystal's naked breasts through her bedroom window. He didn't know exactly how yet, but he suspected it would happen soon. Maybe he was in horror-movie mode because it was only two days until Friday the 13th.

On silent mode his phone vibrated, rattling against the

metal top of the cooler he'd pulled from the wreckage of the deer stand. He knew without looking that Richie had sent him another jittery, almost too dark to see, video. Richie was doing F13 test runs, and wanted to be sure Dale knew how much fun he was missing out on.

The clips were all similar. They started with Richie's hand lit by a streetlight, strategically placing flakes of tuna at the roadside edge of the sidewalk by the park. Then they bounced to the nearby swing set, and Richie grasping the Danowski family's enormous black cat.

As strollers enjoying the night air, and kids hurrying home to make curfew approached the shreds of tuna, he released the squirming Muffin. The huge cat shot out to claim his bribe, rushing in front of the startled pedestrians. Dale could hear Richie laughing at the screams and curses. In one of the vids a man scurried to the other side of the street rather than have a black cat cross his path.

Richie and Dale had been doing it for years. Muffin was used to the routine and seemed to enjoy acting like an omen of bad luck. Richie still got a jolt out of it. Dale was tired of going for the cheap scare and hoped he could redirect Richie's attention to some other mindless prank this time.

Dale checked his watch again. Almost ten o'clock. Right on schedule he heard a rumbling engine in great need of a total replacement. He jumped up and stared at the spot where the thing would appear. Beacons shining through the brush sent out crazy shadows as the vehicle jostled closer over the rough terrain of the old deer run. It rounded the base of the hill, looking as if it might drive right into the lake. Dale held his breath as it stopped a few feet from the rocky bank. He'd first noticed the racket and lights a few weeks ago. That's exactly where he suspected it parked. Now that the trees were down and he had a clear view, he knew for sure.

It sat on Swenson land. Crystal's dad owned the last good stretch before reeds took over. More than eight hundred feet of smart investment, someday it would be carved up into prime vacation property with the family mansion sitting on the high ground, as if to remind the lesser lords who ruled here.

In two years the princess will drive off in her daddy's Mustang convertible to a private college, and I'll still be here, Dale suddenly thought. *And I'll never see her again.*

It hurt. Lots. Almost a physical pain.

If only his parents owned the land all the way down to the shore instead of just to the bottom of the hill. Then he could stroll to the lake on his own property. He'd have the right to wave to Crystal as she lounged on her patio reading. He could invite her for a boat ride—if he had a nice one that didn't smell of decaying fish.

Mostly he wanted control of the space below him where that monstrous vehicle now sat, so he could block off the rutted road and keep the invader out.

Was he wishing again? He had to stop that.

An invisible line marked the border between the Swenson property that rolled gently to the water and the Steinhaus vertical acres. It might as well be a wall.

He grabbed the binoculars resting beside his phone and peered at the vehicle. He hadn't been able to see it until tonight. But the very first time he'd heard it prowl up to the lake, he'd recognized the grinding engine and shrieking gears. Now the headlights gave enough illumination to confirm the clear picture he already had in his head.

Butt toward Dale, the beat-up old truck sat like a rusty toad, right where he wanted to build his own dream cabin. Parts had been replaced and improvised, so it was difficult to tell the original make and model. A homemade topper fitted with an old storm door enclosed the back. Everyone in Glacier Falls knew the dappled olive green, tan, and brown paint job meant to imitate camouflage. They knew the driver, too.

Owen Norquist.

Although the good citizens of the town were divided over churches, the strip club, and whether or not a stop light was needed at the intersection of Main Street and Highway 72, they were united in one thing. They all hated Owen Norquist.

Dale wasn't surprised to see the man at Beauty Lake after dark. He'd observed the guy out poaching and night fishing often enough, but Owen usually worked out of a spot on the north end where he could shine deer in the cornfields and where he kept an old boat hidden in the reeds.

Richie and Dale had gone looking for the boat, planning to punch a hole in the bottom. Richie seemed to know exactly where to find it, snuggled against a berm heaved up by lake ice. At the last minute they decided it was too much work to puncture the aluminum hull. Truth was, they chickened out, afraid the guy would somehow know they'd done it.

You didn't want Owen Norquist mad at you. The man had committed worse crimes than illegally hunting and fishing. He was a liar, thief, wife abuser, and small-time drug dealer. What else? Rapist? Murderer?

Dale thought of the Floater. The glacier that had scraped across this area millions of years ago had carved Beauty deep. It was an ideal place for someone like Owen to sink a body.

Just thinking about the sleazy creep so close to Crystal gave Dale the same queasy feeling he'd had when he'd swallowed a chunk of chewing tobacco—which was doubly Richie's fault for insisting they try it, and then for making Dale laugh so hard he had to take a giant inhale.

The truck cut its lights. Dale clenched his teeth and stared hard. This was the part he speculated about, the part that zigzagged around in his mind spawning crazy theories, each scarier than the last. This was what he didn't want to see but needed to know to prove all his freaky thoughts wrong.

Trembling so hard he couldn't hold the binoculars steady, Dale lowered them and took a breath. To the right, a light bobbed around the corner of the Swenson house. The beam crossed the bridge over the deep ravine cut by a creek. Dale raised the sturdy Leupold to his eyes and followed the glow that seemed to move by itself. Whoever carried it was hidden behind the blaze.

He heard the truck door squeal open, and the rustle of the driver getting out. There was no sense swinging the binoculars in that direction. The cab light on the patchwork monster had never worked. Besides, the driver could be no one but Owen.

What Dale wanted to know, what he *needed* to know, was the identity of the phantom flashlight-wielder.

The creaky truck door closed with a clunk. Dale braced his elbows against his knees, gripping the rubber-coated tubes so tight his fingertips went numb. The flashlight bounced to the back of the truck and slid across a form in a camo jacket and brimmed hat. Dale always got a kick out of Owen's ride being fashionably coordinated with his ensemble.

The beam appeared to aim itself at the storm door. The metal rectangle with blacked-out windows pivoted on its hinges, showing nothing but darkness beyond. Camo Owen and the flashlight climbed in. The door banged shut.

Shit. Nothing more to see.

Dale swiveled to scan the Swenson house. He gasped, almost sucking in a mosquito. Crystal stood like the portrait of a goddess framed by her bedroom window. An aura of soft light glowed behind her. She brushed back shoulder-length blond hair with a graceful hand. She faced the lake, faced the truck squatting on the shore in the dark.

She suddenly turned toward the hill. She tilted her chin, moving her gaze up to the exact spot where Dale sat. He froze. She stared straight at him.

Impossible. An illusion. She was looking in the general direction of where he was, at the gap where the once stately trees were now a field of giant toothpicks, not actually at him.

His brain told him she couldn't possibly see him in the moonless night.

Still, it felt real. He wanted it to be real.

Crystal wasn't supposed to be home. Not on such a nice summer evening. She was usually on a date or out with friends or at band practice. He knew because he regularly checked her media page for selfies and check-ins.

She had a boyfriend. Todd Ashland. *Shit, who named their kid Todd?* She always had a boyfriend, always a guy who was popular who wasn't Dale. Maybe they'd split up. Maybe Crystal finally realized Ashland was just another strutting ego, not worthy of her beauty and her mind. Dale knew it was dangerous, but he let that thought and all its implications surge through him.

The euphoria didn't last long. He took in the whole wide-screen view the storm had cleared for him. The truck. The house just a short walk over the bridge. The window.

Owen, so close to Crystal.

And there was nothing he could do about it. He might as well be watching YouTube. He was strictly an observer here and not one of the players.

Dale could feel his own personal trickster-god snickering at him. He swallowed down a lump that had forced its way up from his stomach. Then he was sorry he had. He should have let the vileness spew from his body instead of holding it in.

He always kept too much trapped inside. As if *that* was a surprise. It was what he saw around him, what he lived with every day, what he'd learned by lesson and example from his father and his father's family. It passed along the generations through the Steinhaus genome along with height and curly hair.

Crystal eased away from the window. The lamp went out in her room. Did she realize she could be seen with the glow behind her? Did she glide back to the glass, invisible now in the dark? He couldn't tell.

At least he knew she wasn't the Swenson in the back of the rusty truck with Owen. Not that he thought that for even a nano sec. But it was good to have proof.

Dale put the binoculars on the cooler, stood up, and paced to keep the insects away. He gave his phone a shake to make the screen light up. Ignoring the messages from Richie, he checked the time.

Minutes crawled by. He checked the numbers again. And again. Doing nothing else. Too afraid he'd miss something if he started playing a game.

He wasn't worried about being gone from the house for so long. His mom was with Father Anderson and the other Vigilants, harassing men going into the Safari Club. His dad was at the fire hall with his Sparks gang, reliving yesterday's exciting almost-rescue of a dead guy.

Eleven o'clock.

The storm door on the back of the truck squealed open. Dale put down the phone and grabbed the binoculars. Palms sweaty against the Leupold's rubber-coating, he strained to see.

The camo-blob that was Owen got out first. The flashlight, pointed at the ground, followed.

Say something, Dale mentally blasted at them. *Let me hear you.*

The flashlight could at least say "Good night, Owen." And Owen could say, "Good night, Insert-name-here."

Despite Dale's urging, the two didn't speak. Owen got into the cab and started the engine. The flashlight glare bounced to the bridge. It stopped. The beam winked out.

Dale tried to control his pounding pulse and ragged breath. He couldn't let the engine's rumbling distract him. There must be light from somewhere. He had to see. He absolutely had to. He had to know.

With brat-zilla Ray Jr. away at camp, only three people were currently in residence at the Swenson house. Crystal, who, except for tonight, was never home. Debbie, with a social schedule full of book clubs and charity wine tastings, who wouldn't walk across unpaved terrain in her designer shoes even to meet Prince William. That left—

Dale hoped he was wrong. The flashlight could be a housekeeper or someone with the lawn service. Maybe it was a random guy who found it convenient to cut across the Swenson estate every week to meet his buddy.

Dale heard footsteps on the wooden bridge, and caught a shadow crossing the ravine. The human form, barely distinguishable from the landscape, crept through the brush onto short-cropped grass then onto the tiled patio. In a blink it vanished. Clattering and thuds echoed up to Dale.

"Crap. Ow ow ow ow ow! Damn. Shit."

An outside flood light snapped on, revealing Raymond Swenson as if he were center stage at the MTV awards.

Raymond. Pharmacist. Key master of drugs.

The man leaned on a rattan chair rubbing a knee. For a moment he looked like a kid caught sneaking in after curfew. "It's okay," he shouted at the person who'd turned on the patio lights. "I tripped. Sorry to scare you, Crystal honey."

Busted. By his daughter.

Dale slapped a hand over his mouth and collapsed to the ground. It was awful and tragic and all that, but right now he wanted to roll in the grass howling until he peed. He shook with stifled laughter, not daring to let a guffaw slip out. Sound amplified around the water basin. He and Richie called it Lake Radio. If Dale could hear Raymond swearing, then everyone along the whole shoreline was bound to hear Dale if he let loose.

Raymond limped through the maze of lounge furnishings, around the corner and out of sight. Dale wondered what explanation he was giving Crystal for taking a walk outside in the dark.

Just checking on the crotch-rocket jet skis we never use.

Making sure a raccoon family hasn't moved into my big-ass, stainless steel gas grill.

Dale lay still. It was funny, but it wasn't. What happened during the past hour? A drug deal only took minutes. He didn't think Raymond and Owen were sharing deep philosophical thoughts, or discussing the stock market, or having a secret Bible study session.

The flood light blinked off. Dale sat up and ran the binoculars across the windows, searching for Crystal. Silently he promised her he would keep watch, like a sacred vigil, to protect her from Owen—and whatever was going on between the town sleaze and her father.

His phone vibrated. He expected it to be Richie again.

It was a text from his mother, sent to both Dale and his dad.

Chapter Nine

HELEN S

Won't be home tonight arrested in jail explain later

Chapter Ten

T**ime for a SunnieChat!**

HOLLY

K saw you tagged in pics with your research team. Are you still in Quito or on the boat?

KAYLA

Boat. Currently off Isabela. Can't believe I'm in the Galapagos!

CASSIE

Who's the hunk leaning toward you like you're a gravity well?

KAYLA

Liam. Phd candidate from Scotland. Our relationship needs subtitles.

ASHLEY

Historically your travel liaisons don't go well.

KAYLA

Can't fight the logistics. Tight quarters. Limited clean underwear. Plus this is a short term grant. Soft money. No future in it. Or in Liam.

Averted Vision

HOLLY

You could at least bring him home for a visit
before you dump him.

ASHLEY

Yeah give your older sisters a thrill.

Chapter Eleven

C assie watched the summer dusk drift into night in its lazy way, as if the sun were reluctant to let the day end. Just before eleven o'clock she set up her telescope on the south-easterly side of the house next to what had once been a vegetable garden. The space had been invaded by creeping Charlie, dandelions, and opportunistic prairie grass. She planned to clean it up—after she got rid of the half a tree bedecked with many branches that rested nearby like a sleeping lizard.

She aligned the tripod to polar north. Polaris was far from the brightest star in the night sky, but it was the touchstone, the focal point the other stars spun around like a calliope at the center of a carousel. The light-clogged sky of Los Angeles had hidden the stars from her. Here they sparkled on full display.

Relaxation didn't come easily. But this seemed like purposeful leisure and that gave her permission to enjoy it.

She'd been so excited to move to L.A. She never thought anything could force her back. According to her sisters, the home-town gossip mongers were sure she wouldn't last long in that sinful place. They'd tossed out theories like Halloween candy.

You wait and see. She'll be a drug addict in no time, with all that cocaine and her-o-in so easy to get. You can practically buy it at the grocery store like bread.

The traffic alone will give the poor girl a nervous breakdown. Smog will do it to you, too. It just isn't healthy out there. She'll collapse from a terrible illness and have to be brought back in one of those med-i-copters.

Some smooth Hollywood type will scoop her up for sure, then leave her shattered and pregnant. She'll have a miscarriage. She'll have an abortion. She'll give up her love child for adoption.

She'll get fired because she's not the smart one. The two oldest got all the brains. And the youngest got all the looks.

Even with Vicky's death and Jordan's trial dominating the local newspapers for months because of the Minnesota connection through Cassie, the gossipers weren't satisfied and continued to speculate about the *real* reason she'd left California.

There's got to be more to it than just that girl's tragic murder.

As if death wasn't enough.

Cassie surveyed her view. The land was treeless to the county road. Beyond that, the field that had chewed up Denny Zunker's truck provided an open panorama. To the west, silhouettes of the disfigured oak and the cabin blocked part of the sky. To the south, trees were periodic barriers. To the north, an unfortunate hill rose up.

Not a perfect vista, but not a terrible one. At least it was far from streetlights and yard lights. The almost new moon had already disappeared below the horizon. No lunar glow interfered with the pinpoints of light scattered across the dark canvas. For a rookie astronomer there was plenty of clear sky to explore.

Mosquitos were her enemy now. The articles she'd read on observing, and the helpful online videos never mentioned how to ward off the pests beyond the standard "smear yourself with DEET." Determined to figure out a solution of her own, tonight she experimented. Taking wardrobe advice from hunters, she wore an anti-bug net jacket and matching pants over a long-sleeved shirt and jeans. To make sure no deliciously veined skin peeked out, she'd tucked the hems of her pant legs into thick socks.

Her innovation didn't stop there. The net jacket's huge hood draped over her face like a wedding veil. She'd donned a baseball cap under it with the brim to the back to keep the fabric off her neck, discouraging over-achieving insects who tried to strike through the open-work fabric. Vinyl gloves protected her hands.

The result was far from fashion forward. Although a light breeze cooled the air, encased in all that gear she was sweaty, and she stunk of insect repellent. She probably looked like a bear and might get shot. Well, she'd be videoed first and then shot. Or videoed and blackmailed. It really was a ridiculous outfit. She'd have to send a selfie to her sisters.

Cassie consulted her star chart by the glow of a penlight fitted with a red gel. The tinted beam helped preserve her night vision. She clicked it off and adjusted a patch over her right eye so she wouldn't have to squeeze it shut or hold a hand over it when she peered through the telescope with her left.

The atmosphere seemed magnificently arid and free from distortion. It was easy to think on such a night. She let her mind take its own path.

Who was the dead man she'd dragged from the lake yesterday? Denny and Raymond didn't know him but someone must, someone local. Maybe even someone who'd stood in her yard discussing tornadoes and boats. The rope attached to the body bothered her. Like the mosquito close to her ear, it buzzed around her speculations, and she couldn't swat it away.

Not far off an angry engine roar shattered the quiet.

Cassie shivered. It wasn't the first time she'd heard that horrible sound.

The Saturday after the Fourth of July. Cassie stood in the yard, trying to get inspiration for a toothpaste ad. She'd been living in her aunt's cabin for less than two weeks. Time and neglect had taken away the familiarity she'd felt here as a child.

She surveyed the mass of rose bushes against the garage. The thorny tangle of spindly canes hadn't been tended in years. Spring had been unusually cold and snowy. The plants sprouted sparse leaves but no buds. She remembered the odd collection of blooms from her childhood—a cluster of delicate pink petals; a massive, crinkly crimson; and a bold yellow. Cassie inhaled the memory of mixed fragrances.

She heard the vehicle before she saw it. The growl and then the gargoyle. Speeding along the road from town, the camo-painted truck, enclosed cargo bed forming a home-made camper, straddled the center line. It came even with her driveway, screeched, and shuddered to a slow roll. The passenger door popped open and a girl tumbled out onto the tar.

The engine revved. The driver popped the clutch with a grinding of metal on metal. The monster charged forward with an oily belch and disappeared over the hill.

Jupiter at her heels, Cassie sprinted to the girl and knelt beside her. "Are you okay?"

Of course she wasn't. She'd just been dumped on the road like garbage. But it's what you say because you're hoping it isn't as bad as the terrible thoughts of gushing blood, broken bones, and emotional trauma in your head.

The girl blinked rapidly as if unsure where she was or how she'd gotten there. "Fuck."

Chin length hair, shocking white with black roots, framed a round face thick with make-up. In a sleeveless tank top and cut-off jeans, she might be as old as seventeen or as young as fourteen. Gravel speckled bloody patches on her forehead, cheek, bare arms and knees. Large pads of skin were scraped from her palms.

Relieved all the wounds looked superficial, Cassie helped her stand. "I can take you to urgent care at the clinic."

She shook her head. "No insurance."

Cassie took her into the cabin and sat her down at the kitchen table. She raided the first aid cupboard. Its contents were well known to her from her own childhood scrapes, and those of her sisters and cousins.

"I'm Cassie, and this is going to sting." She dabbed alcohol on the girl's hand.

The girl winched. Her name was Glenna Lowery. "Glenna. I didn't make that up. It's the only good thing my folks gave me. It sounds like a fairy princess. I used to pretend that's what I was. It can be hard sometimes to get people to hear it right. I usually have to spell it."

With Cassandra on her birth certificate, Cassie knew something about the good and the bad of having an uncommon name.

Glenna hitchhiked to Glacier Falls from Minneapolis last September. "I heard about the Gentlemen's Club opening up. That's what they were going to call it then. It's the Safari Club now. More wild sounding, I guess. I thought I could get a job as a dancer. But the manager, he told me he brings the girls in from places in the Twin Cities that are owned by the same guys. It's real cool. They get to ride all the way here in this humungous, awesome stretch limo with a chauffeur and everything. I bet it has music and they drink Champaign. I've seen that in movies."

She met Owen Norquist, the guy who shoved her out of the truck, at the Crow Bar downtown. "He said he had connections and could get me hired at the place, but it didn't work out. The guy he knew left town, or they had a fight or something."

"What he did to you is assault," Cassie said. "You should report him to the sheriff. We can call right now."

Glenna stroked Jupiter with the back of a gauzed hand. "Naw. Owen's just blowing off steam. And it wouldn't do any good anyway. It'll be okay."

Cassie knew it wouldn't be okay. She could barely think of anything except Vicky—beaten, raped, and killed by her abusive ex-boyfriend/boyfriend.

Cassie worked on Glenna's cheek, and then her arms and legs, cleaning away clotted blood and covering every wound that needed a cushion.

Glenna ran a stubby fingernail, shiny with glitter, over the star chart spread out on the kitchen table. "You must be really smart."

"I just know basic first aid." Cassie moved the supplies to the counter.

"I didn't mean—" Glenna took her hands off the table and leaned against the back of the chair as if she'd done something wrong. "Yeah, I get it."

Cassie was puzzled by the reaction, but she let it go. She felt compelled to wade into a tough issue. "I had a friend. She was serious about this guy, but he, he wasn't good for her. He hurt her. Physically. He told her she deserved it, but she didn't. And she didn't need to stay with him." The roar of a truck interrupted her. Tires crunched to a gravely stop.

Glenna vaulted from the chair. "That's Owen." She rushed out the screen door.

Cassie followed her. The mottled pickup idled in her driveway. A man dangled an arm out the window. Unkept hair the color of rags stuck out from under a camouflage boonie hat. His beefy face looked bored, as if this was just a common occurrence. "Bitch, you get back in this truck. What you doin', jumpin' out like that, you crazy bitch."

"Glenna," Cassie called to her.

The girl turned and gave her a little smile. "It's okay. If he was still mad, he would've made me hitch home."

Cassie wanted to grab the girl and beg her not to get into that truck. She wanted to warn her what could happen, what inevitably would happen. "Please, come see me and we'll talk."

"Thanks," Glenna said. "You're nice and your dog is really sweet. I hope your friend is okay."

Cassie turned and trudged back to the cabin. She couldn't watch Glenna being driven away by her abuser. She called the sheriff's department and relayed what had happened. The girl was making her own choices, so there probably wasn't much that could be done. Still, Cassie felt the need to get it on the record for when—she forced herself through that thought— for when Glenna's bloody body ended up in a ditch.

The officer she talked to sounded sympathetic. "We'll investigate," Rhonda Olson said. "It's not like it used to be when that sort of thing was considered meddling in people's private concerns. Policy now is to check out all domestics. We can even charge him without the woman's cooperation. Don't expect too much to come of it though. Abuse is hard to prove without a medical report."

"She's probably a minor," Cassie argued.

"I know the girl," Rhonda said. "Her ID says she's twenty-two. No missing person on her or outstanding warrant. Sorry."

Sitting under the night sky with her telescope in her improvised anti-mosquito, star-gazing gear, Cassie tried to shake off the memory.

Averted Vision

The rumbling of Owen Norquist's truck grew louder, closer. She didn't bother to check the time. If the truck was on schedule, it would be just after eleven. Sometimes the vehicle charged along the road like an angry bull. Sometimes it slowed, crawling past her place as if it might stop.

Which would it be tonight? She wouldn't let her fear push her indoors. Not with Cygnus, the Swan, gloriously glided overhead, and Jupiter the puppy rolling in the grass nearby.

A beautiful instrument, the black on black telescope stood nobly on its heavy-duty tripod. Her first, and possibly the only one she would ever own. It was powerful enough to keep her satisfied and interested for a long time. She certainly couldn't say that about a lot of things that had been in her life.

She gazed through the finder and clenched her teeth, determined not to let the distant, growling truck distract her. She put the cross hairs halfway between the two stars that marked the short southern segment of the constellation Lyra's parallelogram. She peered through the scope's eyepiece and adjusted the focus. The telescope mount purred, slowly moving the tube to compensate for the Earth's rotation.

A fuzzy wreath glowed against the velvety background. The foggy blob of the Ring Nebula stubbornly refused to take form no matter how intently she stared. The blur was disappointing compared to the tidy oval of gases with a white dwarf at its core that she'd seen in photos.

Using a technique she'd read about called averted vision, she shifted her gaze slightly away from the ghostly splotch. The action defied logic and felt physically wrong. To her amazement, it worked! The image resolved itself into a cool, unblinking eye, glaring back at her.

She marveled at the beautiful light, the old light that started its journey toward Earth two thousand years ago.

The thunder of an unmuffled engine grew deafening. Headlights invaded the landscape. Cassie looked up from the eyepiece. The rusty pickup aimed toward town appeared, rumbling with a menacing laugh. Jupiter rushed to her, snarling from deep in his ribcage. She whipped off her eye patch and slapped it over the ruby light of the mount's drive so it wouldn't give her away.

Her resolve to be fearless evaporated. She abandoned the scope and crouched in the long grass where tomatoes and peppers used to grow. She grasped Jupiter's collar, her fingers sweating in the vinyl gloves.

Cassie could feel Owen Norquist staring at her house as he prowled toward it, his eyes trying to penetrate the sheer curtains hanging over the dark windows. She told herself she should be glad the snakes were so obvious in a small, rural community, so she'd never delude herself into thinking this Garden of Eden was reptile free. She had come here for a less complicated life. That didn't mean it was safer.

She stayed low, tugging the net hood tighter over her face to ward off whining mosquitoes unintimidated by the sharp odor of DEET. The night appeared deep and diffused through the tiny grids. As long as the vehicle kept its course on the tar road, she and the black telescope would just be shapes, no more remarkable than the giant lizard tree limb.

That's what she hoped.

The pickup slowed as it approached. She couldn't see the threat behind the wheel, the beefy face and ragged hair sticking out from under the broad brim of the camo hat. The monster slid out of sight, obscured by the garage. Headlights illuminated the road on Cassie's side of the building and lit up her driveway, sending a skewed shadow of the structure toward her. The harsh white froze, no longer moving.

Cassie's legs ached from the strain of crouching. She eased a knee to the ground in a sprinter's position, ready to spring and flee. Hidden behind the garage, the truck roughly idled. She held her breath and listened for the metallic creak of a rusty door opening. Seconds passed.

The cold beams shifted as their source inched into view.

The truck crunched at an angle from the tar to the gravel driveway, swinging its beams across the fallen limb and directly at her. The shafts of light imprinted the telescope's distorted shadow on the cabin siding.

She should have scurried away when she had the chance. She couldn't jump up now and run. Clutching Jupiter's collar tighter, she curled against the ground so her shadow would not join the scope's. The puppy struggled against her grip.

The pickup's angry motor roared. Gears scraped. The truck jerked back onto the tar. With a grinding screech it shot away, leaving behind the stench of exhaust fumes.

Cassie released Jupiter, who gave himself a great shake. She plopped into the dirt, watching the ruby taillights grow smaller as the truck sped toward town, not moving until they disappeared.

Chapter Twelve

Here's Your SunnieChat!

KAYLA

Cass don't know why you won't send pics. Bangs sound cute

CASSIE

Not just bangs. I splurged on a styling. The look is kind of a bob.

ASHLEY

Roaring twenties, F Scott Fitzgerald?

KAYLA

Did he have a bob?

ASHLEY

K I know your childhood focused on frogs but you must have absorbed some culture from being around the rest of us

KAYLA

Not just frogs. Snakes and spiders too

CASSIE

And a turtle and Mr. Nibbles the guinea pig

Averted Vision

HOLLY

Cass you haven't had bangs since you were
a kid

KAYLA

Fringe or sweep? I hope it's sweep

CASSIE

Fringe

ASHLEY

Fringe bangs! What were you thinking

Chapter Thirteen

Dale drove his dad's Sierra pickup to the local VFW Post, Veterans of Foreign Wars, to visit his incarcerated mother. With the real jail in bits, scattered across a ten-mile swath, he wasn't sure what he would find at the make-shift one. He prepared himself for armed guards and coils of barbed wire.

Instead red flags outlined the lawn where the memorial tank used to be. The place looked like a family reunion picnic. It seemed most of the town was under arrest. The Pizza Heaven delivery car idled near his mother's Mazda. Dale parked at the curb and just strolled right into the crowd.

A long table displaying an assortment of hot dishes separated double rows of tents. The loose arrangement didn't seem to be putting any innocent citizens in danger.

The only trouble appeared to be Edgar Tvrdik. The short, wiry man pushed his way into the wall-less jail and through the crowd like a charging bull. Dale knew he was not a Vigilant. Except for being a volunteer firefighter, Edgar wasn't a joiner, and he definitely didn't do organized protests. He preferred to object to everything and everyone as a solo act.

A strip of gray hair circled Edgar's mostly bald head. He

stalked among the tents yelling for his daughter Linda. He found her setting out paper plates at the potluck table.

"What the hell are you doing?" Edgar demanded. "Just like you to walk out on me. Any foolish, air-head excuse to get out of work and off you go like some God-damn rich super star with nothin' to do but strut around for people who don't give a shit about you."

Linda carefully adjusted a stack of napkins. "I have to be here, Daddy," she said in a small voice. "I'm under arrest."

"The hell you are," Edgar yelled. "Get your fat ass back to the store right now."

Dale felt embarrassed for her. From the way her father treated her, you'd never know Linda Tvrdik Ergen was a grown thirty-something woman with a husband and kids. You'd never know it from the way she reacted either. She hung her head and took it like a beaten dog.

Her husband Greg was a manager at the Falls Market, the big grocery store in town and the main competition for Tvrdik's Goods and Groceries. Dale guessed that made for some brisk conversation around the dinner table on holidays.

Maybe Linda stuck by her dad because her mom had died a long time ago, and her brothers and sisters had all moved away. Edgar took the desertions hard and disowned his own kids. Linda probably felt obligated to stay and take care of him.

That was stupid, Dale decided. He couldn't think of any reason for putting up with the abuse and humiliation her dad piled on her.

Smoky gray clouds rolled across the sky, obstructing the bright summer sunshine. Dale thought it was as if Edgar caused them to form. He and Richie usually didn't go into the store when the old guy was working behind the counter. The minute they walked through the door, Edgar gave them his usual warning, "Get what you need, pay for it, and get out. This ain't no public library or social club. Find somewhere else to do nothin'." Sometimes he tossed in swear words in case they were unclear about his lack of delight at seeing them.

"Move it. Now!" Edgar shouted, turning his back on his daughter. He stomped across the VFW lawn and headed toward the store. The crowd parted before him like a flock of geese.

Linda hunched as if trying to curl up into a ball and followed him. She stepped past the border of red flags and onto the sidewalk, officially becoming a fugitive, apparently more afraid of her dad than the law.

Dale was no fan of the woman. She treated him and Richie as if they had a disease, but as least she tolerated their presence and didn't yell at them. Maybe he sympathized with her because of his own fears. Like her, he was the baby of the family. His two brothers and one sister were much older. They had no interest in the farm and had moved away soon after graduating from high school.

Not that the operation was much of a business anymore. It would never again be the sole support of a family. His dad had trouble accepting that reality. He acted as if Dale would take over someday. He wasn't as mean as Tvrdik, but he had hard expectations for his son. Dale had mostly given up trying to meet them.

Dale watched Edgar practically sprint away from his waddling daughter. Although Linda put all her effort into it, she fell farther and farther behind.

Me and Dad could end up like that, Dale thought.

For Linda's sake, he wished Edgar would drop dead. He wasn't surprised when the guy continued on his way without so much as a trip. Dale no longer put much energy into his wishes. Which reminded him, he wanted to check prices on a spotting scope, something more powerful than binoculars.

The crowd's uncomfortable silence settled back into chatter. Mrs. Glavin offered him a red plastic cup of lemonade, which he took. Mrs. Callahan shoved a plate of tatter tot hot dish at him, which he declined.

He knew his mom would be close by, busy doing something. She took her role as a founding member of the Vigilants seriously. The combined Catholic and Lutheran group was bent on driving the evil strip club from pure, holy Glacier Falls. Wednesday and Saturday nights she took her turn picketing the parking lot with other members of the self-anointed morals squad. She'd be there on Friday's, too, except the drug store was open late. She usually took that shift so the clerks with young families could get home for supper.

Dale found his mom cutting a pan of marshmallow-topped lime Jello into serving-sized squares. "Hey." He held out a scrunched-up cloth grocery bag. "Here's the stuff."

His mom had called his dad that morning and given him a list of things she needed. Dale's dad shoved the items into the sack, cursing under his breath the whole time. He refused to set foot in town as long as his wife was a criminal, so he sent his son to be embarrassed in his place.

It didn't bother Dale that his mom had been arrested and he had to visit her in the sort-of jail. But he felt all sweaty at having to bring her personal items, including hair supplies and a change of underwear.

Helen Steinhaus put down the knife and took the bag. "Thanks, Sherman. Gretta's going to do my hair for me."

Dale kept his face chill against the itchy irritation. His parents insisted on calling him by the first name given on his birth certificate. So did most adults in town. Anyone who wanted to stay his friend knew better.

He got his size from his dad, and his blue eyes from his mom. She seemed so much shorter today. Usually a tower of teasing and sticky spray, her hair lay flat against her head, probably deflated from sleeping on a cot. She wore yesterday's tight jeans and an oversized t-shirt with the Vigilants' logo on it.

"Wells did pretty good setting all this up on the fly last night," Dale said. "How did he move the tank?"

"Tornado did that for him," Helen said. "Justin's a practical guy. He saw an open space and he used it. I'm going to vote for him again next election. I might even campaign for him."

"Yeah, but about this arrest." His dad had kind of explained, but not really. Talking to his mom about stuff was always easier. More relaxed. Less drama.

"When we were waving signs and collecting license plate numbers it was just trespassing and disorderly conduct. Apparently putting bumper stickers on other people's cars is vandalism."

"Bumper stickers?" Dale asked.

"'I'm a sinner Pray for me.' I'd show you one, but Justin confiscated them." She put on a pious expression of mock remorse. "As evidence of our terrible wrong-doing."

"You nail anybody's car?" Dale asked.

His mother gave a wicked smiled. "I did my share."

He chuckled. "My mom the vandal."

"I suppose your dad's mad at me." She wasn't smiling now.

"Yeah, I guess." He ran a hand through his hair, once again caught in the middle of parental conflict. "He says you've gone from being Vigilants to being vigilantes."

"That's pretty good for your dad."

"Witty, even." Dale watched Father Anderson's lively discussion with Sheriff Wells. The priest at St. Mary's Catholic Church was getting more agitated by the second. "Is Wells guarding everyone by himself?"

"Not guarding exactly," his mom said. "We're on the honor system. We drove ourselves here, too. Most of these people weren't even at the protest. They just came over to bring food and show support."

The argument between the priest and the sheriff

escalated. "We want our day in court," Father Anderson shouted. "That place is selling sin. It's the home of the devil, an offense against God."

"God gave us all free will," Sheriff Wells said. "Some folks exercise it by watching skinny women take their clothes off. Father, I realize preventing people from enjoying themselves is part of your job description, but they're not breaking the law."

Dale knew that was part of the conflict. The Glacier Falls' residents were caught off guard by a strip club suddenly getting a business license and flinging open its doors. The town didn't have an ordinance restricting adult entertainment establishments. It had never occurred to anyone that they needed such a thing. Since the Safari Club already existed, the new regulation quickly passed by the city council didn't apply to it. The only way to get rid of the place was to force it to close down.

Father Anderson continued, "We have a First Amendment right to voice our opposition."

"Free speech," the sheriff said in his slow way, "that's exactly what the club owners are claiming."

A crowd formed around the argument. Reverend Gunther of Faith and Hope Lutheran Church rushed to support Father Anderson. Dale had heard stories about the feud between the two congregations over real and imagined insults that went back to when the corner stones of each church were set in place on the same day. The competing theologians had only recently become allies to battle against evil.

"What's that about?" Dale asked his mother.

"We've been released," Helen said, "but we're going to stay for a while to protest being arrested."

Dale wondered if his mom recognized the irony in objecting to being locked up by staying locked up, especially when there weren't any real locks. He felt a little better knowing Linda Ergen hadn't committed a second crime by leaving.

Billowing charcoal clouds headed toward them. He figured a minor sprinkle would be enough to wash away any reverse prison revolt. "What about your job? Don't you work today?"

"Becky's handling my shift right now. Later, one of the girls is coming over here to take my place while I go to work."

By "girls" she meant the women in pink smocks who staffed the drug store. None of them was under the age of forty. Dale imagined them designing a schedule with color-coded time slots, so his mom's spot in jail would always be filled.

Helen shook the bag at him. "I need to find Gretta and get major reconstruction done on my hair. You should get something to eat. Try the kale and green bean salad."

"Yeah, okay." Dale watched her rush off. He wandered around and found the tent that had gotten the pizza delivery. The Petrosky family crowded into the little fabric room. Mom, dad and six daughters were eating, laughing, and talking at the same time. One of the twins invited Dale in and offered him a slice of black olive and pepperoni.

He liked the Petrosky sisters. Ranging in ages from fifteen to nine, they seemed perpetually happy and excited about life. They were also tall. He felt positively normal in their midst. Unfortunately, they were basketball players. The coach of the boys' team had given up begging Dale to come to practice. Dale had turned the guy down every time, pretending he was too chill for sports. Truth was, he couldn't dribble a ball to save himself from hell. When the girls started talking shooting averages, he thanked them and left.

Outside by the untouched kale and green beans Father Anderson seemed determine to continue the fight. "We will rid the town of Satan and his minions," he boomed into a microphone clutched in his hand. His amplified voice competed with thunder.

The rain Dale had anticipated plopped down in huge drops, dampening the electrical cord that snaked across the ground to the preacher. Lightning strobed against muddy clouds. Dale considered staying, in hopes of seeing some real fire and brimstone.

Reverend Gunther grabbed the mic and wrestled with the priest for control of the off switch. "Getting electrocuted will not serve the Lord!" rang with ear-busting volume across the VFW lawn like a celestial announcement.

Dale hurried to his dad's pickup and climbed in. The sprinkle quickly escalated into heavy drops pounding on the metal roof. Rain trickled off the tents and formed streams that cut channels through the DIY penal colony. The scene lit up as if a giant had taken a photo using a huge flashbulb.

Dale counted. *One thousand one. One thousand two. One thousand three.*

He reached six. A thunderous boom burst around him. Six seconds from flash to thunder. The lightning strike had been close. The next one would be closer.

It seemed the protesters suddenly decided to accept having the charges dropped. Dale watched them collect soggy hot dishes and form an exodus to their vehicles. His mom, a garbage bag held over her head to protect her refreshed hairdo and a casserole dish tucked under an arm, dashed to her car and ducked in. She drove away toward the drug store.

Dale made a mental note to reminder her the Mazda needed new tires before winter.

Chapter Fourteen

S unny SunnieChat Day!

CASSIE

My dead guy was on the news

ASHLEY

Saw it. Dad says you're insane for staying at the lake alone. He wants me to get a Rottweiler and move in with you. Cause I'm so scary

CASSIE

That would scare me. Seriously. Don't do that

KAYLA

You could move in with me

CASSIE

Me or Ashley?

ASHLEY

You realize you're on a ship 3,000 miles away

KAYLA

Ash with a big Rott. Cassie's puppy would have to cute someone to death

Averted Vision

CASSIE

Give him time

HOLLY

Don't underestimate the power of cute. My kids cute their aunties out of wild gifts every chance they get. YKWITA. Disney character costumes with wigs. Life size castle Lego kit

KAYLA

It wasn't life size and I did so of my own free will

HOLLY

That's what they want you to think

CASSIE

I passed up the backyard pirate ship. Maybe I should reconsider

ASHLEY

I'm thinking bagpipes and drums this year so they can start their own band. Who's with me?

Chapter Fifteen

The Floater dominated Wednesday's front page of the twice weekly *Falls Press*. Cassie cringed at the newspaper's use of the nickname Sheriff Wells had so casually tossed out. The main article identified him as Russell Sworski from Golden Valley, a suburb of Minneapolis.

The accompanying photo showed a fiftyish man, stoically professional in a suit and tie. He seemed more like a desk jockey than the outdoor type. He'd been missing since October. The cause of death was still unknown.

Cassie's name was given, along with a description of her heroic swim to save a guy who was already dead. The reporter used several of the terse responses she'd made to his questions during the short phone interview. From her past horrific experiences with the press, she'd developed the ability to spew generic comments that meant nothing. Any seasoned journalist who was used to misdirection would never let her get away with such bland statements, but a small-town intern was too polite to press her for more substance.

According to a sidebar, the deceased was a partner in the corporation that owned the Safari Club and a similar establishment in the Twin Cities. That was sure to provide the springboard for a lot of conspiracy theories. The company also operated several elegant restaurants in the Minneapolis and St. Paul area. Sworski was the manager for one of them.

Even a small paper like the *Falls Press* was online. The media vultures must have some kind of spy-like trace for any mention of her name. She ignored the calls from any phone number not in her contacts, and she deleted the voice messages that tried to lure her into interviews.

They weren't really interested in a lake-washed corpse. The current body was just an excuse to trick her into recycling details of Vicky's bloody death that they could pitch as new revelations.

The attention made Cassie want to stay secluded in the cabin permanently. She only lasted until the next day. During her excursion into town she noticed whispers and a bit of pointing, but people gave her space. No cameras were shoved at her. No paparazzi.

She stopped at Prairie Drug, the only drugstore in town, to get ibuprofen. In L.A. she'd taken it mostly for stress-induced headaches and sinus pain. Now she needed it for aching muscles from house and yard work. It was a satisfying difference. Cassie selected caplets and headed toward the checkout counter.

A wide figure was suddenly in front of her. Owen Norquist. His dirty-rag hair looked as if it hadn't been combed since long before he'd leaned out of his truck window in her driveway.

His sunken brown eyes appraised her with amusement. "Well if it isn't the new bitch in town," he said loudly. "I wondered how long it would take you to zero in on the only real man in this county." He looked around, as if assessing the audience.

A few shoppers watched wide-eyed. One scurried out of the store. The cashier picked up the phone and punched a button.

"I expected it sooner since you think you can mess with what's mine. You like to stir up trouble. Well, I've got plenty of it for you." Owen grabbed his crotch and jiggled his hand, seemingly delighted at having another victim to terrorize.

Cassie wrinkled up her nose. He smelled of week-old fish. She knew his lewdness was supposed to make her panic. She clenched her jaw, ashamed she had cowered in the grass by her very own home.

This was not in the dark on a lonely country road. This was in daylight in a public store. She stood her ground. His behavior might be shocking in Greater Minnesota, but it was a common occurrence on metro streets. To Cassie, the ones who yelled and screamed were far less terrifying than the quiet ones who moved silently up behind you and gently whispered vulgarities in your ear then slipped away before you could get a good look at them.

A bleached blonde—not Glenna—quickly walked to the door. She paused before pulling open the glass rectangle. "I'm leaving," she said without turning to look at Owen. Cassie guessed she was Judy Norquist, his wife.

Owen laughed. "I'll get around to you later," he told Cassie. He swaggered toward the woman as if expecting applause. He put an arm around her then slid his hand to her buttocks and gave a possessive squeeze.

Trembling with anger, Cassie stepped to the counter to pay for her purchase.

The pink-smocked cashier hung up the phone and scanned the price. "You want some water so you can take a couple of these right now? Seriously, we've got a break room in the back. You should sit for a minute."

"Thanks, but I'm okay." Well, she would be after some deep breathing and yoga.

"I'm Helen Steinhaus. We're neighbors." Barely five feet tall, she had at least four additional inches of hair teased into a style country-western singers used to wear. She had a sturdy build. One look in her direct blue eyes, and Cassie knew who kept the Steinhaus family on track.

"I did call the manager," Helen said. "I don't want you to think I didn't do nothing to help. He might come charging out of his office in an hour or two, acting all brave. My husband Irv's a volunteer with the fire department. He was over at your place with the Sparks. Said you found that man from the Cities."

Cassie immediately liked the woman. She seemed more friendly than probing. "Strange no one around here knew who he was, or that he was missing, even if he wasn't local."

Helen shrugged. "You might see someone in town a couple of times, doesn't mean you know them. I've seen you around, and you've been in here before, but this is the first time I've had a chance to introduce myself."

"I'm really glad you did." Cassie couldn't help doing a little probing of her own. "Do you remember Russel Sworski coming in?"

"The Floater," Helen said with flare. "I bet Sheriff Wells came up with that handle. All of us girls here looked at the picture in the paper and agreed he hadn't been a customer. We were thinking he couldn't have been staying at any of the resorts. The owners watch out for their guests, and would know if one disappeared. More likely he was at a private cabin. Some of them are pretty tucked away."

"Seems he would have been with his family. Or friends. Not on his own."

"Probably with some buddies," Helen said. "You know, cold beer, stinky cigars, and a little fishing."

"And these buddies just went home without him."

"Or they drowned, too," Helen said cheerfully.

Cassie imagined more blobs rising to the surface and drifting to her shore. "I am never going swimming in Beauty Lake again."

"Sorry," Helen said. "I shouldn't have put that thought in your head."

"It's okay," Cassie said, but she had to change the subject. "Tell Irv I really appreciate the Sparks cleaning up the mess in my yard. Now I need to hire someone who can handle a chain saw and a weed trimmer." She was determined to get the neglected property back into shape. If she could find a reliable person, and if her finances stayed healthy, the position could turn into a steady job. "Got any recommendations?"

Helen had a quick reply. "I know a young man with a lot of experience. Sherman, my son. He's done everything there is to do on a farm. Taking down trees, roofing, mowing."

Cassie exchanged phone numbers with Helen. She stepped out of the store into the sunshine, feeling recovered from her encounter with Owen, until she saw Judy Norquist waiting for her.

The woman ran a hand through her bleached, wavy mane that hung to a blunt cut at her shoulders. She wore shorts and a shirt that were clean and crisp but as tired looking as she was. Three more pieces of inexpensive jewelry than a trip to town warranted weighed her down. "You're Glenna's friend. The one who helped her when she got scraped up."

When she got tossed onto the road like an empty beer can, Cassie wanted to say. She didn't. "I was glad I could help."

"Thank you for doing that. Most people wouldn't." Judy seemed uncomfortable but determined to speak her piece. "Glenna's a good girl. She hasn't had things easy and she's doing the best she can."

Cassie wondered if Judy was also talking about herself.

The woman glanced over her shoulder at the hardware store. "It means a lot that someone was nice to her. But she can't call you or come over to your place or anything. It isn't she doesn't want to. She does. It's just, Owen doesn't want her to."

Judy bit her lower lip. "I don't want you to think bad of

him. He wasn't like that so much when he was doing liquor delivery. It was mostly down in the Cities, so people up here don't know he ever had a steady job, but he did. And things were really good. Then he got hurt and had to take it easy. Even that was okay as long as he could see this doctor in Minneapolis. But after a while he couldn't do the lifting anymore so he was let go. No one around here will hire him for anything. He has to make his own jobs."

Illegal jobs, Cassie thought. She wondered if the prescription just filled for the Norquist household was for Owen.

"I just wanted to tell you about Glenna." Judy shifted so she could more easily watch the store front. "And to say I'm sorry about Owen just now." She put her head down and leaned toward Cassie. "And, I guess, to warn you. Owen's serious about making trouble for you. You don't want that. We don't either, Glenna and me. So be careful. Please." She started to leave.

"Wait." Cassie reached for the woman's arm.

Judy pulled away from the contact "I have to get back to the truck. Owen will get real mad if he sees me talking to you."

"You don't have to stay with him, you and Glenna," Cassie said. "You don't have to be afraid."

Judy looked down at the sidewalk. "It's best if you just let things be the way they are."

The woman hurried away. Cassie watched her climb into the ugly pickup and sink into the seat. Barely a second passed. Owen strutted out of the hardware store swinging a plastic bag. He chucked his purchase at Judy through the open window and hoisted himself into the driver's seat.

Cassie closed her eyes to the familiar rough growl as the truck drove away.

Maybe her dad was right. Maybe she did need Ashley and a Rottweiler to move in with her.

Chapter Sixteen

Celebrate your day with SunnieChat!

HOLLY

> Looking for deep philosophical meaning in good night moon and hop on pop. Not what I imagined my life would be when I got a masters in 19th Cen Brit Lit

ASHLEY

> Life isn't Jane Austin. For which I'm grateful. I couldn't handle a regency waistline right under my boobs. And all those ribbons. I'd burn my bonnet

HOLLY

> It's Austen with an e. See how my years of study just paid off

KAYLA

> Cass needs a pop to hop on

CASSIE

> Not everyone has access to a swim trunk clad hunky Scott

Averted Vision

Chapter Seventeen

Dale's mom clattered lunch dishes from the sink to the dishwasher. Dale should have done it before she got home, but he hadn't and neither had his dad. He thought she looked worn out after her night at the VFW jail and her shift at the drugstore.

At the kitchen table his dad charted the path of the recent tornado on a county map. His parents moved around one another in silence, pointedly not discussing The Arrest. In a strange way the eerie atmosphere reminded Dale of that prickling on your skin when bad weather starts moving in.

"Sherman, I've got a job for you," his mother announced, "working down the road for Cassie Windom, Renee and Steve Schroeder's niece."

The stormy mood burst into a twister. His dad shoved himself away from the table. "Dale works on the farm. He doesn't get all his chores done as it is. And now you want him off doing favors for someone."

His mom added a smeared plate to the rack. "Not favors. Paid employment. And if you didn't spend so much time with your Sparks pals, you could get more done around here yourself."

His mom wasn't wrong. His dad had been at the fire hall a lot lately working on plans for the annual Tornado Daze festival. At least that's what he said he was doing. Dale wasn't so sure. Maybe his mom wasn't so sure either.

"How's he going to learn the business if he's working somewhere else?" his dad shouted.

The yelling would probably go on for a while, and supper was at least an hour away. Dale slammed the door as he left the house, not that anyone noticed. He took the ATV and went to find out what his new boss wanted him to do.

Funny not funny, whenever his parents were mad at one another, they always ended up fighting about *him*.

He saw her right away when he swung into the driveway. She was in the garage fiddling with an awesome telescope. He'd never seen a big fat one like that before. It was nothing like the spotting scopes used for hunting and bird watching, or the long skinny tubes they want you to buy for kids at Christmas time.

"Hi, Ms. Windom. My mom said you need some work done." A red brindle puppy crouched and grr-ed at him, making him laugh. "I like your guard dog." The farm should have one again. But after Old Hunter died, his dad said they were too much trouble. His father had raised the black lab from a pup and trained him to be the best birder in the county. Dale figured his dad just couldn't handle seeing another dog in Old Hunter's place.

"His name's Jupiter," Cassie said.

"Like the planet. Yeah, I see it."

"Call me Cassie." She stuck out her hand.

A little surprised, he gave it a quick shake. "I'm Dale."

She looked confused. "I thought——"

"Yeah, my mom and dad call me Sherman. But I use my middle name." She wasn't bad looking, despite her ugly haircut. He pointed to the chunk of oak sprawled lazily across the lawn. "I suppose you want to get rid of that."

"I could keep it as yard art, but it isn't really my style. So, yes, that's a priority. And the place could use mowing, trimming, tidying up." Cassie gestured to a scruffy spot by the garage. "I'd like this to be a flower garden again, but I don't know what to do with it for now. Any ideas?"

Wow. She asked him for advice. Jupiter tugged at the laces on his work boots. Dale took it as a sign the puppy thought he was okay. "The roses need major trimming. I know how to do that. It's late in the season, but there's plenty of time to put perennials around them, if you know what you want. Or plant annuals just to get through the summer."

"Annuals sound good."

They talked snapdragons and marigolds. She'd get a bunch and he'd plop them in the ground. He might have pretended he knew more about landscaping than he really did. He was more of a crop-seed guy, but he'd picked up plenty about flowers helping his mom give the farmhouse what the DIY shows call curb appeal. Not that there was a curb. Or a ton of people driving by to impress.

It seemed Cassie trusted him right away. That's why he felt sort of guilty about the idea floating around in his head.

Dale returned home to an unnatural quiet. The fragrance of reheating meatball hot dish left over from the prison buffet hit him as soon as he entered the kitchen, making his stomach growl. His mom selected a jar of beets to go with it. His dad silently rolled up the county map.

"The job at Cassie's wouldn't mess up my chores" Dale announced. "And I've already started."

There. If they wanted to fight, they would have to find a topic that wasn't him.

Chapter Eighteen

S unny SunnieChat Day!

HOLLY

Emma is a snowflake in the dance recital. A
snowflake. In July

KAYLA

Send pics

CASSIE

She has to wear her costume at Christmas

HOLLY

At the rate she's growing, she'll be three
inches taller by then. The skirt barely covers
her ass now

ASHLEY

You sew. Add more tulle

CASSIE

Costumes. This is me in my astronomy outfit. I
think I look like a Pirate Bear

ASHLEY

Still can't see your haircut. Are you hiding it on
purpose?

KAYLA

Pirate bear sounds like anime. I'd watch
that show

HOLLY

The kids will want to dress up like Aunt Cassie
for cosplay

CASSIE

I should have gotten them that pirate ship

KAYLA

Sept 19 talk like a pirate day

HOLLY

How do you even know that?

KAYLA

The islands were a big hangout for pirates. I'm
very connected to the seafaring counter
culture. Arrrr!

CASSIE

Anyone remember a guy named Owen
Norquist? Older than the cousins. Or not.
Can't tell

KAYLA

I'm too young to remember anyone

ASHLEY

Nope. But the Denny thing got me thinking.
What guy had a crush on Holly?

HOLLY

OMG my first Stalker!

KAYLA

There've been more?

Averted Vision

ASHLEY

Greg. Is that right?

HOLLY

Grug the bug! I couldn't stand him

CASSIE

I met him. Manager at the Falls Market now

HOLLY

Does he still have great hair?

Chapter Nineteen

Windows down, tunes up. That's how chill guys roll.

Dale twisted the radio knob, dialing in an all-rock station out of Fargo as he and Richie cruised the streets of Glacier Falls in the Fart Bomb. Richie's car wasn't much more than a Toyota frame on bald tires propelled by a tiny engine about as powerful as a pair of hamsters spinning their little wheels. But it was transportation. And it was more than Dale had.

"F13 today. There should be a big-ass full moon," Richie complained to Dale. A scrawny five feet six, his dark blond hair hung to his chin and almost matched his pale brown eyes.

Dale leaned an arm on the window sill and squinted into the dusk. He scanned the deep shadows under passing shrubbery for Muffin. Fifteen pounds of fat and fur, the Danowski's black cat moved like a cheetah when it wanted to. They'd set up their traditional Friday the Thirteenth Freak Out. After only a couple of tuna runs the cat bolted and now commanded its own game of hide and seek.

Dale agreed about the moon. In honor of superstitions, it should be bright and round as a soccer ball, sending out scary shadows. Instead it was new moon, no illumination. He and

Cassie had talked about it while he took a break from chain sawing the downed limb into carriable bits. She'd shown him a calendar of July with moon phases pictured on it. For the second time, he tried to explain it to Richie. "The moon orbits the Earth. You get that part?"

"Sure," Richie said.

"Right now, tonight, it's between the Earth and the sun. Earth on one side. Sun on the other."

"Okay."

"The sun side gets all the light, and the Earth side doesn't get any. If it was right in front of you in the sky you couldn't see it because it's all dark on this side."

"So the moon's invisible," Richie said.

"It isn't invisible. We just can't see it."

Richie eased the Bomb onto Central Avenue. "Duh, invisible."

Dale gave up. Richie didn't get it. Mostly because he didn't give a shit. Although a year older than Dale, they were in the same grade. Dale didn't think his friend's being held back in kindergarten had done him much good. Richie was in deep danger of not having enough credits to graduate in two years.

Tvrdik's Goods and Groceries was on the next block. "We should check the alley behind G. and G." Dale said. "Muffin might be dumpster diving." He really hoped the cat had already scampered home so they could be done with the F13 thing.

"Yeah," Richie said. "And when we find Muff, we should run up to the front door and shove him inside. The old man always works the late shift on Friday. He'd piss his pants."

No, he wouldn't, Dale thought. *More like, he'd bludgeon the thing to death and make his daughter clean up the mess.*

Blocks ahead Owen's unmistakable truck swung onto the street.

"Shit," Dale breathed out.

"Double fudge shit," Richie said.

The pickup charged along Central, defying the modest speed limit. Almost to Tvrdik's, it suddenly braked to a crawl. The rolling camo-monster crept over the pavement as if sneaking up on a prey.

Richie clutched the steering wheel, his knuckles sticking out like mountains from the strain. "I don't think he slowed down to look for a cat."

Dale felt a sickness growing in his gut. Here the block stretched extra-long on both sides due to a zoning dispute going back decades. Cars parked along the curbs made it impossible to turn around. The only path was straight ahead.

"You can make it to the corner. It's not that far," Dale said, but the next cross street seemed a galaxy away. "If he tries to play chicken, you just let him win, Richie. You got that?"

"Get out, Dale," Richie said quietly.

Dale punched off the radio, silencing a neo-techno group he used to like. "What?"

"Seriously. Get out and run behind a tree or something." Richie stared at the pickup edging toward them.

Dale couldn't bale and leave his friend. "Is Owen pissed at you? I mean more than he's usually pissed at everyone?" What had Richie done now?

The camo truck inched closer. A long, metal-blue shotgun barrel slid out of the passenger window. Even at a distance, Dale knew it instantly. Owen's projection of his own exaggerated manhood, a Beretta 686 Silver Pigeon.

"Fuck." Richie slammed on the gas. Rebuilt a dozen times using questionable parts, the Bomb hesitated and coughed. It sputtered, about to die.

The engine boomed and caught hold. The Toyota exploded straight for Owen, the truck, and the shotgun.

Dale braced himself against the dashboard. The seatbelts were purely decorative and wouldn't stop him from vaulting through the windshield even if he'd buckled in, which he hadn't. He wished he had more life to flash before his eyes. Or at least a more interesting one, so his last moments would be entertaining instead of boring.

Shit. I survived a tornado so I can be sprayed with buckshot and mashed like a potato in the bent grill of a rusty pickup.

Richie cranked the steering wheel hard to the right, aiming for the side street. The Fart Bomb skidded in an arc. The back balding tires bumped over the curb on the far edge barely missing a fire hydrant.

Shotgun blasts burst behind them. Dale counted. *One. Two.* Reload.

The Bomb bounced back onto the tar at a slant and vaulted over the sidewalk on the other side, taking out a bird feeder and grazing a planter outside Smile Dentistry.

Richie overcorrected to the left, sending the rear end swinging. The Bomb sprang into the street, completing a U-turn.

Dale stared out the windshield, shocked they were heading back toward Central

Boom.

How many was that? He couldn't remember. He couldn't think. Was another round in the chamber ready to be fired? Or did they have a few precious seconds during a reload to try to salvage their botched escape?

Unseen behind a row of thick lilac bushes, the truck's engine screeched, as if grinding its teeth before pouncing on a meal.

Richie shoved the shift lever into reverse. The Bomb complained then sped backward.

Dale dug his fingers into the dashboard, watching for the mottled monster to turn the corner in pursuit. One of them should be looking in the direction they were actually traveling, but he couldn't pull his stare from where the beast would appear. And he doubted Richie had even glanced at the rearview mirror.

Owen's rumbling pickup shot out from behind the hedge. It flashed past, keeping a straight course on Central, and zoomed away.

Richie fishtailed to a stop. "Holy fuck."

"Holy fuckin' hell." Dale's heart pounded so loud he thought Richie could hear it.

"That was awesome," Richie said. "The Bomb was awesome. My driving was, I mean, man, *really awesome.*"

Dale didn't share Richie's adrenaline-fueled joy. He pulled out his cell to punch 9-1-1. Sirens screamed toward them, making the call unnecessary.

"We gotta' slip," Richie said. He guided the Bomb through a controlled U-turn. No bumping over curbs this time.

That idea Dale had yesterday at Cassie's rocketed back into his head. It was wrong. It was so wrong. This morning he'd decided to never think of it again.

Now he knew he had to do it.

Chapter Twenty

It was hard to imagine anything could so quickly dislodge the Floater and Cassie's "heroic" swim as the primary focus of the *Falls Press*, but a four-day old drowning story couldn't compete with a fresh shooting right on the main drag.

Cassie read the account at the paper's website on Saturday, glad she didn't have to wait until Wednesday for the physical copy.

Last night someone fired four rounds from a moving vehicle into Tvrdik's Goods and Groceries, shattering the large front window. Edgar Tvrdik, the owner and only eye witness, was unharmed. The sheriff's department was investigating. No arrests had been made.

A drive-by shooting on Friday the thirteenth! Cassie was relieved to be old news. She popped a pod in the coffee maker and punched the button. Other people might have the weekend off to lounge on the deck and drink margaritas. Self-employed, she worked when she had a job and was grateful for it.

Oh, to move to Europe. Travel from city to magnificent city, studying the masters. Settle in Florence, Italy, near the

Uffizi museum. She'd paint serious, richly detailed works sure to ignite a new Renaissance.

Of course, she could do the traveling and painting parts now. The Renaissance thing would take more time. But the starving artist role was not for her. She saw nothing noble about it, and didn't feel the least bit creative when she was hungry.

She'd have to continue to pay the rent, keep the electricity flowing, *and* carve out time for personal projects.

Ideas flooded her. Still-life water colors, even though they didn't fit into current art trends. Landscapes in chalk. Abstracts in cloth and beads. She'd made sketches for three-dimensional clothing with the wearer as part of the design. Not a radical idea, but a stretch of her skills and that was what mattered.

Cassie grabbed the steaming coffee mug from the machine and settled into the spare bedroom she'd transformed into her office. Since her departure from Fontana Media, Prentice Royer, her former boss, channeled enough contract work her way to keep her financially stable.

She opened her electronic tablet and pulled up the scene of truck taillights on a desolate country road. The battered vehicle recklessly careens away from the viewer, leaving wavy tire tracks. Towering, ominous, rock formations flank a winding path stretching toward a fiery horizon and ending at a ragged, severed edge that appears to drop into nothingness.

Cassie enthusiastically layered colors onto the burning sky and sharpened the lines of the truck. The image had nothing to do with the product, which made it very high concept. She knew it was therapy, but she grabbed the inspiration before her, even—maybe especially—when it was generated by terror. She added the last highlight.

Drive off a cliff, Owen.

She sent a note and the digital image winging through the air to Prentice.

Knowing she couldn't rely on Fontana forever, she'd been cultivating other clients. An email popped up from the owner of a candy shop. The company had a tiny brick-and-mortar store in New York City and a drab online presence in need of a major makeover. The owner-president was looking for an "invigorating theme" that would "boost our unique brand."

He'd probably picked up the language from a high-powered advertising firm—like Fontana—that had given him some preliminary sizzle he'd been excited about until he looked closely at the string of digits following the dollar sign attached to it. "The graphics have to look rich and yummy." Now, *that* was the chocolatier speaking.

Boldly, she replied to the sugar mogul that she shared his vision of a gooey, tasty electronic presence. Typing a confident response to a stranger half a continent away was easy. Having that confidence was harder.

Designs she'd done for Fontana clients were all over the Internet; but at the agency she'd been part of a team, with multimedia specialists to guide her. Now she was on her own. She desperately needed this experience to build her resume and stretch her skills, yet it terrified her. She wasn't ready for it.

But chocolate! Oh, the joy of research!

Prentice's quick response to her illustration flashed at the top of her email list. "Love it. Give me two more with this theme and style for the same campaign. Send preliminary sketches ASAP. When are you going to come back to Fontana?"

To celebrate, Cassie drove the Mini Cooper into town to grab something frozen for supper. She parked outside the Falls Market and put on a jacket. Like most air-conditioned stores, when she walked in, the place was a cold shock on a hot day. She started on the most direct route to the freezers. A high, screechy voice she recognized came from the produce section.

Mrs. Finster. A skinny crane of a woman, her permed,

slate-blue hair curled tightly against her head. Nurturer of scandal and self-appointed guardian of the town's immortal soul, she never let a small thing like hard evidence prevent her from presenting spicy speculation as fact.

Her gaggle of loyal followers gathered around her, hanging on her every syllable as if she were an online influencer. Cassie didn't want to see or be seen by any of them. She swerved down the canned-goods aisle.

"That Owen Norquist," Mrs. Finster said.

Cassie halted and listened.

"He jumped out of his truck in the middle of the street outside Edgar's store," Mrs. Finster proclaimed. "Climbed out with a gigantic machine gun, all bold and cocky. You know how he is. Fired twenty times straight through the window. Edgar saw him right away, plain as could be. He knew the gun was aimed directly at his head. Real quick, he dropped behind the counter. And that saved his life.

"Edgar told me everything himself. He's lucky to be alive, you know. And that poor excuse for a sheriff we have refuses to do a thing! Someday Edgar's going to make his own justice and flat out kill Owen."

Her royal court made appropriate noises. "Be doing us all a favor."

A chill surged up Cassie's spine. The prophecy was still on her mind when she returned home with frozen lasagna and discovered the empty spot in her garage.

Chapter Twenty-One

Sun Sun SunnieChat!

HOLLY

K please. We agreed emoji lite only. I get enough of that in picture books. Use your adult words! If you're having sex just say so. Don't turn it into a rebus

KAYLA

Ok I'm having sex with the hunky Liam. Anyone else having sex or am I the only one?

ASHLEY

Does sex with the ex-husband count?

HOLLY

Ash again! Stop that!

CASSIE

Not having sex. Sigh

HOLLY

Me neither. We're both too tired. Anyone want to babysit so my husband and I can spend time alone in the bedroom? We'd be sleeping but it would be as good as sex and we need it more

KAYLA

50% of us are having sex

Chapter Twenty-Two

"Just the telescope," Deputy Adam Berger said for the third time.

"And tripod with a motorized mount," Cassie said for the third time. They stood in the garage. AKA: the scene of the crime. The equipment had been beside the workbench where a padded nylon bag sat undisturbed. Easy to grab, it could have held something more valuable than the two eyepieces, red-gel flashlight, and star chart that were in it.

The manual next to it was untouched. The thief would regret not taking that important bit of literature. Cassie struggled to understand the settings, even with the instructions in front of her. "None of the eyepieces are gone, except the forty millimeter that was in the starback. Not the battery or controller." The perpetrator would have to adjust it by hand without the aid of the motor.

Serves you right, asshole.

"You're sure the garage was closed and secure."

"Yes." Cassie clung to her big city habits and locked up everything.

The deputy examined the service door. "Probably got in through here."

Cassie had already figured that out for herself. Because of the summer heat, Jupiter had been in the basement while she'd been in town. He'd probably gone crazy during the robbery, but a barking dog in the country was fairly common and mostly ignored. Only Charlie the ATV Riding Sentry would have noticed the puppy's yips and an unfamiliar car parked in her driveway. The theft must have happened between his regular tours past her place.

She'd let Jupiter out right away and made sure the intruder hadn't gotten into the house. She'd called the county sheriff's number and been routed to the temporary quarters at the VFW. Rhonda answered, the same person who'd taken her report about the incident with Glenna and Owen.

Deputy Berger arrived twenty minutes later. Cassie was fairly certain he hadn't been born and raised in Granite County, although she had no idea what led her to that conclusion. He seemed to be in his early thirties. His light brown hair was buzzed close to the scalp. A bit under six feet, he had a muscular, hockey-player broadness that would probably lapse into pudgy if he ever let up on what must be an extensive exercise routine.

He had nice brown eyes, and wasn't wearing a wedding ring. Of course, that didn't always mean a man was unattached. She wished he'd been sent to recover the Floater instead of the sheriff so she could have met him sooner.

She was quickly disgusted with herself for that line of thought. Aside from the circumstances of meeting a potential date over a dead body, until she had a lot of other things in her life sorted out, she was determined to stay relationship free.

Plus, she wasn't impressed by his manner. She couldn't tell if he was being professional or purposely annoying. Based on no tangible evidence whatsoever, she suddenly had the feeling he'd gone through a tough divorce.

It seemed Jupiter hadn't decided how he felt about the

khaki-clad man either. Wherever the officer went, the dog made certain he got in the way. Berger appeared to interpret it as wanting attention, but Cassie knew it was the puppy's attempt to keep the stranger from roaming too freely across his territory.

Officer Berger examined his notes. Again. "Nothing taken from the house. Cash, jewelry, TV, computer, all still there?" Jupiter sat at his feet staring up at him. He leaned down and gave the Akita a cautious pat on the head. "Good thing you have your watchdog here guarding the place. He's a pretty big pup. He'd make me think twice before I stepped through the door uninvited."

"That's the idea," Cassie said. Jupiter weighed twenty pounds when she got him. Like bread dough, he seemed to have doubled in volume since then.

The deputy straightened and looked around the garage. "I don't know. This doesn't seem like a typical robbery. Most thieves are lazy. They want things they can toss in a sack or tuck under an arm. From the way you describe it, the telescope is big and heavy. It would take a lot of effort to move it. And it's not something you could easily sell around here."

Cassie crossed her arms impatiently. Besides the telescope accessories being left behind, the garage was full of her uncle's tools, all untouched. The deputy had taken a long time to reach a conclusion immediately obvious to her.

A grin broke through Deputy Berger's detachment. "Off hand, I'd say whoever nabbed it just wants to take it for a celestial joyride."

Cassie gave him a cold stare. She didn't want to think of someone doing a quick spin around the sky then trashing her beautiful scope.

The deputy flipped a page on his notepad and snapped back to a neutral expression. "Who knows you had it?"

"A lot of people, I'm afraid." Glacier Falls was a small town, after all. Cassie was a curiosity, a warm-climate city dweller transplanted into a four-season rural speck on the map. Sure, she had Minnesota roots, but she was a woman with a murder in her past. She was practically exotic by local standards, a prime candidate for the chatter groups.

Cassie had overheard some of it in Lorraine's Cafe while waiting for her BLT to go. The speaker was sitting in a booth with his back to her, so she couldn't see him. He probably looked like most of the men in town. Short hair under a cap he never took off. Shirt with two pockets, one for a tire gauge and one for the list of things to get from town that his wife had given him. Wide-legged jeans to fit over heavy boots with thick-treaded soles.

"The gal that's renting the Schroeder place. One of the nieces, isn't she? Too bad none of Steve and Renee's kids want the place. She's got one of those telescopes, the niece does. Hate to be her neighbor. Guy couldn't take a piss from his own tractor without worrying she might be spying on him."

"You don't have to worry about that," another guy said with authority. "She'd need the Hubble to see something that small." The laughter spread across several tables.

"Say," a third voice chimed in, "them Vigilants could use something like that. Then they wouldn't have to stand around in the parking lot. They could snoop on sinners from across the street at the bingo hall."

"Naw," the first man said, "Father Anderson likes to look 'em right in the eye so he can tell 'em to their face they're going to hell. Makes him feel like Christ driving the merchants from the temple."

Cassie was surprised they knew about the Hubble Space Telescope. Then she reminded herself her bias was showing. Just as she'd learned not to overestimate people in L.A. because of their slick appearances and sparkling use of language, she was reteaching herself not to underestimate the people here because of their casual approach to—well, to everything.

She tried to apply that same philosophy to Officer Berger. She relayed an edited version of the conversation she'd overheard in the cafe.

Berger gave an unimpressed nod. "Who might have actually seen it?"

"Anyone who's been here." Cassie didn't add that hadn't been too many people. Let him guess how much she entertained. "Anyone who's driven by at twilight and seen me setting up in the yard. There are other people who could figure it out. Maybe someone at the post office was curious about my subscription to *Sky and Telescope*."

"Maybe," Berger said. Cassie knew he really meant the chance of that was nil. "Could I get a list of people who might have seen it in your garage or on your property?"

A list. A confession of her dismal social life committed to paper.

The closest thing she'd had to a neighbor over for coffee was when she'd patched up Glenna. Could she count mingling with the volunteer firefighters when they'd collected the Floater as a soiree?

Oh. Yeah. Those things happened. "Some—maybe all—of the Sparks were here after the tornado," Cassie said. "I don't think I'll be able to remember many names. And the sheriff was here. And the hearse crew. The telescope was in the open garage. They would have seen it."

"That would be a good start," Berger said.

"They could have told other people about the crazy astronomer on Beauty Lake. Locals are always curious about new people."

"You've been pretty good at avoiding saying too much about yourself." Deputy Berger clamped his lips together. "Sorry, Ms. Windom. That was out of line."

"You might as well call me Cassie. The truth isn't nearly as interesting as the stories told at the Falls Market over cartons of blueberries."

"That would be Mrs. Finster and her cronies. Why don't you call me Adam."

"I reported a domestic abuse situation with Owen Norquist and a girl named Glenna Lowry. This could be retaliation."

Adam nodded. "I heard about the incident at the drug store. I made a note to check on him. This isn't his type of thing, but you never know."

"He seems to prefer open harassment." Cassie told him about the rusty truck that all too often cruised by slowly. She hugged her arms to her chest. She hated that it spooked her. At the deputy's insistence, she promised to call 9-1-1 if Owen set foot on her property.

"What about Sherman Steinhaus?" Adam asked.

"You mean Dale. He prefers his middle name. He's doing yard work for me. Cleaning up from the tornado, mowing, that kind of thing." He'd been there this morning but left before she went into town. She should add that, but decided not to. She expected the officer to caution her about the young man. Dale liked to project a rebellious image. She wouldn't be surprised if he'd been arrested for petty crimes. She preferred to judge him on what she observed for herself.

Dale was a good worker who appeared to get satisfaction from a job well done. Beneath the sometimes-cavalier manner, she sensed a deeper character. Although he tried to hide it, his intelligence slipped out. He had an interest in the world beyond Glacier Falls. And he read. A lot and in secret, she suspected.

Jupiter accepted Dale immediately. And Cassie liked him. She just did.

Adam walked out of the garage into the heat toward his car. "Maybe you could put together that list. Friends, electrician, plumber, someone who stopped and asked for directions." He squinted at the bright sunlight. "Jehovah's witness."

Cassie smiled. "I'll do what I can." She thought it to his credit that he didn't warn her Dale might be trouble.

"How about I stop by tomorrow and pick it up. You work at home, right? So you'll be here?"

She nodded. "That part of the rumors about me is true."

Chapter Twenty-Three

Cassie watched the dust-laden patrol car pull out of the driveway and wondered why she was attracted to Deputy Adam Berger when his casual attitude toward her stolen telescope infuriated her.

Was it his soft brown eyes and easy manner?

That he towered over her by at least an entire inch so she'd be able to wear heels on their dates if she wanted to?

Might be the uniform. Who could resist a guy in khaki?

The absence of a wedding ring?

Clearly, it was simpler than that. She'd gotten used to swimming in an ocean of potential partners. Here the pool of eligible men was a shallow puddle.

She banished Adam from her mind, but it was still hard to concentrate on the two new pieces Prentice wanted. She'd never had anything stolen in Los Angeles. It had taken a move to safe, rural, middle America for her to become a victim.

But then, there were many ways to be affected by a crime. You didn't have to be in the line of fire to feel the shot pierce your soul. You didn't have to be the victim to be victimized. Jupiter at her heels, Cassie strolled to the mailbox.

Wild prairie roses twined around the post, canes dotted

with pale pink blooms. Cassie pulled open the scarlet box. Aunt Renee had painted it the bright color so Uncle Steve wouldn't blissfully drive past, listening too intently to his favorite Minnesota Public Radio station to notice where he was.

Cassie retrieved the delivery for the day, being careful not to disturb the spider that had taken up residence in the domed rectangle. She walked back toward the house, sorting the junk mail from the gardening catalogs addressed to Aunt Renee.

A long, stark-white envelope stuck out from the clutter, her name and address neatly typed on the expensive stationary. Jordan thought he was clever, giving it to his lawyers who then posted it to her with the law firm's return address, so it would not be branded as from the Los Angeles County State Prison. Did he think she could be tricked into reading the handwritten pleas for her to believe in his innocence?

The thick contents required extra postage. She felt the pages crinkle through the covering. His letters were getting longer.

Vicky and Cassie joined Fontana Media at nearly the same time. Both workaholics and new to the city, at first their friendship was a convenience. They shared take-out when trying to meet a deadline, bounced ideas off of one another, and enjoyed complaining about men together. Conversations turned toward Impressionist painters and art deco architecture, noir films and underappreciated literature. Like twins separated at birth, sisters of the soul, their finding one another seemed inevitable, even predestined.

Vicky encouraged Cassie to experiment with her art. Cassie supported Vicky's wacky literary style. Together they produced sharp, effective ad campaigns.

Cassie met Jordan through art gallery friends she and

Vicky hung out with. His pale-streaked surfer hair was more from a salon than the sun, and the intense blue eyes, were more contact lenses than nature.

The compliments that bubbled out of him were much too smooth for Cassie's taste. His casual, witty comments sounded rehearsed, as if he practiced them in front of a mirror. She guessed he spent a lot of time gazing at his own image, perfecting little nuances of expression and the tilt of his broad shoulders.

At first she only saw him when they went out in a group. She deflected his efforts to separate her from the others. Then unexpected encounters happened at odd places. Cassie had the prickly feeling they were staged rather than accidental.

Jordan seemed baffled by her cool reaction, as if shocked that the country hick wasn't flattered by his attention and dazzled by his sophisticated, urban charm.

Cassie started dating Chad almost as a way to avoid Jordan. They worked in the same building. His friends were spreadsheet jockeys and database geeks. He was cute and thoughtful and deserved someone who cared about him more than she did.

Rebuffed by Cassie, Jordan turned his attention to Vicky. Not surprising. She had perfect cocoa skin and a profile worthy of worship. The relationship began with candlelight and roses then turned controlling and abusive.

Vicky threatened to get a restraining order but she didn't. Not then. Not yet. She accepted his excuses and forgave him. She even believed him when he blamed her for his sudden explosions.

Cassie watched the scenes repeat and repeat, like a macabre horror film on a loop. The audience knew what was going to happen, while the star on the screen refused to see the danger. The inevitable climax was far from the end of the story for Cassie.

Six months after Vicky's death as Cassie tried to flag down

a cab to get to a late dinner with Chad, a power outage hit a large section of California. In the middle of honking motorists freed from traffic signals, and panicky pedestrians without the security of street lights, she stood on the sidewalk and stared straight up at the sudden display of stars.

Despite the danger of taking her attention from the street, she ignored everything around her and gazed at the bright specks. Under the startling and beautiful canopy of diamonds sparkling against black velvet, Cassie finally acknowledged to herself that she was deeply and profoundly unhappy with her life.

Two weeks later an earthquake shattered every bit of glassware she owned and caused her apartment building to be condemned due to structural damage. She released Chad to find someone who could appreciate such a wonderful guy. And she decided to go back to Minnesota. The process took almost nine months of gestation, like a birth. They should have been the worst days of her life, but she soared through them like a wild bird.

She moved into an inexpensive apartment miles from the ad agency. Although car-less for years and used to public transportation, she purchased the sunflower yellow Mini Cooper. The building was owned by a Turkish family who spoke fractured English. Cassie never figured out how many of them there were or how they were all related. She only knew they kept the place spotless, drank wonderfully strong coffee, and cooked with a great quantity of cinnamon and olive oil.

Mamma, papa, kids, aunts, uncles and other assorted relatives hugged her when she left. Eyes clouded by tears, mamma shoved a tin full of honey-thick baklava at her. The sticky treat kept her on a sugar high during the entire drive from the Pacific to the Mississippi.

Walking across the dandelion speckled lawn from the mailbox to the cabin, Cassie ran her thumb across the finely textured envelope holding Jordan's latest missive. The letters started arriving soon after his arrest when he gave up on the unanswered calls and texts. She read them at first. After his conviction, her courage and energy depleted, she came up with a different way to deal with them.

She went into the house and dropped the flyers and catalogs in the kitchen. Forcing herself to be numb, she descended to the basement, unsealed the plastic bin and slid the envelope in with the others.

In pain and rage she'd come close to destroying them. Pyre made, she struck the match but couldn't bring herself to touch the flame to paper.

If the endless legal appeals resulted in a new trial, if the horror that followed the nightmare started all over again, the letters could be important.

She couldn't go through the courtroom grilling a second time. The first had broken her in ways that would never mend. Each day was like clawing a scab off an infected wound and feeling it ooze sickness. She had no words for Vicky's parents. Drained, she had no spirit left to share with them.

The letters could save her from that. Somewhere in his declarations of innocence, Jordan might have slipped, incriminating himself. In his own words. In ink. On paper.

As long as the envelopes stayed sealed, they fed her resolve and her hope that within them he'd written something, *something* that nullify any legal twist that would otherwise give him another chance before a jury.

Deep down, Cassie knew she needed more from Jordan. A confession. Clear and precise.

I killed Vicky.

In writing, so there would be no doubt.

That's why she protected the fragile papers instead of turning them into a bonfire and scattering the ashes.

Cassie snapped the lid back on the bin. She went upstairs to her office and sat at her design table. On automatic, she let pencil lines find their own path.

Her beautiful telescope, an elegant masterpiece of engineering, was gone. It had opened up a vista of excitement and light. It had been teaching her how to find what was hidden from the naked eye. Her world felt suddenly small again. Small and invaded.

She sketched in heavy strokes, the shapes of her drawing too, too familiar. They formed the landscape of her recurring nightmare. Tears blurred her vision, softening the thick graphite but not the memory of the image it imitated.

The landline rang. She let it roll to voice mail. "This is Rhonda from the sheriff's office. You're an artist and you use a computer, right? Have you worked much with websites? The Sparks might have a job for you."

Chapter Twenty-Four

Here's your SunnieChat!

HOLLY

What are the two bright stars I'm seeing WSW?

CASSIE

Vega. Altair. What are you doing up at 1am?

HOLLY

Kid has the flu

CASSIE

Which one?

HOLLY

Emma. Others will follow soon. They're not good at sharing except stuff like this. Flu in the summer. I think the snowflake recital brought it on. I hope you're not working this late

CASSIE

Out with binoculars. Dark night. Clear sky

HOLLY

Not your scope?

CASSIE

Not tonight

HOLLY

So you can't sleep. This dead guy stuff isn't good for you. Come visit for a few days

CASSIE

Oooh I can share the joy of flu

HOLLY

Just come

CASSIE

Can't. Working on a gig for my old boss. And I've got a line on a local job. Meeting about it tomorrow

HOLLY

My sister the entrepreneur. Glad that came up in auto suggest so I didn't have to spell it myself. Good luck with the job

CASSIE

Tell Emma I send her a hug

HOLLY

Sure. From a safe distance

Chapter Twenty-Five

"Dale, why are we doing this? Richie hefted the heavy top part of the tripod and let the legs drag on the ground. "Explain it to me again."

Dale stumbled in the fuzzy glow from a thin moon low to the horizon in a cloudy sky. He grasped a flashlight in one hand and cradling the telescope in his arms. He didn't trust Richie with either of them, but he wasn't doing such a great job himself. The beam refused to go in the right direction, making the heavy-duty Rayovac close to useless. Only muscle memory kept him on his usual path to what had been the deer stand.

They'd gotten the two pieces up most of Red Hawk using the taboggan-ator. They'd worked out the system when they were kids. The cargo—they always called it that, like a code word—was strapped to an old wooden toboggan. A rope ran from the curved front up the slope, around a tree, then back down to the ATV. One guy, usually Dale, guided the cargo while the other guy, usually Richie, drove the ATV away from the hill. The toboggan slid upward as if it were an escalator. Toboggan-ator!

The system took a lot of rope, and it was limited by how

far the all-terrain could motor away from the hill without running into buckthorn. For the last part of the incline they had to use AMVs—All Muscle Vehicles. Which meant themselves.

Dale felt bad about relocating Cassie's telescope without her permission, but he did it anyway. "I told you. There's something I have to check out." Dale intended to get the hardware moved and set up in daylight, but Richie screwed around and was way late picking him up. And now the guy was being a jerk.

"I was hoping for details," Richie said. "I know it's not for star gazing. Or to enjoy the awesome view. What can you see in the dark anyway?"

"It's a telescope. For looking at stuff in the dark. That's what it does."

"Oh. Yeah." Richie stopped and grabbed quick breaths. "I'm remembering why we only brought a keg of beer up here once."

The big, fat cylinder mounted on the sturdy tripod hadn't looked that heavy sitting in Cassie's garage. Dale was a strong dude. He'd planned on scooping up the whole thing and carrying it to Richie's car parked at the tractor access to the corn field. He was sure he could do it.

Except that he couldn't. The thing was more than heavy. Things stuck out and twisted, like a little kid having a tantrum. Richie had to break it down so they could haul it across the road. Once they got it to the Bomb, Dale realized he would have had to dismantle it anyway to fit it into the trunk.

Stowing it in the backseat would have been easier, but he couldn't leave it exposed. And covering it with a blanket make a suspicious lump. If they got stopped, he didn't want a mound of probable cause for a search sitting right behind him.

Mostly Sheriff Wells ignored them or gave a little speech about proper behavior then walked away, as if they weren't worth the bother of much else. But Deputy Adam Berger hadn't been worn down by years of dealing with the same people for the same things over and over. At every opportunity he harassed them in a-cop-is-your-friend tone, as if he were doing them a favor.

Richie had been driving around with the telescope in his trunk since yesterday when they'd snatched it. Because Richie was Richie, Dale worried about it every minute. But he couldn't keep it at the farm, where his dad might come across it. Even though The Event wasn't until Wednesday night, it was safer up on Red Hawk than in the Bomb or hidden in the barn.

Setting it up now was good too because he'd never used a telescope, and he needed to practice.

It was all about collecting intel. Dale tried to think of what Owen and Raymond could be doing in the back of the pickup that took a whole hour. He needed a good look, a really good look, at the meet up.

And, despite Richie's skepticism, he thought he *would* look at the stars.

"I can figure out you want to spy on something," Richie said. "But we've scanned this whole place with binoculars a million times and never seen anything more interesting than a little poaching and some disappointing skinny dipping."

Yeah, Dale was going to spy all right. He'd be like Mrs. Finster on Cedar Street, peeking through a gap in her curtains at the comings and goings of neighbors, then relating boring, everyday incidents as if they were absolute proof of, you know, sexual encounters. But this was different.

This wasn't because Dale was tired of cable and didn't have Netflix or Hulu. This was real. "Don't make so much noise. Lake Radio, man."

"Not on this side of the hill," Richie said. "Not until we get to the top. Hey, remember when we were up in the deer stand and we could hear every stupid word those guys in the boat were saying about how they were going to catch Old Mossy Back and it would be the biggest Muskie anybody'd ever seen and it was like the Lock Ness Monster and they'd be famous."

Dale remembered. That day he'd wanted some time by himself to sit on the cooler and read whatever his hidden book was at the time, but Richie's dad was on a rip and Richie needed a place to be that wasn't home. And that was okay. That's what you did for a guy. Richie had done it for him.

He would have told Richie about the weekly meet-up on the shore of Beauty Lake, except that it involved Owen. It would have been a neat mystery to share. Something epic to investigate together. But then, after seeing—well, almost seeing—Owen shoot up Edgar's, and Richie acting like the dangerous bully was gunning for him personally, with a real gun, Dale didn't want his best friend to know anything.

It wasn't just that Richie could be a dumb ass. It was more than that. The shooting had shoved everything having to do with Owen across the line into serious shit.

Richie didn't do well with serious anything.

Dale leaned into the terrain, feet slipping on the long grass. The more he struggled, the more he just wanted to get to the top, and the less concerned he was with the condition the scope would be in when he finally got it there.

He didn't know how fragile the innards were. Composed of mirrors that bounced light around, the device might already be broken from riding in the trunk with only a packing blanket as a cushion.

Richie reached the crest. He balanced the tripod on the three legs folded together and brushed stringy hair out of his eyes. "Holy shit. Holy mega-maxa, penultimate shit."

"Stop admiring the scenery and give me some help," Dale said.

"But there's so much of it now. Even with no sun or moonlight or anything I can tell. When you told me all that shit about the tornado, I thought you were making up half of it. And, hey, I got my own burden here." Richie spread out the collapsed legs and extended them to put the mount chest high.

Dale held the tube while. Richie, working by touch, guided it into the dovetail and turned the knobs to clamp it down. Even in the dark, he could figure out how it fit together. Many things seemed to mystify him, but a gizmo with moving parts he could fiddle with was as comfortable to him as a teddy bear and as irresistible as popcorn foaming with lava flows of melted butter.

Dale automatically looked toward Crystal's window. Tonight it was just a big black rectangle, like an unplugged flat screen. Maybe it was his mood, but the lake seemed just as flat and dark.

On the opposite shore a single mercury light hanging from a utility pole gave off an annoying harshness. He and Richie hadn't broken into the cluster of rustic cabins it guarded since they'd turned thirteen. By then they'd advanced from fishing shacks to places with heat, running water and cable television all winter long. Mostly they didn't take anything. Just ate chips and snacks left behind and watched R-rated movies.

Dale ran the flashlight over the restored telescope. He guessed it had made the journey okay.

Richie patted the mount. "This thing has a motor. We should have taken the battery and controller. I bet they were sitting right there and we didn't even notice. Can't go back and get them now."

"What we need are instructions on how to use this thing," Dale said. Technical manuals were a foreign language to him, but they were Richie's native tongue. He'd tried to do some research online, but he'd gotten distracted by fantastic photos of planets. Saturn circled by a plane of rings. Mars, all red like in science fiction stories and movies.

He could never tell Richie he was interested in faraway worlds. Increasingly he thought about a lot of things and did a lot of things he never shared with his best friend. While he felt the urge for new experiences, Richie seemed way too excited to go on doing what they'd already done a thousand times.

"What're we looking at?" Richie demanded. "Shit. We've never relocated anything that's this much trouble before. It better be really good."

"Relocated" was more code. They'd done petty stuff— magazines, candy, things you could shove into a pocket. Mostly they'd pulled pranks, like taking Mrs. Finster's garden gnomes and adding them to the statues in St. Mary's Catholic Church. Dale tried to think of something—anything that wasn't' the real thing—that would satisfy his partner in crime.

Headlights appeared on the mile-long driveway to the Swenson pseudo-mansion. Dale fumbled for the switch on the flashlight. It seemed forever before the yellow spot winked out.

One of the three garage doors slid up as if by royal command. The automatic overhead light flooded the interior. Dale could see the back end of a white car next to an empty stall. Beyond it were shapes that could be bikes and tools and whatever rich guys stored away.

"No one's driving the Beemer tonight," Richie said. "I bet Swenson's got a lot of fun stuff for an old man."

"I think he was in high school the same time as our dads," Dale said. "He's not that old, not older than our dads."

A red Mustang convertible cruised up the drive. "Crystal's home early," Richie said.

The car slowed as it approached the garage. At this distance in the dark, Dale couldn't tell if the driver was Crystal. Maybe he could see who it was with the telescope. He took off the round plastic covers and aimed it at the building.

"Hey, think Todd dumped her?" Richie asked.

"Todd's on vacation with his family." Dale wished Richie hadn't mentioned his would-be girlfriend's almost-steady boyfriend.

"On vacation?" Richie seemed shocked by the concept.

"All of them together? Even his bratty sisters? It's good to know he's suffering. Where'd they go?"

"Orlando." Dale said it too quickly. "Maybe." He didn't want to seem sure of his information. "Visiting relatives. And Disney World. Or something. I guess." Richie didn't have to know he learned about Todd's movements through Crystal's media posts.

"No shit," Richie said. "I've always wanted to go to Disney World."

"Lake Radio. Keep your voice down."

Richie whispered, as if in church, "I bet that garage is a man-cave toy store. Hurry or you'll miss it."

Dale clenched his teeth in frustration. The tube moved in a weird way. In an arc rather than a straight line. He'd watched a video. Well, part of one. If he could get the parking spot for the Mustang centered in the finder, a pirate's spyglass kind of thing attached to the tube, it would magically show up in the scope's eyepiece. He scrunched down and squinted.

The shiny white BMW hung upside down in the tiny circle of the lens. Shit. They'd broken the spyglass thing. He hoped the big tube was okay. He switched to looking through the telescope's eyepiece. Semidarkness filled his view. The strong light from the garage bay cast a glow to one side. He twisted the scope to find the glow's source. It wouldn't go where he wanted it to. He was trying too hard. Mechanical things only worked for him if he didn't force them.

The Mustang's purring motor went silent. Dale heard the wide door rumble and bang against concrete. He straightened. The garage was closed.

"Did you see anything?" Richie asked, forgetting to whisper.

"No," Dale said. "I can't get it to work right. I've got to practice."

Richie gazed out over the lake. "With this garage thing, we'd move into some major shit, wouldn't we." He said it in the same semi-joking tone he used when he asked his mom—really his step-mom, his bio-mom had died when he was little—to bring him a beer from the fridge, knowing she never would.

"Richie, that's not why I want the telescope."

"Yeah, it's probably just crappy old TV sets, Nerf noodles, and snowshoes anyway," Richie said.

Dale took a breath, ready to blurt out the whole thing. Noises below the hill at the lake stopped him. A door screeched open and slammed shut. Dale grabbed Richie. "Shhh."

The familiar truck started up with a sputter. Headlights snapped on, spreading a glow over the shore. Dale swallowed hard.

No. This was the wrong night.

"Looks like Owen's been out night fishing," Richie sort of whispered.

"Shhh," Dale insisted.

"Why do I have to be quiet. He couldn't hear himself fart over that engine."

"Flashlight." Dale pointed at a beam bobbing from the truck toward the ravine, moving too quickly for Dale to catch it in the telescope. What would he see if he could? Raymond's pockets bulging with cash from a drug deal?

The truck grumbled away. The narrow light crossed the bridge, bounced swiftly toward the Swenson house, then winked out.

Flood lamps snapped on, washing over the patio. Dale had a flashback to the scene last Wednesday.

Raymond was smoother this time. No tripping over plastic patio furniture textured to look like rattan. He was suddenly perched at the top of the stairway to the lake, facing the house as if he'd just trudged up from the water. His light-colored polo shirt and dark knee-length shorts irritated Dale. The man looked so normal, not like an asshole who allowed a monster on his land, near his house, where his daughter lived.

"Fuck me with a rocket ship," Richie said softly. He lowered himself to sit in the grass.

Raymond disappeared into the house. The flood lights snapped off. Interior lights came on, sending bright blocks through the glass door onto the paved patio.

Dale sat beside Richie and leaned against a leg of the tripod. "I'm guessing it's a drug deal."

"Pharmacist meets scumbag. Yeah." Richie hugged his knees. "You going to prove it with a relocated telescope?"

"I just want to make sure Crystal is okay. You know. With Owen so close." There. Dale practically confessed to his best friend that he was totally smacked for a girl who wouldn't notice him even if he got hit by a meteor and it was all recorded and posted online.

"Scary. Yesterday," Richie said.

"Yeah." Dale again felt the tightening in his gut and heard the blasts in his head. They should have told Wells or Berger they sort of saw it happen. But they'd agreed it was a bad idea to rat out a guy with a shotgun.

"I've done some stuff," Richie said into the dark. "Stuff you don't know about."

Dale found it hard to believe Richie would have, or could have, kept anything from him. It hurt a little that his best friend had secrets, even though Dale had his own.

It was clear Richie wanted to spill. Dale was afraid to hear, but it was kind of his duty to listen.

Hell, this was Richie. How bad could it be? "Stuff? Like what?"

Chapter Twenty-Six

SunnieChat is here for you!

ASHLEY

I'm sending you info on online dating services. You need to get out there

CASSIE

Don't bother. I'm seeing someone

ASHLEY

No you're not

CASSIE

Seriously. He was here Saturday

ASHLEY

Even in a text I can tell when you're lying

CASSIE

Chad was the love of my life. I'll never get over him

ASHLEY

LOL. You're not even trying to be convincing

CASSIE

I don't want a relationship right now

ASHLEY

It's ok to just have fun. Not everyone's into the spouse and kids package. I'm not

CASSIE

Ash I can tell when you're lying too you know

Chapter Twenty-Seven

Cassie nervously clutched the steering wheel as she drove into town. She thought about the ways she'd spent most of her Monday evenings before moving to Glacier Falls. Concerts, plays, museums, and movies were available to her in L.A. She'd experienced little of it. Usually she'd just gone home after working late and collapsed, still burdened by deadlines.

When she'd decided to move back to Minnesota, she'd imagined lazy nights inhaling breezes rich with the smell of lake instead of smog. She'd eat off of real plates rather than out of cardboard containers. She'd watch the sun slowly melt into the horizon, without human-made constructions cutting off the day as if natural time were obsolete.

Had she ever envisioned herself walking into a bingo hall? She was pretty sure that scenario hadn't been in any of her day dreams.

Well, here she was. The concrete block rectangle squatted south of town alongside Highway 72 like a giant Lego box built by a creatively challenged adult. Cassie parked the tiny Cooper at the end of a row of SUVs.

On the other side of the highway gaudy lights spelled out

"Safari Club" across the front of a wooden building. According to Glenna, the original name had been the Gentlemen's Club. That would have been a longer sign. There wouldn't have been room for "Girls Girls Girls" flashing around it. A string of placard-waving protesters stood on county property at the lip to the strip club's parking lot. They seemed like an orderly group, not likely to scare anyone away.

Although the bingo hall had no blinking lights or protestors, Cassie gathered her courage before approaching it. She bravely crunched across the gravel and pushed open the heavy glass door. One large room took up most of the space. Wrapping paper adorned with wreaths and smiling Santas covered the row of huge, display-style windows, as if to keep out the taint of the place across the highway. Fuzzy squiggles of flashing neon leaked through the barrier.

Rows of cafeteria tables and folding chairs faced a podium where Ryan Miller spun a cage full of clattering balls. Had she remembered to put him on the list of her visitors for Deputy Berger? Some of the other men looked familiar too, although she couldn't put names to the faces. They circulated through the hall handing out bingo cards and collecting the per-game per-card fees. The legal charitable gambling was run by the Glacier Falls Volunteer Firefighters with the help of the auxiliary organization, the Sparkles. Translation: the wives, daughters, and girlfriends of the Sparks.

She flinched as a wiry man brushed past her. "Hey there, Cassie. Glad to see you here." His Danowski Family Polka Band t-shirt was different from the one he'd worn when he'd steered her around like a bumper car while The Floater lay on her shore.

"Hi, Boomer." Funny how quickly she'd gotten used to solitude. She'd almost chickened out when she saw the parking lot was nearly as full as the one at the Safari Club. In contrast to the clientele at the adult entertainment establishment only a double-lane of asphalt away, this was a family group with males and females of every age.

Except teenagers, she noticed. That didn't surprise her. Bingo was soooo mid of last century.

Cassie couldn't believe she'd actually agreed to meet Rhonda here to discuss a potential job. In preparation she'd visited the Sparks' website. The unorganized jumble of unlabeled photos and blocks of tiny font horrified her. She was certain she could improve the design, but was shaky about the rest of it. To get started, like in all good advertising, she had to understand the clients' expectations.

She squared her shoulders and stepped deeper into the room. If the Sparks wanted a jazzy, isn't-fire-fighting-fun image, that's what she'd deliver. If they insisted on flaming pink bunnies dancing across the screen, she'd make them the fluffiest, flamiest, most delightful capering rabbits in all of web-dom. *If* she got the job.

No, *when* she got the job.

Cassie held onto her determination against the chaos swirling around her. A round, red-haired woman in a silver Sparkles jacket shot her a wave. Cassie had spoken to Officer Rhonda Olson several times on the phone, but hadn't met her until now.

The woman sat to the left of the dais at the opposite end of the room. A cashbox dominated the table in front of her. A Spark handed her a bundle of bills, taking her attention away from Cassie. She rifled through them quickly then efficiently tucked them away.

Cassie felt eyes follow her as she walked the length of the very long space toward Rhonda. Probably startled by her appearing in their nineteen-fifties bubble, where nothing ever changed, the bingo players openly gawked.

She tried to ignore the attention. She'd been treated like a traveler from the future before—usually as the lone woman in a boys-only treehouse-conference room. She told herself this was less intimidating than facing a bunch of entrenched males who stared at her anatomy rather than at her well-endowed advertising plan.

In reality it wasn't, but she could get through it.

Please, don't let them want flaming pink bunnies, she thought hard to the media gods. *Please, please, no anthropomorphized firetrucks with huge, rolling eyes and a grinning grill.*

"Glad you made it." Rhonda offered her a folding chair. She appeared to be in her early fifties. A touch of red tinted her brown eyes. Her bare arms were rosy with sunburn. Although her hair was dyed now, the ruby color must be close to the shade she'd been born with. "I thought this setting might give you some ideas. Community coming together and all that."

A new game started. Ryan Miller spun a rattling cage, plucked up the ball that fell free, and announced the letter-number combination.

"I'm trying to talk them into an electronic set up," Rhonda said. "We can afford it, but some of the guys like the old crank system."

The place looked more lucrative than a gold mine to Cassie. Most of the players had multiple bingo cards arranged in front of them. Building maintenance was low, and all the workers were volunteers. She did an estimate of the contents of the cashbox. "That's a lot of money."

"About average," Rhonda said. "We just do Mondays. Summer's the best. No school events going on. We get a few vacationers, but mostly it's locals. That includes the snow birds back from their winter homes in Arizona and Florida. Some of the proceeds go for prizes and to support the fire department. The rest we route into donations. Uniforms for the high school band. A granite memorial at the city park. On the website you can highlight all the things Sparks bingo has financed for the town."

Cassie, who'd just had her telescope stolen, wondered about the building's security system. She used her calm, "dear client, you're going in the wrong direction" voice. "Those are great things to feature, but I think we should avoid advertising on the Internet that bingo is that successful. You might end up getting robbed."

"We've got cameras like most places," Rhonda said. "There's a vault in the back." She flipped a hand toward the Staff Only door behind her. "And everything except what we need for change I take to the bank depository when we're done for the night."

The flaming hair, the iron-ore eyes, and the way Rhonda carried her solid figure should be enough to deter a thief. Unfortunately, some people were desperate enough to chance anything. And others had no instinct for self-preservation.

As if ready to prove that point, a handsome man with slickly coifed, caramel hair swaggered up to the table. Cassie was certain she hadn't met him. He shoved a wad of bills at Rhonda. "Put this in your bra, honey, and we can count it together later."

Rhonda took the money without missing a beat. "Now you know that's out of line, Rodney Fluge."

A reasonable person would have apologized, but he grinned. "Ah, come on, Rhonda, I'm just fooling around."

"The law takes sexual harassment seriously and so do I."

He continued to smile. The longer he held the pose, the more his good-natured expression looked fake. "Ah, come on, we don't need all this politically correct stuff between friends."

"Yes, we do," Rhonda said. "Don't think you can get away with it just because we went to school together. Now go sell more bingo cards."

"Later then." He sauntered away, the smile still stuck on his face.

"That was his idea of showing off in front of you,"

Rhonda told Cassie. "Makes you want to puke, doesn't it. He keeps running for mayor and losing. He can't wait for Mayor Bob to retire or drop dead so he has a shot at being elected."

Harry Ziegler, owner of Chewy the dog, greeted Cassie. He turned in a stack of bills to Rhonda. "How's your mom doing at Sweet Meadow?"

"It's been tough going, but they take good care of her," Rhonda said.

While the two chatted, Cassie watched the crowd. "There seems to be as much socializing as playing," Cassie said to Rhonda when they were semi-alone again.

"Gossiping, you mean. People's imaginations are working pretty hard on how a restaurant owner from Minneapolis ended up dead in Beauty Lake. Especially since his upscale, must-wear-a-suit-coat-and-tie eatery belongs to the same company that owns that den of decadence across the street."

Irv Steinhaus loomed over them. He nodded to Cassie and slapped down a bundle of cash. "So, Rhonda, how did Owen kill the guy? Shoot him? Stab him? Beat him to death?"

Rhonda fixed the man with a stare that would have stopped a charging rhino cold in its tracks. "No one did anything unless the crime lab says so. Don't go spreading any wild stories you can't prove."

"Wouldn't think of it," Irv said and walked away. Cassie watched him pick up a conversation with another Spark. Except for the height, she didn't see much resemblance between him and Dale. Maybe he'd been sullenly handsome once like his son, but now his features seemed burdened by a perpetual disappointed in life.

Rhonda stored the bills in the cashbox. "People have got Russell Sworski murdered by everyone from the FBI to Father Anderson."

"How exactly did he die?" Cassie cringed at what had just popped out of her mouth. "Sorry. I was just thinking out loud. You probably can't say anything."

Rhonda gave her a smile. "Finally, a sane person who asks a question instead of trying to guess the answer. The victim suffered a blow to the head and then drown in lake water. Maybe he fell against something. Maybe someone hit him. It could have been an accident, except it wasn't reported and there are indications the body spent a whole winter under the ice."

Cassie remembered the fragment of rope attached to the body. "Anchored to the bottom of the lake."

"Must have been. Otherwise, it would have shown up right away. Which means foul play."

"What about his family?"

"He's got a current wife, an ex-wife, and a grown daughter. All the wife knows is he was up here for a week on business. She didn't have an address. Said she didn't need one. If she wanted to get a hold of him, she could just call his cell. But she didn't try that until two days after he was supposed to be back."

"That doesn't seem normal," Cassie said.

"Nothing about this has been even close to normal. It took her another day before she contacted the police. That was last October. I remember when the Minneapolis PD notified us."

"What about his business connections up here?"

"He told his partners he was going deer hunting with some pals. Thing is, the season hadn't started yet. I'm trying to find out who those pals are.

"There was no wallet. It could have been stolen or it could be at the bottom of the lake. The same goes for his phone. His clothes were new and expensive, like he'd never hunted before. Like he bought them just for this trip 'up North,' as the Twin Cities folks say. I've started checking the gun shops that carry high-end gear. I'm hoping he and the pals went shopping together so we can get an ID on them.

"I appreciate dealing with gun shops. The owners are behind the counter every day with their personal hardware on their hip, protecting their inventory. They know their customers, they know their stock, and they cooperate with law enforcement."

"What about his car?" Cassie asked.

"We've got the description and the license plate. The killer has had plenty of time to dispose of it. I'm guessing it went through a chop-shop months ago."

"Hey, more for the box." Denny Zunker surrendered a handful of bills. He turned to Cassie while Rhonda flipped through the cash. "I hear you're going to help the fire department with the website."

"Well, I don't know the tech part," Cassie said, "but I can do the design work." She hoped that sounded confident without bragging or building up expectations beyond her expertise.

"We've got a high school kid who does the tech," Denny said. "He takes care of the newspaper's site, too."

Cassie was relieved she'd have an experienced computer nerd to work with.

Edgar Tvrdik set a stack on the table. Despite Mrs. Finster's version of the shooting, Cassie had read in the paper that there wasn't enough evidence to make an arrest. Edgar's questionable eyesight and possible bias against Owen tainted his account of the incident. Owen claimed his truck was stolen with his shotgun in it then returned without the weapon.

Edgar pulled a slip of paper from his shirt pocket and flapped it at them. "I want you all to watch, so no one thinks I'm stealing." Cassie got a flash of blue ink against a dull portrait of Washington. "I'm exchanging this one dollar for —" He took a crisp bill off the top of the stack. "—this one dollar." He shoved the first single into the middle of the pile. "Didn't do me any good anyway. Don't know why I thought it would." He stalked away scowling. He grumbled at Greg, his son-in-law, as he stalked past him.

"Wonder what that was about." Rhonda riffled through the bills and put them into the cashbox.

"Beats me," Denny said. "He's real upset about the store. I think it pushed him over the edge. He's been saying all kinds of crazy things about Owen paying off the sheriff and about having to make your own justice. It's been a real strain on Linda and the family. Heck, you can see it in Greg's face." He looked toward a red-shirted Spark speaking into a cell phone through a clenched jaw.

Cassie had met the man at Floater Fest; now she remembered the boy from those summer days when she was a kid. Holly would be glad to know that, yes, he still had great hair. Thick and wavy, it flopped to the side in an almost anime way.

Denny shuffled a few bingo cards. "Looks like things are rough again, Rhonda. I'll try to settle him down." He gave Cassie a nod and a grin, then set a course to intercept Edgar.

"That might be a long intervention," Rhonda said when he was too far away to hear her above the crowd murmur. "It'll be another low-sales night for Denny." She tilted her head at Cassie. "He's eligible. He's dated a girl from Hewitt on and off for years. If something was going to come of it, it would have by now. He's not rich, but he's got enough of an income from renting out farmland he owns near Marshall that he doesn't have to hold down a job like the rest of us. Men don't know what to do with money. He sure could use a wife to help him spend it."

Cassie hadn't reviewed the information Ashely had sent her on online dating services. She hadn't deleted it either. "Boomer already made that pitch. But I don't want a relationship right now."

"Well, that's just wrong. What do you think of Adam? I knew you two hadn't met, so when you called about the theft, I sent him out for you to take a look at."

"Rhonda!"

The officer of the law shrugged. "We don't have much to offer. You should at least see the whole buffet."

Cassie searched her brain for anything to divert the conversation elsewhere. "I see getting arrested hasn't stopped the protesters across the street."

Rhonda laughed, probably aware she was being redirected. "I used to be a Vigilant but I had to back off. I did the signs and marching. And taking photos of the vehicles in the parking lot was okay. We'd find out who owns the cars then call the wives and mothers and tell them where their sleaze-ball men have been spending their evenings. Don't worry, I didn't abuse my position with the sheriff's department by running license plates through the DMV. Didn't have to. We pretty much know what people in the area drive."

"Like Owen Norquist's truck," Cassie said.

"He's been there," Rhonda said. "That wasn't a surprise. But some others were. Like Irv on the first night we started doing it. Fortunately, his wife wasn't with us. That was one phone call I could never bring myself to make. Father Anderson handled it."

According to Rhonda, the strategy was only partially successful. The Vigilants had forced business from the locals to drop off. But the out-of-towners were harder to track down and intimidate. "Father Anderson came up with the bumper-sticker idea. A little something for guys to explain to their families. I told him it was vandalism and they'd end up in jail. Father figured it was worth it, so they went ahead.

"I've stayed away since that decision was made. It's not just because committing a crime would jeopardize my job. I believe in following the law. I'm still with them in spirit. I'm no prude or Bible thumper, but I want that porn palace out of my town."

"It seems there are people who want to do more than drive away the clientele in order to make that happen," Cassie said. She noticed Rhonda never referred to the Safari Club by name. She had read the letters to the editor on the issue. The ones signed D. E. Kinsley stopped just short of calling for a mob with pitchforks and Tiki torches to get rid of the "den of the devil."

"I wish the tornado had smashed it up," Rhonda said. "At least then it would have been an act of nature and not one of man. I worry someone's going to douse it with gasoline and flip a match. And sometimes I wonder if Sworski ended up in Beauty Lake because he was part-owner of that rat hole."

Cassie watched Denny talking earnestly to a glowering Edgar. It seemed, even with his friends, Edgar's communication skills were dismal. She hoped he appreciated the support the Sparks gave him.

Electronic tones shrieked across the hall. In unison, the Sparks reached for their phones in response to the automated alert. The siren mounted on the fire station a few blocks away wailed like a banshee.

Ryan jumped down from the dais. Rhonda rushed up and took control of the microphone. "Hold your cards. We're going to pause a moment while we make a personnel shift. Most of you know how this goes. Just sit tight."

The men passed off their cards and money to women in Sparkle jackets and t-shirts. Denny rushed over and handed Cassie his bundle, as if she were his personal Sparkle. She was too surprised to do anything but take it from him.

Boomer extended his arm in the air and wiggled his hand. "I can take four to the station in the Buick."

The exit jammed with bodies as the men funneled through the single door. Rhonda's amplified voice came over the speakers. "Let's send off our brave guys with a round of applause. The Glacier Falls all-volunteer firefighters! The best crew in the entire state!"

Enthusiastic clapping rang through the room. A woman Cassie didn't know climbed onto the dais, accepted the microphone from Rhonda, and took over spinning the bingo cage.

Rhonda returned to the table. Cassie shoved bingo cards and bills at her. "These are from Denny." Rhonda gave her a sly smile that almost made Cassie blush.

Chapter Twenty-Eight

Dale sat in a plastic booth punching holes in his chocolate-nut-something Blizzard with a straw while he watched each minute Richie was late tick away on the fake antique clock.

He was really pissed at Richie. Again. His muscles ached from hauling the telescope up Red Hawk, on top of farm chores and yard work at Cassie's. Mostly, he was brain sore from worrying about what Richie had confessed to him last night.

His dad was at the bingo hall. His mom had dropped him off at the Dairy Queen on her way to rally with the Vigilants. Usually the protesters maintained a smaller presence on Mondays when Sparks and Sparkles were needed to run the game, but the group was riding a tsunami of publicity and needed extra outraged citizens to march around with you're-going-to-hell signs.

Videos of the bumper-sticker arrests had gone flash viral. It was every TV anchor, blogger, poster, and click-baiter's wet dream. Oooh, sexy, nude (well, sort of) women, and greedy club owners ruining a small town versus pious crusaders for morality.

The clips were mostly of the pot luck spread, complete with apple pie, at the on-your-honor tent-jail. #tattertot. Hardened criminals tossed Frisbees at one another or watched sports on their phones, using the VFW's wi-fi. Interviews with the pastors were especially teeth grinding.

And, yup, there was Dale in several sweeping shots of the crowd. He'd never be able to tell anyone he was from Glacier Falls ever again.

Dale didn't understand why his parents had to drive separate cars tonight. The Vigilants couldn't legally park in the club's lot because they weren't customers, so his mom's Mazda would be across the street sitting right beside his dad's Sierra. But their son wasn't allowed to use one of the family vehicles because he didn't have a *real* reason for needing it. That was adult code for he wasn't going to a specific place for a specific purpose that they approved of.

They never asked him if he approved of where *they* went and what *they* did.

The minutes ticked away on the big-ass clock. He'd had the whole evening mapped out. This once in a lifetime opportunity would never come again and was more important than spending the night on the hill practicing with the telescope. Unfortunately, it was totally dependent on the Bomb for transportation.

Dale's phone chimed. Richie was finally replying to the multiple texts he'd sent. Dale sorted through emojis and shorthand. Translation: the stupid jerk got himself picked up for driving under the influence before he even made it to the DQ.

At least there wasn't a stolen telescope in the trunk.

Bridget, Richie's very unsteady—in more ways than one—girlfriend, slid into the booth across from Dale. Petite and curvy, this week she had a startling candy-pink streak running through her artificially dark hair. She'd gotten the same text. Well, it was probably a different text with similar information. "I'm going to visit Richie in jail. Want to come?"

"I got shit to do," Dale lied. He had nothing now. He'd had his fill of the sheriff's tent prison, and he didn't want to end up as the audience to Richie and Bridget's inevitable grope-fest.

Besides, he was too angry and deflated. With Todd on a family road trip, Crystal was going to a movie in Alexandria with her girlfriends. Dale planned to accidentally bump into her there and ask her what flick she was going to and did she want some popcorn and—

Now he was stuck in town waiting for hours before he could hook up with a Parent Uber.

Bridget pouted. "Whitney's around. She can come with us. You like Whitney, don't you?"

"Yeah. But I really got other stuff." Dale had been with Bridget's friend a few times to make Richie happy. The girls always smelled of raspberry vapes and wore makeup that made them look like vampire clowns. No one did smoky eye and blood-red lipstick anymore. It said so at a blog Crystal had commented on.

Whitney was a little shorter than Bridget. Dale felt like a freaky giant next to her. She was pretty and pleasant enough. The awkward, fumbling, physical stuff was okay but not what his imagination told him it should be. She was just a bod-dub, a body double, a substitute for who he really wanted to be with.

They didn't have much to talk about. She only read teen-gossip blogs. Her online posts and tweets were mostly about celebs. On all other topics, her memory went back about a month. She laughed too much, sounding like a chirping bird. Dale wished she could be serious at least part of the time.

He felt bad for being so critical. Whitney and Bridget behaved the way people expected them to, just like everyone else. Dale saw it all around him—with his parents, Richie, and himself. You got a label and that's how you acted, even if it really wasn't the whole of you or how you thought of yourself.

"You can give Richie this." Dale got up and shoved the Blizzard at her. The tall paper cup would probably be empty before she reached the VFW. He left the DQ and wandered along Central. When he reached Edgar's store, he realized he'd been heading there without consciously knowing it, drawn to the place like some people go out sightseeing after a tornado.

Plywood filled the space where the window used to be. Red spray paint ringed holes in the siding. Maybe it was to mark them for the official investigation. Maybe it had been done by kids so they'd show up better in selfies.

Dale thought he might go in and really buy something this time. Linda would be working while her dad enjoyed himself at bingo. Light spilled through the undamaged glass door. The come-on-in sign formed a rectangular shadow on the sidewalk.

He punched the flat metal door handle. A sharp pain shot through him from wrist to elbow. "Damn." He gave his arm a shake. He'd expecting the panel to easily swing inward, like always. Instead it held firm. Locked. He rattled it to be sure. Worried, he cupped his hands around his eyes, pressed against the cool glass and peered inside.

Candy bars, beef jerky, and bags of chips lined the shelves facing the door like good little snacks. No tipped over displays or pools of blood. He stepped back. It didn't feel right just to leave. He pulled out his phone to call his dad and have him check with Edgar.

A mass blocked the light coming through the door. Linda puffed up to the glass, keys in her hand. A sour grimace twisting her face, she let him in.

"Sorry," Dale said. "The sign says you're open. Everything okay?"

"I had to get a case of soup out of the storeroom and

didn't want to leave it unlocked. Especially since—" She gestured toward the plywood.

"Want help with that?" Dale asked.

"Naw, I'm used to the lifting." Linda smeared the back of her hand across her wet, sweaty cheek.

Yeah, Dale knew that. She'd been hauling cases of canned goods, bags of cat food, and jugs of laundry soap her whole life. Although with the huffing and puffing noises she made, it seemed just walking around took all her strength.

Linda didn't say thanks for the offer. He didn't expect her to. He didn't see any cans of Campbell's Chicken Noodle laying around, waiting to be priced and shelved. She'd probably been in the bathroom. He felt he should say something about the shooting. "The place doesn't look so bad."

"You came to gawk, too," Linda said. "Suddenly everyone needs gum."

"People want to be sort of supportive." Dale scanned the candy display. There was no way he could buy gum now.

"The sheriff's acting like shooting up this place was nothing. My dad saw the truck. He *saw* Owen, same as I'm looking at you. That bastard grinned at him with his finger on the trigger. That should be enough. It should be plenty. But Wells said my dad has a beef with Owen so maybe he convinced himself he saw more than he did."

Dale put KitKats and crumpled bills on the counter. "There's got to be evidence. Like the shotgun."

"Surprise, surprise." Linda rang up the purchase, took the dollars and slapped change next to the candy. "They can't find it. More like they're not looking."

Dale scooped up the bars and coins. "Owen could have stashed it lots of places."

"He could put it on a gold chain and wear it around his neck. Wells still wouldn't find it."

"Have a good night." Dale bolted out the door away from

Linda. He tried to shake the memory of the shotgun sliding out of the passenger window.

Two people were in the truck. Was Owen the driver or the shooter? Or neither one. He and Richie had been too far away at first to tell, and then too fixated on the Beretta 686 to actually look inside the cab.

Dale crossed the street as Greg Ergen pulled into the alley that ran behind the store. The guy practically had a second job at his father-in-law's place, helping out his wife. It must be tough for an ambitious, workaholic to be married to a woman who wouldn't move away from daddy. Especially *that* daddy.

Dale headed toward the pretend jail. He'd find a way to ditch Bridget, so he and Richie could talk about last night. The harder Dale tried *not* to think about what Richie had told him, the more he thought about it. And the more he wanted to spew his guts out.

On a hot night last summer Owen pulled up beside Richie in his churning truck and asked if he wanted to have some fun. Anyone else would have immediately seen a toxic-waste warning sign flashing over the guy's head.

Not Richie. The gene that told you not to smear ice cream on your face to get a grizzly bear to lick it while you livestreamed the event was missing from his DNA.

Owen drove Richie to a construction site across the highway from the bingo hall. The future home of the Safari Club was a hole in the ground lined with concrete blocks and surrounded by piles of building materials. Owen pointed out the lumber he wanted.

Richie shoved the boards through the narrow storm door into the make-shift camper on the back of the truck. Most of them stuck out, too long to fit inside.

"It was, you know, a safety hazard," Richie told Dale last

night while stars played hide and seek behind the clouds over Beauty Lake and dew gathered in the grass.

"Owen didn't care about strapping them down or putting a red warning flag on them. And then, I mean, the whole thing didn't feel right. Not legal, you know. And it's dark, which is good, but we're right out in the open by a busy road. I say that to Owen. He says he has a connection. That a guardian angel sat on his shoulder, watching out for him. Then this other guy shows up in a big Ram, mad enough to shit nitro."

Dale knew that kind of pickup. Built for heavy payloads, it was a magnet for middle managers who wanted to give the impression they actually worked for a living. Sitting next to it, Owen's rolling rust and camo must have looked like an outhouse.

The guy and Owen moved away from Richie. "Owen usually blasts out every word," Richie told Dale, "but he's talking low, like he's trying to calm the guy down. But Ram Truck is on a full-blown rant. I figure he's the connection. But he wasn't no guardian angel, or any other kind. He swears up a storm and calls Owen names I've never heard. It was kind of educational.

"That's when Owen gets loud. He says the boards came from somewhere else in the first place, and they didn't belong here anyway. Then he says he got a better price and he'd get Ram Truck more later but this was an emergency for a special customer. That's what he says. Special customer.

"Ram says he don't take shit from no one and they'd never do business again. He throws his arms all around and stomps all over. He says he's ratting out Owen to the cops. And if that don't work, he's got friends who'll 'take care' of Owen for him.

"Owen, he just laughs. For a big guy, he's got this squeaky, high pitched chuckle." Richie demonstrated the irritating snicker.

"Then I don't hear anything for a while," Richie said, "just cars going by like it's a regular night. I guess Owen is talking soft again. The other guy is real still, like he's listening hard. They must've reached a deal 'cause the guy climbs into his big-ass truck, and, zoom, he's gone."

After the argument Owen took Richie to another construction site where he had him unload. If it had been anyone but Richie telling the story, Dale would have thought he was lying about where they delivered the stolen lumber.

Owen dropped Richie off at the same place he'd picked him up. Richie got some cash and a six-pack out of it.

"You dumb shit-head," Dale told him, "messing with Owen like that. He only brought you along to do the lifting. There are better ways to earn some bucks, and your dad lets you have beer any time you want." The Dalheimers had their own unique philosophy of parenting. They didn't care how much their son/stepson drank as long as he didn't use "drugs."

"Yeah, I know," Richie said. "But it was something to do."

The night suddenly seemed a whole lot darker to Dale. "You've got to stay away from Owen. Double-snot promise."

"I figured that out," Richie said, "especially after I saw the Floater's picture in the paper."

Dale didn't want to ask, but he had to. "Who was it, Richie?"

"It was Ram Ass," Richie said. "The non-angel. Owen's connection."

Chapter Twenty-Nine

Richie had actually seen the Floater. When he was alive. He'd seen Owen arguing with the guy. And now the guy was dead.

Dale walked faster toward the fake jail. He had to convince Richie to tell Wells or Berger. Richie was still a minor. He could handle whatever theft charges came out of it.

Dale slowed, giving himself time to think it through. Owen would know it was Richie who snitched, putting him in the cross hairs of the man's temper. And maybe his shotgun, for real this time. At least Richie hadn't been the target on F13 when Owen shot up the G and G.

Dale backtracked to the big box gas station, the only place in town where you could rent movies anymore. He scanned the video disc packages lining a side wall. The manager, a college kid home for the summer, watched as if he expected Dale to pull out an AR-15 and drill the place.

Dale pretended to consider an adventure flick. He'd seen it a few times. This high school kid, played by a twenty-something actor Whitney adored, didn't want to get involved but he had to save his friend. And there's a girl. Lots of guys but one girl. Hard to maintain a population that way.

An alarm wailed. "My God, another tornado," a customer said softly, as if shouting would somehow invite a twister down from the sky.

Not the steady blast that warned of severe weather, the whine rose and fell in a cadence of hills and valleys.

Fire.

Dale's whole body clenched. He forced himself to saunter outside, pretending only a casual interest. A chocking stench fouled the air. He strolled toward a dark plume spiraling from a residential neighborhood on the other side of town.

Emergency vehicles screamed a short distance away. His dad would be on the long red and white. The scars, where his father's skin had melted to lava, were always covered by clothing, but Dale never forgot they were there. He broke into a jog, then a sprint.

The firetruck sirens became stationary. Dale reached the flashing lights and stopped dead cold, as if he'd smashed into an invisible barrier.

Smoke billowed from Edgar Tvrdik's front door and second-story windows. Mature trees and bushes surrounded the building, sprawling across property lines toward other homes. An out-of-control blaze had the potential to devastate the entire block.

Irv, in full gear, attached a hose to a hydrant. Edgar ran the wide, flat snake to the smoldering house with the rest of the team.

The house was empty. His dad didn't have to run through flames to rescue an unconscious victim. Not on this call. Not tonight. Dale forced slow gulps into his lungs, tasting acrid soot. Tightness eased out of his muscles.

Watchers stood on porches, lawns and sidewalks. Dale mixed in with them, hoping his dad wouldn't notice he was there. He moved away from the crowd to where high schoolers he knew clustered around a bunch of cars. They drank from aluminum cans and joked as if they sat by a campfire instead of a burning house. A couple of them shot videos and took selfies.

"Hey, want some pop?" Shawn Miller pulled a red can from an ice chest in the trunk of his car and handed it to him.

Dale snapped it open and took a sip of the liquid sugar. Shawn, a senior, rambled about a trip his family had taken to the Boundary Waters. The Millers were heavy into outdoorsy stuff. They all hunted. Broad-bodied and shorter than Dale, the older boy's eyes were on the smoking house where his dad, Ryan, sprayed a fountain of water on the old wooden structure.

Dale liked the guy. But he didn't really fit in with the ball-jockey, class-officer crowd surrounding him. Todd would be with them if he wasn't in the Magic Kingdom.

Crystal would, too, if Todd was here.

At the moment Dale couldn't say where he belonged. He'd never be part of Crystal's group. He didn't have the hard cash or the optimistic future. Part of him knew he couldn't stay with Richie, the usual guys, and the girls like Bridget and Whitney forever.

It wouldn't be easy to break away. He sort of owed them, like a debt, because they accepted him without question. But he wasn't as much like them as he pretended to be. He wanted something different, something more, something he didn't have now and wasn't sure how to get.

He knew what he wasn't. He didn't know what he was.

"We're going out to Eagle Lake," Shawn said. "Hot dogs and s'mores. We've got plenty of food. You should come with us."

"Thanks, but I'm meeting Richie." Dale hoped Shawn didn't know about the DUI and jail thing. Far from any flames, his dad hefted the hydrant wrench onto a shoulder.

Dale turned his back and walked away, just another guy in

the crowd. No one his dad would notice. A block later the air still stung his lungs.

"Real shame, ain't it."

Dale jumped.

Owen Norquist leaned against a maple, arms folded across his chest. The olive, black, and tan jacket he always wore didn't camouflage his beer belly one bit. The brim of his boonie hat shadowed dark, sunken eyes. "Tvrdik's had himself a stretch of bad luck, wouldn't you say, Sherman?"

He laughed like the devil himself, squeaky and irritating, exactly the way Richie had mimicked him. Then he coughed up a hunk of phlegm and spit it into a bed of geraniums. "You and that skinny friend of yours with the ugly car seem to be around when my business is going down. Better be careful you don't fall into a big old pit of someone else's trouble."

Dale clenched his fists and kept walking.

"You didn't see nothin'," Owen shouted at his back. "Got that, Sherman. You didn't see nothin'."

Dale turned left at the corner so a row of mock orange bushes obstructed Owen's view of him. A shot of adrenaline propelled him into a run. He slowed at Faith Lutheran Church.

The gleaming white structure held a rose tint from the low, evening sun. The main building and the bell tower pointed skyward, as if to speed the congregation's prayers to heaven. A less lofty appendage stuck out from the back. The Community Center matched the pure white of its host; but, a single story, it crouched low to the ground, like a humble disciple.

Or a penitent sinner.

Last night on Red Hawk Hill Dale asked Richie where he and Owen had delivered the stolen lumber.

"To church," Richie said, as if the confession would absolve him and at the same time get him struck by holy lightning.

Dale didn't understand right away. Church to him was St. Mary's. But Richie wasn't Catholic. Their religious differences had been a great source of discussion when they were growing up. Each denomination professed to be the exclusive keeper of God's truth. Only its members would be saved come Judgment Day. A weighty thought for first graders who'd sworn a blood oath to be best friends beyond forever.

Which one of them would make it to the bliss of heaven and which would burn in hell?

They'd spent hours comparing services and hymnals but didn't find much difference, except some stuff about Mary. The Bible didn't say if the Apostles were Catholic or Lutheran. Jesus walked around Galilei making friends with everyone. He never asked what church they went to. Some of them must have been Catholics and some must have been Lutherans, but Jesus didn't care.

Dale and Richie decided they'd both be okay.

Father Anderson and Reverend Gunther reinforced the boys' conclusion, espousing a more modern philosophy than their predecessors. They were all about reaching out to your neighbors, whoever they may be. The men practically turned inclusion into an Olympic sport. The Lutherans won gold, beginning construction on a community center before the Catholics reached their donation goal.

Where did you and Owen take the lumber, Richie?

To church. To Faith Lutheran.

"Gunther was there looking at a bunch of stuff piled up for the new addition," Richie said last night on Red Hawk. "He saw Owen's truck pull up, and he just walked away. He didn't see me, which is good, 'cause I was, you know, doing something wrong."

The complexity of the situation was lost on Richie, but Dale saw it like a revelation. In the rush to beat the competition, the Lutherans were caught short. With pride and commitment on the line, Reverend Gunther sought the devil's help.

Dale gazed at the result. He wondered which boards were supposed to be part of the Safari Club. It seemed they should stand out somehow, but they blended right in.

Chapter Thirty

Sitting on a squeaky folding chair next to Rhonda, Cassie no longer felt as if she were the in-house entertainment. The bingo hall buzzed with guesses about the location of the fire. Anything flammable was given serious consideration. Grass fire had the most support. Trash bin behind Pizza Heaven was a close second.

No smoke billowed from across the highway. Rhonda's prediction about arson at the despised building she would not name hadn't come to pass.

"Should we do this another time?" Cassie asked.

"This is the time I've got." Rhonda checked her phone. "I haven't been called in, so the department doesn't need me. An emergency during bingo doesn't happen too often, but it's nothing new and this group can handle it" She puckered her lips at a message, then stood and signaled the number caller. "Hold your cards for an announcement," the woman said.

"Sorry to interrupt," Rhonda shouted. "In case you're wondering, the fire is at Edgar Tvrdik's house." She put up her hands to stop the concerned murmurs. "You all just saw him, so you know he's okay. The Sparks have it under control. Nothing to worry about."

The caller spun the cage and the next ball rolled out. "Here we go, folks!"

"I read about the shooting," Cassie said. "And now a fire. That's terrible!"

"Suspicious timing for sure," Rhonda said. "Every speck of ash will be examined on this one. That could be info on the website, how a local fire gets investigated."

Cassie made a note of that. This job would shove her outside of her professional comfort zone. Writing copy. Photography. Skills she hadn't used in a while. Isn't that what she'd hoped for?

"You mentioned you want to have notices of community events and to spotlight the charities the bingo money supports. What else would you like to see?"

"There should be a whole page about the annual lutefisk and lefse dinner," Rhonda said. "The event is a lot of effort and not much profit. But it's tradition, so we keep doing it. And a big spread on the Tornado Daze Festival."

Rhonda relayed that the Sparks preferred to be called firemen instead of firefighters, although it was understood the website needed to use the gender-neutral term. "They know they shouldn't, but they discourage females from applying. Instead they want a donated hot dish and brownies from time to time. Personally, I think they're missing out on some good candidates."

They'd had one female member and figured that was enough to get them off the hook for any discrimination lawsuit. "It would be a nice highlight," Rhonda said. "Amy Miller is Ryan's oldest." At least six feet tall with oak-tree thighs, she'd played sports alongside her brothers since she was a little tyke. No one could say she wasn't strong enough to haul fire equipment.

"Behind her back some of the guys wondered if she had the guts to do what needed doing when the smoke was so thick you couldn't see, and you could feel the heat through your protective gear."

That was settled when faulty Christmas tree lights turned Junior Rasset's place into a deathtrap. His wife was working the late shift at the Kraft cheese plant in Melrose. Junior got four of the kids out then went back for the fifth. "I was first officer on scene," Rhonda said. "I got there the same time as the firetrucks. Eighteen below zero. I wrapped those kids in blankets and counted heads, and I came up short. I shouted that Junior and little James were still inside.

"All suited up, Amy rushed straight into the place. That century-old wood frame burst into hell itself. I thought we'd lost the three of them as quick as you could blink. Then Amy charges out the front door. She's got little James tucked under an arm and Junior thrown over her shoulder. She was a hero, plain and simple."

"That has got to go on the website," Cassie said. "I'd like to interview her."

"She's in Montana fighting forest fires for the summer," Rhonda said. "I can get you her number."

"That's a good angle, too," Cassie said. "Something like 'Spark continues to make home town proud.'"

"I like it," Rhonda said. "When she left for college last fall, the Sparks chipped in and gave her a really nice, expensive hunting knife. It was a special order. Denny drove to Minneapolis to pick it up in time for the party." Cassie got the feeling the comment was another of the woman's efforts to nudge her toward romance.

While they talked, Sparkles handed Rhonda wad after wad of bills, providing plenty of enticement for a would-be thief. Cassie tried to put it out of her mind. She was being overly sensitive because of her missing telescope. The security system would deter her imaginary robber. Cameras dotted the ceiling. Alarm wires framed the windows and doors.

But how long would it take Adam or Sheriff Wells to

answer the signal? "Rhonda, I hope you aren't alone when you close for the night."

"Irv, Denny, and I do the receipts together most times. We have a pretty smooth process worked out so it goes fast. Becky and Helen will help out tonight when they get done protesting across the road. It will take longer than usual because they don't do it every week. Well, that and I'm sure we'll have a larger take than normal by about a hundred. People get excited when there's a fire, and they spend more money. And I think the Sparkles are just better at selling cards than the Sparks."

Rhonda leaned in close. "I don't let just anyone touch the cashbox. Some folks I wouldn't trust with that much temptation. They think they'd never do anything wrong. And mostly they wouldn't. But it's different when it's right in front of you, and you're sure no one's watching. Anyone can have a moment of weakness. Some are more inclined to give in to it than others. I wouldn't want to put certain people in a potentially bad position."

Despite the smooth purr of air conditioning, the room was suddenly overbearingly hot. Cassie dabbed perspiration from her upper lip. Rhonda was right. Anyone could end up doing something wrong. Something horrendously, horrifyingly wrong.

You didn't plan it. How could you? You never imagined being in a situation so far, so very far, from anything you've ever experienced.

Then suddenly there you are. Your life is changed forever. And you're changed in ways you'll never figure out. She snapped her attention back to Rhonda. "Someone goes with you to the bank, right?"

"Honey, I don't need an escort. Remember, I'm the one with the gun." She gave Cassie a sly look. "If you're so worried about it, maybe you could help out next week. I have other plans, so the boys will be on their own. They both have a serious streak when it comes to money and are just as particular about who they do the accounting with as I am. I've got a feeling they'd welcome you. Denny would anyway."

"Rhonda, will you stop."

"You don't have a date for next Monday, do you?"

"No, and I don't want one, either."

"Bull." Rhonda lowered her voice. "Maybe you've got a hunk you keep secret. That's okay with me. I've been seeing a guy, but I don't want these jokers to know about it. Instead of saying I can't work bingo because I have a date, I tell them I'm babysitting for my sister's kids over in Long Prairie. I know I can't keep it quiet forever; but so far, so good."

Oh, great. A confidence. A secret. Cassie didn't want it, even though she knew Rhonda could become a good and loyal friend—something she'd been desperately missing since Vicky.

Cassie made her escape long before bingo ended at the respectable hour of ten o'clock. Out in the parking lot a mercury light bleached out the sky. Neon letters glared at her from across the road. Muffled music pulsed with a sensual beat.

If someone wanted to snatch the bank deposit, they wouldn't go into the building where there were cameras and alarms. They'd do it out here. She climbed into the yellow Cooper and locked the doors, not at all certain she should take a job highlighting a set up for a quick robbery.

Chapter Thirty-One

Celebrate your day with SunnieChat!

ASHLEY

Either Zach gets a hobby or I get a divorce. There is such a thing as too much togetherness

CASSIE

You're already divorced. Kick him out

ASHLEY

Yeah but he's a really good cook

CASSIE

Come visit me if you need space

ASHLEY

I'd need an excuse

CASSIE

OMG I'm having a crisis!

ASHLEY

What kind? Artistic. Financial. Existential. Malfunctioning toning shoes

Averted Vision

Chapter Thirty-Two

"You're not a suspect," Deputy Adam Berger assured Cassie.

"Person of interest?" Cassie heard that in crime shows all the time. It always meant suspect. She certainly felt like one. A folding table in the main room of the VFW separated them.

Adam was being overly polite. He'd already thanked her several times for coming into the station when she was probably really busy and all that. The brief casual moment they'd had in her garage was not likely to repeat itself here.

"You're more like a witness," Adam said.

He'd called early and requested she make a formal statement. She'd thought it was connected to the stolen telescope. But no. This was a separate event.

"There was a robbery last night," Adam said.

"At the bingo hall. Yes, you said that when you called." She remembered their repetitive conversation from before. Was repeating himself habit or a strategy? "Is Rhonda okay?" She'd asked him that on the phone, but he'd avoided giving a straight answer. He'd promised to explain everything when she came to the station, dangling a carrot in front of her to get her cooperation.

She'd followed the dancing bait. Here she was.

"Why do you ask about Rhonda?" Was there wariness in Adam's voice?

Cassie stood. It seemed he expected her to be the only one giving information. "I know she takes the money to the bank. Was she hurt? You're going to tell me right now or I'm leaving."

"She was not injured," he said calmly.

Cassie sat back down, hoping he was telling the truth. "I'm hardly a witness. There wasn't any robbery while I was there. I was gone before bingo ended." Come as you are grilling. She wore a short-sleeved t-shirt, shorts, and cheap slip-on shoes, far from her former designer footwear. Her wayward bob was barely combed. It felt good that she didn't care. She was done dressing for a job, and for an image of herself she'd left behind.

And she wasn't in the mood to try to impress Adam Berger.

"I'm interviewing everyone who was there," Adam said.

"Especially if they asked about security." In retrospect, her behavior last night must seem suspicious. She'd practically announced she was plotting to snatch the gambling receipts.

"No one thinks you took the money."

"You're sure Rhonda wasn't hurt." Now she was doing the repeating, but she needed more reassurance.

"Not a scratch on her." Adam slid a yellow pad and pen at her. "It would help if you'd write down who you remember seeing. In the building. In the parking lot."

Great. Another quiz on the town's residents. It was like a dementia test. Maybe he could just use the list she'd given him before. "I'll put down the names I know. I hope spelling doesn't count." She started with Rhonda Olson.

"Did you notice anything unusual?"

"I've never been there before so I don't really know what would be unusual." She wanted to cooperate, she really did, but she couldn't shake the attitude. She was irritated by Adam's manner and angry at herself. She should have stayed last night, adding another presence to the cash counters when they closed up the place. A larger group than the robber expected might have prevented the attack.

"Just tell me what you remember."

"Okay." Cassie launched into it. Job interview to redesign the Sparks' website. The mayoral candidate's sexual harassment. Great-hair Greg (She didn't describe him that way to Adam.) talking on the phone. Edgar's drama-queen dollar exchange. Denny promising to talk Edgar off the ledge. The fire was a biggie, lots of shuffling around. Protesters at the Safari Club would come over later. Helen and Becky would help Rhonda count the cash.

And, oh yeah, she had asked a lot of questions about the alarm system. And the cameras. And the money.

She left out Rhonda's efforts at match-making.

"So it happened in the parking lot." Cassie added "Becky Somebody who I never saw" to her list.

"Why do you think it happened there?" Adam asked.

Adam's avoidance made Cassie certain she was right. "That's the spot I picked for *my* heist."

Adam's nice brown eyes were cool and observant. She was being evaluated. Judged. "Maybe you saw someone who looked out of place?"

When the other people being interviewed were asked that same thing, Cassie wondered how many of them named her.

Cassie peeked around the open door. Rhonda clicked away at a computer on a real desk, not a card table. A fresh breeze wafted through the window into the bright room. The red-haired woman looked up and smiled. "Come on in and see my new digs."

"Very nice," Cassie said. "I expected a dingy storeroom with you in the center of a beer-keg maze."

"I made the arrangements. I picked my own space."

"I heard about the robbery. You're okay, aren't you?" Did that sound too desperate?

"Hale and hearty," Rhonda said. "Sweet of you to ask. The sheriff ordered me to take it easy for a few days, but he still expects me to do everything I was doing before. I've got an alert out on your telescope to pawn shops and law enforcement all over the state. Adam's checked with some of his contacts about stolen goods activity. No hits yet."

"Well, it's only been three days," Cassie said.

"You talk to him?" Rhonda asked.

"I just got done being roasted over a slow fire."

Rhonda flashed her bright blue nails and gave a sly smile. "You were at bingo, so you had to be interviewed. Sorry about that."

"No, you're not." Cassie suddenly saw the situation from a different perspective. "You set it up so he'd be the officer to call me."

"Just giving you and Adam a chance to get to know one another better."

Cassie laughed. "And to think I was feeling guilty about leaving you with all that cash, practically with a Rob Me sign pinned to your back."

"No offense, but you wouldn't have been much help, unless you have martial arts training, which I don't think you do. I've got to admit, I didn't see it coming. Helen and Becky helped me count the take for the night and get the deposit ready. We left together. I had the bag, as always.

"Some of the Sparks' cars were still in the lot. When there's a fire, they carpool to the station. Helen drove away while Becky locked the door with my key. I walked to where our cars were parked side by side.

"The guy popped out from behind Becky's SUV. Kind of

hunched over, wearing heavy clothes, like he wanted to look like the Hulk. He ran straight into me. Knocked me into the dirt, wrestled the bank bag from me and took off. I chased him but it's been a long time since I've done a marathon. Becky was too surprised to do anything. Which is okay. It's just money. She could have gotten hurt if she'd tried to fight him."

Cassie felt no comfort at being right about where it happened. "Did it feel planned or more like someone was watching and hoping for a chance?"

Rhonda tapped her blue nails against a yellow pad filled with official-looking notes and unofficial doodles. "Hmm. Good question. I'll give that some thought."

Chapter Thirty-Three

It's always sunny at SunnieChat!

ASHLEY

I think I'm pregnant. Don't tell H and K

CASSIE

I'm calling you right now. You better answer

Chapter Thirty-Four

The Swenson house sat like a serene pale sculpture at the crest of a gentle slope. It's second-floor windows, at a slight angle to Red Hawk Hill, were symmetrically placed, four in all. In the deepening twilight the two center ones glowed with interior lights.

Dale watched the bright one on the right through binoculars, catching glimpses of Crystal moving around in her bedroom. Unfortunately, he couldn't see details. She was probably peeling off her clingy knit top this very minute, and he was missing it. He felt sort of ashamed at the perv-y thought.

He tried again to aim the telescope at her window. The fancy device didn't work, at least not the way he wanted it to. Trying to reconcile the upside-down image in the cross hairs of the finder—which might be broken—and the right side up view through the eyepiece was disorienting. He fumbled to make the adjustments by touch in the dark. He didn't dare flip on the flashlight for fear of being seen.

It was a crazy night. His parents were at an emergency, decoder-ring only, meeting of the Sparks and Sparkles officers. They wouldn't tell him what it was about. As if he couldn't guess the only agenda item was the bingo robbery two days ago.

Richie kept sending him texts punctuated by excited, almost joyful, emojis with cracks about Dale's mom being a suspect. It wasn't funny. Not even a little. He sent Richie vivid death threats to let him know just how not humorous it was.

Dale tried aiming the telescope again. No matter how careful he was, he kept ending up at the wrong rectangle. A den or office with a green-shaded desk lamp provided enough light for him to make out mallard wallpaper. Raymond must have decorated it himself. The man had a saggy face, balding head, and beer-gut body now; but Dale had seen early photos of the guy. He used to be the handsome, wavy-haired, captain of the Glacier Falls High School football team. Go Icebergs!

A big star in a little sky, Raymond went off to college and found out he was no more than a speck of glitter on a rhinestone studded jumpsuit. He wasn't big enough or quick enough to compete at that level. Small injuries added up, and probably hurt a lot. Eventually he must have accepted that he should actually study, and train for a real profession.

Along the way he snagged beauty queen runner-up Debbie. The two of them spent money as if buying stuff could compensate for faded mini-fame, and deteriorating looks.

Seems Raymond's personal space should be a shrine to the high school hero he used to be, not an ode to ducks.

All his hopes now rested on Raymond Junior.

Six years younger than Crystal, brat-zilla Raymmy was spending the summer rotating through expensive sports camps, designed to turn him into a scholarship athlete with a promising pro career.

Trying to live through your son much? Dale thought. Did every dad secretly want to do that?

Past dusk, the moon wouldn't rise for hours. Although protected by darkness, Dale feared the man would suddenly appear at the window and discover him trying to catch his daughter undressing. It was a stupid thought. He always expected to get caught. Guilt did that to him.

Dale didn't think of his observing Crystal as *spying*, exactly. More like watching over her. She'd posted she was staying in tonight with an awesome book.

Just as important, she *hadn't* posted joy at Todd's return from Florida. Dale should be elated by that void. Instead it worried him.

He imagined she was sick. With a contagious disease. Something exotic, tragic, terminal.

And it was Wednesday.

Dale hoped Ray was smart enough to cancel tonight's Bible study with Owen. After the drive-by and the fire, he'd have to be bat-shit loco to let that guy near his house. There couldn't be anything, not in the great scope of the history of the world, more important than protecting his daughter.

Dale tried again to zero in on Crystal's window. Healthy or ill, she might be propped up by a bunch of pillows on her bed reading. He hoped the book was a novel. If he could see the title, he could pick up a copy for himself from the library—he knew how to get around the limp security system.

He'd read the whole thing. Study it. Hell, he'd memorize it. Then when school started, he'd carry the volume around, casual like. Crystal would notice it, and maybe not actually talk to him about it right away with her two faithful companions Jessica and Melissa watching, but she'd be impressed.

Later, in the hall or somewhere, she'd say something to him. Or he could see her noticing the book and he could say to her, "You ever read it?" And she would be like, "Yeah." And he would say, "I'm just at the part where—" and he'd pick something about in the middle. "What did you think of it? Did you like it?" And then a day or two later he could say he'd finished it and something about the characters and the plot and all that stuff.

Yeah, if he could just catch the title of the book.

And seeing her naked would be good, too.

Damn. He kept ending up back at the mallards.

Dale heard the labored engine of Owen's truck. Not ten yet. The guy was early.

He wanted to punch something. Swenson must need money real bad to deal drugs right in front of his kid.

Crappy shit-head of a dad. How could he put that mega-sleaze so close to his own daughter? Owen could rape and murder Crystal—Princess Debbie, too. Raymond wouldn't be able to stop him.

It would be just like Owen to slaughter them all then drive to the Municipal for a beer. The skunk had a wife and a girlfriend living in the same house. He was mega sure of himself or not very bright. Or both. The stolen snowmobile he left sitting in his front yard last winter was proof of that. Either way, he did as he pleased to everything and everyone. And he got away with it.

Headlights jumped as the vehicle bounced over ruts. It backed into its usual place, butt to the lake. That was weird. Different from the last time. Even before the trees went down when Dale couldn't see clearly, he was sure the beacons always skimmed the water then quickly went dark. Tonight they made a ghostly path across crushed grass, continuing to shine after the engine died, taxing the weak battery.

Dale felt itchy, and it wasn't just the mosquitoes. Why keep the lights on for a secret meeting? Was Owen making a vid to post online? Typical cock-strut, ego-pop?

Hey, here's me at my recent drug buy waiting for my supplier/best bud Big Ray. #lovemymeth

A figure suddenly stood on the driver's side at the edge of the glare. Whoever it was had been waiting for the truck. The guy was too short and too thin to be drug-runner Ray. The truck's door opened. As usual there was no interior light. A form got out from behind the wheel.

In a panic Dale spun the telescope and struggled to sight in the view below. He peered through the eyepiece with one eye and played with the focus knob. The magnified light was harsh, eerie. As with the Swenson house, the image didn't look right. At least he got part of the truck and the two figures, who had moved around to the other side while Dale battled with the hardware.

The slight man waved his arms around. "I been here a good fifteen minutes," he shouted loud enough to be heard even without the Lake Radio effect. Dale had been yelled at by that voice more than once.

Edgar Tvrdik.

"Might as well have a big arrow pointing at me," Edgar railed, "and a sign in mosquito. 'Free Food.' You alone? You screwed it up, didn't you. Well, you better come up with something else fast or you and your buddy will both be camping out at Wells' kiddy-land jail."

Owen stepped into the headlights, a silhouette wearing the usual camo jacket, loose pants, and brimmed fishing hat. He leaned against the hood between the headlamps, becoming a black lump.

Edgar stomped back and forth, flapping his arms like a horny whooping crane. His movements sent shadows dancing. Dale stifled a laugh. The old guy was really chewing Owen's fat up one side and down the other. That just showed how bum-dumb Edgar was, talking like that to a guy who already had some kind of grudge against him.

What *was* Edgar doing out here at night meeting the guy who'd fired a shotgun at him and probably set fire to his house?

Old man Tvrdik bordered on psycho. But even a loony, raving son of a bitch knew better than to yell at Norquist alone in the dark far from help.

Dale could almost hear the corny organ music of a horror flick getting louder and louder, telling you something really, really bad was about to happen.

He should do something. Owen wouldn't hurt Edgar, not too bad anyway, if he knew someone was watching—would he? Sure he would, and then he'd come after the witness just as he always did, which was why charges against him were quickly dropped.

But if he didn't know who the witness was—

Lake Radio. "Row, row, row your boat," Dale sang in a falsely deep voice. It was the first song that popped into his head. Shit, it was limp. "Gently down the stream—" The tune rolled around the basin. No one would be able to tell where it came from.

He looked through the eyepiece while continuing the rhyme. It was like reciting the ABCs while writing out the Gettysburg Address. Edgar jerked his head up and looked around as if trying to find the source of the singing. Owen slowly took a step toward Edgar.

Dale saw a stick with a bulging end in Owen's right hand. He heard Edgar swear. Dale sang louder and faster. "Life is but a dream. Life is but a dream. Life is but a dream." The false bass slipped into crackles and squeaks.

Owen raised the hammer high over his head. He held the tool suspended for what seemed like forever. Dale panted, unable to keep the song going. The arm swung down, slashing through the truck's beacons.

Dale heard a wet smash, then a thump, like the fall of a rotted log. Owen dropped the hammer into the grass. He grabbed Edgar's arms and dragged the body out of view.

Like a powerless god, Dale continued to stare at the empty, harshly lit scene. Splashing echoed up from the lake. His stomach churned. He swallowed down a bitter lump. Water swished and then grew calm.

Owen strolled back to the front of the truck into the

eyepiece's circle. From the knees down his camouflage trousers clung, darkly wet, to his legs and boots. He scooped up the hammer in his left hand and stood like a grotesque Sasquatch, torso tottering on stilts that swelled into giant, booted feet.

Dale suddenly found himself face down in the grass, an arm tangled around a tripod leg. A metal door screeched and slammed shut. The growl of an engine with a sick muffler vibrated up the hill as the truck prowled into the night. Something oozed toward Dale's eye. He swiped at it with the back of his hand and felt a wet gash. He must have fainted and cut his head open on one of the many knobs sticking out of the telescope mount.

Dizzy, he teetered to his feet, using the tripod for support. He grabbed the flashlight and rushed—hell, fell—down the hill, rolling through sumac and ironwood. He scrambled over fallen trees, shoving his way through their cracked branches. Beam careening like fireworks, the flashlight was just something to hold on to.

Dale wished Edgar to be alive. He willed it. Waves licking his scuffed kicks, he stopped at the shore, panting. He ran the Rayovac across the gray waves. Edgar bobbed facedown, clothing undulating around his thin body.

Dale balanced the flashlight on a beached log and slogged thigh-deep into cool liquid. He grabbed Edgar under the arms, heaving him up so air reached his face. The dripping, water-heavy form resisted. Dale twisted to straighten the body. He lost his footing and staggered. Edgar slipped from his grasp with a sploosh that propelled him toward shore. The flashlight cast a shaft across vacant eyes staring from the slack face.

Dale recognized how overly optimistic he'd been. The old man seemed surprised too, to be a floater on the surface of Beauty Lake.

Damn. Another one.

This wasn't someone else's snowmobile sitting in Owen's

front yard, or bullets shot through a window, or an empty house set on fire. This was way beyond that shit.

And Dale watched it happen. He was a witness.

He couldn't walk away. He'd have to tell Wells.

I am mega screwed.

His own blood trickled down his face. He couldn't stroll into the police station, report a crime, and admit he'd hit his head on a telescope he stole from Cassie. He'd say it happened when he tumbled down the hill. Or he fell off the ATV. Something like that unrelated to the—

It wasn't so easy to think just now. He couldn't find the right word. Then it was suddenly in his head and there was room for nothing else.

Murder.

Chapter Thirty-Five

There's always a friend on SunnieChat!

Averted Vision

CASSIE

> Falls Market is for sale. Great retirement
> project for dad

ASHLEY

Lots of walls to paint. He'd like that

KAYLA

Each wall a different color

ASHLEY

Won't happen. Mom has veto power. Which is
and always has been a good thing

Chapter Thirty-Six

Aquila, The Eagle, flew in the southeast. Cassie thought the constellation looked more like a big kite than a bird.

Wrapped in her anti-mosquito gear, she sank into a camp chair resurrected from the basement to replace what the tornado had sucked away. She struck a match and lit the citronella candle on the unfolded snack tray beside her. Maybe the fumes kept away the blood-thirsty insects. Maybe they didn't. She was willing to try almost anything.

Her legs straddled an old camera tripod with an adapter that held binoculars. She balanced a sky chart on one knee and studied it under the red glow of her flashlight. Bright Altair was easy to find in print and in the sky. She peered at the brilliant gem through the Pentax 10 x 50 she'd found in the same box as the eyepieces.

Out on the lapping water loons called to one another in their strange, eerie language. Cassie had talked to Ashley again today. It was hard keeping a secret as monumental as a pregnancy from Holly and Kayla. But for now, she had to honor her sister's wishes.

Cassie kept her ache in a special place she'd built after the second miscarriage. Wait and see. Listen and hold Ashley's hand. Be there if things go wrong again. Or if they go right this time. It was all she could do.

She was just a regular bear tonight, using both eyes. Not a pirate bear with an eyepatch. It would probably be another hour before Mars rose above the corn stalks across the road. She had plenty of time to enjoy star hopping around Aquila's four main points before the planet came into view.

If only she had her telescope. Cassie let herself be depressed by its disappearance. She'd never find another deal like that one. "You can have it cheap as long as you promised to take *everything*," the astronomer's widow had insisted. Cassie foolishly agreed before she saw the stacks of journals and ring binders full of notes that must have been penned over decades.

"Bad enough he spent all that time out in the dark," the woman said. "Then he'd have to scribble about it, too. Silly waste of time."

Cassie had crammed cardboard containers into the Mini Cooper until it wouldn't hold anymore. She'd hauled that load to the cabin, then gone back for the last of the boxes, the telescope, tripod, and two bins of assorted thingies. The widow wouldn't let her put the good stuff in her car until last. Cassie wouldn't pay her until the equipment rested at the curb, waiting to be wedged into the Coop.

Someday she'd sort through everything. Some rainy day when she finished reading a really good book and wanted to think about it before she started another one. Or when she needed a break from a project. Or when she just wanted something semi-productive that wouldn't tax her mind.

Okay, so she might never dump the boxes on the floor and paw through them. But she just couldn't chuck the man's lifetime of work into the trash. Who knows what gems might be hidden amid the yellowing pages. With luck he'd written out detailed instructions for how to use the thingies.

A breeze off the lake whispered away humidity, leaving

pleasant air. She absorbed the quiet and the stars, and mostly the solitude, enjoying the indulgence of being alone in her own cocoon. She was still shedding the tension of the noisy, populated bingo hall. And the guilt.

She should have stayed until the end to provide an extra set of watchful eyes. She should have cautioned the three women not to let the familiarity of the situation lull them into a false sense of security. When you've done something a bunch of times and nothing's gone wrong, it's easy to think nothing ever will.

And it hadn't. Not for Monday after Monday going back years. Not for all the bingo nights past with fat bags of cash being transported to the bank by a lone person.

Then two nights ago it had.

Hmm. Why that night?

Opportunity? Did the thief think it would be easier to rob the place when there was a fire and the Sparks were gone?

Cassie swatted a mosquito that didn't understand what the citronella candle was for. Did the thief *make* the opportunity by setting Edgar's place smoldering?

Would the thief have charged out from behind a car and grabbed the bag even if there had been no fire, and Denny, Edgar and Rhonda had walked out into the parking lot?

To Cassie, the thief seemed motivated by desperation and an immediate need for cash. She guessed a lot of people fit that description.

How could she showcase the wonderful things funded by bingo on a public website without attracting other desperate souls? She'd toyed with the Sparks proposal, wanting it but not wanting it.

Working with the fire department would anchor her to the town, force her to interact with people. She and Rhonda might become friends. Although she hated to admit it, she needed human contact that went beyond texting with her sisters. At the same time she craved privacy. With discovering the Floater, she already had more attention than she wanted.

She'd turn it down. *Thank you, but I'm too busy with my current assignments.*

Except she needed to build up Internet experience on her resume. And she had to expand her clientele. She couldn't rely on her former employer forever.

For tonight, she avoided committing herself to either path. As she climbed toward a very changed life, it felt important to rest for a moment and see if the view was what she'd hoped for.

She scanned the heavens for revelations encoded in the glittering patterns. Not expecting to find any, but enjoying the search.

A grating engine sent a shiver through her in the warm July night. Jupiter raised his head, ears at attention. He gave a low, disapproving woof from deep inside his ribcage. Cassie quickly switched off the flashlight and puffed out the candle as the rusty vehicle crested the hill. She held on to Jupiter's collar to keep the giant puppy from running out to the tar road. This was the truck's fourth trip by her house since sunset. Pointed toward town this time, it slowed and swerved onto the shoulder with a rocky crunch. The vehicle idled beside Cassie's mailbox.

Anger had dissolved Cassie's fear. She sat still, visible if your eyes were adjusted to the darkness and you knew where to look. This time she wouldn't hide. Had Owen stolen her telescope? Had he prowled around her place until he found something to take that he thought would really hurt her? Maybe he planned on stealing more things, one at a time, just to terrorize her.

The engine suddenly boomed. The truck shot away as if purposely spraying dust into the air so it would seep into the cabin's open windows.

Her courage melted into relief. She had her solitude back,

although it occurred to her that too much of it could be dangerous.

That worry didn't last long. A few minute later every vehicle in the county with flashing lights and a siren ripped past her place. Sheriff. Ambulance. State troopers. It reminded her of when she'd discovered the Floater.

What catastrophe had triggered the circus this time?

Chapter Thirty-Seven

Happy SunnieChat Day!

HOLLY

Now Evan is sick. He's worse than the kids. I feel like crap

CASSIE

I can come. I'll bring crackers and popsicles

HOLLY

Thanks but I've been fighting off dad's threats of invasion. I'll just give in

KAYLA

He'll pile up dirty dishes in the sink and claim he doesn't know how to load a dishwasher. Spoiler: he does

ASHLEY

He'll repair stuff that doesn't need fixing

KAYLA

You'll have to send him to the store then change the locks before he gets back

CASSIE

He knows that trick. He'll never leave

ASHLEY

Just hope he doesn't show up with paint
samples

Chapter Thirty-Eight

Before entering the Falls Market, Cassie remembered to pull on her windbreaker to defend herself against the air-conditioning. As expected, the over-eighty crowd was using the place as a social club. She maneuvered her cart around the aisle blockers. At least she knew she could beat the slow movers to the checkout line.

Last night she'd stayed out looking at the sky long past common sense. Perhaps it was in defiance of Owen's obvious threat, or a reaction to the convoy of vehicles with piercing sirens and flashing lights that zoomed by her place.

The turmoil had carried into her dreams. Once again, she was at the museum with Vicky. Together they observed the bedroom murder scene with their usual analytical detachment.

Then her friend led her past Impressionist paintings and Rodin metal masterpieces to another display. The Floater rested like a sculpture in the center of the room. Parchment white, he posed on a patch of sand representing her beach. A constant wet drip came from hidden speakers. They walked around the scene, discussing its composition.

Vicky stopped and stood very still, a beautiful ghost in a

sparkling dress, her hair twined into intricate braids. "No one should get away with murder."

Navigating the grocery store aisle, Cassie hung on to the memory of the nightmare.

Ahead Mrs. Finster held court for her attentive subjects beside a bin of oranges. "That Sherman, he saw the whole thing." Today her strands of short bluish hair stood straight up from her head then curved into quick claws in what Cassie thought of as Gray Punk. "He's got a terrible wound on his forehead and probably a concussion. He should really be in the hospital, but you know how kids are. You can't tell them a thing."

It took a moment for Cassie to realize the busybody was talking about Dale. She maneuvered around the blockade of carts controlled by senior drivers to reach the lettuce. Feeling like a hypocrite but doing it anyway, she lingered over her selection of Romaine or Iceberg so she could listen.

"He didn't try to fight Owen, did he?" a man in a plaid shirt asked. His cap had a logo of the North Stars hockey team, which years ago had deserted Minnesota for Texas. "He's a tall kid but all skin and bones."

Cassie packaged the Romain and dropped it into her cart. Dale in an altercation?

There was no doubt who the Owen was. When people talked about Owen Knutsen, they said Owen Knutsen. (Can't call him Knute because that's his grandfather.) When they talked about Owen Nelson, they said Rocky's boy Owen (even though the boy was in his thirties). When they just said Owen, they meant Owen Norquist.

Cassie cautioned herself not to be alarmed. Any narrative Mrs. Finster promoted required thorough fact checking. Silently she disagreed with the hockey fan's description of Dale. He was definitely tall, but she'd seen him hauling big chunks of wood.

"I'm sure he tried to save Edgar's life," Mrs. Finster said, as if it were gospel instead of her own gossip.

Dale injured protecting Edgar Tvrdik from Owen? Ridiculous. Cassie grabbed lemons and limes then moved farther away to the apples, deciding not to believe a word of it.

"There were sirens!" Mrs. Finster threw a hand in the air to show her shock. "And police cars racing through town all night long and way into the early morning. I swear, I didn't get any sleep at all."

"Well, I live in town, too," one of the four women clustered around Mrs. Finster said. Unlike the other three—who had short, tightly curled, blue-gray 'dos similar to their idol—her silvery waist-length hair was tied with a scarf at the nape of her neck. "There were sirens about eleven and that was all."

"You must have fallen asleep," Mrs. Finster said. "I bet you missed the emergency medical tearing out of the fire station. I seen it real clear from my living room window."

"You sure do spend a lot of time at that window," Scarf Woman said, apparently not one of the nodding sheep.

Mrs. Finster ignored her. "When they come back, the ambulance didn't use sirens, since Edgar was dead."

Suddenly queasy, Cassie put down a luscious, green Granny Smith. It hit her that she'd been more of a witness to the event than the teller of the tale.

Last night her little country road had turned into a noisy speedway for screaming vehicles with strobing lights because of a murder.

And before that, she'd been sitting in her yard staring at Owen's truck, ready to face his harassment head on. Had she been a breath away from taking on a killer?

After the drive-by shooting at G. and G., it was a logical straight line from Owen to Edgar's death. Cassie wasn't the only one to follow that thread.

"You suppose they got Owen locked up in a tent?" Hockey fan chuckled.

"If they do," Mrs. Finster proclaimed, not acknowledging the humor, "none of us is safe in our beds."

Dale injured. Edgar murdered. Owen arrested.

Had Owen really done the deed with Dale as a witness? Cassie didn't wish anyone dead, but a first-degree conviction would certainly solve a lot of the town's troubles. And a problem of her own. Owen wasn't likely to get out of a crime that severe—if true.

"That boy is a hero, is all I can say," hockey fan said, "risking his own life like that. Fine boy."

Cassie wanted to point out that Mrs. Finster only speculated Dale had tried to save Edgar. She hadn't actually said he'd done anything. And how would she know one way or the other? She couldn't have gotten that information from looking out her window.

Cassie's frustration went beyond the primary source. Hockey fan and the three ladies who nodded their heads in agreement were more interested in a good story than in reality. The Finsters of the world would be powerless without their armies of repeaters and embellishers.

Cassie and the single hippie-haired skeptic were outnumbered. As far as the Produce Social Club was concerned, Dale's bravery was now fact. His superhero feat would be spread all over the county by supper. At least Dale would get some *good* publicity out of it.

"It's a miracle he turned out so well," Mrs. Finster said, "what with that family he comes from." She launched into a litany of sins committed by the Steinhaus clan, starting five generations back.

Cassie clenched her teeth, stashed a quart of strawberries in her cart, and moved on. Around the corner in the next aisle Glenna Lowery stood with a hand resting on a shelf beside the saltine crackers. Her face looked as stark as her bleached hair. Cassie abandoned her groceries and put an arm around the girl, feeling how skeletal she was under the sleeveless knit top. She worried that, in addition to everything else, Glenna might be anorexic. "Do you feel like you're going to faint?"

"I just—I want some oranges," Glenna said. "It's not a crime is it, wanting oranges? Those old witches keep standing there like they own the place, and only people they approve of can buy fucking oranges."

"In that case," Cassie said, "the store's never going to have to restock *that* display."

Glenna gave a weak smile and uncomfortably slipped out of Cassie's grip. "I'll be all right."

"How many do you want?" Cassie asked. "They don't know me well enough to disapprove of me yet."

"Six. And they don't have to know you at all to decide you're not good enough for this damn town."

Cassie adjusted herself into a friendly-assertive posture, one she had often used in her L.A. life. She left her cart and strolled back around the corner.

"If Bob and Sandra can't find a buyer," Mrs. Finster said, "they'll have to shut down. And then where would we get our groceries? Thank goodness for Greg. He's practically taken over the Market since Bob's stroke."

"Bob didn't have a stroke," Scarf Hippie said.

Mrs. Finster stuck to her narrative. "Oh, I'm certain he did."

"Excuse me," Cassie said with a smile, feeling like chum in a pool of pariah. The blue-gray blockade parted. She pulled a plastic bag off the roll attached to the side of the bin and shoved oranges into it.

Mrs. Finster pounced on her as if she were the last mint on the plate. "Oh, you don't have that lovely dog with you."

"He's not allowed in a grocery store," Cassie said.

"Having an animal that big would scare me half to death. You never know when they'll turn on you. But I'm sure he's a good watchdog. Too bad he couldn't stop that thief who broke into your place and took your things."

"Yes, too bad." It was amazing. Cassie and Mrs. Finster had never been introduced, never spoken before today; yet they knew more about one another than Cassie had known about most of her California neighbors. Compared to Mrs. Finster, earthquakes didn't seem so bad.

"I don't know how you can live so far out in the country," the sweetly aggressive woman said. "It seems so dangerous, you being alone way out there, without a husband. And now with *two murders* practically in your own home. You must be terrified!"

Cassie gave a smile she had frequently relied on in staff meetings when she wanted to punch out her client—or her boss. "Danger feeds the soul." She made her escape, the whine of refrigerated air and cold human silence at her back.

You fool, she told herself. *You should have kept your mouth shut. Instead you supplied meat for the carnivores. You'll be branded a psycho-killer by nightfall.*

Shelving filled with an assortment of boxed crackers provided a comforting barrier. Cassie handed Glenna the plastic bag.

"Now who looks like she's about to faint," Glenna said.

"I survived."

"Thanks. They're for Jessie. He's Judy's youngest. He likes oranges. He doesn't want the juice from a box or anything like that. He has to have the real thing. I cut them in half for him and he sticks his whole face in it." Glenna gave a little sob and couldn't seem to take her eyes off the bag. "How do you tell a little kid his father's in jail, and this time he might not be getting out?"

That confirmed for Cassie that Owen was being detained by the authorities. "Want to go over to the cafe and get a cup of coffee?" She didn't understand Glenna, not one bit. And she certainly didn't get her relationship with Owen.

Averted Vision

According to Laurel, Owen and Judy started living together when they both dropped out of school at sixteen. Somewhere along the years they got married—at least, that's what people assumed. No one recalled a wedding. That wasn't surprising since Owen was unlikely to have a church ceremony with a reception at the VFW.

Owen and Judy had three children. Now Glenna was part of the family. The women cooked and cleaned and took care of the kids. They hauled Owen home from the bar when he got drunk, and bailed him out of jail when he got arrested.

It nauseated Cassie to think what else they might do for him. And she wasn't thinking sex. Owen didn't seem the type to conduct his illegal enterprises alone. He would want others to take care of the hard parts while serving as audience to his triumphs.

Glenna shook her head. "I gotta get home. Besides, people stare at me—more than usual I mean. We've even had reporters trying to get us to answer a bunch of goddamn questions."

"You know you can stop by my place any time," Cassie said.

"I'm not supposed to. You know, like Judy told you, because of Owen. But I almost did," Glenna confessed, "lots of times." She clamped her mouth shut and put a hand over her eyes as if fighting off tears.

"Next time you will. Next time—when you want to— you'll come to the cabin. We'll sit and look at the lake and chat." Cassie fought off the urge to give her a mandate. *You will absolutely come to my place tonight!* She knew it was counterproductive to push. The girl would have to take the next step herself.

Glenna lowered her hand and gave Cassie a puzzled look. "You're smart. You see how things work around here. You know you're not supposed to be nice to me. Why are you doing this?"

It was a fair question. Cassie wasn't sure she could explain, even to herself. The reason included the injustice of men getting away with abusing women. And the tragedy of women who were cornered into being abused. "The only one allowed to pick my friends is Jupiter, and he likes you."

"It isn't 'cause of what you *saw*, is it?" Glenna whispered.

"What I saw?" A vision of Vicky's body flashed through Cassie's mind. The sudden image knocked the breath out of her and she gasped to get it back. That's really what made her want to help. She feared the girl would end up dead, wrapped in blood-soaked sheets. But Glenna couldn't know that.

"You don't have to keep it a secret from me." Glenna spoke as if Cassie was the one in need of a friend. "I could feel it, like electricity, when you bandaged my hand. But it's okay. I know you'd say if I was going to get hit by a semi or something. Thanks again for getting the oranges." She turned and walked toward the checkout counter.

Cassie shivered under the harsh fluorescent lights. What had Glenna said? A secret and a semi? She couldn't make sense of it. The air conditioning droned. It was too cold. She finished shopping and loaded the reusable cloth bags full of groceries and the insulated bag holding frozen goods into the backseat of her car.

Down the street she saw Rhonda talking to Denny. Hoping to get a factual version of whatever had happened last night, Cassie walked over to join them.

Rhonda greeted her somberly. "Denny and I were just discussing including safety information on the webpage." She obviously had no doubt Cassie would take on the Sparks' project.

"There's a brochure we put together a few years ago." Denny seemed detached, as if his real thoughts were far from the sunny sidewalk. "I'll get you a copy. You should have one anyway, since you're in a new house—well, new for you. It tells you all the things to check and that you should have escape routes planned, just in case. I know you've got smoke detectors. You should check the batteries."

"I'll do that." Cassie remembered Laurel saying the Sparks had installed the devices for free when her aunt and uncle built the place. It was part of a program to ensure every dwelling in the township had them.

She didn't want to talk about the job she might or might not take until she'd had more time to think about it herself. "I heard about Edgar. I'm so sorry for your loss." She knew from her own experience how inadequately words dealt with death, especially when you had no grief of your own to offer. She'd only seen the man a few times, while he had been a part of Denny and Rhonda's world their whole lives.

"It's so strange," Denny said, his thin lips tight. "I think Edgar expected to live forever. I'm starting a collection for the family."

"That's a good idea, Denny." Rhonda pulled bills from her purse and handed them to him. "I've only got thirteen on me."

"Much appreciated," Denny said. He pulled out his wallet. "I don't have a donation envelope set up yet."

Cassie had to start carrying cash since moving away from a city that ran almost exclusively on plastic. She still wasn't used to it and needed to replenish her supply. Good thing the Falls Market took credit cards. She grabbed her last bit of currency then shoved the billfold back into her purse. "I don't know what's correct in this situation." She handed Denny the ten.

"That's too much. Five is good, since you didn't really know him." He handed her the three singles Rhonda had given him plus two more from his wallet. "A lot of people each put in a little. We can get a real nice Butterball, a card, and still have plenty for flowers."

Cassie shoved the change into her pocket.

"Who's going to turn on an oven in July and heat up a whole house to fix a turkey?" Rhonda asked gently.

"Mrs. Callahan," Denny said. "That's Father Anderson's housekeeper," he explained to Cassie. "She'll roast it on the gas grill then take it over to Linda's when Edgar's brother and his family get here from Wisconsin. I suppose the other kids will come, even though they haven't spoken to their dad in years. They'll figure there's some inheritance in it for them."

"Be fair," Rhonda said. "Don't go turning Edgar into a saint just because he's dead. He was hard on everyone around him, and hardest on his own children. He drove those kids away. Linda should have left, too."

"I know." Denny pulled a note pad and pencil stub from his shirt pocket. "I'm writing down your names so I don't forget. Mrs. Callahan will put them on the card in calligraphy. Sorry to take off, but I have to get to the fire station. We're planning a memorial service for Edgar."

Rhonda gazed after the lanky man. "Poor Denny. He's far too occupied with tragedy since the Sparks got into charitable gambling."

"How's that?" Cassie didn't follow the connection and hoped Rhonda wasn't working around to Denny needing a good woman to take care of him.

"He used to organize a lot of the fund raisers in town. Once we got bingo, the money started rolling in almost on its own. We could pay for firefighting equipment and still have plenty to donate to other groups. Suddenly the town didn't need as many raffles and pancake breakfasts. That left Denny with nothing much to organize except donations for funerals. It took him a while to find other things that needed doing. He almost single-handedly revived the fire safety campaign."

Rhonda shifted her big purse from one arm to the other. "He's pretty broken up about Edgar. When the harassing stuff with Owen got bad, he practically became Edgar's bodyguard.

In a strange way that vile man's having it in for Edgar was the best thing that ever happened to the old miser.

"Except for the Sparks, Edgar didn't do much outside of running his store and complaining. His business has been dropping off for years. He didn't exactly make customers feel welcome, and he was too stubborn to modernize the place. After it got shot up, he found out he still had good friends, like he used to before his wife died and he forced them all away. People who haven't set foot in G. and G. for years have made a point of going in and buying something."

"Do you know what caused the fire?" Cassie asked.

"Arson. No doubt about it. Time-delay incendiary device. The smoke detectors were disabled. Too bad his neighbors didn't notice anything sooner. It must have smoldered for a bit."

"Long enough for the person who rigged it to be somewhere else?" Cassie asked.

"Not long enough to get to South Dakota," Rhonda said, "which is where Owen claims he was that night, although we think we've got witnesses who saw him at the fire. That's not proof, of course. And witnesses tend to lose their memories when it comes to Owen."

Across the street Cassie watched Dale go into the drugstore, bandage strips plastered above one eye. She remembered why she needed to talk to Rhonda in the first place. "I saw Owen drive by my place four times last night. All before the emergency vehicles and the sheriff cars came out from town."

"You should make a formal statement."

"Did Dale Steinhaus see Owen kill Edgar?" Cassie had to ask.

"Under investigation. That's all I can tell you. I'd say more if I could." Rhonda checked her watch. I've got to get back to work. If I leave the sheriff alone too long, he'll try to move into my great office. You can call in your statement when you get home. Be sure to say you want to speak to Officer Berger," she said with a wink. "And don't worry about Dale."

Cassie drove back to the cabin doing exactly that, worrying about Dale. Strangers waved hello as she passed them on the road. Absently, she waved back.

The Floater, her telescope, arson, the bingo robbery. Edgar murdered and Dale a witness. A crime spree in Glacier Falls!

Statistically, living here wasn't as safe as it used to be. She swung into the driveway and punched the opener for the garage door. The panel groaned in protest as it rose. Cassie slammed on the brakes and crunched to a stop.

Sitting inside the garage was her telescope.

Chapter Thirty-Nine

SunnieChat is here for you!

CASSIE

K the pics are amazing. I want to go there!
Sisters trip to the Galapagos!

HOLLY

Lizard?

KAYLA

Marine iguana. I could stay here forever but
the grant doesn't last that long. I might have a
gig in New Zealand after this. A doc I know
got a five year grant. He wants me on
the team

ASHLEY

Just you?

HOLLY

Not drop dead gorgeous Liam?

KAYLA

Just me. Dilemma. Just when I'm getting used to his accent. Before I didn't understand most of what he said. Now we have real conversations

ASHLEY

Any surprises? A wife and four kids?

KAYLA

He's a Whovian

HOLLY

From Whoville? I've read that Seuss a few million times. To the kids. I read it to the kids

KAYLA

Different doctor. From the Tardis. Doctor Who

CASSIE

Does he have a tattoo in Gallifreyan?

KAYLA

No. In Greek

CASSIE

What does it say?

KAYLA

Not telling

ASHLEY

Where exactly is this ink?

KAYLA

Definitely not telling

ASHLEY

Send pics

Chapter Forty

Although the murder rate in the county was up, the theft rate was down. Cassie put away the groceries then went to the garage to check out her returned telescope. Apparently Deputy Berger was right, someone had simply taken it for a celestial joy ride. Clever phrasing. She could laugh at it now.

Tufts of dried grass and clods of dirt stuck to the legs and feet. Other than that, it was just the way it had been when she last saw it. With relief she knew she'd been wrong to suspect Owen. No one who allowed his own truck to deteriorate into a rolling pile of junk would return someone else's property intact.

She called the sheriff's department on her cell. She didn't recognize the name of the officer who took the call. "Stolen telescope," he said crisply. "I know the case. I'll send someone out as soon as possible."

"As long as I've got it back," Cassie told him, "just forget about it."

"We can't do that," the officer said. "A crime's been committed and reported. Leave the article alone so you don't disturb any fingerprints. Since it's evidence, the crime lab will have to examine it." He sounded authoritative but bored, as if automated. "An officer will take it into custody."

Cassie bristled at his calling her beautiful, precision instrument with the power to elevate human kind beyond itself to the stars a generic "article," and declaring it had to be, in effect, arrested. It was a victim, not a criminal.

"You want it," Cassie said, "you have to send Adam Berger."

"Deputy Berger is not available."

"Give him the message," Cassie said. "You got that?"

"Yes, ma'am."

She hung up on Officer Robot.

Jupiter sniffed the legs of the tripod. Up and down. Up and down. Up and down. He seemed curious but not agitated by the scents.

Cassie walked a circle around the scope. "What do you smell, Jupe?" The odors of strangers made him edgy. Some people he barely tolerated, like Deputy Berger. The puppy's behavior convinced her the scope had been taken by someone he was used to, someone he liked.

She scrutinized a spot Jupiter found especially interesting. Reddish-brown smears dulled the silvery metal. She searched for similar marks. A smudge marred the shiny tube. Dark blotches speckled the matte-black surface of the mount.

Someone's soft flesh had made forceful contact with the solid mass. That someone put a hand to the dripping wound, trying to staunch the flow. Then he touched the telescope, tainting it with his blood.

Gosh, who could it have been? How about the hero with bandages on his forehead.

Cassie felt betrayed. She thought she had built a real friendship with the young man. They'd talked about *Kidnapped*, the book he was currently reading. While great stories had been shoved at Cassie like bright berries by parents and two older sisters, Dale had discovered them on his own. He'd done a good job of it. *Frankenstein. The Count of Monte Cristo.* Not easy reads.

Although illogical, she still trusted him. After all, he'd returned what he'd taken. She wondered what he'd wanted it for. If it was star gazing, he could have asked to use it right here. It must have been for something specific. And terrestrial. And special, since it wasn't an easy thing to haul around.

If he'd asked to borrow the scope, would she have lent it to him? No, she had to admit she wouldn't have. The beautiful device was still too new. It was part of her escape to a different life. She needed to keep it her own for a while.

Well, that was shot to hell now. But she could make sure it didn't go any further. If there were no clues, there'd be no way to charge anyone with the theft, and no reason to keep the "article" as evidence. Right?

Besides, as an eye witness to Owen killing Edgar, Dale had enough to deal with. He didn't need to be arrested for stealing, too.

Eyewitness. *From how far away?*

She patted the elegant combination of lenses and mirrors. The Floater had already been dead when she'd seem him through it. How much more terrifying it must have been to watch a magnified murder in real time.

She went into the house and collected a bucket, cleaner, and rubber gloves. Rags were a problem. She hadn't lived here long enough to accumulate an assortment of worn socks and stained sweatshirts. Her designer corporate uniforms were stored in the closet of the spare bedroom, now her office. One of the crisp Egyptian-cotton blouses seemed appropriate. She sniped off a sleeve with great satisfaction.

In the garage Cassie removed the tube from the mount. She rested it on a towel on the workbench and gave the black surface a gentle polishing with a non-toxic, plant-based, naturally produced, certified green, all-purpose cleaner.

She wondered what story Dale had told to explain how

he'd seen the murder. He must have kept the telescope out of it, otherwise it would already be confiscated. The device was no good for close viewing. It would have been set up far from the actual scene. That made her confident she wasn't washing away any critical DNA samples that might convict the murderer.

Cassie hauled the tripod and mount onto the hard-packed driveway. She carefully spritzed and wiped and rinsed away the clods of dirt and grass. She dabbed at the dark smears, knowing she couldn't scrub off all traces of blood. Maybe the crime lab would only check for fingerprints. And it was Dale's blood anyway. Not the victim's or the killer's. She could come up with an explanation.

Oh, Officer, I remember now. Dale cut himself with the chainsaw.

Damn blood. Once the stuff got into something—like your dreams—it refused to let go. There'd been droplets in arching swaths on the walls of Vicky's bedroom. Splatter patterns, one of the detectives had said, not knowing Cassie was close enough to hear. She'd closed her eyes, wishing he hadn't given the abstract design a name. Since then, she saw them mimicked in paintings she'd once loved.

The murder hadn't just been one thing. It had caused a long chain reaction of loss. The collateral damage still surprised her.

Finished, she put everything back into the garage the way she'd found it. She pulled her car forward to cover the puddle. The cleaning items were out of sight by the time Officer Adam Berger arrived and parked behind her Mini Cooper.

Cassie had mixed feelings about seeing him so soon after the bingo interview, but she was glad Officer Robot hadn't flown over on his integrated helicopter like Inspector Gadget.

"This is where it was when you came home?" Adam examined the black and chrome without touching it.

Jupiter paced territorial circles around Cassie. "Yes," she said truthfully.

The concrete floor was dark with small rings of moisture outlining each of the tripod's button feet.

"You're sure you found it exactly here and not, say," he pointed to her wet front tire and trickles of water that had splashed out when she'd driven through the puddle, "where your little wind-up toy of a vehicle is now?" He definitely seemed more relaxed out here in the wild than sitting behind his card-table desk.

"Hey, the Cooper got me to Minnesota, along with everything I own, all the way from California. Show some respect." This was the land of all-wheel drive SUVs, and heavy-duty trucks with optional snowplow attachments. She was used to smart-ass comments about her car, and she was not going to let this one go unchallenged.

Adam kept his gaze on the scope. "And you didn't move it?"

"Now, why would I do that?" She knew he avoided eye contact because he underestimated her. He didn't have to worry. She could look him full in the face and lie without giving herself away. It was one of her best corporate skills. "It's been returned and it's perfectly fine. There's no need for the sheriff's department to put any more time into it."

"Do you really want to drop the matter?"

"I don't see any reason to pursue it. Investigating two deaths and the bingo robbery is far more important."

Adam grinned but still didn't look at her. "This is where I'm supposed to tell you there are no small crimes, and law enforcement treats them all with equal seriousness. But I'd have trouble saying it convincingly and you wouldn't believe it anyway."

"How about some iced tea?" Cassie offered, her way of waving a truce flag.

He made eye contact and smiled. "Sounds good."

They went into the kitchen and sat at the table that had been there since the place was built. She made Jupiter stay outside. The furry ball sat on the step and stared at them through the screen door. "How's Dale?" she asked. "Is he okay? And safe?"

"Norquist is being held for questioning, if that's what you're asking."

"Partly, I guess."

He took a sip of tea and put the glass down thoughtfully. "Before you called in about the telescope, I'd already planned on coming over to see you. You live close to where Edgar was murdered."

"And I'm the expert on dead bodies at Beauty Lake."

"Rhonda said you saw Owen last night."

"I didn't have my telescope, of course, but I was out star gazing with binoculars." Cassie told him about the truck making two round trips past her place, including the part about it stopping by her mailbox. "Technically, I suppose he was on the property, but it was only for a moment. He didn't yell anything or spit out the window."

"What about a black 2008 Jeep Wrangler?" Adam asked.

"I don't remember anything like that, but then it doesn't sound as memorable as some other vehicles that go by. Is it Edgar's?"

Adam nodded. "We found it parked not far from the crime scene."

"Do you think you can make a murder charge stick?"

Adam shrugged. "A defense attorney is going to pick at Dale's testimony pretty hard. We've got a hammer found in Owen's truck with what appears to be blood stains on it. But it isn't blood, and it isn't Edgar's blood until the lab says so. It's being fingerprinted, but if it's established the hammer belongs to Owen, no jury's going to be swayed because his prints are on it."

"But if there's evidence the truck was at the scene, wouldn't that help?" Cassie asked.

"Stolen, and then returned, according to Owen. Tire

tracks show it has been there a lot, not just last night. That's not surprising. Everyone knows he night fishes. That's probably one of his spots."

"Everyone seems to know a lot of things, but Owen still bullies the town and no one's been able to stop him." It came out harsher than she meant it. She hoped he didn't think it was a criticism of his abilities.

Adam didn't seem offended. "He's been arrested dozens of times for petty crimes. He's paid fines when forced to. Done jail time. Even performed community service."

"Now that's a scary thought." Owen didn't seem the type to play cards with senior citizens or pick up trash at the public park.

"I went through a lot of frustration over that man when I first came here," Adam confessed. "Eventually I had to accept that, as much trouble as he is and as much as I wish he would be gone from my town, it's hard to get evidence of a crime serious enough to force a judge to put him away for long."

"Until now."

"Maybe." Adam stirred a touch of sugar into his half-finished iced tea.

"You don't think he's capable of killing?" Cassie asked.

"He could. Anyone could. I don't think he'd do it because it isn't as satisfying as shooting up a guy's store and knowing he'll be scared of you for the rest of his life."

Cassie remembered the look on Owen's face when he'd leaned out of his truck in her driveway and yelled at Glenna. He'd been more amused than angry. And in the drugstore he'd seemed delighted he could terrorize Cassie in front of an audience. He enjoyed the power and the attention, no doubt about that. Yes, Owen would be disappointed if one of his playthings died on him.

Still, abusers got tired of the same-old, same-old and escalated their torments. Some of them eventually snapped.

"Owen did kill Edgar," Cassie hoped Adam would give her confirmation.

"Guilt or innocence depends on what you can prove in court." He ran a finger through the condensation on the side of his glass, causing drops to roll down onto the tablecloth. "I hope you don't mind my throwing around my personal opinions. I guess I feel it's safe to talk to you. I know you won't go blabbing all over town."

Cassie hadn't noticed much of either personal or opinion in anything he'd said. "Translation: I have no friends and I never go anywhere."

"You've got a city-caution about you. And you're smart. You know Owen's lawyer is going to focus on how Dale could see so well from way up on top of Red Hawk Hill."

The kitchen faced lake-side. They couldn't see the garage from here, but Adam's glance moved in that direction. If he had x-ray vision, he'd be looking through all the walls to the telescope sitting a building away on the concrete floor. He slowly brought his gaze back to Cassie. "Unless something miraculous happens—and I don't expect it to—this case hangs on Dale's testimony being accurate and believable. Might be a good idea for you to mention that to him. Maybe the two of you will remember something important."

Adam thanked her for the cold drink and left, trying to give Jupiter a pet on the way to the patrol car. The dog dodged out of reach and bounded into the house.

Cassie could barely manage a polite goodbye. She slumped to the kitchen floor and let Jupiter snuggle into her lap.

Abusers snapped.

Through his lawyer, Jordan had begged Cassie to visit him in prison.

She shouldn't have gone.

But she did.

Once.

Chapter Forty-One

The Los Angeles County State Prison felt both sterile and grimy at the same time. Cassie vomited twice in the rest room.

"Here, honey." A woman handed her a baby wipe. "First time?"

She shook her head yes then scooped up water from the running faucet and rinsed out her mouth.

"I wish I could tell you that you get used to it," the woman said. "You don't. Not really. But you'll be fine. Just go easy on yourself and give yourself time. Whatever your guy did that put him in here, it's not on you."

The woman's kind words made her stomach heave, but she had nothing left to expel. In a haze she followed signs and instructions from guards.

She was suddenly sitting opposite Jordan, a plexiglass partition separating them. She picked up the telephone-style receiver hanging on the wall and put it to her ear.

On his side of the divider, Jordan spoke into his own. "Hi, Cassie. You look wonderful."

His warm, friendly greeting compounded the bizarre situation. He acted as if they'd last seen one another at a party instead of in a court room. Cassie couldn't manage a standard social response. Conversing with her best friend's murderer was not normal and she wouldn't pretend otherwise. "What do you want, Jordan?"

"I want to see you. To talk to you. I miss you so much." With the change in lifestyle, his hard edges showed. Gone was the shy, boyish appearance, so perfect he could have trademarked it. His bright hair and summer tan had faded to fall.

Cassie remembered his inviting eyes, intensely blue from vanity contact lenses. Now they were a chilling steel. "We're not at Starbuck's, and this isn't a date. Tell me what you need to, so I can leave."

Jordan gazed at her with the sad, sincere expression he'd perfected during the trial. "I want you to understand. You know Vicky was always pushing me." He spoke with no remorse, innocent as a lamb. "She did things on purpose. To upset me. As if my anger proved I loved her."

"You went beyond anger," Cassie said.

"I got a little rough at times," Jordan said. "I admit that. Vicky wanted it that way. But I didn't kill her."

The tilt of the head was just right. His lips quivered ever so slightly. "I'm so glad you came. I hoped so much you would." He aimed that cool gaze at Cassie like a precision weapon. "Vicky was a mistake from the beginning. I wouldn't have been taken in by her if you hadn't been so afraid of our feelings for one another. If we'd been together, this wouldn't have happened. You know that, don't you."

Cassie got the message: I'm in prison because of you.

Jordan's performance shook her like an earthquake. She shouldn't have come here. She slowly moved the phone toward the hook to hang up.

"Wait. Wait." His lips moved in front of her as he spoke into the receiver on his side of the transparent barrier. Eerily his voice came from the molded plastic frozen in her hand. "There's something I have to tell you. About Vicky."

She closed her eyes and put the phone back to her ear.

"I don't care what other people think, but it's important to me that *you* know the truth. I should have left her immediately when she started doing things she knew I hated and saying horrible things to hurt me." He paused as if expecting Cassie to ask for details.

She didn't.

"I stayed with Vicky because I wanted it to work out between the two of us, even though—" He gave a little half-sob.

Cassie felt she was supposed to fill in the blank. *Even though I'm in love with you, my darling Cassie.*

"That night she was on a rant. She wanted more. She wanted me all to herself, but she knew there was part of me she could never have. I slapped her, yes. It was wrong. I shouldn't have done it. But I hit her once. *Once.* And then I left. You understand? I left. She was alive."

That was nothing new. Cassie had heard it over and over at the trial.

"You see it, don't you? It's obvious when you think about it. I should have figured it out sooner. I can't prove it. God, I wish I could. But now *you'll* know, at least. And that's more important to me than anything because—"

Again, the unfinished thought for Cassie to complete with romantic words, as if this were the perfect fantasy.

His illusion couldn't touch her. The glitter he spewed was just sparkly bullshit. There had never been a dream with him in it, only the nightmare of Vicky's death.

She opened her eyes. "Tell me." Behind the facade of his earnest, vulnerable pose, she could see he expected her to accept everything he said.

Jordan spoke softly and slowly. "Vicky set me up. She

planned the whole thing. She baited me into that fight, because she was always jealous of us, Cassie. You know she was. She wanted what we have between us, but she knew it would never be that way for her. She didn't expect me to leave, but I did. When I walked out, she couldn't handle it. You know how depressed she'd get. She broke down. She broke down and she took my bracelet and put it in the bed beside her to incriminate me. Then —" He halted, as if overwhelmed by what he must say next.

Cassie gripped the phone. The pause was a strategy to draw her into his sphere, to dangle her from a thread before he severed it, plunging her into shock at his revelation.

Jordan let out a great sob. "—she killed herself."

The plastic was too heavy to hold. Cassie let go. It hung from the coiled cord, shouting at her. "How else did the chain get in the bed, Cassie? How else? It was on the desk in the living room. I put it there. No one believes me, but it's true. You believe me, don't you, Cassie. I know you do. You have to. Because I'm telling you the truth.

"Please, pick up the phone, Cassie! Pick it up and listen to me. Pick it up, Cassandra! Listen to me, bitch! This happened because of you. Because of you, Cassie! Because of you!"

Jordon banged the receiver against the transparent barrier, lips moving, his muffled voice coming from beside Cassie, as if a demon whispered to her. She sat still as stone, her limbs too weak to move. Guards dragged away a raving Jordan.

She sat in the tiny cell, more alone than she'd ever been.

Chapter Forty-Two

Exhausted by the memory of the smothering cubical buried inside the vast, grim building, Cassie sat on the floor of the cabin's sunny kitchen hugging Jupiter.

The incapacitating flashbacks enveloped her less frequently now than during the trial; but, like the nightmares, they would not go away. Her sisters continued to urge her to get professional help. Holly sent her articles on PTSD and phone numbers for trauma help lines. Ashley gave her the names of psychiatrists recommended by her own shrink. Kayla, knowing her older sisters had the traditional mental health angle covered, gave her a subscription to a yoga magazine and sent her CDs of Gregorian chants, Tibetan singing bowl music, and humpback whales calling to one another in the ocean.

Cassie ruffled Jupiter's thick fur, pushed him off her lap and got up. She was grateful she hadn't collapsed until after Adam left. She carried her glass of tea, lemon, and melted ice into her office.

Although she didn't really know Edgar, she felt connected to his death through Dale. And through Owen. She knew she shouldn't equate Owen with Jordan and Glenna with Vicky.

Unfortunately, her mind had formed the links and she didn't know how to sever them.

The *Falls Press* sat on her desk, folded open to another letter to the editor about the Safari Club. According to D.E. Kinsley, it would be right and just if that Sodom and Gomorrah was struck down. "The good folks of Glacier Falls must not tolerate the den of the devil in their midst." The writer urged those good folks to take it upon themselves to "do God's work." The inflammatory words didn't exactly tell the town's citizens to commit violence against the strip club, but they came close.

Rhonda's concern that someone might firebomb the place seemed justified. Maybe Russel Sworski, the Floater, had been killed because he was one of the owners, as Rhonda speculated.

Saving souls from sin had a long history as a motive for violence. It opened up a lot of possibilities for suspects. All of the Vigilants. The Father and the Reverend, in their new holy alliance, could have a plot to bump off each owner one by one. Perhaps Kinsley, the agitator, had done more than pen letters. Or could the killer be one of Mrs. Finster's groupies?

Enough of that. She dumped the paper with Kinsley's inflammatory rhetoric in the recycling bin. Then she checked her email.

A message from a small but trendy company that specialized in all-natural skin care products popped up. She'd done a pitch to them a few weeks ago. She hadn't gotten that gig, but they liked her work. They were launching a new line of fruit-inspired bubble bath beads. Could she whip up some bright—but mellow—packaging?

You bet she could! As she typed an enthusiastic response, her mind danced with vibrant green limes (that was the bright part) frolicking in creamy foam (very mellow) against a background of fat water droplets (even more mellow).

Her cell rang. Glenna. The girl wanted to—needed to—

talk. Right now. Cassie set aside the images of colorful—yet relaxing—citrus. Following the directions the girl gave her, which no map app could rival, she navigated along county roads west of town where the Norquist mailbox sprouted from a rusty milk can, marking the entrance to the driveway.

Front door punctuating a broad porch supported by pillars, the three-story house had been stately once. With her artist's eye, Cassie could see the old beauty under the faded ghost with a sagging roof. She guided the Mini along tire ruts that wound past a garden rich with tomatoes, squash and beans, then parked by the back door, as Glenna had instructed.

The dirt trail continued toward a neglected barn surrounded by knee-high weeds. A generation ago this had been a working farm. Now the only tended part was close to the house. A patch of mowed grass provided a lawn. Shocking purple pansies spilled from an old bathtub. Golden California poppies sprouted from a propped up rusty wheelbarrow with no wheel. A sandbox held toy farm equipment. Beside it, a swing set squatted over brown ovals where grass had been worn away.

Wooden pins dangled from the ropes of a clothesline, showing it was used regularly. Cassie remembered helping her cousin Laurel and Aunt Renee hang out the wash when she came to visit. She had hated the work but loved the smell of wind-dried sheets at night when she snuggled into bed.

Cassie got out of the car. Dogs barked not far away. She wasn't sure if she should let Jupiter loose. It was stupid to bring him, but she appreciated the company. She was a little shaky about going to Owen's, even though he was locked up in a proper brick and mortar jail in the next county.

A child exploded from the house, screen door banging behind him. "Can I play with Jupiter?" the boy shouted as he ran to the car. "Glenna says I can if it's okay with you."

Scabs dotted Jessie Norquist's knees below shorts that were

too big for him. His shirt was streaked with dirt and grass stains. He had an alert, round face sprinkled with summer freckles and topped by unruly blond-brown hair. He was too fresh and shiny to look anything like Owen.

Glenna appeared in a sleeveless blouse and cut-off jeans. Her short, snowy hair stuck out like straw, and she wore her usual thick make-up. "It's okay to let Jupiter run. I put the mutts in the barn."

Cassie let the puppy out of the car. Jessie threw himself down on the ground, and buried his hands in the dog's thick, reddish coat.

"I bet he plays fetch," Jessie said. "Does he play fetch?"

"He's not very good at it," Cassie said. Jupiter liked toys but didn't have the attention span to stay with them for very long. "You'll have to give him some practice."

Jessie rolled an old tennis ball across the lawn. Jupiter scrambling after it. Cassie followed Glenna into the house. The kitchen was tidy but in need of new paint and wallpaper. A plastic-coated cloth abloom with sunflowers covered a metal-framed table. Cassie sat on a matching metal and vinyl chair.

"Jessie just loves dogs." Judy put a steaming mug of coffee in front of Cassie.

Glenna fussed with a cigarette, as if trying to work up the courage to explain why she'd asked Cassie to come over.

Cassie imagined any woman who lived with Owen would be fidgety, as if she received random electrical shocks. Glenna could certainly be like that. Judy had seemed that way, too, when she'd spoken to Cassie outside the drugstore. Now she showed a natural calm. Maybe it was because Owen was out of the way at the moment. Or perhaps because she was on her own turf.

Seeing the two women side by side, Cassie was struck by the resemblance. Owen obviously went for a certain type. Both of them wore heavy make-up on a warm summer day in their own kitchen. A fortyish version of her husband's girlfriend, Judy stood slightly shorter than Glenna and was not as anorexic looking. Today she only wore two necklaces and a bracelet, much less jewelry than when she went to town. Cassie wondered if the woman's long-sleeved shirt and jeans, out of place considering the weather, covered bruises.

"I would've come over to your place," Glenna said, "but the sheriff's got the truck 'cause it's evidence and everything, and the Dodge don't work so good." She stopped as if suddenly struck mute.

Cassie heard children older than Jessie arguing over a video game in another room. She was surprised and dismayed that Glenna was still here. With Owen under arrest the girl could have left if she'd wanted to. She was definitely skittish enough to bolt when there was trouble. Was that how she'd ended up with this life? Considering the current circumstances, running away seemed like a good idea. So what was keeping her here?

Judy put a hand on the younger woman's shoulder. "Get to it." There was a gentleness in her voice. Cassie had wondered about the relationship between these two women who shared the same house and, presumably, the same man. Soap opera standards said they should be bitter rivals. Instead they behaved like sisters.

"Since you and Berger are dating and are probably going to get married and everything," Glenna said, "I figure I can tell you and you can tell him."

"We are not dating," Cassie said.

"You guys broke up?" Glenna sounded genuinely distressed.

"No," Cassie protested. She should have been prepared for this. The man had been to her house more than once. Naturally half the town expected wedding invitations. "We've never been on a date. We're not even really friends. I've talked to him a few times, but it's all been about sheriff department business." She purposely didn't mention the telescope. Until she had a chance to get the whole story from Dale, she wanted to be careful.

"But you're still helping Berger with old man Tvrdik's murder. Because that Sherman kid works for you and you're psychic and everything."

Psychic! Where had that come from? "Glenna, I'm not—"

Glenna brushed away her words, black polish thick on her chewed fingernails. "That's okay. I know you can't say nothin' about it. That you have to keep your secret and everything."

That was the second time Glenna made a cryptic remark about a secret. Cassie didn't understand it now any better than the first time in the grocery store over oranges.

"Anyway," Glenna went on, "you can tell Berger what happened, and then he'll let Owen go, 'cause he didn't do it. I know he didn't. I mean, the thing with the truck was all my fault. I always have the truck on Wednesday nights. Sometimes other nights, too."

Cassie sipped her coffee. The thick liquid was almost too strong to choke down. There was no cream or sugar to cut it with, so she swallowed it straight, like a good Minnesotan. Her mind was stuck on psychic and secret. She had to get those issues resolved before she left, but she was afraid to interrupt the girl. Now that the locomotive had built up speed, Cassie didn't want to risk derailing it.

Glenna traced one of the sunflowers on the tablecloth with her little finger. "I went to the Municipal to get a six-pack of Bud. Oh, and I got cigarettes, too. Not vapes. Real cigarettes. You've probably never been in the place. They have the off-sale part where you can buy beer and hard liquor and wine, and then they have a bar with tables and a TV for watching baseball and sports. Most people are in the bar part.

"Off sale's never very busy. That witch Mrs. Hanley waited on me right away. It didn't take more than two minutes, even though she always asks to see my ID, like she don't remember me from one week to the next. Mr. Hanley, he's not like that. He just tries to get a look down my blouse and sells me the beer. I think that's why his wife always gives me a hard time. Like it's my fault her husband's a pervert. Anyway, when I come out, the truck's gone. Just like that." She snapped her fingers.

"Was the truck locked?" Cassie asked.

"The locks have been broken for years," Judy said. "Besides, no one locks their cars around here."

Except me with my citified ways, Cassie thought.

Glenna took a drag, her hand shaking. She blew a column of smoke toward the ceiling. "I just stood in that parking lot with the cold six-pack under my arm thinking Owen is gonna kill me when he finds out, and then he's gonna kill the guy who ripped off the truck. And I'm thinking that it must have been on purpose. I mean, the place is full of trucks that are a whole lot better, and some jerk takes Owen's piece of junk? The only one I can think of who's dumb enough to do such a thing is Tvrdik." Glenna slapped a hand over her mouth, as if she said something wrong. Then she lowered it to play with the figure of an angel dangling from the gold-colored chain around her neck.

"Oh, don't tell Berger that part about Owen killing Edgar for taking the truck, 'cause I know he didn't. He couldn't have. Owen was here. Judy can tell you and so can little Jessie."

Judy added, "I told Sheriff Wells when he came to arrest Owen, but he don't believe me. I suppose no jury would either."

"Did you call the sheriff that night?" Cassie asked, "about the truck?"

"It might be hard for someone like you to understand," Glenna said. "You know stuff so you can make the breaks go your way. But for me the cops don't solve trouble, they just make things worse. I called here. You know, maybe Owen came into town and took the truck, even though that didn't seem likely. Well, Owen answered. I hung up quick, like it was a wrong number or something. Then I went into the bar. I had a Bud and tried to reason it all out. And, like I said, I'm thinking the only one who's dumb enough to steal anything that belongs to Owen is Tvrdik, 'cause he's so mad at him and blames him for every little thing."

"You don't think Owen shot up Edgar's store?" Cassie asked.

Glenna and Judy looked at one another. Glenna tucked her lower lip under her front teeth. "He was alone," she said quickly. "He wasn't aiming right at the guy like people are saying. And he didn't hurt anyone."

"It's okay." Judy turned to Cassie. "I was driving. Owen had me go past the store slow while he popped off a few rounds at the place."

"It's not her fault," Glenna said. "Owen made her do it."

"He didn't start any fire though," Judy said. "He would've told us about it if he had."

Glenna flicked her cigarette ash in the general direction of a much-used ashtray. "Hell, bragged about it, you mean. He went on and on about shooting up the store and stuff like that as if it made him some kind of big, brave superhero, like in a comic book."

The smoke was making Cassie ill. She was beginning to regret having encouraged Glenna to confide in her. She wanted to help the girl break out of an abusive relationship, not become confessor to a litany of crimes. Or to hear a slime ball being defended by women who should be glad he was gone.

She wasn't sure she believed the part about Owen being home when the murder was committed. It would be more like him to take the truck himself from the parking lot and then say Glenna had it, so she would be the prime suspect.

"Anyway," Glenna said, "I finished the beer and figured I'd have to, uh, call this friend for a ride or hitch home. Judy would've come and got me, but, like I said, the Dodge don't work so good. I wouldn't want her to get stranded somewhere. But when I went outside, the truck was, well not exactly where I parked it, but pretty close. You get it, right? Someone took the truck and killed Edgar and then put it back, and it couldn't have been Owen 'cause he was here the whole time."

"Why do you have the truck on Wednesday nights?" Cassie asked.

Glenna seemed knocked off balance by the question. She swirled her cigarette, sending out miniature tornadoes. "Well, I just do. It's my night to get out, you know, have some fun."

"You buy a six pack." Cassie leaned forward. Glenna's free hand rested on a field of sunflowers. Cassie touched it lightly. "Then where do you go?"

Glenna pulled away as if Cassie's fingers were flames. She stabbed out her cigarette. "Look, I just wanted to tell you about the truck. That's all."

Judy came to her rescue. "Where she goes has nothing to do with this. Honest. And it would get Glenna in trouble."

"Oh, God," Glenna said. "Berger, or that cow Wells, is going to ask me that." She turned to Judy. "She's not being mean. She just wants me to be ready for all the questions. I told you she was smart." Glenna turned wide-eyed to Cassie. "And people like you, with a gift, you have a code, right? You don't just go around telling on people unless it can save a person's life or something."

Another psychic comment, Cassie realized. "Glenna—"

The girl studied the wallpaper, thick with ivy spilling out of copper pots. "Okay, okay, I'll say I just went into town this one night to get beer and come right home."

"Mr. and Mrs. Hanley are going to tell the sheriff you're a regular Wednesday customer." Cassie had no intention of getting trapped in a scheme, yet she felt the spring ready to snap, closing jagged jaws around her.

"Yeah, the witch would," Glenna said. "Bet the old man wouldn't if I asked him."

Cassie winced. Add one more potential member to their little conspiracy club. She tried to convince Glenna and Judy of the virtue of telling the truth. They were adamant Glenna's weekly activity had to be kept out of it.

"I buy beer and come straight home," Glenna said. "You can tell Berger that."

Cassie promised to relay Glenna's story to the authorities, but she didn't actually commit to a particular version. She felt drained when she stepped outside. Panting, Jupiter hopped into the car with her. At least *he'd* enjoyed the visit. Jessie yelled good-bye then ran into the house, to his mother and his father's girlfriend.

It wasn't until Cassie was miles down the road that she remembered she hadn't dealt with Glenna's misguided belief she had a floating crystal ball hidden in the linen closet.

As soon as she got home Cassie called the sheriff's office. Rhonda answered. Cassie relayed only the skeleton of the truck theft. Glenna would have to provide the details herself. She still felt as if she'd been tricked into supporting a lie. Throughout the rest of the day, while she worked on drawings of dew-speckled lemons and limes, the term "sin of omission" kept popping up in her thoughts.

Chapter Forty-Three

Dale arrived Friday morning on the ATV with a cart rattling behind it. He didn't come up to the house to say hello and pet Jupiter. Instead he went straight at what was left of the lizard log with a chain saw, slicing away at its core. He heaved chunks into the cart. As part of the deal he would take them home and turn them into sellable firewood.

Cassie noted his presence through the window of her office. She let the pitch for the bubble bath account marinate in her mind while she plunged into the candy shop project. She'd decided on a cottage garden motif, inspired by what she hoped to accomplish next spring in her aunt's neglected beds.

Funny, filling the spaces around the house with living, breathing greenery seemed so obvious that she hadn't noticed the permanence it implied. Putting a plant in the ground was a promise that went beyond her one-year rental agreement, yet the idea felt as natural as embellishing the outlines on the tablet screen before her with floral colors.

Persian blue irises and velvety scarlet cardinal flowers bloomed from her stylus. The tones set off the textured browns of the products and would brighten advertisements, gift boxes and shopping bags—and the company's website.

She finally admitted to herself she had to take the Sparks' job.

Really, truly, make the call to Rhonda and no backing out.

The decision went beyond adding a client and gaining experience. She needed to move forward.

She would pick up the phone any minute now to make the commitment. She absolutely would.

Adding a rosy highlight to a petal, part of her balked at the evolution to digital. Her heart craved the tangible. Textured paper and chalk. Stretched canvas covered with thick dabs of paint. Later she would reward herself by creating a landscape in oils.

When she was satisfied with her progress—at least for the moment—she grabbed two cold Cokes and went outside to ambush Dale.

Chapter Forty-Four

Make your day bright with SunnieChat!

ASHLEY

Not yet. It's too soon

CASSIE

No hurry. Whenever you want

ASHLEY

I wish I wasn't so scared

Chapter Forty-Five

"I'm glad you found time to come over. You're probably really busy at the farm," Cassie said.

Dale took the pop can she offered him and flicked it open. He'd hoped to get the yard cleared and motor off without having to talk to her. That wasn't going to happen now. "It's a big old monster of a tree. Lucky it didn't do more damage."

"How'd you hurt your head?"

He knew she was going to ask. He resisted touching the butterfly bandages holding together the gash. "I fell. No big deal."

"Looks like you fell against something."

"Just a rock." Dale took a sip. A breeze couldn't cover the awkward silence. They watched Jupiter sniff at twigs and snap at a grasshopper.

"My telescope was missing for a few days," Cassie said. "I thought it was stolen. Then I remembered I probably said you could borrow it, and I just forgot. I'm a little embarrassed about the whole thing. I made a big fuss and had Officer Berger come out here and write a report and do an investigation. But there wasn't really any crime, was there?"

If the topic came up, Dale had planned to bluff his way

through. He hadn't expected her to offered him an escape hatch.

He couldn't take the easy way out. With just the two of them standing in her sunny yard, he couldn't play along. He had to confess. "It was stupid. I wanted to use it to look at some—some stuff."

It seemed Cassie was one of the few people in town who thought he was an okay guy all the time. Not just when he'd done something they thought was brave, like snitching on Owen so the man got arrested. For the moment they patted him on the back and called him a hero because he'd cleaned up a rat problem they were too scared to take care of themselves.

Once the rodent was locked away for good, Dale would just be "that Steinhaus kid" again with little present and no future.

He couldn't tell Cassie he was trying to protect a girl he was sort of stalking. He couldn't risk having her look at him the way other people did. Or worse, looking through him like he didn't matter. "I wasn't going to keep it or trash it or anything. And I am so sorry I took it."

He wouldn't have said that to Richie and definitely not to his dad. Maybe because his dad acted as if he should be sorry about everything, from being born to outgrowing his shoes to not being like his older brothers. Or even like his older sister.

Somehow it felt okay to admit it to Cassie. "I mean, I'm saying I'm sorry to *you*. An apology, okay? And on top of that I'm sorry because all it did was get me into a big mess."

Dale recounted his crime and what happened Wednesday night. He even included fainting like a wimp and hitting his head on the tripod. "It was so weird watching Edgar just stand there in the headlights. Like I could feel what was going to happen. I wanted to look away or blink, but I just stared."

By the time Dale finished, Jupiter had dropped two chew toys and a plastic sandbox shovel at his feet. The knot that had been living in his stomach since the night on Red Hawk loosened a little. "I sure never expected to see a murder."

"What did you expect to see?" Cassie asked. "What's the stuff you wanted to look at?"

"Owen goes to that spot a lot," Dale said. "He parks his toad of a truck at the shore and waits and another guy meets him. I've seen them absolutely, for sure, twice. But I know they've been doing whatever it is they're doing more times than that. For months maybe. I wanted to figure out what was going on. You know, in case it was more illegal than his usual stuff. And maybe dangerous."

"This other guy is not Edgar?" Cassie asked.

Dale didn't want to say the name. "If I tell you who it is, you'll think I made a mistake—or I'm lying."

"I promise to be honest," Cassie said. "That's the best I can do."

Dale took a big breath. "Raymond Swenson."

"You saw him through the telescope?"

"No. And not that night. Not when Edgar was killed. But two times before that. In patio lights." He didn't say who flipped on the bright floods.

Cassie gazed at the lake. "Okay. This is what I think we should do—"

Dale listened. When adults said "this is what *we* should do," they usually meant "this is what *you* are going to do because I say so." But he could tell Cassie's "we" really did mean the two of them. Together.

"Yeah, okay," Dale said.

Cassie pulled out her cell. The number was in her contacts. She clicked it and handed the phone to Dale.

The red convertible sat in the Swenson driveway like a holiday ornament. Dale stood beside the waiting-to-be-rebuilt deer stand, wondering if Crystal was home. He rolled his shoulders to loosen the muscles. It had been just as hard hauling the star-gazing equipment up Red Hawk Hill the second time as the first, even though Cassie had efficiently stripped it down into parts and Berger had guided the toboggan-ator.

Jupiter, delighted by the change of scenery, sniffed at exciting new scents and chased squirrels, real and imaginary. Berger stood with his hands on his hips. He turned, surveying the entire three-hundred and sixty degrees. "Dale, show me where you saw Raymond."

"He moved along there." Dale pointed from the shore, across the bridge to the patio. "Twice."

"Through the telescope?"

"With binoculars," Dale said. "And without binoculars."

"But not the night Edgar was killed."

"No." Dale had already described what he saw. He couldn't tell if Berger was making sure he got the details straight or if he was trying to trick Dale into contradicting himself.

"Berger!" The sound carried around the basin and bounced back amplified. It took a moment for Dale to pinpoint Sheriff Wells as the source. He stood below the hill at the edge of the lake—the murder scene—his head cranked back looking up at them.

"We're setting up now," Berger said into his radio.

Dale stifled a laugh. Both of the officers had the devices, but the sheriff had shouted anyway. Wells didn't like flashy gadgets. The department might never have gotten computers if Rhonda, new to the force at the time, hadn't stuck the purchase order under his nose and ordered him to sign it. The veteran lawman was an immovable boulder when confronted by most people, but he turned into gelatin—transparent and jiggly—when Rhonda faced off with him.

Dale set the tripod where it had been on Wednesday night. Cassie put the puzzle pieces back together, hefting the tube into the dovetail vise. Dale felt like a dork-o, standing around while she did the work. He'd been taught you always carried heavy stuff, groceries and things, for older people. But he'd also learned not to get between a mamma moose and her calf. He scratched at the edge of a bandage on his forehead. What a shithead he'd been for taking it from her.

She had more muscle than he'd expected. Well, she was a lot taller than his mom, who was pretty strong. And he guessed she wasn't really old or anything, not near as old as his mom. She seemed as un-excited as he was by the sheriff's skepticism of the whole telescope story, and his wanting a reenactment. Like on a reality cop show.

"All set," Cassie said.

"Just how far can you see with this thing?" Berger asked.

"It depends on an object's size and brightness. The star Altair is about sixteen-and-a-half light-years away. The planets are a lot closer, of course. How well you can see them depends on their diameter and ability to reflect sunlight."

Adam grinned. "I was thinking more of how far you can see on Earth."

"Sorry," Cassie said.

Dale wondered that too. How far could you see if there were no trees, hills or buildings in the way?

To where ships disappeared over the curvature of the earth, he supposed. He'd like to take it to a beach on the ocean to try it out.

Hmm. No, he wouldn't. Not after this. And that still wasn't what the deputy wanted to know anyway.

Chapter Forty-Six

A breeze whipped across the hill, carrying the smell of water and leaf mold. Below, Beauty Lake sparkled like a star cluster. Cassie wished she was here to sketch the scenery rather than reenact a grisly event. "I'll show you what you can see," she told Adam.

She angled the scope and peered across the lake through the small finder mounted on the tube. The hours she had struggled learning to accommodate for the uncorrected image paid off. Without thinking up-down and right-left she centered on a hunter-green A-frame that appeared to teeter on the point of its roof. She locked down the mount then checked through the eyepiece. The cabin was exactly where it should be, a dollhouse set in the magnified circle. Thanks to the starback, which flipped the view on the horizontal axis, the scene was right-side up.

She adjusted the focus, transforming a blur into a door symmetrically flanked by windows. She offered the view to Adam.

"I know that place," he said. "Belongs to summer people from South St. Paul. It's a little spooky. Almost enough to make a person paranoid."

"That's with a forty-millimeter eyepiece. In this telescope it magnifies the view fifty times," Cassie said. "I can write out the math equation for you."

"This is exactly the way it was when Dale borrowed it?" Adam asked.

"Yes." Cassie was glad he didn't sound sarcastic when he said "borrowed."

Adam turned to Dale. "The set up look okay to you?"

Dale shrugged. "Sure."

Adam radioed Sheriff Wells. "Ready for you to get into position." He didn't get a response and didn't seem to expect one. He turned to Cassie, "Can you show the sheriff and the squad car in that thing?"

Cassie shifted the scope's angle. The sheriff's balding head gleamed in the sun. He held a stick in one hand and scratched his posterior with the other. Either he forgot he was being watched or he didn't believe the telescope could really show what he was doing. It was probably the later. Residents of L.A. high-rise apartments tended to shrug off a neighbor in the building opposite them with a modest Newtonian reflector. They would stitch their drapes closed if they understood what even an inexpensive brand with low-quality optics can show across the short span of a city street.

"You'll probably be called as a witness," Adam told Cassie.

She straightened from the scope. He was only an inch taller. In the uneven terrain, they stood eye-to-eye. "Why?"

"The defense is going to target Dale's testimony. If I was Owen's lawyer, first I'd destroy the credibility of the sharp-eyed young man who claims he saw the crime. Then I'd go after the equipment he used, piece by piece. I'd do my best to convince a jury that this telescope couldn't find an elephant across the length of a football field. At the least, you'd need to explain the magnification. That's when you'll have to do the equation."

Adam spoke into the radio. "We're all set here." He

turned to Dale. "The sheriff's going to go through the movements like you described them. You tell me if it looks right and if you remember more details."

Dale put an eye to the lens. Adam raised an arm to signal the sheriff. Without optical aid, Cassie could see the squad car and a khaki man in front of the passenger side. The figure could have been any pudgy person in tan clothing. At night he would have been illuminated by the headlights, but that wouldn't have helped much with identification. The man made some motions; it was hard to tell what he did. He walked to the shoreline and stood there for a moment. Then he went back to his original spot. He bent down. He straightened up. He looked up at the hill and held his arms wide to indicate he was done.

Dale pulled himself up to his full height and clenched his fists. He stalked to face Adam. "Do you expect me to be fooled by that? Do you think I'm such a screw up that I don't remember what I told you?"

"He did it just the way you said." Adam pulled a small notebook from his shirt pocket and flipped through a few pages. "Stood in the headlight on the passenger's side, gave one blow with the weapon in his right hand, dropped the weapon. Dragged the body out of your sight toward the lake. You heard splashing. He came back into your sight and picked up the weapon with his left hand. And that's when you stopped looking through the telescope."

"You switched it all around." Dale's face flamed. Adam kept a balanced stance and dangerously calm expression.

Cassie maneuvered between them, hoping the situation wouldn't escalate, with her in the middle. It was an unwise position. She couldn't believe she put herself there on purpose.

Try to trick Dale? Would Adam do that? Was he that kind of person?

Like Mars coming into focus Cassie understood the reason

for the confusion. "Dale, Adam, listen to me. Owen is left handed, isn't he." She wasn't sure how she knew that. Something during her two encounters with the man must have given that impression. Maybe that was the hand he'd used to lewdly jiggle his junk at her in the drug store.

Fixed on one another, the males ignored her. She was tempted to step aside and let them work it out while she protected her telescope from the scuffle.

No, she couldn't do that. How would she explain Dale being arrested to his mother?

Cassie wanted to yell, but she forced herself to speak like a sane, reasonable person. "I'm guessing from what Dale reported, the thinking is Owen held the weapon in his right hand when he hit Edgar, so it would seem that the killer was right handed."

"Yeah," Dale said, "then after he ditched the body in the lake he gave himself away by picking up the hammer in his left hand." He seemed a fraction away from pushing past Cassie and slamming his fist into Adam's face. "You guys did it the opposite to see if I'd notice. You don't believe a kid like me can tell the truth."

Dale had told the truth, *as he'd seen it*, Cassie knew. The sheriff had followed Dale's description of the murder without variation. But they were both wrong. She hoped she got the chance to explain before the young man took a swing at an officer of the law. She suddenly wished her passion was fly fishing or collecting refrigerator magnets instead of astronomy.

"I follow the evidence," Adam said.

Reaching over Cassie, Dale stabbed a finger at Adam. "You'd believe me if I came from the right family and had the right friends."

From a fist to a finger—Cassie took it as a sign of de-escalation. The misunderstanding was her fault. How best to explain the error?

"Dale," Cassie said sharply. "Dale!" She waited until he broke eye contact with Adam and looked at her. "Can you see the license plate of the squad car through the telescope?"

"Seriously? The license plate?"

"Yes," she said emphatically.

"I didn't see it that night," Dale argued. "I didn't have to. Everyone knows Owen's truck. The plate is too dirty to read anyway."

Curiosity seemed to be winning over adrenalin. Hoping it was safe to remove herself as a barrier, Cassie went to the telescope and adjusted the view. "License number. Right now," she ordered.

Dale and Adam exchanged expressions that communicated *Is she trying to put something over on us?* and *Beats me, I guess we have to go along with it.* They shared a grimace, as if to mutually indicate *This better be good because we were right in the middle of something.*

Dale hunched his six-foot-three frame and peered through the eyepiece.

"Read it." Cassie was not happy with either of them. A moment ago they'd been a heartbeat away from a boxing match. Now they were pulling silent guy-bonding on her.

"Hey," Dale said, "it's all mixed up, like it's in a mirror."

"Because it is," Cassie said.

Adam checked it out for himself then stepped back as if the ground crumbled beneath his feet. Cassie explained the basics of the Schmidt-Cassegrain design, including left-right reversal. "Mostly, it doesn't matter when you're looking at stars and planets. You can use a different starback, that's the part that holds the eyepiece, to correct it, but I don't have one."

"You didn't know about this?" Adam asked Dale. "So you thought the sheriff and I had worked out a scheme to try to shake your story?"

"Yeah," Dale said.

Cassie swiveled the scope back into position. Over the radio Adam instructed the sheriff to reenact the crime again, this time starting out in front of the driver-side headlight and holding the stick in his left hand. Wells complied almost cheerfully, as if enjoying the reality-TV action.

Dale watched intently through the lens. "That's it. That's what I saw."

"This matches better with the blood stains and marks on the ground," Adam said, "and with the results of the post-mortem. Frankly, your original story didn't fit the details. That's why it was necessary to go through this."

"Did you actually see the person's face?" Cassie asked.

Dale shook his head. "Owen was wearing that fishing hat he always has on. The one with the brim all the way around it. You know, a boonie."

"Could the person have been female?" Cassie had to ask. She didn't want to hear the answer.

Dale thought about it. "A girl walks different from a guy."

Adam nodded. "More sway."

Cassie felt they were doing that male-thing again.

"I didn't see much walking, so I couldn't tell from that," Dale said. "But it would take muscle to drag a body into the lake." He took a moment. "Or would it? Edgar was a little guy. Not much to him."

"Cassie's strong enough to do it," Adam said.

Dale shook his head. "No, it couldn't have been a girl. Because it was Owen."

Cassie asked Adam, "Was the blow the cause of death?"

"It contributed to it," Adam said. "The official COD is drowning."

Cassie felt a shadow creep over her. Dale's eyewitness account of a faceless, camo-clad murderer didn't clarify anything. With the left-right issue straightened out, it even exonerated Owen. A left hander as big as the main suspect would have struck a killing blow. Even someone who was ambidextrous had enough power to accomplish the gruesome task. Edgar would have died before he became the second Floater.

A left-handed blow from a right-hander would be weak, less lethal. It seemed someone was trying to frame Owen. Any lawyer would latch onto that theory like a bulldog.

Cassie knew the man had done plenty wrong. He treated the women closest to him no better than he did his truck.

Why couldn't he absolutely, without a doubt, be guilty this one time? Why couldn't there be some scrap of evidence that pointed at him and only him?

Cassie sank through fog. Hands supported her, slowing her descent. Muffled voices faded into the distance. In her mind she didn't see Owen standing over Edgar's body. She saw Vicky's desecrated bedroom. Dread enveloped her like a plunge into deep water.

Then the numbness came, as it had that day.

Cassie observed the horrifying scene with an artist's eye, finding the formal composition rich with bold hues and textures. Ruby blood. Azure sheets. Vicky's cocoa skin. A sculpted ode to jealousy, possession, entitlement, ego. Jordan's performance-art masterpiece.

But it was incomplete. It lacked a signature, a flourish that would forever link it to its creator.

Cassie drifted to the living room, propelled more by instinct than plan. On the desk the bracelet Vicky gave Jordan for his birthday sparkled blindingly. Vicky insisted Jordan pick out the chain of thick gold links himself, of course. That was the only way to ensure he would be satisfied with the expensive trinket.

The clasp shattered against Vicky's teeth when Jordan back-handed her for another imagined flirtation. Cassie took

Vicky to the emergency room to get the sprained wrist, cracked ribs, facial lacerations, and multiple bruises tended to. Vicky promised she was done with him. She promised through the shock that left her devastated and almost unable to care for herself. She promised.

Jordan's calls wouldn't stop, so Cassie blocked them from reaching Vicky's phone. She disposed of the tsunami of roses he sent. She returned the gifts in their elegant boxes from exclusive stores. She shut down Vicky's online media profiles when the messages turned sick and threatening.

Jordan followed Vicky as she went to work, to the deli, to the dry cleaner. And he made sure she knew he was there.

Cassie held Vicky's hand through the process of getting a restraining order, thinking this was finally the breaking point. Vicky was rid of the man. Her friend would be okay.

But Cassie was wrong. Her stomach churned when Vicky told her Jordan swore counseling had changed him. They'd started dating again, casually, to see if they could work things out. And the cycle began again.

The bedroom tableau, powerfully depicting Jordan's obsession, reached out to Cassie like perfume as she stood fixated on the masculine gold bracelet.

He'd guilted Vicky into getting the clasp repaired for him, as if she'd intentionally damaged the ridiculous chunk of metal.

Cassie took a pen and pushed the shiny links onto a periwinkle-colored note pad. Slowly, calmly, she carried the glittering tangle to the bedroom. She lifted the sheet with the pen and tumbled the golden snake onto a crimson stain, putting the signature in place. Completing the sculpture.

Cassie returned the pen and pad to the desk, and called 9-1-1.

"You back with us?"

Cassie blinked at harsh light that drained color from the landscape, turning it into a starkly inked sketch. She squeezed her eyes shut to erase the sting.

"You left us for a while." Adam's voice, soft and concerned.

Yes, I do that.

She battled a dichotomy, unable to resolve her image of herself as an honest person with what she had done. The strain spread thin cracks through her sanity. Someday she would shatter like an aging china vase.

But she felt no compulsion to confess, even when the bracelet became the key piece of evidence against Jordan. The nightmares that plagued her sleep seemed like justified punishment. And also like a reward, since they kept Vicky with her.

Hypocrite. Just yesterday she'd agonized over a little lie Glenna and Judy wanted her to support. It was certainly more benign than what she'd done to Jordan. Had she rejected it for ethical reasons or because a stolen truck and a phone-call alibi helped an abuser?

Cassie wished to do nothing to aid Owen, yet she'd alerted the authorities to Glenna's story. And now she'd blown the prosecution's explanation of how the despicable man committed the murder. The man might end up free because of her.

What if she'd been the witness instead of Dale? Would she suddenly remember the hat tumbling off as the killer bent into the beam of the headlight, revealing Owen's fleshy face? Did it matter that he might not be guilty of *this* crime?

Cassie felt dizzy-sick, as if she'd twirled and twirled in place until she'd collapsed. Cautiously, she opened her eyes to a canopy of sky. She was flat on the ground. Adam knelt beside her, two fingers pressed against her neck, checking her pulse. Dale was on the other side, peering at her as if she were a corpse. A whining Jupiter struggled in his arms.

Adam helped her sit up. He kept an arm around her, ready to support her if she relapsed. Cassie wondered how often he had lent his strength to someone in crisis. His worry made her feel worse. The terrible bangs stuck to her damp forehead. She swiped at them with the back of her hand, brushing away the perspiration but doing very little to control the short wisps.

Dale gave her a crooked grin. "Must be the altitude." He tapped by his bandages, peach slashes against his tanned skin. "I had the same trouble. At least you didn't hit anything."

"My scope!"

"It's okay," Dale assured her.

"This is embarrassing," Cassie said. "I'm fine." But she wasn't. She let them help her stand.

"It's forgotten," Adam said.

They packed the equipment onto the toboggan-ator. Going down the hill was only slightly less difficult than going up. With the backseat of the Mini Cooper folded down, the scope, mount, tripod and peripherals fit neatly into the hatch back.

"You're not driving," Adam said flatly.

"So much for it being forgotten." Cassie could decide for herself what she was capable of doing. "I'll drive myself home."

"Then I'll have to arrest you for public endangerment," he said sternly.

Cassie knew she wasn't going to win this one. But she wasn't about to be chauffeured by law enforcement.

She would give in on her own terms. "Dale, you're driving."

Chapter Forty-Seven

Dale crouched over the steering wheel of the yellow Cooper and hung a right onto the tar road, fully aware of the two Glacier County vehicles behind him.

Sheriff Wells gunned the motor on the squad car and shot past. Berger's cruiser stayed behind the Mini. He was probably making sure they didn't turn around and go to the Steinhaus farm where Cassie could drop him off then drive home by herself.

"Does it make you nervous having a patrol car behind you?" Cassie asked.

Dale gave a little laugh. "I'm sort of used to it." He thought Berger had really blown his chances with Cassie. Ordering her not to drive was a big mistake. Tailgating them was another.

"And you're driving slow to make a point?"

"Berger doesn't know when to stop being a cop."

Riding in the back with the telescope, Jupiter gave a shake. Wispy tufts burst around him. The ginger snow drifted onto the upholstery. The dog was a fur factory. He hung his huge, fluffy head into the front between them.

"What really happened back there?" Dale asked keeping his eyes on the road.

"It was nothing."

"You won't tell me because you think I'm a kid," he challenged, but not too hard.

"Did I tell Officer Berger?"

"You might have a different reason for not telling him."

"Just like I have a different reason for not telling you," Cassie said lightly.

"You didn't blab about the telescope, so I'd keep my mouth shut about this."

"Allergies. I've been in the city too long. I can't handle all this nature. A half-calf skinny latte with a hazelnut shot will take care of it."

"Don't try dusting me with coffee code. Glacier Falls may be at the ass end of the world, but we're still less than an hour from a Starbucks and two Caribous."

She tapped a finger on Dale's cheek. "Jupiter, lick!"

The dog sloshed his gigantic wet tongue across the side of Dale's face. So far, this trick and shedding were his only talents.

"No fair!" Dale batting away the puppy. "Berger thinks you got all fairy-princess faint-y because of Wells' little play-acting. You know, pretending to kill a guy." Dale gave Cassie a sideways glance. "He doesn't know you as well as he thinks he does. Or maybe as well as he wants to."

Cassie smiled. "Are you trying to give me advice on my love life?"

"Berger doesn't like me. I don't always like him, but you could do worse."

"Once you eliminate the married men in this territory," Cassie said, "there aren't enough options around to rank them."

"I bet there're some married guys who've come on to

you." Dale thought his father might be one of them. He wasn't going to ask. She wouldn't tell him anyway, and he liked that about her.

"Actually, less here than other places."

"Was it Owen or not?" Dale asked. "He's the only one who's tried to kill Edgar."

"I don't think shooting up the store was a murder attempt. He wanted Edgar scared to death, but I don't think he wanted him dead."

"I should have figured out that mirror thing. I had all kinds of trouble zeroing in on what I wanted to look at. Now I know why."

"Can you tell me what you saw again? Exactly the way you saw it. Don't worry about the left-right thing."

Dale went through the whole scene in the truck's headlights. She never asked him if he was *sure*. She never acted as if he was just a farm kid. She looked him in the eyes —well, except now when he was driving. She listened to him and she noticed the quality of his work, even if it was just cleaning up a downed tree.

She treated him better than she did Berger.

He parked the Mini Cooper in the garage. Berger's patrol car sped up as it went by, like a greyhound who'd finally been let off leash.

Dale draped both arms over the steering wheel. "What would you do if someone told you something that made you bone-cold afraid for him?" Before he could stop himself, he spilled about Richie helping Owen, and about Reverend Gunther and the community center competition.

Cassie didn't tell him he should report it to Berger. She didn't warn him Richie was a bad influence, and he should stop hanging out with the guy.

"It hurts when your best friend makes dangerous choices," Cassie said.

Dale got the feeling she knew a lot about that.

Now that Berger wasn't watching, Cassie offered to drive him home. He turned her down. The ATV was back at Red Hawk. That wasn't so far to walk.

Chapter Forty-Eight

un Sun SunnieChat!

HOLLY

Mom and dad took care of Evan and the kids so I could hurl without an audience. Andi's not sick. Don't know how she got such a tough immune system

KAYLA

Are all of your appliances intact?

HOLLY

Mom directed dad toward less invasive projects. Grill scrubbed, cars washed, every hinge in the house oiled

ASHLEY

Lucky. Last time they were here dad painted the bathroom while I was at work

CASSIE

I remember that. What was the color? Mauve. Sunset blue

Averted Vision

ASHLEY

Bridesmaid dress lilac. Perfect with my red
towels

HOLLY

Ash you called it. He came with paint chips.
Checked to see how they looked in every
room. Mom ended that. I'm glad she skipped
garden club and library board to come with
him. She had to get back for a macular
degeneration fund raiser. Dragged a reluctant
dad home. They left enough jello and chicken
broth to last a month. Now I have to put
things back in order

ASHLEY

Hope she got dad out the door before he
messed up the sacred alphabetized
spice rack

Chapter Forty-Nine

After Dale left, Cassie doodled notes about what he'd told her. She put "Dale" at the top of the page and "Edgar" in the middle. It would be convenient for Owen to be the killer. She put a large "O" toward the bottom. The more she considered what Dale saw and what Glenna told her, the more she knew it wasn't that tidy.

What would happen when Owen was released? She drew an arrow from the "O" to "Dale." Would the man be satisfied with tossing threats at his accuser? Or would he feel obligated to hurt the boy badly enough to teach him a lesson and to show the whole town he was still untouchable?

She turned the stick arrow into a dagger. This was supposed to be paradise, away from greasy smog, earthquakes, a neurotic on every corner, psycho-snipers pretending to be normal people, and grid-lock traffic that felt like a metaphor for your life.

Until now she hadn't realized how much the move to Minnesota was less a strategic retreat and more a panicked flight. Determined to take her mind off murder and harassment, Cassie put aside the legal tablet and pulled out her sketch pad. She might as well have told herself not to think about spiders.

She tried to depict a pleasant bubble bath filled with vibrant, happy kiwis. A green oval surrounded by suds morphed into Glenna's face framed by shocked hair.

So that's how it was going to be.

She had to plow through the whole mess and get it out of her system or it would just keep crawling through her brain.

Like spiders.

On a fresh page she sketched the basic bones of Owen's truck. Wednesday nights Glenna drove the rolling rust bucket. She bought beer, did something that could get her into trouble that she wouldn't talk about, went home, and passed the keys to Owen.

Then he drove the camo-sprawled vehicle to Beauty Lake where he met up with Raymond. And did what? Delivered something? Maybe a package Glenna had picked up earlier. What did a semi-wealthy pharmacist need that he had to get illegally?

Last Wednesday nothing went as planned. Someone snatched the truck from the liquor store parking lot while Owen sat on the couch at home watching TV, waiting for Glenna to return from her weekly errand.

Who stole the truck, disrupting the schedule? Who *knew* about the schedule?

Who wanted Edgar dead?

If the murderer was not the abrasive, arrogant, bully who ignored laws and social rules and neglected personal hygiene, then Cassie had to expand her field of view to a wider range of suspects, like switching from a twenty-five-millimeter eyepiece to a forty millimeter in order to see a larger circle of sky.

Her pencil decorated the page as she considered the Minnesota-nice, law-abiding citizens of Glacier Falls.

The murderer was someone who came to a full stop at intersections; who gave Harry Ziegler's roaming dog the right of way; who counted change after every purchase and returned the extra if an error was made; who brushed their teeth and wore clean underwear; who got the oil changed according to the instructions in the owner's manual; who gave a cheerful hello to everyone while on the way to the cafe or the lumber yard where they held down a full-time job to keep the bills paid.

A Spark? A Sparkle? The bingo thief? The Floater's still unidentified killer? Mrs. Finster, as revenge for a love affair with Edgar that soured half a century ago?

Okay, not the last one. Now she was just making things up.

Cassie set aside her montage of the truck surrounded by a drooling dog, coins and bills, a bingo card with missing numbers, a valentine heart pierced by an arrow, and boxer shorts hanging from a clothes line.

She decided it would be a stargazing night. Adam and Sheriff Wells had taken photographs of her telescope, but they'd let her keep it. The moon was a pale ghost in the sunlit sky and wouldn't set until after 1 a.m. She'd check out its craters and mares. Then she'd hit a few stars bright enough to hold their own against the satellite's illumination, which would be at fifty-seven percent tonight according to her chart.

The ambitious project required appropriate nourishment. And her brain screamed for chocolate.

After seven o'clock. It was too late to shop at the Falls Market. She drove into town, thinking the candy rack at the smelly gas station was the only option for satisfying her craving. To her surprise, a "We're Open" placard hung on the door of Tvrdik's Goods and Groceries.

In honor of its deceased owner the place should be closed while the family gathered together in mourning around the donated Butterball.

Maybe the Tvrdik clan wasn't that kind of family.

The funeral hadn't been scheduled yet. Holding it this weekend would have disrupted Tornado Daze activities.

Can't mess with Tornado Daze.

Cassie pushed through the door and nodded to Linda who stood behind the counter. Did she own G. and G. now, or was it shared among the siblings?

Her husband Greg conferred with Ryan Miller, bright in a flaming Sparks polo shirt, beside the canned vegetables. They greeted her then went back to hushed tones over a case of string beans.

The shop showed signs of a transformation. The scrubbed floors almost gleamed. Boxes of mac and cheese adorned the shelves in precise rows. A new window replaced the temporary plywood. A special display of potato chips punctuated the end of an aisle, enhanced by a brightly colored sign proclaiming "Coming Soon! Pay with Convenience of Major Credit Cards!"

Cassie grabbed a twelve-pack of Coke, a jar of chunky peanut butter, and a bag of pretzels. After much deliberation, she selected an assortment of candy bars, all with chocolate as the main ingredient. She took her items to the cash register. Linda manually punched in the prices.

"I remember you and your sisters." Linda's voice was too harsh for simple conversation. "You and your cousin Laurel, you all had your own little club. That Holly, she still strut around like some super model?"

Cassie was stunned. Where had that come from? "I don't—"

"You all have weird names. You're Cassandra, right?"

"I go by Cassie."

"Yeah, Cassandra." She said it like a dirty word. "Greek mythology. Bet you didn't think I knew that. Always predicting doom and gloom." Linda's slumped posture indicated "Doom and Gloom" would be the title of her autobiography.

Cassie tried to lighten the mood. "And cursed by Apollo so no one would believe her." She handed over some bills.

Linda scowled. "People believe you, all right. That's why my dad's murderer is out of jail."

So soon? Owen Norquist freed? Cassie's heart paused in mid beat.

Linda made a show of counting the bills, as if making sure Cassie hadn't shorted her. "Charges dropped. All because you said Sherman Steinhaus lied."

"He wasn't lying." Cassie stiffened. She felt it more necessary to defend Dale than herself. "He just didn't know he was seeing things switched around."

Linda plopped coins into Cassie's hand. "Want a bag?"

"No. No bag. I have my own." She shoved the peanut butter, pretzels, and candy bars into the cloth bag she kept folded up in her purse. She dropped the change in after them and scooped the pop into her arms. Called soda in California; here it was always pop.

Ryan Miller held the door for her and stepped out behind her into the sunny evening. When his dad retired a few years ago, he took over the family accounting business. He had an easy, relaxed manner. Cassie supposed it was useful when dealing with people who were under stress around tax time.

"Linda isn't usually like that," Ryan said. "It's just when she's upset, she starts acting like her dad." Dark hair prematurely sprinkled with distinguished gray, he had a handsomeness guaranteed to increase with age. "She's afraid Owen is going to want revenge and will come after her, Greg, and the kids."

Cassie wondered if he and Greg had been planning a defense. "This war between Edgar and Owen is hard to understand."

"It was like a game to Owen," Ryan said. "He would come into the store. Sometimes he'd take something. Sometimes he'd just pretend to then laugh when Edgar accused him of shoplifting. It's been going on since last winter or fall. Edgar kept reporting it to the sheriff's office. There wasn't much Justin, or anyone, could do, especially the times Owen didn't do anything except be obnoxious. It got so Edgar trusted the law as much as he did out-of-town checks. Greg told him he should just let it go, but Edgar never listened to other people much, especially Greg."

Ryan shook his head as if trying to make sense of it. "Then the strangest thing happened. About a week ago Edgar started bragging he didn't have to put up with Owen anymore. Said he'd told the SOB never to set foot in the store again."

Cassie thought that was a pretty empty directive unless he had a way to enforce it. "It sounds like he had something on Owen."

"Guess Edgar thought so. But I can't think what would shame or scare Owen." He paused, as if selecting his next words. "I don't want you to think badly of Linda. She tried to help her dad. We all did."

"You mean the Sparks?"

"It wasn't easy. Edgar had his own ways. He didn't want anything that looked like charity or pity. Funny, he was real involved with bingo and giving it everything he had when there was a fire, but he never went to the Municipal with us for a beer."

Maybe he couldn't afford a drink out with the boys, Cassie thought. Maybe he could only handle being around people when there was a common goal, and he didn't know how to simply socialize. It was easy to get out of practice. It can happen without you even realizing it.

"This little store could get a big boost if no one takes over the Falls Market," Cassie said.

"The Market's a great business opportunity." Ryan shifted into accountant mode. "You don't get those very often in a small town. Edgar should have snapped it up right away, but he wasn't a risk taker when it comes to money."

Cassie thought Edgar had gotten pretty risky around Owen. But money was different. Money was always different.

"You're coming to the fair tomorrow, aren't you?" Ryan asked.

Tornado Daze. Cassie had skimmed the articles in the newspaper. Every store window had a poster inviting her to join the festivities. Interesting how people liked to commemorate tragedies. Or maybe it was the survival of tragedies they celebrated. "I haven't really thought about it."

"I highly recommend the band concert and fireworks."

"Sounds like fun," she said, careful not to make a commitment.

On the drive home, she thought about isolation and losing the ability to connect with other human beings. Was she headed in that direction? Maybe she should go to the fireworks. Be with people. Socialize without the presence of a dead body.

When she opened the cabin door, Jupiter bounced around as if he thought she would never return. She moved the single cold Coke to the front of the refrigerator and put the warm cans in the back. She had a late supper, by Minnesota standards, of a peanut butter sandwich and pineapple chunks with a candy bar chaser.

Her eating habits had changed since moving here, but she would not describe them as having improved. She no longer passed a line of restaurants and delis with take out on her way home, and she lived outside the delivery range of the only pizzeria. She ate too erratically and in uneven amounts, snacking for days then devouring a multi-course meal.

She resolved to embrace healthier habits. Recommended daily requirements of fruits and veggies from now on. And an exercise routine. She would figure one out and start right away. Well, maybe not right away, but soon.

Barely past sunset, the moon arched in a slow descent to the horizon. She set up her tripod and mount in the yard and attached her phone to it with a rubber band. Using an astronomy app as a guide, she adjusted the unit toward the North Celestial Pole, aligning it to Polaris.

The North Star sat in its stationary position. Even though it wasn't dark enough to see it, it was still there. Stars were always in the sky. Planets always cruised overhead. Nebulae. Galaxies. It was easy to forget them when a bright Sol dominated the heavens.

She shifted a tripod leg a fraction of an inch. On her phone's screen, a glowing dot representing the not-yet-visible Polaris moved into a red circle. She nudged the leg another tiny, tiny bit. The dot rested in the center of the target.

Perfect.

She stood back and surveyed the telescopes position. She should mark the locations of the feet. Put in pegs, or spray paint around the prints, or—

Or she should just breath and relax. She shouldn't have to tell herself, will herself, to enjoy a beautiful evening.

She'd thought leaving Los Angeles would automatically release her from a compulsion for precision, that it would free her from the subconscious belief that her actions could transform the flawed world into an orderly paradise. She had blamed the city for her quest for excellence: the pace and pressure, the deadlines that left her dissatisfied with even the best of her work because it felt prematurely torn from her hands, the personal relationships that likewise seemed perpetually under developed. But the city was thousands of miles away while the feeling remained with her.

L.A. had not infected her with perfection. She'd carried the kernel of it with her to the West Coast where it thrived, then brought the virus back with her.

Perhaps she'd expected lake life to act like a vaccine.

Instead, the murders, her wonderful telescope becoming a window to tragedy, Dale in danger, and her sisters' rollercoaster lives added new strains.

She behaved as if managing the details, like shoving the warm pop into the back of the refrigerator and moved the cold to the front, would somehow straighten out the big things.

She looked at the dot of Polaris centered in the bullseye of her phone app, wondering if she would always need a device rather than instinct to find true north.

Chapter Fifty

Time for a SunnieChat!

CASSIE

K do you know if the New Zealand gig is going to work out?

HOLLY

Is Liam working out?

ASHLEY

I'd like to see that. Send pics

KAYLA

Don't know yet. Not sure. About either one. Liam applied for the position too. There's only one spot. Him or me. Or someone else

CASSIE

Any chance Galapagos grant will be renewed?

KAYLA

No news

HOLLY

No news is good news

ASHLEY

No news is no news

HOLLY

Code Red. Dad's figured out Facetime

CASSIE

He needs a community ed class on meditation

KAYLA

Yoga

CASSIE

Goat yoga

ASHLEY

I tried that. Goats eat your purse. Then they
poop on your yoga mat

KAYLA

Mom and dad can do acroyoga together

CASSIE

I'd like to see that

ASHLEY

No you wouldn't

Chapter Fifty-One

According to a text Dale got from Richie, Owen celebrated his release from jail by swaggered through town to make sure everyone knew he was out and still doing as he pleased. Camo truck still being held as evidence, he cruised the streets in an ancient Dodge that belched plumes of oily smoke, while he swore loudly and regularly. At least, that was Dale's interpretation of Richie's abbreviations and creatively spelled words punctuated with emojis.

Tornado Daze gave everyone something to fuss about besides murder. The annual festival memorialized the twisters of 1849, 1902, 1966, and now the new one. Dale really wanted to be all hermit-y and stay out of sight. After rising to the town's favorite local celeb, he'd suddenly fallen back to pond scum, as if it were his fault the evidence against Owen hadn't held up.

But he had to shed lone-wolf mode to go to the parade, mostly to see Crystal.

Okay. Exclusively to see Crystal.

He had no other interest in the spectacle. He hadn't stuffed napkins fluffed up to look like flowers into chicken wire stretched over hayracks. He wasn't a member of any of the clubs or teams getting ready to ride on the floats or grin from shiny convertibles and antique cars. He wasn't an organizer with a clipboard, lining up clowns and handing out paper bags of wrapped candies to be tossed to the children along the route.

He belonged to nothing, hadn't volunteered for anything, and hadn't been asked to help out by anyone. He stood on the sidewalk outside the bank with kids too little to be organized and parents too busy taking care of them to be involved.

A blanket of clouds covered the sky. The air, heavy with moisture, couldn't decide if it should burst into rain or not. Around Dale, many of the locals wore t-shirts stating "I survived '66." Other shirts had "Tornado Daze" with the first three visitations listed, but not the "I survived" part, since the earliest one was over a century ago. Most of them had updated their ensembles with "I survived 2018" buttons.

Owen wasn't in the crowd lining the street. This wasn't his kind of thing. Still, Dale scanned every man in the area. Then he scanned again.

From the back of a pale blue 1966 Impala, Sandra Meirer waved enthusiastically. Her husband Mayor Bob held up his hand like a frail, overweight Pope, signaling the start of the festivities. Dale wasn't sure the man would live long enough to sell the Falls Market and retire.

As if anticipating the mayor clutching his chest and needing an escort to the hospital, the newest fire truck crawled after the Chevy, lights blinking. Dale's dad had been excited when the volunteers purchased it because it was a greenish-yellow. The shade was in style for a while, but now it wasn't. The town bought it used and cheap. It was supposed to be easier to see than the traditional red, making it safer to tear around in.

Dale figured anyone who didn't notice the siren, lights, and size of the vehicle wasn't suddenly going to pay attention to the color. It looked so much worse in the muted daylight than it had the other night at the fire at Edgar's. The strange hue reminded Dale of vomit. He didn't know why people weren't puking in the street as it went by just from looking at it.

Oblivious to the color, Greg Ergen draped one arm over the steering wheel and the other out the window. Ryan Miller rode next to him. Both stone-faced, they seemed unmoved by the people who sat on the curb or in lawn chairs flapping American flags left over from the Fourth of July. Instead they looked as if this was Mayor Bob's funeral procession.

A block up on the other side of the street Dale spotted his mom in her rosy smock outside the drugstore, watching the parade with other pink-clad women. He crossed his arms over the Metallica t-shirt, which she hated. He avoided eye contact, hoping she wouldn't notice but sure she would. Mothers had radar for that kind of thing.

To his mom, heavy metal was evil noise. Country western, her reverberation of choice, was somehow more wholesome and spiritually uplifting. Dale failed to see how singing about drugs, sex and bad relationships accompanied by screaming electric guitars was an invitation for the devil to enter your soul, but singing about drugs, sex and bad relationships accompanied by twangy steel strings would deliver you to God.

In contrast to both musical styles, the Danowski Family Polka Band blared out a schottische on accordion, guitars and drums from a tractor-drawn flatbed. Poster board signs stapled over crepe paper fringe rustling around the edge like a grass skirt declared "Polka Mass Tomorrow St. Mary's Catholic Church Sponsored by Knights of Columbus."

A small projectile stung Dale's arm. Richie grinned at him from the green and white, balloon-infested 4-H float. He chucked another miniature Tootsie Roll as if launching a fast ball. Richie's dad was a believer in the power of the youth club. He thought it would save his son from bad influences, like Dale. As long as Richie stayed a member, his dad let him drive the Fart Bomb.

Dale raised a protective arm to his face and felt the impact of a wax-wrapped pellet on his bare skin. The weapon bounced onto the road. A little kid with a possible future as a short stop snatched it up. The boy smirked at Dale as if daring him to claim the candy.

"Hey, that's mine!" Dale yelled in a monster-deep voice. He faked a lunge. The boy squealed with glee and ran after the decorated hay wagon to score more treats.

"Somewhere Over the Rainbow" in marching tempo with heavy brass blared from upstream in the parade's flow.

Don't look, Dale told himself. *Ice it. You're an indie, drum-solo kind of guy, not a pop-culture, movie-musical fanboy.*

Clowns cavorted in front of the Glacier Falls High School Marching Band banner. Okay, he could look in that direction if he was watching them.

Junior Rasset in a blue wig and floppy shoes pointed a giant pistol at Boomer, still recognizable in white face paint and an exaggerated red mouth. Junior pulled the trigger. A flag popped out with "Bang" on it in bright letters. Boomer staggered in a dramatic death scene and slowly eased himself to the pavement. He tossed red scarves into the air, signifying spurting blood.

Junior held a bucket over the body. The prone clown's foot shot upward. Junior tapped the metal pail with the barrel of the gun. Clunk. Kicked the bucket.

Dale didn't laugh with the crowd. The skit seemed limp and insensitive considering recent events. He pretended to watch the scene while focusing beyond it.

Encased in a heavy brass-buttoned jacket and pants marked by a shiny strip down each leg, Crystal stomped through the summer humidity. Her flute, level with the horizon, touched her lips. A pale strand escaped the rest of her hair, tucked under a tall, braid-draped hat.

She should have been anonymous in the straight lines of musicians clad in the blue, white, and black school colors; but, to Dale, the determination in her step and the swish of her hips set her apart. He was sure he could pick out her trills from those of the other two flutists beside her.

As the band reached him, it swung into that song from *Gone with the Wind*. Dale imagined Crystal's hat flying away on the sweeping notes, freeing her long locks to float about her angelic face like a halo.

Too quickly she was past him, with only a forward stare and not a single glance his way.

Does she know I'm here? Does she know I'm alive?

A John Deere tractor pulled the American Legion's contribution into view. It was the same as last year and every year Dale could remember. Cobweb-like gauze swirled around a spiral frame, giving the impression of a funnel cloud. Within the wisps, miniature houses, barns, and cows wobbled on wires that you were supposed to pretend you didn't see.

In front of the filmy terror, seated on mounds of green indoor-outdoor carpeting to simulate rolling hills, the Tornado Queen and her escort King Twister, flanked by two pairs of runner ups, smiled at the crowd. All six had graduated from high school in June and were hanging around with minimum wage jobs until the technical colleges and universities started in another month.

Of all the boys and girls who'd ridden on that float, Dale couldn't remember a single one who'd stayed at home, working on the family farm for the rest of forever. It seemed having plans to leave Glacier Falls was a requirement for the honored positions.

Two years from now Crystal was sure to be queen. Dale knew there was no point in his even filling out an entry form for king. Clique membership wasn't strict, as it might be in a larger school. A small town with a limited number of teens had to tolerate some cross-over, but everyone knew their true rank. Only total pops became Tornado Daze royalty. Dale didn't qualify.

Beyond the tiny cows bobbing in old Halloween cobwebs, came the horseback riders. They were last as always, so the marchers and the clowns didn't have to step over piles of greenish-brown shit. Mostly oldsters and parents with their little kids, they wore Western hats and shirts, jeans, and leather-tooled boots.

The few high schoolers in the group were all boys. Girls were quicker to catch on to the social scene than their male counterparts. The riders were aggies, as in agriculture, like Dale. They knew engines, crop rotation, seeds, and animal breeding. They didn't know about—or didn't want to know about, or couldn't afford so why bother knowing about—trendy watches that told you how many steps you'd taken, and that could pay for your over-priced expresso.

The guys held on to the reins as if the horses really needed their guidance to plod down a straight street. They doffed their hats and waved them in the air, pretending to be in the same strata as the royalty ahead of them.

To Dale, their performance seemed pointless. When school started, they'd be eyebrow-deep in reality. It wouldn't take much. The first football pep fest. The history quiz on chapter one. Maneuverings for dates to the Homecoming dance.

He shouldn't be so hard on them. For a few brief moments slowly riding down the main street on the backs of powerful animals in front of an applauding crowd, they must feel as adored as King Twister. He was sure they were more appreciative of the attention.

The parade route was the same every year. Central Avenue from the courthouse to the state highway, which was just a regular street here in town. Take a left past the lumber yard then left on Fourth to the school, where it officially ended. Since the spectators always camped out on Central or the highway, the orderliness usually dissolved like a wet sugar cube once each event rounded the corner onto Fourth.

Except for Crystal's group. As Mr. Stokely the director often reminded his students, marching band was about discipline. No one was allowed to break formation until the last note faded away.

If Dale took Pine Avenue, he could beat them to the school grounds. He'd happen to be entering the building for something—he could think up a believable story on the way— at the same time Crystal was going in to change out of her uniform. He'd say a quick "hey" to her.

Then—more importantly—he'd be leaving just as she'd be coming out with her flute case. He could hold the door for her and say something clever. No, something ordinary, as if he talked to her every day.

In the direction of the courthouse some jerk revved his engine and pounded on his horn in long blasts, causing the horses to whinny and prance in fear.

A shiny red Mustang convertible shot forward, screeched to a halt then jerked ahead again and again, forcing riders out of the way. Blue-gray smoke and gravel shot into the air with each lurch.

Behind the wheel Owen Norquist launched kisses from his extended middle finger at the startled crowd.

Parents, while trying to control their own skittish mounts, grabbed for the reins of their children's horses. Owen sped toward a teen cowboy then slammed on the breaks, cranking the steering wheel. The car skidded sideways. The horse bolted, charging past the American Legion's mock tornado straight for the marching band.

Panicked animals reared and stomped. A palomino, reins hanging loose with a tiny girl clutching its mane, clopped wild-eyed onto the crowded sidewalk, heading toward the drugstore.

Dale sprinted into the street, through an obstacle course

of crazed horses. The sports car roared at him and smoked to a stop, blocking his path. Defiantly he locked eyes with the driver, barely registering that the asshole threatening to run people over was Owen.

Dale smashed his fist into the candy-red hood with more anger than he knew he had in him. Owen flinched in surprise. The reaction wasn't much, but it gave Dale a world of satisfaction. He rushed around the front of the car, feeling the engine heat. Briefly, he wondered if the bumper was about to crash into his kneecaps.

As he ran, he searched the scattering crowd for his mom, hoping she had sought the safety of the store yet knowing she hadn't.

A semi-circle of women in pink smocks spread their arms, corralling the palomino. The animal sputtered and threw back its head. Its tiny rider shrieked in terror. Dale's mother grabbed a dangling leather strip. "Easy, easy." She clutched the rein and gently coaxed the snout closer to stroke the white blaze. "Shush now," she cooed.

The convertible horn blared. The horse jerked against the restraint, attempting to flee its pastel captors. The women stood their ground. His mom kept a firm grip. "Sherman, get Alicia," she ordered.

Dale ducked around the pink ladies. "Come on, honey." He held out his arms to the little girl. She let go of the horse's mane and lunged. The force knocked him back a step. "That was pretty good riding." He carried her out of striking distance of the hooves.

"Stardust didn't mean it." A loose red star barrette dangled from Alicia Glavin's short, strawberry-blond hair. It matched the glittery silver stars on her red shirt, and her shiny red boots. "He got scared. He didn't mean to be bad."

"Of course not," Dale said. "I bet he's a really nice horse."

"The best in the whole world."

A patrol car wailed, coming closer. The convertible careened onto a side street. Stardust reared. Now that its rider was safe, the drugstore ladies backed away, letting the horse break free. It torn off, hooves clopping against the pavement.

"Stardust!" Alicia shouted after it, her blue eyes watery.

"He'll be okay," Dale said. "He just has to stretch his legs a bit, then he'll get tired and find some nice yummy grass to munch on."

He envisioned the other runaway horse knocking down the band's uniformed marchers like bowling pins. If Crystal lay in the street bleeding, trampled into a coma, he would never forgive himself.

Idiot. He'd had the option of protecting the girl of his dreams or his mother. He'd picked his mom, who could take care of herself. Instead of rescuing the fair maiden, he had his arms around a six-year old.

Larry and Monica Glavin ditched their mounts and rushed to their daughter. Dale passed Alicia off to her parents. He faded into the teary-eyed mob that surrounded them, hoping to make his getaway. He couldn't escape that easily.

"Sherman." His mom caught his arm.

"That was pretty gutsy, Mom. Are you okay?"

His mother patted her tower of curls. "Fine. When you grow up on a farm, you learn how to handle a spooked horse."

"I didn't." His grandparents always had horses when his mom was young. Dale had seen the photographs. When he was little, he'd wanted one of his own more than anything; but, to his dad, they were just expensive pets. So that was that.

"You came running to help just the same," his mother said. "That girl could have been carried halfway to Eagle Bend by now."

Does that mean you're proud of me? Dale wanted to ask. He didn't. Sirens danced around them. Every patrol car in the fleet seemed to be on the streets.

"Owen almost got people killed," his mom said. "He's dangerous, and he's stupid. With luck Wells will have him in handcuffs soon. In case that doesn't happen, you watch out for him. Promise me, you see him, you go the other direction."

"I promise," he quipped automatically.

His mother wouldn't let him get away with the programmed response. She locked him in a powerful stare from her parental arsenal.

"Seriously, Sherman Dale Steinhaus."

"Seriously, Mother." She'd given him "the look" and invoked his full name. He was totally trapped. "I promise."

"I've got to get back to work." She looked at his chest and frowned. "Sherman, did you have to wear that shirt?"

Dale's mother gathered the pink-smocked ladies like a flock of flamingos and herded them into the store. Larry Glavin swung into the saddle of his gray. Monica lifted Alicia up to him then mounted her pinto. The family rode off after the errant Stardust, not exactly into the sunset since it was still early afternoon; but it sure felt like the end of a movie.

Only he hadn't gotten the girl. Not even close.

Adrenaline from the rescue dissipating, Dale tugged at his sweaty shirt sticking to his skin like duct tape. The humidity felt about ninety-nine percent. He set off to find out what had happened with the other runaway horse that had charged toward Crystal.

No bodies littered the street. No blood stained the asphalt and ran into the gutter. He heard brass and drums blaring "Let's Twist Again" in the direction of the lumberyard. The disturbance hadn't stopped Mr. Stokely's well-trained crew.

Feeling like a fool, Dale jogged in the direction of the school to get ahead of the band. The idea of intercepting Crystal was still in the back of his mind, but it had lost its urgency. He'd been so careful to watch out for Owen, then he'd ended up right in the guy's path at the wrong end of three-thousand pounds of Ford metal, practically daring the psycho to squash him like a bug.

And, yeah, the car.

Mustang.

Convertible.

Red.

Dale had been in reptile-brain panic and still recognized it in all its sleek, scarlet glory. His fist hadn't slammed into the hood of the smoke-coughing Dodge. It had hammered Crystal's dad's attempt to time-travel back to his youth.

He caught up to the 4-H float. The giant four-leaf clover on the back wobbled as it turned on Fourth Avenue. Richie jumped off and handed Dale a tiny Tootsie Roll. "My pockets are full of them. I bet I've eaten a hundred of these little suckers." He popped another into his mouth. "What was all the shouting and sirens and stuff behind us? And did you hear the band go all off key? Crash and burn! I bet Stokely was spitting fire."

"I'll tell you about it later," Dale said. The empty sidewalks were free of spectators in tornado t-shirts cheering, applauding, and flapping flags. The parade seemed more stupid than usual without an audience. "I need to get out of here. Do you have to do 4-H stuff?"

"Not if I flit right now."

Chapter Fifty-Two

Happy SunnieChat Day!

ASHLEY

Zach is on a health kick. Steamed veggies with quinoa and avocado for supper last night. After he went to bed I binged Ben and Jerrys

HOLLY

Cherry Garcia or Red Velvet Cake?

ASHLEY

RVC

HOLLY

OMG your pregnant

KAYLA

Ice cream as a pregnancy test?

ASHLEY

Don't start stock piling diapers. It might not happen

KAYLA

Sounds like it already has

Averted Vision

HOLLY

How is Zach taking it, besides the veggie rampage?

ASHLEY

In shock

KAYLA

I'm doing a happy dance!

HOLLY

No reaction from C? You already knew! WTF Ash. Tell one, tell all. That's the pact

CASSIE

I had to pledge secrecy with a blood ritual

KAYLA

Blood ritual? You mean you drank a glass of cabernet

CASSIE

Two glasses actually. These things have very rigorous requirements

ASHLEY

Don't judge. I couldn't deal with you all at once. Still can't

KAYLA

Ash however it goes we're with you

HOLLY

Sis whatever you need

CASSIE

Always

HOLLY

If you plan on painting the spare bedroom in nursery colors I know a guy

Chapter Fifty-Three

Technically the fairgrounds hadn't opened for Tornado Daze yet. Dale thought most of the town was already there anyway putting out flags and looping crepe paper across the booths. The Lions Club fired up the brat and burger grill but wouldn't be ready to serve for another twenty minutes.

Killing time, he and Richie just happened to stroll past the gazebo, where the concert would be held. Their musician-classmates dotted the lawn surrounding it. Mr. Stokely was big into having a BB, a Band Brand. His flock had swapped the tall hats and thick uniforms for pale blue, band-logo t-shirts with shorts or jeans. Dale scanned them. Crystal must be close by but he couldn't spot her.

Collapsed chairs, and music stands that looked like the skeletons of prehistoric fish leaned against the hexagon's railings. Mr. Stokely wiggled a finger at the stacks, counting. Wire-rimmed glasses with round lenses gave him an owlish appearance. He stopped and smiled at Dale and Richie. "Hey, guys, got a minute to help out?"

Some teachers wouldn't have dared ask, afraid uncivilized, non-band, aggies would very rudely and crudely say no, especially during the summer without the threat of detention for mouthing off. The refusal would be an embarrassing challenge to their authority, and a reminder that their control over students was an illusion.

Mr. Stokely had no such fears. He was a band director. He directed. It's what he did.

Dale carried a folding chair in each arm up the steps into the gazebo. Crystal snatched one from him. Shocked, Dale tried to come up with a conversation starter. After all his mental preparation for this very situation, his mind was like a wiped hard drive. What had happened to those casual phrases that came so easily to him in his daydreams?

"Damn," Crystal said softly. She fumbled with the chair as if she'd never seen one before. Her single yellow braid swung forward over her shoulder. She flipped it back with enough force to knock a guy out if he'd been standing too close. "Damn," she said banging the metal puzzle against the floor.

Dale set down the other chair and grasped the one Crystal clutched. "How about I handle the unfolding and you line them up."

She held firm. "I can do it."

"I've got it." Dale tugged at the frame. She jerked it back. He couldn't let go. They sawed the air with the chair. She didn't want his help, Dale realized, didn't want to be anywhere near him. But this was the opportunity he'd hoped for.

"We do it together," Dale said. "Okay?"

"Okay," she snapped. Crystal held on to the back. Dale popped out the seat and legs. They set it down in unison with a clunk.

"That's one," Dale said. "How many to go?" He wanted her to smile. She didn't. "You okay?" Shit. Her dad was sure to be in trouble for his meetings with Owen. Did she know Dale was the one who snitched to Wells and Berger?

"Is it true?" she skewered him with those blue eyes. "Was Owen driving my dad's car?"

"Yeah," Dale said before he could stop himself. He should

have played it sub-zero and said something like, well, he was driving a red Mustang. Is that your dad's? Instead, with a single word he'd blurted out evidence that he kept track of the Swenson fleet.

Except if he said he didn't know who it belonged to, he'd look brainless. The rolling bling was the only one of its kind for miles around; everyone knew who owned it.

Richie and a freshman delivered more flat chairs. Dale made them three dimensional and passed them to Crystal.

"I wish he *had* killed Edgar." Crystal slammed chairs into a curved row, as if daring them to crawl out of alignment. "Then he'd be locked up forever and gone, gone, gone."

"Owen been bothering you?" Even voicing the question sent an Arctic wind through Dale.

"He's been acting like my dad's best friend." Crystal kept her voice low but her words were like screams. Her shoulders shook but he didn't dare touch her. "He even came to the house. That filthy-mouthed, filthy-minded creep was in *my* house talking to *my* dad."

Dale swallowed hard. "Actually in your house? Why?"

"I don't know. Some kind of business deal, which makes no sense. I mostly couldn't hear what they were saying. Something about payment. Owen wanted a payment."

"It's probably nothing," Dale said without believing it. He couldn't tell her about the Wednesday night book club, or whatever it was. "Owen's a poacher. Maybe your dad bought off-season venison from him."

"It sounded way more serious than that. And now he has the Mustang."

"Grand theft auto means jail time for sure," Dale said. "With what happened at the parade, he must be under arrest. It'll get straightened out."

Crystal plunked into the chair she'd just placed. "The thing is, I don't think he stole it. I think he forced my dad into giving it to him." She looked up at Dale. "You saw Mr. Tvrdik get killed? You really *saw* the murderer?"

She didn't ask it the way Bridget and Whitney would have, like a reaction to a tabloid headline. *It's horrible! Tell me every detail.*

Crystal wanted hard facts. Dale leaned back from the intensity, just a bit, just a centimeter. But those eyes had a gravity of their own. Drawn in, he sat beside her. "I didn't see a face."

"But you saw it happen?" she whispered.

"Yeah." A vision of it suddenly filled his head. He felt as he had that night, as if he watched something too real to be true.

"Would you take me to where you were when you saw it?"

Dale was startled. Was she really asking that they go someplace together? "Right now?"

"After dark so it's the way it was then." She looked about to cry or slam her fist into someone. Dale couldn't tell which, but he knew it wasn't a good idea to be too close to her if she did either one.

"I wish I could skip this," Crystal said. "If only I didn't have a solo."

Out on the lawn Mr. Stokely looked up. "Chairs," he yelled. "Chairs!"

Dale stood and grabbed one of the gray metal frames that had piling up, despite Richie and the freshman delivering them as slowly as possible. "I-I-I could meet you, you know, after the concert. We could watch the fireworks then go out to the lake." He knew it wasn't a date, more like date-adjacent, but he tried to make it sound like one. It was probably his only chance to show her he was smart and fun to be with and maybe even romantic.

"We have a break after the regular concert then we play right at the end of the fireworks. *Stars and Stripes Forever* and the *1812 Overture*. The American Legion fires guns for the cannon blasts. Is after that okay?" Loose strands of golden hair fringed her forehead. Her braid had swung forward again, like a lemon-yellow vine on her shoulder.

Okay? Was Crystal really, truly asking him if that was okay? "Sure," Dale said, as if it didn't matter one way or the other to him. After all, he was a guy who came and went as he pleased.

Crystal took command of the chairs with a new passion. "Don't forget."

Mr. Stokely clapped his hands. "Music stands. Get those music stands in place. Let's go, people. Rehearsal in three minutes. We'll start with the Sousa."

Dale left the gazebo to the band geeks. He didn't know what a sue-saw was. He'd look it up on his phone before the fireworks ended so he could work it into the conversation with Crystal.

He had to plan this all out. Stuff to say. How to be standing when she left the gazebo tonight to meet him. Maybe he should go home and change his sweaty shirt.

What was he going to do for transportation? Crystal might not have a car. Either Owen was out tearing around in the Mustang or Wells had it confiscated for evidence, so the Swenson family was short a set of wheels.

It would be more like a date if he drove anyway. Drove what?

He had a lot to figure out. His dad and mom were both here. His mom managed the Sparks command center, and his dad worked security. They'd arrived separately, but he didn't think either one of them would surrender their keys, especially since he didn't want to explain why he needed a vehicle.

Richie fell into step beside him. He'd forgotten about Richie. How could he do that? Five minutes with Crystal and his best friend for his whole life vanished from his mind, like a guy who disappears in a horror movie and everyone says how awful it is, then for the rest of the flick they act as if he never existed.

"Saw you talking to Crystal," Richie said.

"Yeah."

"She tell you to fuck off?"

Dale thought it might not be such a tragedy if Richie disappeared. "I'm meeting her after fireworks."

"Right. Me and that Penny babe from *Big Bang* will double with you. We'll go to Vegas and gamble away her money."

Dale thought that, should hell freeze over and his night with Crystal really happen, he would climb the water tower and shout it to the world. For now, he wanted to keep it private, a delicious taste in his mouth and a tingling on his skin. He didn't even try to convince Richie. Let him think it was a joke. "I need to borrow the Bomb."

"I'm meeting Bridget by the cotton candy. Whitney's with her."

"Dude, I really need the car. Like now and later tonight. You can get a ride with Bridget, right?"

Richie handed over the jangly Power Rangers key chain. "You're loss."

Dale jumped into the Bomb and made a quick trip home. Overlapping sheets of sooty slate clouds layered the sky. The radio crackled with static. His Code Red app beeped with threats of a thunderstorm. He showered and pulled on clean jeans. A Grateful Dead t-shirt replaced Metallica. His mother wouldn't be happy, but girls went for the classics. When he got back to the fairgrounds, the whole town seemed squeezed into the few acres of booths and carnival rides.

Richie ambushed him by the Knights of Columbus bean bag toss. "You're in deep shit," he practically sang.

"What now, Richie?" He was working on a strategy. He

needed the perfect place to sit to watch the concert. Somewhere far enough from the gazebo to show a casual attitude yet close enough so Crystal had to notice him.

"Owen's here." Richie grinned, as if the situation was enormously entertaining.

I'm in deeper than deep shit, Dale thought. Then he forced himself to be calm. After the stunt at the parade, Owen *had* to be in jail, didn't he? If he'd somehow managed to elude the entire sheriff's department, cops in the whole state would be after him. "You saw him?"

"Junior Rasset told me. Somebody told him. Said I should warn you." They walked past the tilt-a-whirl and wove through the kiddy rides. "Owen left Swenson's man-toy in old bat Finster's tomato patch then nicked her Eldorado. Bet it hasn't been out of the garage more than twice in the last hundred years. Finster must be having a fit. At least it's easy to spot."

"Richie, are you sure this 'Owen on the loose thing' didn't come from Mrs. Finster?"

"I told you. It came from Junior."

"But who actually saw him?"

"I don't know. Everyone," Richie said. "The Sparks are on high alert. Man, Owen's a whole lot of tunes short of a playlist. You better stay with the crowd tonight, hero-boy, 'cause I don't think I can stop him if he decides to kick your ass."

"Thanks all to hell." Great, he was being protected by skinny Richie and a bunch of volunteer firemen.

Damn. True or not, if the Sparks knew, his folks knew.

"You better hope he don't find Cassie either," Richie said. "He's been mouthing off how she made up that left-right shit about her telescope 'cause she's hot and heavy for him. Owen wants to give her a reward."

Dale felt as if he'd been hit by a taser. "Did Junior tell you that, too?"

"Somebody did. Don't remember."

"Is Cassie here?" He hadn't seen her at the parade. For having lived in a huge city, she sure didn't like to be with people much.

"I saw her talking to Owen's wife and girlfriend. Ain't that like irony, like from English class, that Cassie's friendly with them? Maybe she'd fit right in at that hippie dump Owen's got going."

"I'd shove your face into the dirt for that, but I don't have time right now. Shit, Richie, never say anything like that again." Dale walked faster, covering ground. He looked across the top of the crowd, trying to spot Cassie's tall figure.

Richie followed like a reluctant puppy. "Hey, are we *looking* for Owen?"

"Shut up, Richie. Your stupid is showing."

Sparks served as the Tornado Daze's equivalent of mall cops. The hook and ladder truck sat next to the fireworks site. Three of the volunteers stood by the display. Others circulated through the crowd with two-way radios. They were easy to spot. Dale and Richie had a lot of Trekkie jokes about their red shirts.

Father Anderson and Reverend Gunther, both in crimson tees, stood at the junction of the St. Mary's cake walk and the Faith and Hope craft booth. They were probably discussing the Safari Club in un-Christian terms. Dale hardly recognized them without their white-collared uniforms. For the first time in the festival's history, their fund-raisers sat side by side, an interesting offshoot of the new alliance.

"Sherman," Father Anderson called when Dale and Richie got close.

"Yes, Father?" In Dale's family a summons from a priest was like a command from God. Richie melted away, leaving him to face the two clergy alone. Yeah, his best bud would be great protection if Owen showed up.

"Have you seen Miss Windom?" Father Anderson asked.

"No, sir." Dale couldn't look at Gunther. Not after what Richie told him. The reverend preached honesty from the pulpit but used stolen materials to build the community center. Worse, he'd sinned for personal reasons, to beat Father Anderson in their petty little competition. And he'd done it through the devil himself. How would Father A react if he knew?

"If you see her, please tell her Rhonda needs to talk to her about a dollar bill she's trying to track down. It has a note from her niece on it. She thinks Ms. Windom might have it."

"I'll give her the message," Dale said. "If I happen to see her."

"Don't forget, Sherman."

"I won't, Father."

"And tell her to watch out for Owen. And you do the same, young man."

"I will, Father."

"This is what I think we should try next," Gunther said to Anderson. Dale felt lucky to escape without being forced to join the holy army in its escalating tactics to rid Glacier Falls of sin.

Crystal, apparently done with the sue-saw (Damn, he'd forgotten to research it), examined heart-shaped picture frames at the craft booth. She looked straight at him and raised her hand in a semi-wave. That little movement almost knocked him over.

Chapter Fifty-Four

It wasn't the crowd and the sticky heat so much as the smells that made Cassie's stomach churn. Greasy smoke from burgers and fries at the Lions Club booth. The choking sweet scent of "tornado twist" cotton candy at the 4-H stand. Burnt flesh of roasting pig at the Port-A-Pork oven on wheels.

She bought a Coke and unbuttered popcorn from a booster club dad. A pony-tailed girl in uniform holding a basketball smiled from each of the large picture buttons clipped to his red shirt. Different in appearance yet all the same, she recognized the faces from the local sports pages. Proud dad Gordon Petrosky handed her the paper cup filled with exploded kernels. Of less-than-average height, his six tall, coordinated daughters were destined to lead Glacier Falls to the state tournament year after year for the next decade.

Only a little after eight o'clock, the sun hung below streaks of lead and shale that threatened to split open and let loose a deluge. The miracle fabric of Cassie's light windbreaker whisked away sweat and would repel any rain. She hoped the wet weather would hold off until after the festivities wound down.

This wasn't her style of entertainment, but she

appreciated the community it fostered—not that every member of the populace fit neatly into the fellowship. Nearby at the 4-H booth Glenna held little Jessie's hand. Judy bent down with a cone of pink spun sugar for the boy to nibble. Cassie had spoken to the women for a few minutes. They knew about the incident at the parade but hadn't heard from Owen.

Cassie's phone chimed and chimed again. Sure, just when her hands were full and she couldn't reach it. The sisters' Tell One Tell All policy was not being followed by any of them. Since Holly and Kayla learned about Ashley's pregnancy, Cassie had been juggling text-versations with all three, plus with each one separately, and a thread with Holly and Kayla but not Ashley.

Cassie retreated to the deserted recreation area at the far end of the fairgrounds, away from the parking lot, food stands, and glare of lights being switched on against the growing gloom. The Glacier River sloshed against the bank, sending out the scent of fresh water. The natural flow bounced over rocks and swept across sand bars, cutting its own path, so different from the concrete waterways of L.A.

She walked through bristly ankle-high grass to a picnic table beside a stone fire pit. Generations of birds had been there before her, marring the brown wood. Deciding to stand, she grimaced at the thought of sitting on the white-splotched surface in her khaki shorts. She set her drink on the clearest spot she could find. How much protection did waxed paper provide against bird doo-doo? She didn't dare set down the unstable popcorn container.

With a free hand, she dug into her purse for her phone. The bag was real calf skin, made doubly expensive by a designer label. She'd spotted it in an exclusive boutique she and Vicky loved to visit. Mostly they'd just looked and drooled, but one day Cassie decided she absolutely had to have the elegant, tan pouch suspended from a thin strap, even though it shoved her budget into the danger zone.

That was back when she had a steady salary to rely on, before self-employment. No splurges allowed now! The tiny admission to the fairgrounds for the concert and "fireworks extravaganza," as it was advertised, fit her current finances. Smaller print on the posters told her "Sponsored by the Glacier Falls Fire Department." Bingo money was paying for most of tonight's entertainment.

It had been a long time since she'd attended an event. Living and working in the same space had advantages, but it was also isolating. She felt good closing the door to her spare-bedroom-turned-office and walking away from projects in various stages of development. Well, that's what she unconvincingly told herself.

One-handed, she fumbled for her phone. Okay, so it wasn't the guilt-free exit she'd imagined. More like a baby step toward gaining balance in her life.

How am I doing so far?

"Cassie."

She looked toward the shout, startled but pleased. Dale usually avoided calling her by her first name. He was still getting comfortable with the familiarity it implied. Of course, at the moment she could see he didn't have a choice. He had a girl with him. The situation required him to appear at ease with this adult female who was not a school employee, a relative, a friend of his mother, or the mother of a friend.

"Funny to see you without Jupiter," Dale said.

"He wouldn't enjoy noisy fireworks." Cassie viewed it as a nervous comment, not at all like Mrs. Finster forcing an opportunity to imply Cassie put herself in danger by having a large pet.

"This is Crystal." Dale flicked a thumb toward the girl at his side. "Uh, Crystal Swenson," he added like a caution.

Swenson. Raymond's daughter. Cassie held out her hand.

"I'm Cassie Windom. It's nice to meet you." Crystal was lovely in face and figure. Some of it was the luck of the draw from the gene pool. Some of it was contrived through the magic of hair and makeup that teen females studied like alchemists and applied like sorceresses.

What was Dale's interest here? Was he investigating or on a date? If the later, she hoped there was more to the girl than her looks. Cassie wanted to think Dale recognized the difference between shiny metal and genuine gold.

Surprised, the girl shifted from one foot to the other before she timidly shook Cassie's hand. "We're sort of neighbors."

"I know it's asking a lot and everything," Dale said, "but could we borrow the telescope? Later tonight? After the fireworks?"

Cassie gestured toward the churning sky. "There won't be any stars visible tonight."

"I don't want it to look at the sky," Crystal said. "I want Dale to show me what you can see from Red Hawk."

Did Crystal know about her dad's evening activities and Dale's spying? Cassie didn't want to outright say she wouldn't let them take it. "It would be pretty hard hauling it up there in the dark. It was tough enough in daylight."

"You've been there?" Crystal asked. "If you look to the north, you can see my house."

"Oh, sure," Dale said as if it had suddenly occurred to him. "You remember," he said to Cassie. "I showed you where the tornado ripped out the pine trees."

Cassie played along, as if she and Dale had visited the hill to star gaze and not to reenact a murder scene for the sheriff. "The light-colored place up the little hill from the lake."

"Champagne," Crystal said. "Beige really, but my mother likes to call it champagne. I could never see much of the hill from my window before the trees blew over. It's hard to believe you can recognize people down at the lake from there, even with a telescope. Do you think—" Crystal hesitated and looked toward the river. "Could I have seen the murder from my house? If I'd looked out the window? Because I think maybe I saw something."

"It was probably too dark and too far away," Dale said. "You couldn't have seen anyone. Not for sure."

"No," Crystal said, "not for sure. I'm not sure at all." She looked at the ground a moment, then lifted her eyes to Dale. "Don't forget about the message."

"Oh, yeah. Cassie," Dale said, "Officer Olson, Rhonda, needs some dollar bill you've got. Her niece wrote something on it."

Cassie handed the cardboard popcorn container to Crystal. "Help yourself."

Two free hands! She flipped through her phone. Rhonda's call came during the pregnancy frenzy. Thinking it was about the Sparks' job, Cassie had let it roll into voice mail. She pressed the triangle and put the phone to her ear.

"Cassie, this is Rhonda. You know when you gave money for Edgar's Butterball and you were given change? You maybe got a dollar with letters on it in blue ink. Check if you still have it. If you find it, tuck it away someplace real safe. It's important." A phone rang in the background. *"Oh, shoot, I've got to answer that. Just find that bill and hold on to it. It's from my niece, remember that. Don't tell anyone anything different. Except Adam, if you see him. But no one else."*

Cassie hit the call button. The unanswered ringing took her to voice mail. Oh, great. Telephone tag. "Rhonda, I got your message. I'll look for the dollar. You'll have to tell me all about your niece over a glass of wine."

She thumbed on the flashlight app and handed the phone to Dale. He held the beam steady as she pulled her billfold from the elegant purse and searched through it. The few crinkly Washingtons in the slim pack showed only U.S. government green and a little grime. "I might have spent it at the Boosters stand on my gourmet meal."

Dale thumbed off the light and handed back her phone.

"I can run and check right now, before it gets passed off to someone else."

"Mr. Petrosky waited on me. I should give you a dollar so you can make the exchange."

"That's okay. If he has it, I'll take care of it and you can pay me later." Dale jogged off toward the midway.

Cassie tucked her billfold into her purse. Crystal handed her the popcorn. "He's really nice, isn't he? At school he pretends not to be."

"I think he is. Jupiter does, too. He's my dog. Well, a puppy really." Cassie guessed that Crystal knew quite a bit about pretending. In the girl's silhouetted profile Cassie observed a lift to the chin and set to the shoulders that she liked.

"Did you grow up in California?" Crystal asked.

"No. Not so far away from here. In Irving River." *Which means I'm right back where I started.*

"That's close to Morris. Did you go to college there?"

"St. Cloud State. I wanted something different and farther from home. Although it's not that far." That was an inadequate summary of how she'd felt at the time, like saying Apollo 11 went to the moon looking for a new vacation spot.

"I want to live someplace bigger," Crystal said. "At least for a while. Here everyone thinks they know all about you. What you want, and what you'll do, and what your whole life will be right to the day you die."

"I bet they get surprised all the time."

"Were you scared? When you first moved out on your own? It would be normal to be scared, wouldn't it?"

Cassie shoved her phone, texts still unread, into her purse and retrieved her pop from the picnic table. "I guess so, but I wasn't. I was excited. I couldn't wait."

"Me, too. I want to go to the University of Minnesota and study American literature or economics. I haven't decided yet."

Dale returned, panting from the quick trip and trying to hide it. "Mr. Petrosky doesn't have it, but it could be in a bundle he put in the till. They're checking, but it'll take a while."

"I have to get ready for the concert," Crystal turned to Cassie. "It was nice meeting you. I hope you'll let us borrow the telescope. We'd be really careful with it, and we'd bring it back right away. Dale, I'll see you later." She headed toward the colored lights.

Dale took a step to sprint after her then stopped and pivoted back to Cassie. "I don't really want to carry the telescope up that hill again. Is it okay if I tell her you were afraid we might drop it or something?"

"I'm more worried about the weather. You don't want to be standing on the highest point around holding on to a huge piece of metal if it starts to lightning."

Dale nodded. "That'll work. You're going to go listen to the concert, aren't you?"

"I can hear it from here."

Dale ground a foot into the grass as if extinguishing a cigarette butt. "That's not a good idea."

"I know. The birds have made sure there's no decent place to sit."

Dale didn't crack a smile. "Things don't feel right."

"Having trouble accepting your good fortune?" Cassie teased.

Dale looked away. Cassie wondered if he blushed. He seemed to do that a lot. He told her about the reports of Owen being nearby and spouting off about her having a thing for him. She got the feeling he softened it, hoping she would still pick up on how deeply serious it was. "Look, I think it's all rumors. Owen's probably in jail or a hundred miles from here. But you should still be careful."

Cassie had to agree. She started walking back toward the carnival with him. "I suppose I could rejoin civilization."

A whistling flare blossomed from the site of the fireworks display. "It's way too early—" An explosion sent a fiery geyser into the air, cutting off Dale's words. He sprinted toward the blast.

"No!" Cassie yelled after him, fearing the entire display would burst into a giant fireball.

She caught movement at the edge of her vision.

A camouflaged blur rushed toward her from the river bank. The figure slammed into her, grabbing the tan rectangle hanging from her shoulder. Shocked, she jerked back, reflexively tightening her grip on the containers in her hands. Popcorn pelted her face like hail. Icy liquid sloshed over the rim of the waxy cup, dousing her hand and splashing her clothes.

The attacker yanked at the purse. The strap slid off Cassie's shoulder into the crook of her arm. She dropped the crushed cardboard, clenched her bent arm against her chest and snatched the thin strap with her other hand.

"Help!" Cassie yelled. "Help!"

Boom. Boom, boom, boom. Fresh eruptions drowned out her cries. Flashes cast light across the mugger's brimmed hat. She glimpsed deeply-colored fabric under the tan and brown pattern of the shirt.

"Ahhhhhhhh!" She screamed in anger at the ski-masked face. The attacker shoved her hard. She fell back, throwing out her arm in an attempt to catch herself. The strap slipped from her straightened elbow. Leather slid through the palm and fingers that still clutched it, burning her skin.

Cassie swung up her free arm and grabbed. She hung on to the strip with both fists. On her back in the grass with her adversary looming over her, she kicked at the assailant's leg with her soft sandals, hoping to make contact.

Reason caught up with her, dampening her instinct to fight. It was only a purse. Just a fancy sack. Its contents could be replaced. It was not her life. Not her soul. Not a link to

Vicky. The designer tag no longer had a connection to who she was or what she wanted to be. She hadn't even thought of it when she'd gathered what was most important to her and huddled under the stairs.

Cassie opened her clenched hands and released the leather. The startled thief staggered backward, recovered footing, then dashed away toward the field of parked cars.

Mind numb, Cassie pushed herself up to sit in the grass. She messaged stiff fingers and adjusted a loose sandal. Dislodged popcorn fell from her hair.

What to do next? Standing seemed like a good idea. She slowly rose onto wobbly legs and gave her windbreaker a shake to rid it of clinging kernels. Dark liquid from her spilled drink rolled off the fabric. Moist splotches soaked into her shirt and shorts. She shoved her hands in the jacket pockets, seeking tissues.

A different kind of texture crunched against her fingers. She slid out the papers and squinted at one. In the dusk a presidential man with a triangular hairdo gazed back. Dollar bills. She'd worn the jacket a lot lately. Mostly when she went into town. Did she have it on when she and Rhonda gave Denny donations?

The accidental fireworks quieted. Cassie no longer had her phone with the handy flashlight app. She needed light in order to examine the bills. She also needed to report the theft.

Laughter bubbled up inside her and spilled out. She could add mugging to the growing list of calamities that had happened to her since moving back to boring, rural Minnesota.

Chapter Fifty-Five

The Sparks' Command Center was the only permanent structure at the fairgrounds. A white-washed, block building on a concrete slab, it stood stoically at the end of the midway. Strains of Bob Dylan's "Blowin' in the Wind," the opening number for the band concert, wafted in with Cassie.

Jessie Norquist contentedly licked an ice cream cone. "Hi, I'm lost so I've got chocolate," he announced to her. Mr. Calhoun, one of the grocery store seniors, sat with a blood-pressure cuff wrapped around his arm while an emergency medical technician checked his vital signs.

Helen Steinhaus, silver Sparkle jacket draped over the back of her chair, staffed the center. "It looks like you could use some help," she said brightly. "You didn't get hurt by the fireworks, did you?"

Cassie stepped up to the massive wooden desk that served as Helen's fortress. "My purse was stolen. I was in the park. The man, woman, I don't know, grabbed it and ran away."

Helen pointed to a line of red droplets oozing down her calf. "Looks like there's more to it than that."

Cassie hadn't noticed the injury. Now that she saw the

blood, she also felt the aches in her shoulders and the painful strips across her palms.

Helen guided her to a chair and fetched antiseptic and a towel for the wound. She forced a cup of fruit punch into Cassie's sore hands and told her Sarah the EMT, who was someone's ex-cousin-in-law, would get to her soon.

"People were injured by the fireworks?" Cassie wanted to asked about Dale, since he'd been running toward the explosion, but she didn't want to alarm his mother.

"Two with minor burns," Helen said, "but they're fine. Mr. Calhoun had a scare, but he'll be fine. Little Jessie got separated from his mother, but he's fine."

According to Helen, everything was fine. And Cassie believed her.

"I'll report the theft," Helen said. "The sheriff is on the grounds, but he's busy investigating the accident. And did anyone tell you? Rhonda needs to talk to you about a dollar with a message on it from her niece. I guess it's got a little heart drawn on it."

"Yes, thanks," Cassie said.

Helen walked away with purpose and soon returned. "I notified the sheriff's department. Rhonda should have answered, but I got routed to the automated system they turn on when no one's in the office. I tried calling her on her cell but had to leave a message. I'm sure she'll get back to us when she can. Good thing we have our own security force." She went to the old wooden desk and picked up a two-way radio. "Spark needed at the CC ASAP."

Cassie pulled five unsmiling Washingtons from her windbreaker pocket. She smoothed out wrinkles and examined them in the glare of the ceiling lights. Clean. Clean. Clean. Clean. Blue ink. She tucked away four bills and peered at the fifth.

There was no cute heart carefully drawn for a favorite aunt. Cassie hadn't expected one. The niece reference was a cover, just like when Rhonda used it as an excuse to get time off from bingo. James Bond spy stuff. A warning to keep the bill's real nature, whatever that was, a secret.

From whom? According to the message, anyone who wasn't Adam. That left about 7.6 billion people. Of course, they weren't all in Glacier Falls.

Block letters obscured the official seal. Admit One GC. Below that in script were two smudged letters. The markings looked like a tacky advertising gimmick someone came up with in a moment of misguided inspiration.

Here you go, Mr. or Ms. GC. Here's a dollar, plus we'll let you into our establishment for free so you can spend your entire mortgage payment.

At bingo the night of the fire Edgar had made a big fuss, exchanging a bill with blue on it for another one from the stack he turned in to Rhonda. Cassie hadn't seen the writing, but her design-sensitive mind had registered how the scribbles were placed. She was sure this was the same dollar. Except Edgar wasn't GC.

Cassie tilted the paper to catch the light better on the smudged script that appeared to serve as a signature. RS. Russel Sworski, part owner of the Safari Club. Only that wasn't the original name for the place. According to Glenna, the working title was Gentlemen's Club. GC.

Cassie held the connection between two dead men in her hand. How did Edgar get it and why did he think it was important enough to hang on to until— What was it he said? He decided it "hadn't done him any good." Whatever that means.

The marred portrait of the somber president gazed up from the cotton and linen canvas.

Georgie, Georgie what path did you take to my pocket?

Okay, she told herself, *follow Georgie with the blue tattoo.*

Cassie wished she could doodle her thoughts. If she was correct about RS being the Floater's initials, the bad-luck bill started with Sworski. It traveled from him to Edgar then to the pile of bingo money, becoming part of the loot in the stolen bank deposit bag.

In her message Rhonda said Cassie received the bill when she gave a donation for the Tvrdik family the morning after the murder. Cassie mentally stepped through the exchange. She and Rhonda were the first contributors. Rhonda gave Denny some bills. Cassie gave him a ten, which he deemed overly generous. He gave her three singles he'd gotten from Rhonda, dug into his own wallet and handing her two more.

Her credit card habits had fostered sloppy cash and coin management. Instead of tucking the money into her billfold, she'd shoved the currency into her jacket pocket.

The five singles came from two people.

Rhonda wouldn't have given Cassie the okay to tell Adam about the bill if it somehow incriminated her.

The GC ticket came to Cassie through the other person. When he realized its significance, he had to get it back. He was the mugger who set up the premature fireworks blasts as a distraction, the one who slammed Cassie to the ground, and snatched her purse.

Denny. Damn.

Under the command center's stark lights, she carefully folded up Georgie's portrait and stored it in a cargo pocket of her shorts, smoothing down the flap for security.

With the "Denny is a great guy" illusion shattered, Cassie considered him more critically. Maybe the steady income that supposedly gushed in from family land was more like a trickle. Rhonda had made a remark about him often bringing in low bingo revenue. Cassie suspected it wasn't because he was doing more aspirational messaging than card pushing, as Rhonda thought.

Denny was using charitable gambling as his personal ATM. The night of the fire he was pulled away before he had a chance to complete his usual withdrawal. With an outstanding bill at the auto body shop from his scenic drive through a corn field, he felt forced to take the whole bingo bundle.

Cassie listened to "Twistin' the Night Away" through the open door. She hoped an officer would arrive soon, and that it would be Adam. Chatter crackled from Helen's radio. "Still unable to reach local dispatch."

It worried Cassie that Rhonda was suddenly missing. It worried her a great deal.

Chapter Fifty-Six

The high school orchestra swung through a mix of the identical tunes the marching band had played during the parade (with the addition of violins and non-portable instruments) interspersed with other compositions. Technically the two groups were separate, but many of the same students participated in both. Dale sat on the grass in a good position, not too close, not too far away.

The performance hadn't been delayed by the unscheduled fireworks. The Sparks, none of them his dad, quickly dowsed the small fires it caused, protecting the rest of the display. Nothing for Dale to see. Nothing for him to worry about.

He squinted at the glaring artificial lights in the gazebo. Duh. His strategy was pointless. Sitting in the bright bubble, Crystal couldn't possibly identify anyone in the natural darkness surrounding the gingerbread structure.

He got up and moved to the fringe where he could look around for Cassie. She was sure to be nearby. She'd been right behind him when he rushed to investigate the explosions, hadn't she? She wouldn't have stayed by the picnic tables all alone after what he told her about Owen, even if it was just a rumor. He searched the faces while keeping an ear to the music, but didn't spot her in the crowd.

He wandered through the booths, screening the carnival-goers for Cassie and preparing for his non-date. When the musical ordeal was finally over, he casually ambushed Crystal with an extra cup of lemonade in hand. "I don't think it's a good idea to borrow the telescope."

"I need to see what you saw." Crystal sipped at the sour liquid as if still playing the flute.

"Well, there's probably not going to be another murder at Beauty Lake tonight." Dale gave a little laugh. It was supposed to be funny, maybe even witty.

Crystal closed her eyes and pressed fingers against the center of her forehead for a long moment as if she had an unbearable migraine.

Dale sobered. "What are you trying to figure out?" Thunder rolled in the distance. Good. Thunder meant lightning. They couldn't possibly go to Red Hawk now.

"I can't tell you."

"You think your dad killed Edgar." Dale couldn't believe he said it out loud.

Crystal put a hand over her face. "Don't. Just don't."

Dale felt frozen in a nightmare. He wanted to snatch the words from the air and shove them back into his mouth. He wanted to tell her it absolutely couldn't have been her dad, but he didn't know that for sure.

And it suddenly sort of made sense that the camouflaged man was Raymond Swenson. The guy had been meeting Owen at that very spot for, shit, a long time maybe. If, as Dale suspected, the pharmacist was selling Owen drugs, and if Edgar found out—

Tvrdik was the type to blackmail a guy. The old miser would feel he had a right to get a cut of anything Owen was involved in to make up for the stuff swiped from his store. It wouldn't matter to Edgar that the payoff actually came through a partner instead of from Owen himself.

Swenson would be scared to death of a drug charge. He couldn't afford to lose his job and his pharmacist license. The guy liked expensive toys, and his wife could out shop the Kardashians. Paying Edgar to keep quiet put a strain on the family finances. Killing the guy solved that problem.

But if Owen knew about the blackmail, hell, he'd figure out about the murder. He'd be pissed Swenson had dressed up in camo and pretended to be him when he did it.

Owen would threatened to tell the sheriff, even though it meant admitting to dealing. He'd go through with it, too, and not even think it was strange.

Poor Swenson, swapping one blackmailer for another who was worse.

Is that how Owen ended up with a shiny red Mustang convertible to call his own?

"There's nothing to see at the lake," Dale quietly told Crystal.

She shook her head, as if to clear it. "Please, don't tell anyone about this."

"Yeah, we wouldn't want people to know the Christmas-card Swenson family isn't so perfect after all." It just popped out. He wanted to melt right into the ground. It was something he would have said to Richie and the guys, or even to the girls they sort of hung around. Never to Crystal. It was too personal. Too close to the truth. Too much what he really thought.

He must be possessed by a sadistic alien sent through a black hole across a billion light years to ruin his life! She was going to slap his face like in an old black-and-white movie. Or drench him with the lemonade he'd gotten for her. Or, most likely, knee him in the balls.

He would accept whatever came. He deserved it, and it might make her feel better.

Crystal lowered her hand from her face. She wouldn't look him in the eye. "If you promise to drop the don't-give-a-shit, hard-guy pose, I promise not to pretend to be perfect."

Dale felt relieved she'd only gotten sarcastic instead of scream-y, ball-punching angry. "You get the easy part."

"Okay, you tell me what my side of it should be," she demanded.

He ticked them off on his fingers. "You have to promise not to be Homecoming royalty, star of the state championship volleyball team, smart-but-not-overly-smart, prettiest girl in school." There was more, but he didn't want to seem like too much of an expert on her.

"It definitely sounds harder now. Can I keep the volleyball part? I work my butt off for that one. I don't mind changing the smart thing. We have that in common. We both pretend to be dumber than we are. Why is that? It's okay to put everything you've got into sports and do everything you can to look awesome, but you're slammed if you study or say something intelligent."

"What makes you think I'm smart?"

"I've seen you trying to hide a real book that's not for school in your backpack. And sometimes you use words that have more than two syllables."

"I hope you haven't been spreading that around." She noticed the books! *This is the best night of my life, even if my future father-in-law will be in jail for the wedding.*

"Our secret," Crystal said. "Although you're not doing much to protect your own image. First you report a murder, then you save a little girl on a runaway horse. How will Mrs. Finster ever handle such respectable behavior?"

Dale laughed. He laughed with Crystal! The whole stupid car and horse thing had put Dale back on the hero list. People he barely knew came up to him at the carnival and told him how brave he was.

It seemed they thought he jumped in front of the speeding

convertible and forcing it to a halt with his raw, Superman strength. Then he bounded into the car, wrestled control of the vehicle away from Owen—who outweighs him by at least a hundred pounds—and parked it safely at the curb. Next he plucked the little girl from the raging stallion as it charged past him. That's when Owen regained consciousness. Not wanting to endanger the curly-haired tyke, Dale allowed Owen to escape. With the convertible.

"The stuff at the parade wasn't much." Dale was pretty sure Richie was the source of the embellishments.

"It is now. It spread through the whole gazebo before the end of "They Call the Wind Mariah.""

"You band kids do a lot of talking between notes." Thunder definitely rolled toward them now. He didn't care. He and Crystal were having a real conversation, not one he'd planned but one that happened all by itself. Maybe they could get past the labels people stuck on both of them. If she wanted him to haul a telescope to Duluth on his back in a lightning storm, he'd do it.

"Sign language. We all knew before the first video went viral."

"First video? How many are there?"

"A bunch of them," Crystal said. "They're on the Tornado Daze website. And YouTube and stuff."

Richie suddenly invaded. "Hey, Cassie got beat up!"

Chapter Fifty-Seven

Wind huffed and puffed at the concrete building like a storybook wolf. Playful at first, it quickly gained power, as if the beast grew stronger. Cassie shivered. She flashed back to the roaring wind when she'd huddled under the stairway with Jupiter.

But that was over a week ago. It was absurd to be scared now. Telling herself that didn't help. Neither did the cloying fruit punch Helen forced on her. She would have preferred ice cream, like little Jessie.

The boy crunched into the cone, sending melted dribbles down the side like lava flows. He seemed unconcerned that he was officially a lost child.

When the EMT finished with Mr. Calhoun, she dressed the cut on Cassie's leg and insisted on checking for a head injury. A nice enough woman, Sarah seemed disappointed she couldn't put on a cast or remove an appendix with a pen knife.

Answering Helen's call for assistance, Denny hurried in, radio close to his ear. Cassie seethed, wanting to shove him to the floor and demand her purse back; but that would give him a chance to escape. He consulted with Helen then walked toward her.

Shit. She had to stay calm until she could get him arrested.

Okay, okay. You're in a meeting with a client who expects an awesome ad campaign immediately and all you have is a stick drawing of a cat. She'd done that before; she could do this.

Denny went down on one knee, putting himself at eye level. "Are you all right?"

Face to face with her attacker, Cassie forced a smile. "A few bruises, wrenched muscles, wounded pride. It'll all heal."

"You're shaking! I'll get you a blanket."

"No," she said too quickly, too loudly. She didn't want anything from him. "It's just adrenaline aftershock. I feel fine." How dare the asshole look at her with concerned puppy eyes.

"Sorry we can't search for the mugger or your purse right now. We're stretched pretty thin with the fireworks accident. It put holes in our big display. Greg's trying to rearrange the order so it won't be too noticeable." He glanced around as if making sure no one else was listening. "Not that it'll matter. A storm's moving in. I'm guessing we'll have to shut down and send everyone home."

"You sure it was an accident?" Cassie couldn't help taking a poke. *And not a distraction so you could mug me?*

"Just one of those things that happen." Denny rubbed a knuckle against a sunburned nose that matched his Sparks shirt. That was the fabric she'd seen under the camo, red darkened to burgundy by the twilight.

"Rhonda wants to talk to you," Denny said. "You might have a dollar bill with a note on it from her niece. Something about a birthday party?"

He'd seen through Rhonda's code. The knuckle to the nose again, his nervous "tell." He'd never make it in advertising. Cassie moved a hand toward her cargo pocket to reassure herself the bill was still there. She stopped and massaged a knee instead. "I looked. I don't have it," she lied. *You didn't find it when you tore apart my purse, did you, shithead. I hope your brain is exploding, trying to guess where that dollar is now.*

A staticky voice came from his radio. "I've got to take care of this. If you're really *really* okay."

"I'm not going to clutch my pearls and swoon," Cassie said.

"Can't image you ever doing that." Denny went to Helen's desk. He flipped through a ring binder labeled Emergency Procedures then respond to the call.

Dale, Crystal, and Richie burst in and descended on her. "It was Owen, wasn't it," Richie prompted, obviously delighted by the drama.

"I don't know who it was," Cassie said, wondering if Denny was trying to catch their conversation. "It all happened too fast."

"Did you figure out where Rhonda's dollar might be?" Crystal asked. "I heard her niece drew a unicorn on it for her."

Cassie kept her hand still. She'd almost made a give-away move with Denny. Now she had more control. "No. I wish I remembered having it, but I don't."

"Sorry your cute purse is gone," Crystal said. "You should put a hold on your credit cards right away."

"I don't have a way to do that. My phone is in my purse, wherever that is." If Denny shoved the bag into a trash bin after riffling through it, some lucky dumpster diver could be posting nude photos in her name, calling her friends asking for money, and texting her sisters by now.

Crystal pulled a glittery rectangle with dangling beads out of her back pocket. "You can use mine if you know your passwords. I probably have the apps."

Richie scanned the windows high up on the walls, a cinder block from the ceiling. He paced to the open doorway and peered at the sky through the glare of midway lights. "It's blowing like a son of a bitch," he announced. "We're going to have another tornado for sure."

"Language, Richie," Helen reminded him in a way that indicated she'd done it many times before.

"Sorry, Mrs. S.," Richie replied in the same tone.

"There's no need to go scaring people," Helen said.

"For real," Richie said. "The air's got that spooky feeling, just like last time."

Wind rattled the roof. Crystal navigated the credit card apps like an admiral, efficiently helping Cassie freeze her plastic.

Adam trudged in, as if he hid a world of concern behind official sternness. He went straight to Denny and Helen. "Looks like we've got lightning moving in. Denny, can you coordinate the emergency shut down with the Sparks? No need to panic anyone. Just tell them to follow the plan. There's an officer already at the road who'll manage traffic."

Denny nodded. He flipped through the ring binder again and got busy on the radio.

Weather warnings echoed from cell phones. "Did I call it or what," Richie bellowed. Helen silenced him with a look. He ambled back to his friends, who thumbed their screens, checking the alerts.

"Helen," Adam said, "sorry to do this to you."

She brushed away his concern. "I know. This is a shelter. We keep the door open till you tell us everyone else is gone and our job is done. Don't worry. I've been through this before. I was one of the Sparkles running this place when the first roof got ripped off."

Jessie reached the end of his cone and started crying. Helen went to comfort him. Wrapped in attention, he sobbed harder.

Sarah said Mr. Calhoun was in no danger of dropping dead any time soon—although she didn't phrase it exactly that way. She asked Dale to escort him to the Lutheran church's bus, which would take him back into town. Crystal and Richie went with them for support.

Finally through the urgent business, Adam walked over to Cassie. Patience gone, she jumped up from her chair. "Where's Rhonda?" she demanded.

"Well," Adam said, "she does seem to be out of touch at the moment."

"I really need to talk to you. Quietly." The dollar weighed heavily on Cassie. It needed to be someplace safer than on her person. She shifted, putting her back to Denny, and eased the folded paper out of her pocket. "Rhonda is trying to track this down. You need to examine it but not right now."

Adam produced an evidence bag and had her slide it in. He sealed it and tucked it out of sight.

"There are initials on it," Cassie said. "RS, Russell Sworski."

"I'll check it out," Adam said.

"You're not the least bit surprised I just handed over vital evidence in two murders, are you?"

"That's speculation."

"The 'not surprised' part or the 'vital evidence' part."

"Both."

Cassie folder her arms and glared at him. "I got mugged protecting what's in that bag you whisked away. Well, sort of protecting it. I didn't know I had it, but still, you owe me."

"I am sorry about that," Adam said. "Rhonda and I tried to get a hold of you, and I looked for you here."

"I got Rhonda's message," Cassie said, "which was pretty cryptic. That's all I've heard from her. And I don't answer if I don't recognize the caller ID." Had he used his personal phone? "The number you called from must not be in my contacts." *We'll have to change that.* She hated that her mind flipped to such a thought. She was mad at him and wanted to stay that way for a while. Which was easy, since he should have immediately offered to give her his number but he didn't.

Instead he said officially, blandly, "Rhonda is following up on some information."

"At least tell me this, was Sworski in town a lot? Did he shop at the Market or go to the hardware store?"

"His bank records show a check made out to Goods and Groceries dated October fourteenth. Linda and Greg said they didn't know anything about it. When I questioned Edgar, he went straight to government harassment and demanded a lawyer." Adam rubbed his short, bristly hair. "Look, I have to get this place cleared out."

"Adam, I have to tell you. About the mugging—"

"Later. Wait for me here. Then we can go to the office. This place is solid but it's built on a slab. The VFW is granite and has a basement like a bank vault, probably the safest place in town if we have another tornado. We can take care of the purse snatching there."

Tornado. Cassie wished people would stop bringing it up. She needed to tell Adam about Denny. And about Richie seeing Sworski and Owen together. Sworski buying groceries at Edgar's had some implications, too. She put those on her mental list for their discussion later.

As Adam left, Dale, Crystal and Richie blew in on a heavy gale. Dale reported to his mother then wandered over to Cassie. "Mr. Calhoun is safely in the care of the Lutherans."

"You'd better go home before the weather makes it impossible," Cassie urged.

"I'll wait for my mom," Dale said. "We can take Crystal home, since she lives so close. If that's okay?" he asked Crystal.

Crystal thumbed her phone. "I'll text Missy and tell her I have a ride."

"Richie, you should head out," Cassie said.

"Okay." Richie didn't move any closer to the door.

Denny alternately spoke into the radio and talked to

Helen. The woman clutched Jessie to her chest. Judy Norquist hadn't been located yet.

"You will find his mother," Helen commanded, "and that's that, Denny Zunker. She must be worried to death."

Cuddled against the comforting shoulder, the boy stuck his tongue out at Denny and made a gesture with an extended middle finger. Dale and Richie laughed. Crystal scrunched up her face in disgust.

While she waited for Adam, Cassie worked on the puzzle of the dead men connected by a defaced dollar bill. Two fuzzy circles bobbing around a central core, they reminded her of the elusive Ring Nebula. Seeing the situation clearly might take the same technique.

Averted vision.

Instead of staring directly at the planetary nebula's faint, reflected light, she had to shift her gaze to the side. Then the smoky rings popped into a sharp oval. Sometimes looking away from the center was the only way to see the real shape of a thing.

Don't look straight at the two men, look at the people and events around them.

Sworski came to Glacier Falls geared up to illegally shoot deer with his pals. Plural. That was definitely an Owen-related activity. According to Richie, they knew one another, probably going back to when Owen delivered liquor in the Minneapolis area. Sworski's restaurant could have been on his route.

Cassie mentally marked Owen as one of the pals.

What if during his poaching trip, Sworski suddenly craved frozen waffles and Fig Newtons? It was too late to go to the Falls Market. Goods and Groceries was the only place open. Used to the city-way of doing things—as Cassie had been when she'd moved back here—he wasn't carrying much cash. He was surprised Edgar didn't take credit cards and only trusted your check if you were third-generation local, could prove you had a job, and didn't have any visible tattoos. Okay. Maybe not the last thing.

Except Edgar *had* taken the check from a Minneapolis bank. What could convince the conspiracy-theory miser to break his own rule?

Sworski couldn't use Owen, aka Pal Number One, as a character reference. Edgar would have told him to shove his worthless piece of paper into an uncomfortable personal location, and perform a creatively painful act involving tender anatomy and innocent wildlife.

Sworski, to show what an honorable, important guy he was, scrawled out a free pass to his strip club on a dollar bill and gave it to Edgar as a good faith gesture, probably declaring it was worth more than his purchases.

What a deal! It was like getting paid double. Who could refuse that?

Edgar could.

He was all about the cash. It would take more than a lone dollar to convince him the check wouldn't bounce.

Enter another member of the poaching gang. Pal Two, a local who was not Owen, assured Edgar that Sworski had oodles of money.

The paranoid store owner accepted the check not because Pal Two convinced him, but because he knew he could collect from PT if the paper came back stamped insufficient funds.

Pal Two must have been relieved when the check cleared with no hitch. Bet that joy didn't last long. Edgar had leverage, and he was one to use it. Pal Two's position in the community would plummet if the Vigilants found out about an association with a scumbag linked to the devil's den they were trying to close down.

Edgar owned PT body and soul.

When Sworski's corpse bobbed to the surface of Beauty Lake, Edgar would have confronted Pal Two. In a panic, Two blamed Pal One, the instigator of the poaching trip. True or not, Edgar believed it and must have been elated with his new power.

Cassie imagined him flourishing the GC bill in Owen's face. *Come near me again and I'll march Pal Two to the sheriff to spill what you did, and you'll be locked up for life.*

Instead of forcing his enemy to back off, the store owner's threat caused an escalation. Although completely unfair, Edgar blamed Pal Two for the shotgun blasts through the window. And he expected PT to help him teach Owen a lesson.

Poor Two, squeezed between a bully and an ogre. Killing Edgar and incriminating Owen got rid of both. All it took was a bit of planning.

The horrible fruit punch churned in Cassie's stomach. If Edgar trusted anyone to vouch for an out-of-town check, it would be a Sparkle or a Spark. She glanced at Denny. He was a thief and a mugger. It sickened her to think he might also be a calculating, premeditated murderer.

Chapter Fifty-Eight

A determined gust propelled Glenna Lowery and Judy Norquist through the open doorway of the fairgrounds building. Heavily outlined eyes wide, ghost hair sticking straight out from their heads, Cassie thought they looked as if they'd just escaped from shock therapy.

Jessie screamed with joy. He struggled in Helen's arms until she released him. He launched himself at his mother, tackling her legs with a force that almost knocked her to the floor. Rain suddenly pinged in waves against the metal roof. Judy caught her breath and used it to yell at Jessie for getting lost. Unaffected by the scolding, he babbled at her about chocolate ice cream.

"Okay, folks," Denny said, "time to vacate the premises. The only ones left are us and the emergency team. Leave everything. We'll clean up tomorrow."

Helen tossed markers and a clipboard into a canvas bag. She sent Dale around the room to turn off and unplug whatever shouldn't be left running. Crystal stashed a pitcher of fruit punch in the refrigerator. Cassie was uncertain what to do. "Helen," I'm supposed to wait here for Adam."

"I'll try to reach him," Denny said.

"Thanks," Cassie forced out.

Judy picked up Jessie and headed for the door. Glenna gave Cassie a little smile as she followed. Ducking in from the rain, Ryan bumped into them. His wet salt and pepper hair had tightened into boyish curls. His jacket and pants dripped dark puddles on the concrete floor. He slammed the door against the outside gale. "Sorry about this, but it's dangerous out there. We'll have to stay put."

Helen reversed her motions, pulling out the markers and clipboard. "Well, this is a good place to be. All safe and cozy. Crystal, why don't you find chairs for Judy and her friend."

The door flew open. Raymond, Greg, Irv and Harry crowded through the opening. Frigid wind-driven rain propelled Father Anderson, Reverend Gunther, Adam, and a few stranglers after them. They stood shivering and dripping, soaked to the bone.

Dale grabbed blankets from the supply cupboard and handed them out. Helen produced an industrial-size insulated coffee pot from under the kitchen counter. Cassie and Crystal toted steaming cups to the new arrivals.

Dale stopped Crystal mid-delivery with a remark that made her laugh. Raymond tossed a blanket around his neck as if it were a discarded towel. With the efficiency of a border collie, he swooped between the two, separating his daughter from an undesirable companion. He grabbed two chairs from the rack and herded Crystal to the edge of the room for a family discussion.

Dale found a piece of wall to slouch against. Cassie splashed out coffee for herself and paced over to Dale. She desperately needed to talk to Adam, but the room had gotten crowded. She'd have to be patient. "Crystal looks trapped," she said softly.

Dale glared at Raymond. "The night of the murder, she saw something. Now she thinks her dad killed Edgar, and Owen knows it and blackmailed him out of the Mustang."

Cassie took a moment to process. That would explain the girl's need to view the scene through a telescope. "Could it have been Raymond you saw?"

"Don't know," Dale said. "Can't talk about it here." He pushed off from the wall and walked over to Richie, who dug through a box of ancient games.

Greg shook his phone. "That's not going to make bars pop up on the screen," Harry said. "We're all stuck with no cell service, and the landline is dead."

Helen tried to hand Greg coffee, but he wouldn't take it. "Is one of the Petrosky girls babysitting your kids?"

Greg nodded, staring at the screen. "Yeah. Heather, I think. Or Jennifer."

"There're level-headed girls," Helen said. "Whichever one it is will have your kids tucked away in the basement safe as can be."

"Linda's at the store all alone," Greg said. "She's scared to death. I told her to close up and head home. I have to stop her, so she won't get caught outside in this." He turned to leave.

Harry grabbed his arm. "Greg, you can't even walk in this wind. You'll never make it to your car."

Greg shook off his hand. "I'm going." He pulling a blanket over his head like a hood and rushed toward the door. Ryan blocked his path. "You'll get killed out there. That won't help Linda any."

Greg pushed past him. Adam stood between him and the exit. "No one leaves until I say so." Irv and Dale towered behind Officer Berger. "I'll arrest you if I have to," Adam said. "Now sit down and drink the damn coffee."

Greg looked past Adam to the father and son, six foot three pillars of farm-hardened muscle. He let the blanket slip to his shoulders in defeat. Helen put a hot cup in his hand. Father Anderson and Reverend Gunther murmured comforting words and escorted him to a chair.

Greg's anguish tightened the tension in the room. Cassie strolled the length of the rectangle, restless. Would she ever get a chance to talk to Adam?

Glenna shook a cigarette from a pack and joined her. "Wish I could light up." She twirled the stick nervously.

Lightning pulsed through the high windows. Despite the noisy storm, Jessie slept in his mother's lap. Glenna had taken the other children home while Judy looked for the lost boy. She'd returned to find Jessie still missing and the fairgrounds being evacuated. "At least the Dodge didn't leave me stranded on the road. It was risky driving it here the first time, but the kids wanted to come so bad."

"I hope they're okay at the farmhouse," Cassie said.

"I'm really worried about them, too," Glenna said. "They're probably standing in the yard watching for funnel clouds." She glanced toward the sleeping child. "Judy gets real upset when Jess does stuff like this. I hope he outgrows it soon."

Cassie didn't think that would ever happen. The system was working too well for the boy.

Glenna tipped her head toward Crystal playing a game on her phone while Raymond tried to have an earnest conversation with her. "That's his daughter, isn't it. She's soooo pretty. I bet her bedroom is all pink and white, and she has a canopy over her bed and her own credit card. Some people are born lucky." She rubbed the angel figure dangling from her necklace as if it could bring her some of that good fortune.

Cassie wondered if that's what Glenna would have if she could. Pastel and cream. Flounces and bows. She doubted Crystal's life was as ideal as the other girl imagined. Still, there was much to envy in being cared for and protected while you're trying to figure out how the world works.

Glenna gestured as if to touch Cassie's arm. Instead she clutched her hands together, the unlit cigarette between two fingers ready for a drag. "I want to say thanks for getting Owen freed. Even though he went off and did crazy stuff as soon as he got out. I knew they'd listen to you." She leaned close without making contact. "'Cause of your gift and everything."

"Glenna, what makes you think I'm psychic?"

The girl bit her lower lip. "Don't worry. You didn't slip or anything and give it away." She spoke as if they were conspirators. "I never would have guessed if I hadn't been inside your house that time Owen got so mad and pushed me out of the truck. It was real sudden and you weren't expecting company, so I saw what I shouldn't have. Books with stars on the cover and a magazine page with the Zodiac.

"Then you talked to me like you saw my whole life in a vision or something, and I knew you had the gift. I didn't tell no one but Judy. She'd never say nothin' to no one, either. She didn't even really believe me until you come to the farm and I was telling you about having the truck on Wednesday nights. You were nice and didn't say anything, but I could tell you saw right into what I was thinking, about meeting *him*."

Now Cassie understood. Glenna confused astronomy with astrology, and she'd lumped in psychic ability as well.

Who was the mysterious him Cassie was supposed to have plucked from Glenna's mind? The girl's sunken, pale blue eyes heavily outlined in smeared black kept flicking to Crystal and her father.

Raymond.

With a jolt, Cassie understood she was wrong about the events on Wednesday nights. Glenna didn't get beer, go home and pass the truck to Owen so he could meet Raymond. It was Glenna, cold six-pack stashed in the back, who drove the truck to Beauty for the secret rendezvouses.

Cassie had been a sliver away from shutting down the psych-astrology thing. Ashamed of herself, she used it. "Owen set you up with Raymond."

"I was real stupid." Glenna's voice was barely audible over the pounding hail. "I thought it was just about the drugs, and that didn't seem so bad. Owen had me meet Ray casual like. You know, just bumping into one another a couple of times like normal.

"And I did that and Ray pretended he wasn't married. And I told him this story Owen made me memorize about how I was in this terrible accident and wrecked my back and it still hurt real bad.

"Then I said I was out of pain killers. That's exactly what I had to say. Pain killers. Not oxy. No drug name or street slang. I couldn't call my doctor in Minneapolis to get my prescription renewed because I don't have insurance and I owe the guy a lot of money because of the accident. Owen gave me an empty bottle with a label that said exactly the kind of pills he wanted.

"I felt like an actress." Glenna gestured with the cigarette. "I bet I could be one if I tried. I told Ray I was in agony and couldn't sleep. I asked, real polite and sad-eyed if he could just get me a half dozen pills to help me out until I got an appointment with a doctor here. I said I'd find a way to pay him and I'd be really grateful. Owen said any screwing was up to me." She gave a tired laugh. "Yeah, as if a guy was going to just do me a favor without a fuck. Even a nice guy like Ray."

At first Glenna gave Raymond a few bucks for the prescription drugs, far less than they were worth. Owen insisted she make Raymond take the cash, no matter how much he protested.

Clever, Cassie thought, *it turned the pharmacist into a pusher, selling drugs illegally to someone who was probably still a minor.*

"Then I said I was broke," Glenna told her. "Ray gave me the stuff anyway. Then Owen made me ask him for money. I didn't want to, but Ray is really rich. Have you seen his house? I've never been in it, but the outside is like what people on TV live in. And we were really involved by then. A permanent relationship, so I guess it was okay. Except Owen took almost all of it and only let me have a little."

Cassie listened with a sinking heart. Money along with sex made it prostitution.

"It's sad," Glenna said. "He's this old, balding guy with a frigid wife, and he's trying to act like a high school stud."

Cassie had a flash of the rusty truck idling in her driveway. A troubled Glenna had sat in the cab, wanting to talk to her psychic friend. "When you went to meet Ray the night of the murder, what did you see?"

"I suppose you know all about that," Glenna said. "I was late, 'cause of the truck being ripped off for a while. There usually aren't any lights on at Ray's, so he can watch for me and know to come meet me. I always park in the same place.

"That night it felt weird, like maybe I'm sort of psychic, too. I didn't turn on the dirt road that goes to the lake 'cause I thought I saw lights already there. I stayed on the tar and kept driving to where I could see the house. The place was all lit up. I was already real nervous and everything, so I got out of there.

"I really wanted to talk to you. Everything was screwed up and I was worried to death about what was going on at Ray's. But I couldn't 'cause Owen would be mad if he knew. Good thing I took off. When I was almost to town there were cop cars and stuff acting like they owned the whole road. I quick made a turn so they wouldn't see me. Glad I didn't know what was going on. Mostly I was just thinking of how to explain things to Owen."

Cassie wondered who, other than the participants, knew about the short-term money maker and long-term scam Owen and Glenna had lured Raymond into. The man seemed so pathetically normal, sitting beside his teenage daughter who ignored him. Not that Cassie had any sympathy for the pervert drug dealer.

The hail blew away, replaced by rain that crashed against the windows like a waterfall. The lights flickered and went out.

"Just stay put," Helen yelled. "Everything's fine."

Emergency beacons positioned near the ceiling snapped on. Glenna shivered like a ghastly ghost in the shadowy glow. "Sometimes I like storms. Sometimes I don't."

Cassie felt the same. "Tonight is definitely a don't."

Chapter Fifty-Nine

So he wouldn't accidentally glance toward Crystal and her dad, Dale watched Cassie and Glenna do laps together. Complete opposites, they still appeared to have plenty to talk about. He wandered over to get coffee, even though Father Anderson and Reverend Gunther stood next to it, discussing Vigilant strategy with his mom.

"We must do more," Father Anderson said. "God is using these storms to warn us. By allowing that den of the devil to exist in our midst, we have turned into a town of sin. We will be struck down like Sodom and Gomorrah, the just along with the evildoers."

"You're being a bit melodramatic," Reverend Gunther said.

Dale wondered if anyone else noticed the similarities between the priest's words and the crap-filled opinions in the newspaper. His mom read them out loud sometimes. They were all written by that low-tech troll nobody in town seemed to know. "You sound like those letters to the editor," Dale said, playing innocent.

Father Anderson sputtered, suddenly speechless. Helen's eyes lit up with the glow of the light bulb that had just gone off in her head. "I should have remembered right away. Your grandfather was Dwight something Kinsley. When we put together the parish cookbook a few years ago, we included family histories along with the recipes."

Reverend Gunther looked as if his pet poodle had pissed on the carpet. "Bill, you wrote those letters?" He launched into a sermon on non-violence and ethics.

Dale wished he dared to hit that hypocrite Gunther with what Richie had told him. Instead he eased over to where the Sparks were talking about the fire at Edgar's, and edged in beside his dad. They'd had a bonding moment, standing shoulder to shoulder, backing up Berger when Greg had tried to run out and get himself killed in the storm; and it felt good.

"Simple delayed incendiary," Ryan said. "Get it ready to go and you can be a block away by the time it starts smoking. Whoever set it didn't even try to make it look like an accident."

"Kids' stuff," Denny added. "Sherman and Richie could figure out how to do it from YouTube."

Greg kept his phone in his hand, as if the contact could bring it back to life. "They had plenty of reasons to do it, too, for all the times my father-in-law had to kick them out of the store."

Irv's face flashed scarlet. "You guys saying my son started that fire?"

Denny held up his hands, as if to declare peace. "Irv, that's not what I meant."

Dale affected a calm bravado, but it was a thin veneer over his anger. "Denny, when you discover scratch marks in the new paint job on your precious Silverado, think of me." He turned to Greg. "Maybe you and your wife set the fire. That night she had the store locked. She was waiting for you, so you could do it together."

"I was at bingo," Greg said.

"I saw you drive into the alley," Dale shouted, "just before the fire."

Greg didn't look at Dale. He spoke to the Sparks, as if they'd all accused him. "Linda called me. She heard a noise behind the store and she was scared because of the shooting. I told her to lock the doors. I ducked out for a few minutes and went to calm her down. When I got there, I saw Sherman walking away. He'd been prowling around outside the store, terrorizing my wife."

"Liar," Dale said.

"Sherman, I'll handle this," Irv said.

"My name is Dale, and I can defend myself." He squeezed his hands into fists and stared daggers at Greg, Denny, and his father. "I didn't terrorize anyone and I didn't start that fire." He wanted to run away so he wouldn't punch any of them, but he was stuck here.

Ryan intervened. "We can straighten this out. Greg, when you got to the store where was Dale?"

"Crossing Central."

"Did you see him in the alley?" Ryan asked.

"No, but Linda heard him. And then he went into the store, pretending he was a regular customer."

"She heard noises," Ryan said calmly. "Did she actually see anyone in the alley?"

"No, no she didn't," Greg admitted.

"So Dale went into the store and bought what he needed, then left." Ryan said.

"I guess," Greg said. "Sorry, Irv. Really. Sorry, uh, Dale. Linda's alone in this storm and I'm worried as hell is all."

"Yeah, okay." Irv stalked away like it definitely wasn't okay. Greg retreated to the isolation of the men's room.

It wasn't okay with Dale either. He'd gotten a half-ass apology and a limp excuse, and now everyone was calling him Dale like it was street slang six months past trendy.

"I wasn't accusing you of anything, honest," Denny said.

"Yeah, I get that." Dale tried not to watch his mom intercept his dad for a whispered conversation. The Steinhaus family dynamics were too raw and personal and, at the moment, too public.

He told himself he wasn't anything like his dad. Mostly it was true. Then bam! His inherited hair trigger went off, and there was nothing he could do about it. He'd done a pretty good job of making a drama scene on his own. His parents not-at-all-private argument was just a bonus embarrassment.

He couldn't look at Crystal. She must be staring at him in horror. "I didn't mean to say that about your truck," he told Denny.

Well, I didn't mean to say it out loud, Dale thought.

Chapter Sixty

"I know who attacked me and grabbed my purse." It hadn't been easy for Cassie to maneuver Adam into a space where they could talk without being overheard.

Emergency lights flooded the shelter with an unearthly, cool light. Dale, Richie, Jessie and Glenna played a kids' game they'd found in a box of castoff toys. The peeling board and plastic pieces appeared older than the four of them added together.

Arms crossed, feet sticking out in front of him, Father Anderson snored in one of the uncomfortable folding chairs. Greg stared at his phone. If the cell towers still stood, it was unlikely a signal could pierce the storm.

Adam seemed to doubt Cassie had figured out the identity of her attacker while drinking coffee and listening to thunder and hail. "It might be hard for you to accept," she told him. "It's the same person who stole the bingo deposit. And I don't think that robbery and my purse were the only thefts. It looks like skimming has been going on for some time."

"Skimming." Adam folded his arms.

"From bingo."

"But who took your purse?"

"The skimmer."

Adam scowled. "A name would be more useful. We both know who's in charge of that money, so don't go saying Rhonda."

The heavens shattered with a deafening crack. The door burst open. Framed in the rectangle, a jagged shaft of molten light divided the sky, silhouetting a great, egg-shaped figure. As if called down from some stellar plain, the woman barreled in, bright and glistening in a yellow slicker with matching floppy hat and boots. Rivulets flowed from her as if she were a fountain. They formed a moat that moved with her as she stepped in and slammed the door shut. She whipped off her hat and shook out her red mane, sending spray flying. "At least we don't have boring weather," Rhonda declared.

"Denny Zunker," Cassie whispered to Adam.

"Denny Zunker," Rhonda said forcefully, "I am taking you into custody for questioning, concerning theft and assault of an officer of the law."

"Me?" Denny's narrow face drained to ash. "All the electricity in the air has messed up your brain, Rhonda." He tried to laugh, but the hard expression on her face choked off his efforts.

Adam commandeered a back corner opposite the kitchenette for a makeshift cell. Rhonda instructed Denny, on his honor and under penalty of severe storm, to stay within a border of folding chairs. Then she recited his rights.

"I'd like to consult with my client," Harry told Rhonda and Adam. When Cassie had been warned to watch out for his dog Chewbacca, she'd thought it was because he was vicious. It turned out Chewy was blind and deaf, and prone to napping in the middle of the street. The local motorists were used to swerving so they wouldn't disturb him.

"Harry, you're retired," Rhonda said. "And you practiced real estate law."

"Still a lawyer," Harry said.

"Find out where he ditched my purse," Cassie said.

Rhonda, Adam, and Cassie positioned themselves so the two officers could watch the prisoner while he conversed nose to nose with his new defender. "I'm glad to see you're all right," Cassie said to Rhonda.

"I was worried about you, too, hon," Rhonda said. "Sorry I couldn't get here sooner. I ran into a downed power line on 28. Had to direct traffic until the highway patrol arrived."

"Remember me," Adam said, "the one without a clue? Rhonda, you've got a lot to fill in."

"The clue is in your pocket," Cassie said.

Adam pulled out the crinkled rectangle sealed in plastic.

"That's what I've been looking for." Rhonda tapped the transparent bag with a bright blue nail. "I know for a fact, this was the only dollar in the bingo deposit with marks that match my polish."

"I'm not hearing a reason to arrest anyone," Adam said.

"I'm getting there." Rhonda shed her slicker and handed her rain gear to Helen in exchange for a blanket. She rubbed a corner of the flannel across her damp hair. "On Monday bingo was robbed. Thursday morning I saw Denny pull a dollar marked with blue out of his wallet and give it to Cassie as change for a donation to the Tvrdik family."

Adam did some quick calculating. "If it's the same Admit One, that's about a sixty-hour gap. Denny could have gotten it when he broke a twenty or won it playing poker. We'll have to put together a timeline of his movements."

"And we need his financial records," Rhonda said. "This is bigger than a couple of shove and grabs."

"You mean like skimming from bingo?" Cassie said.

"Very clever of you to figure that out, Ms. Windom," Rhonda said. "I feel foolish not realizing it before this. Whatever else is going on, Denny's done a lot of good for this town. Of course, that doesn't make up for breaking the law.

Allegedly. I didn't click to it until I got a call back from the owner of a gun shop in Minneapolis."

Adam looked bewildered but patient. "A guy from the Cities tipped you off?"

Rhonda gave a wicked grin. "You know I have a way of getting intel from gun shop guys. Sworski bought more than fancy hunting gear. He also wanted a scrimshaw-handled knife, just like the one in the photo his hunting buddy showed him that had been purchased from that very store."

"Oh." Another chunk fell into place for Adam. "You mean the *famous* knife. The Sparks' going away present for Amy Miller."

"Special order. Clay sent me information on it," Rhonda said.

Adam gave a slow smile. "Would that be Clay Geisler? You two on a first-name basis now?"

"We are, but it will stay professional—when I'm on duty." Rhonda seemed more than a little pleased. "Adam, remember how expensive the knife was? It actually cost eighty dollars less than Denny said it did, eighty dollars less than he collected."

"I suppose no one asked to see a receipt," Cassie said. The Sparks ran into blazing buildings together. That was a pretty strong trust-building exercise.

"I doubt anyone even thought to," Rhonda said. "It made me think of all the times Denny's collected for charities and events. Over the years he's had access to a lot of unrecorded cash."

"Did he do fund raising for the Faith Lutheran Community Center?" Cassie asked.

"He practically ran the committee," Rhonda said. "Why?"

"I'll explain later." Cassie wondered if that was the reason Reverend Gunther had to creatively acquire lumber.

"Cassie, I didn't mean to put you in the center of the bull's eye," Rhonda said, "but I needed you to hang on to that dollar. And I couldn't just put out an APB for Denny. My fellow officers would have thought I'd gone bat-guano crazy, and too many of the Sparks are scanner junkies. I didn't want anyone to accidentally tip off Denny."

Cassie could imagine it happening. Ryan or Greg—or Irv or Helen or any of the other Sparks or Sparkles—hears the radio call and says, "Hey, Denny, there's something screwy going on. Why would Rhonda be ordering your arrest?"

Rhonda scrunched up the damp blanket and dropped it on the floor next to her chair. "Cassie, when you didn't answer the phone or respond to my message, I used the network I had. I thought I was being clever with the stuff about my niece. I hoped you'd tumble to it. I didn't think Denny would, but he must have figured it out. Maybe my secret isn't so secret after all."

Adam looked like he was still trying to squeeze the pieces into a coherent picture. "What's this about your niece and a secret?"

"That's personal," Rhonda said. "Forget you ever heard it."

Adam shook his head. "That's not likely to happen. And you can't keep secrets for long in a town this size."

"You'd be surprised," Rhonda said.

A banshee wailed, long and steady. The warning siren fought to be heard through hail pounding on the metal roof.

Tornado.

"They spotted one," Irv said wistfully, as if he wished he was the brave hero out in the rain and wind, catching first sight of a terrifying twister reaching down from the green sky to touch the earth.

"Everyone, listen up," Helen shouted. "Safest place is in the bathrooms. I think we can all fit."

Cassie thought she was overly optimistic about the side-by-side spaces. Out of habit and embarrassment, they'd probably split up by gender. There were more males than females. It would be interesting to see how this went.

Rhonda deposited Denny and his real estate lawyer in the Gents. "Stay put. I don't want anything to happen to my prisoner." She and Adam herded the strays who'd gotten stranded at the fairgrounds through the matching doors and got them settled. "Let's go, guys," Adam yelled at those left in the large room.

Greg and Ryan fumbled with batteries and flashlights. "One more minute," Ryan called.

"Gents is full," Rhonda shouted.

"I want to see the tornado," Jessie shrieked.

Judy tugged at his hand. "Do this and you can have oranges and Fruit Loops when we get home."

Jessie plopped onto the floor, spread out like a petulant snow angel, and wouldn't budge.

"We should pray for God's mercy, that this disaster will pass us by and we will be spared." Father Anderson said.

Reverend Gunther looked startled, as if he wished he'd thought of that. "Let's join hands," he added.

"You can join hands in the bathroom." Rhonda rushed them into the Ladies.

Dale and Richie hung back, as if they'd rather die than be crammed into a toilet. "We're good out here," Richie said.

"Yeah, me too," Crystal said.

"Stop being a stubborn fool," Irv yelled at Dale. He left his son and squeezed into the packed men's room.

"Get in there," Raymond barked at his daughter, "or I'll carry you in."

Crystal stood her ground. "Why was Owen Norquist driving the Mustang, Dad!"

Raymond tackled his daughter and slung her over his shoulder as if she were a bag of laundry. He streaked toward the shelter of porcelain and pipes, paused before the two doors, then swerved into the Ladies.

"You can put sugar on the Fruit Loops," Judy cooed at Jessie, trying to coax him off the floor.

"I'll cut the oranges for you, just the way you like them," Glenna said.

Cassie scooped up the boy without a word and carried him to the only bathroom that still had space. His entourage scurried after them. She passed him to Judy then shoved the three through the narrow door.

Juggling flashlights, Ryan and Greg secured the cupboards. Adam gestured to Richie and Dale. "Come on."

"I can't," Richie said. "I've got that closet thing."

"Claustrophobia," Dale said.

"Yeah, that." Richie took a flashlight from Ryan.

"They're both full anyway," Cassie told them.

Adam surveyed the room. "Okay, next best place is the kitchenette."

The emergency lights faltered, but held. The wind suddenly vanished. Hail ceased its assault.

"Damn," Rhonda whispered.

Adam corralled them into the slim nook between the row of drawers and appliances lining the wall, and the Formica-covered counter sticking out into the room.

Cassie sat on the bare cement floor between Dale and Ryan. Knees scrunched up to her chin, she leaned back against the refrigerator. What was she doing here? Sandwiched between laminated shelving and a Kenmore, when she could be in a nice, smog-choked metropolis on the ocean side of the San Andreas Fault.

She could go back. Her lease on the cabin was only for a year. It would mean returning to a tiny apartment. And shutting down her own business, since she couldn't earn enough independently to pay California-level expenses. And giving up Jupiter. And her telescope. What would she do with the jumble of boxes the widow had forced on her? She could offer the star charts showing the constellations to Glenna.

Cassie slapped a hand to her horrible bangs. *Oh, crap!*

She'd packed Glenna into unforgiving, tight, sweaty quarters with Raymond and Crystal.

Maybe the two preachers snuggled into the women's bathroom with them could provide guidance.

Not likely. The cramped space and cloying fragrance of potpourri was not conducive to slogging through relationship dynamics. Besides, before Crystal dealt with her father having an under-aged mistress, she needed to resolve the "my dad might be a murderer" thing.

What had Crystal witnessed that made her think her dad had killed Edgar? Cassie couldn't quiz Dale about it. This was no place for a private conversation.

She closed her eyes and panned across the scene as she'd viewed it from Red Hawk. Champaign (not beige) house with a patio and large, second-floor windows. Foot bridge over a gap in the terrain. Sumac bushes, unidentifiable shrubs, tall grasses. Wells by the patrol car, playing out the scene so it matched forensic evidence.

She imagined the view at night. From the Swenson house, movement in the truck's headlamps would be stark highlights and deep shadows void of detail. To see the real action, to see the killer's face, you'd have to be on the murder side of the bridge.

And someone was.

"Adam, Rhonda." They were hunkered down past Dale and Richie at the opening to the kitchenette. Cassie got her feet under her and crouched.

"Stay down," Ryan told her.

"Adam!" She pushed up higher to see him, her head rising above the counter top. This couldn't wait. "Edgar's murder, there was another witness. Not just Dale. Someone close. *Really* close."

The roar of a rushing train bore down on the shelter. The corrugated roof rippled like a giant gray-winged heron. It twisted and tore with a woeful screech, struggling for freedom.

Suddenly loose, it fluttered off into the night, drawing the shelter's air with it.

Cassie gasped like a fish in the desert. Wind rushed into the vacuum with an angry bellow. Chairs, paper cups, and plastic toys spun in the turbulence and smashed against the cinder-block walls.

A dislodged emergency light sent a beacon upward through the gaping hole, as if searching for the culprit who'd caused this chaos.

In the beam, Cassie saw a bright silver Chevy pickup cruise overhead like a blazing meteor.

Chapter Sixty-One

A flying truck? Well, that was just begged for drunken word play.

Cassie wondered if she'd really seen it. Is that what had knocked her down? She felt as if she'd been hit by something bigger.

She pushed away debris, braced herself against a solid, flat surface and slowly rose. The light was too dim, too slanted, too blurry. She swiped a hand across her forehead and felt wet bangs stuck to her skin.

Arms supported her staggering steps. Metal clanked. A cold, hard chair was suddenly under her. "Stay right here. I'll get Sarah."

Where would I go? She'd already sprinted across more than half of the United States. Pacific Ocean to Mississippi River. Western Expansion in reverse.

Tangled voices chaotically buzzed around her. One detached from the rest and spoke close to her ear, soft and soothing. "You're hurt. I'll take you to the hospital."

Arms helped her stand and urged her forward. Were they the same as before? That was only a moment ago, wasn't it?

She let herself be guided. A muggy breeze pressed against

her. She smeared a trickling warmth above her left eye. A step and a step and a step. How many had she taken?

Hardness turned mushy under the soles of her sandals. It was darker than before. Tendrils tickled her ankles. Grass.

Grass and grass. It was such a long, long walk to the hospital. She bumped against a rough-barked pillar felled by some giant.

"Climb over," the voice said. "You can do it."

"I'll jump it. Like a hurdle." *Like the Olympics.*

"Don't do that. Just sit on it and swing your legs over."

"That's a better plan." Cassie followed directions.

She tried to blink away the blurriness. Abstract shapes filled a monochrome world. All objects seemed equally close and equally far, like a painting without perspective.

It will be brighter when the clouds go away. "Waxing gibbous moon. Sixty-seven percent illumination. Sets at 3 a.m." Had she said that out loud? She thought so, but it might have just been in her head. Which felt wrapped in yards of flannel. Yards and yards.

Water lapped in a slow rhythm. She smelled the wet algae of the river and hesitated. There were supposed to be straight-edged shapes here. "No picnic tables."

Numbness floated through her body like a weary ghost. What was she doing again? Oh, she remembered. "Do you think we'll find the hospital soon? I'm pretty sure I'm going to faint. Or vomit. Either one." *Maybe both.*

Cassie's escort kept a firm grip on her arm and held her tightly around the waist. "You're doing great. We don't have to go all the way to the hospital, just to the ambulance. It's waiting for us. You can do this."

The voice was so calm and comforting. "Who saw Edgar's murder?" it asked.

She batted away the question with a floppy hand. "I know that part. I'm still trying to paint the rest of the picture." She made curlicues in the air. *Doodle, doodle, doodle, doodle, doodle,* she sang in her head. "Like why was Sworski killed?" She laughed. "It sure wasn't about poaching."

She stopped, jolting her supporter. "I have to sit down." She let her knees buckle and sank toward the inviting grass.

Awkward arms kept her upright. "We're close now. A few more steps."

"I can't. Honestly. The ambulance will have to come to me."

"There's no road here."

"This is the country. People drive into corn fields. And park on a meadow. And make their own roads because they want to go to a special spot at the lake."

A wind blew past her ear. Or maybe it was an exhausted sigh.

"We'll make a deal," the voice said. "If you keep walking, I'll tell you something important I know about Russ Sworski's murder. Then you'll tell me something important you know about Edgar's murder."

"That sounds really, really fair." Light-headedly happy about the arrangement, Cassie let herself be shoved across uneven terrain. Maybe they were going to the mountains. That could be fun.

"There's this liquor warehouse in Minneapolis," Voice said. "Russ knew a guy who worked there. It was simple. Just go to the place, load up a few cases and drive away. Then deliver them to Russ' restaurant. Owen had done something like it for him before. Not exactly the same, but sort of."

Lumber. First it's here and then it's there. And then it's another there. Cassie wasn't sure why that popped into her head.

"Shit." The person tripped then recovered. "You've heard this before? Who told you?"

"No, no. Don't stop. What happened next?" She liked this bedtime story.

"Owen said he wasn't going to drive his truck all the way to

Minneapolis when there was a whole lot of liquor a whole lot closer. The Municipal would be easy to break into. Seems Owen had thought about it and just never gotten around to doing it. Russ could come along for fun. Then he could take the booze back to the Cities himself. Russ didn't like that. The guy he knew at the warehouse would do a thing with the inventory and no one would know stuff was missing. But the Municipal would report the theft to the sheriff's office, and there'd be an investigation."

Adam. There was something she was going to tell Adam.

"And Justin, Sheriff Wells, he doesn't let go of a thing once he's got his teeth into it. Owen said he'd do it his own way or not at all. And liquor cases are heavy. He'd get a kid he knew to do the hauling."

Richie. Cassie worried about Dale worrying about his friend.

"Crap." The arms lurched. Cassie's support was gone. "Sorry," Voice said. She thumped to the ground. It seemed like a good place to take a nap.

The figure loomed over her. "How do you know so much?"

Cassie scraped around for leaves to pile into a pillow. "I read a lot. And I have sisters. It's sort of self-defense."

"No, I mean about—" There was a huff of frustration.

Darn, she'd upset Voice and broken the story. The arms hoisted her back to her feet.

"You're heavier than you look. You have to help me out here."

Sure. Sure. I'll walk if you talk. Russ must have been really mad. Wow, she'd never met the guy and she was calling him by his first name.

"He was beyond mad. In a flash Russ switched from buddy to boss. He told Owen there would be no kid. Owen would do exactly as he was told or Russ would turn him in for stuff he did before. Owen called him crazy because Russ was more guilty than Owen, and had a lot more at stake. Russ laughed. Right in Owen's face."

You shouldn't laugh at Owen. Everyone knows that. How did she know that?

"Yeah, that was a mistake. Russ said he had lots of lawyers. They'd make sure Owen took the fall. Russ would be sitting in his hot tub sucking on a cold beer while Owen served hard time. He said it a lot cruder than that, but you get the idea.

"Then Russ did the dumbest thing you can imagine. He turned his back on Owen. Owen grabbed him and yanked him so hard. Like he was tossing him out of his way. Like the guy was garbage and not a person. I can still hear his skull crack when he slammed into the tree."

And the body went in the lake. Splush! Strange, her escort was panting but she felt fine. Weightless as a dancing snowflake in a tulle tutu.

"It wasn't as easy as that, but, yeah, the body ended up in Beauty."

Ohh, she'd said it out loud. She'd ruined his punch line. Bad manners. What else had she said that she thought was only in her head?

"Your turn. Tell me about the other murder."

The other murder. *Vicky.* Cassie wanted to lie down again, so she could spend time with her friend. It didn't matter that the dream always turned into a nightmare.

Vicky!

"Shh, you have to be quiet," Voice said. "We're almost at the hospital. Don't disturb the patients. I don't know Vicky. Was she at the lake? Did she see it happen?"

I miss her. Every single day.

"You need to focus."

I'm not sorry about Jordan. It was wrong. I shouldn't have done it. But I'm not sorry. And I can handle it.

"Who's Jordan?"

Damn, you shouldn't know that name. "He's from another life, not from here."

"You've got blood on your hands."

True. But he's not dead.

"Let's wash it off. There's water right here."

It isn't that easy. Just ask Lady Macbeth.

A coolness seeped into her sandals and covered her ankles. Her feet slipped on a rocky riverbed. She and the voice waded deeper until swirling liquid reached mid-calf.

"Who saw Owen kill Edgar?" Voice was so soothing, so practiced at being calm and reassuring.

Owen didn't kill Edgar. "Someone can look guilty and be innocent." *Shit, Jordan, you deserve what you got, even if you didn't do it.* "If you look out the window of the Swensen house, it's too far away. No details. Just camo."

"No one else saw it happen?" A sharp anger crept in. "Only Sherman?"

You mean Dale. "You can't stare straight at it. You have to look to the side. I bet ambushing Owen was Edgar's idea. Or he was guided into thinking it was. That's what Edgar was expecting. Ambushing Owen, I mean. Pal Two was supposed to lure Owen to the lake for some night fishing." *Lure. For fishing. That's funny.* She'd have to text her sisters. "Edgar's waiting so he and Pal Two can beat up Owen." *Fight violence with more violence. As if that would teach him a lesson, which it wouldn't.* "Edgar really thought it would make up for the window and end the harassment." *Revenge stories always go wrong. Edgar didn't know Pal Two had a different plan.*

"Paul Tu? Is that a name? You're slurring."

"Pal. Two. *The other one.* Russ and Owen's friend."

"Owen doesn't have friends. Just people he uses."

"And abuses. He and Edgar were alike that way."

"Yeah. But the old man had his demons. Owen is an asshole because he likes being an asshole."

"Owen has his pain, too." Cassie breathed in fresh, moist,

smogless air. *Location, location, location.* She laughed. The water made her shiver in a good way.

She squeezed her eyes shut against the fuzzy scene and increasing dizziness. *The killer drove Owen's truck right to where it was supposed to be.* "Paul Tu parked by the lake with the headlights on. Didn't know it was a signal."

"What signal?" Voice demanded.

Not very subtle but better than Glenna shouting, come down to the truck, Ray, and bring drugs.

"Ray and that white-haired girl and drugs."

Don't forget sex and money. "You know about that, too? Damn. It's a secret. Don't tell anyone."

"I won't tell a soul."

"Bet Raymond dove into the bushes in a terror when he saw Edgar walk up to the truck. The second biggest bully in the county discovers an underaged girl with a link to Owen sneaking onto your property." *Zap! Your job, marriage and social standing, suddenly melt to a slag heap.*

But it wasn't Glenna who got out of the cab. Another fit of laughter hit Cassie. *Imagine, expecting to have sex and then fft! Mur-der. Right there. Can't miss it. You're saved from a scandal but loaded with a new dilemma. With your moral compass already bent pretty far from true north, any way you play it, you are dead center in shit city.*

"Sounds like you've put it all together," Voice said. "Too bad you got bonked on the head during the tornado, wandered away and fell into the river."

"I got bonked?" Cassie opened her eyes to the hazy shadow on shadow landscape. She probed her forehead and found a gooey gash. "Is that blood?" *Oh, yeah, out, out damn spot.*

People called her name from far, so very far away, as if she'd gotten herself lost and they were trying to find her. None of them was Vicky.

I tried to wander away. It didn't work. I don't feel lost at all. I feel— I feel overly found.

Her escort forced her to move, feet skidding on submerged

rocks. She shuffled, as if slogging through pudding. Water reached her knees.

We do things sometimes. Unexpected things. Because. Because there should be justice. The world should be set right.

"The world is very wrong," Voice said. "Always has been. Always will be. We can't change that, no matter how hard we try. It's a crooked universe."

Oh, the universe is amazing! Gigantic and beautiful. And it's around us in all directions. That's so awesome.

"Cassie," the Voice said, suddenly in a panic, "did Ray tell you who he saw that night?"

She smooshed a finger against her lips. "He didn't say a word," she mumbled. "I figured it out myself." *Pretty proud of that. Even though it took me a super long time.* Her finger was so heavy. She let her hand fall. "Russ and his paper trail." *I hope he's okay with me calling him Russ.*

"He'd love it," Voice said.

"For a while Edgar thought he was king."

"More like a dictator."

"Power is hard to hold on to," Cassie said. "He was losing his grip." Cassie swished a bloody hand through the air. "Then a bonus floats into my front yard, giving Edgar the ultimate golden leverage to stop you from buying the Falls Market."

Thick, floppy hair topped an echoing silhouette that refused to resolve itself into a single image.

Cassie didn't have to look directly at him to know who it was. "Ring Nebula, Greg. You killed your father-in-law."

The supporting arms vanished. Cassie teetered. A blow struck her chest, slamming her backward. She smacked into the water and plunged to the bottom. Her head slammed against a rock. She flailed at the hands pressing her down.

Submerged, she smelled nothing, yet she recognized Jordan's surf-boy scent of sand and ocean. She saw nothing, but she knew the monster she fought had sun-streaked hair and intense blue eyes.

Jordan had approached her first. Handsome and charming and attentive. She'd turned him down because he was too—too *everything* to be real. Why hadn't Vicky's predator alarm gone off, as Cassie's had?

Why, why, why had Vicky gone back to him after she knew what he was?

Jordan loomed over her, forcing her into silence and submission as he had Vicky. Killing her as he had Vicky. Dulled by the heavy water, his furious words rang clear. "It's your fault! It happened because of you! Because of you!"

Cassie punched and clawed, the way she wished Vicky had. Air. She needed air. She braced her hands on the rocky riverbed, curling her fingers around sand-polished stones. She heaved, propelling herself upward. Her mouth broke the surface enough to gasp. The force knocked him away.

He pounced, shoving her back down into the silty fluid. His hands grasped her throat. Precious oxygen escaped her lungs.

She could have been the body tangled in the crimson-stained sheets. She could have been the corpse in the blood-smeared bedroom.

She could have been the lifeless victim.

But she wasn't.

She wasn't then. And she would not be now.

She stiffened her arms straight out from her shoulders, as if preparing for a loving embrace. She allowed herself to sink to the river bed. He came down with her, leaning close.

She grabbed a stone in each fist and swung upward, hard and fast. A jolt trembled along her rigid arms as she smashed the rocks against Jordan's temples.

Even through muffling liquid, she heard the sharp crack. Again and again in a fury, she drove her grief, her frustration and guilt into the blows.

The vise around her throat eased.

Cassie let the weights drop. They sank with small gurgles. She pushed aside the limp form that pinned her in place.

Released, she floated to the surface and filled her aching lungs. Water swirled around her, cool and comfortable and welcoming. Overhead, the clouds parted. Cygnus the swan, wings stretched wide, soared through the glittering banner of the Milky Way.

Cassie absorbed the peace and let the open river take her.

Chapter Sixty-Two

The Glacier Falls Clinic was packed. Cassie tried to sit still as ordered, while a nurse dressed the wound on her head.

In addition to the staff and the actual tornado patients, she identified people who seemed to be relatives and/or friends of the wounded, and/or volunteers who spontaneously showed up to help. That seemed to cover the town's entire population.

The small medical facility had quickly annexed the insurance company next door to accommodate the crowd. A harried doctor evaluated Cassie, then sent her to the boring ecru-on-ecru office. She tucked herself into a chair and waited for her turn to be transported to the Prairie View Hospital in Esker.

The bright lights helped clear her thinking. Her wet clothes didn't bother her as much as her squishy sandals. A volunteer wrapped her in a fresh blanket. She wasn't sure how she'd gotten the first one, which had grown soggy and smelled like wet dog.

With a clean comforter around her, she realized she was what smelled like wet dog.

She tentatively poked at the gauze covering the gash on the back of her head, then she ran a finger over the bandage on the front. The possibility of a skull fracture or a concussion —or both for all she knew about medicine—put her on the priority list somewhere after chest pains, labor contractions, and broken bones.

Reluctantly she accepted she might be spending the entire night here. She needed to let her parents and her sisters know she was okay, but the location of her phone was still unknown. The platinum white land-line phone on the insurance company's cream counter was tied up with more important calls.

At least the people-watching was entertaining. The patients had matching blankets. Mrs. Finster, arm in a sling, held court as if this was her usual kingdom. "That giant twister swooped out of the sky straight at me. Almost scared me to death."

Blanket tossed over a shoulder, Dale plopped into the chair next to Cassie. "Almost doesn't count. Too bad it didn't drop a house on her." He looked as if he'd been caught in a downpour.

"Are you okay?" Cassie asked him.

"I'm good. I'm supposed to make sure you don't fall asleep. You know, head injury."

"Can I borrow your phone?"

"Dead. It needs your thoughts and prayer, and two days in a bag of rice."

Dale must have gotten drenched in the rain. But that didn't seem right. He'd been in the shelter with her when the deluge hit. Cassie was sure of it. Maybe. Her vision had straightened out but her memory was foggy. "How much damage is there?"

"Tornado slammed the fairgrounds pretty hard. Stripped away everything that wasn't bolted down. And some things that were. All that's left is trash and the cinder-block shell that saved our butts. Another funnel went through town. It's kind of bad some places. Like bombs went off. Lots of injuries. As far as I know, no one died."

"The Norquist kids at the farm? Jupiter?"

Dale shook his head. "No major damage in those areas. They should be good."

"Everyone who was with us, are they okay?"

"Better than you. Except for Greg."

Cassie's heart stopped. "Is he—? Did I—?"

"Sorry to tell you," Dale said, "he survived. You roughed him up good though. He's in the hospital. Not fair he got to cut in line in front of all these other people."

"But he's been arrested, right?"

"For trying to drown you? Yeah. And the other stuff, too. The guy spilled his guts to Berger before he was even in handcuffs. Wah-wah, Edgar treated Linda like shit. Wah-wah, forced me into free labor at G. and G. Wah-wah, threatened to say I was mixed up in the Floater's murder if I tried to buy the Falls Market."

"This seems to be less about Linda and more about purchasing the grocery store," Cassie said. "I think Greg got involved in shady deals with Owen to raise the capital."

"Buying your father-in-law's competition," Dale said. "And I thought family dinners at my house were tense. Hope he saved up a lot. He's going to need a mega-wad for lawyers. Now, after Greg tried to nix you and everything, now that scum Swenson says he saw the guy kill Edgar. He's making an official statement to Wells."

"That must be hard for Crystal."

Dale looked away. "She's with her mom, I guess. It looks like the end of the family Christmas card photos."

Cassie swallowed down a wave of nausea. Was Raymond spilling the whole story? She hoped no one would quiz her about why she suspected he'd witnessed the murder. Glenna had told her in confidence about their relationship, thinking

Cassie was bound by some psychics' code. Although that wasn't a real thing and she wasn't psychic, Cassie felt she had to honor it, like the seal of confession.

Oh, shit. She may have let the details slip to Greg while stumbling around in a shock-induced haze. "I'm having trouble remembering what happened."

"That's probably normal with the trauma and all. We couldn't find you after the tornado. I heard you shout something from down by the picnic tables. Well, where the picnic tables used to be."

Cassie remembered splashing, and Dale shouting at her. "Did you pull me out of the river?"

Dale shrugged. "No major. You're tall, but you don't weight much. You were just floating along like you were enjoying it."

"I think I was." So, she'd been a Floater, too. "Thank you, Dale. I suppose I should give you a raise."

"Good thing I didn't hang back and let Berger try to rescue you. He's a shitty swimmer. He tried to do this little kiddie arm-paddle thing. I almost had to save him, too. I seriously thought about letting him drown, even if you do have a thing for him."

She should protest. Her romantic interests were none of his business. She was too drained to put up a fight. And it felt good to have her defenses gone. "In light of this new information I'll have to review my options. I mean, a Minnesotan who can't swim? And I think he's afraid of dogs."

"Jupiter doesn't like him."

"Well, that does it. He's off the list."

"You know," Dale said. "Denny probably won't do much jail time. He might be able to get over the whole you-testifying-against-him bit."

Cassie dreaded going into another courtroom. "I suppose I'll have to do that. He did knock me down and steal my stuff. I used to like that purse."

Dale flicked a thumb toward the glass doors. Richie and Glenna stood outside in the flood lights. The girl took a drag from her cigarette and blew out a plume. "When Richie's dad gets here, we can take you to the hospital."

"Just get me to the Mini. I'm sure I'm okay to drive if someone is with me."

"Got a key? License? Proof of insurance?"

Cassie groaned. Fob and license were in her purse. Somewhere.

Dale grimaced. "Not that it matters."

"Oh, no. Please, no."

Dale made an up-ward fluttering motion with one hand. "Off into the great unknown. Richie's Bomb is MIA, too."

Through the glass doors Cassie watched Adam walk up the sidewalk from the street. Damp marks streaked his tan uniform. "He looks like he ran through a car wash," Cassie said.

Adam stopped to talk to Richie and Glenna. It seemed like a concerned chat, that he was making sure they were okay. That he was asking about Judy and Jessie. That he wanted to be sure Richie had a ride home. That he was being a nice guy and a good officer of the law. He smiled at Cassie as he came in.

"Maybe he has a phone you can borrow." In a smooth motion Dale was out of the chair and strolling past Adam with a quick "Hey." He was through the door before it swung shut.

"I'm your Uber to the hospital," Adam told her. "The car's outside. I'm sure you'll recognize it, since it's been to your place a few times. I've just got to round up a couple of other people."

Don't let one of them be Mrs. Finster, Cassie thought. This time she was sure she hadn't said it out loud. She stood and settled the blanket on her shoulders like a cape. She rubbed her sore neck. Did she have bruises from Greg's hands squeezing her throat?

Richie held the door open for her. Glenna grabbed her arm as if she needed guidance to go the few steps to the curb. It was nice to have people who watched out for you. Friends who searched for you after a disaster. Who pulled you out of the river. Who gave you a ride when your car was in an unknown location.

But was this the right place for her? There were ten more months left on her lease. Ten months to decide if the move here was the best thing she'd ever done or a gigantic mistake.

Cassie took the front-seat, passenger position in the patrol car. Adam settled three people—none of them Mrs. Finster—in the back.

He got behind the wheel and started the engine. "I've got good news, sort of. Someone discovered your purse hanging from their mailbox near Esker. It should be waiting for you at the hospital."

He guided the cruiser away from the curb. "And a state trooper found a yellow Mini Cooper."

Chapter Sixty-Three

It's always sunny at SunnieChat!

ASHLEY

In a tree

CASSIE

Yes. The mini is in a tree

HOLLY

Hope you have good insurance

KAYLA

The pics are so cool. The yellow really pops out from the leaves that are left

ASHLEY

That's how dad taught me to park too

HOLLY

Glad mom taught me

KAYLA

It could be a birdhouse. For Big Bird

Averted Vision

HOLLY

Treehouse. The kids would love it. You'd be
their favorite aunt ever

CASSIE

I thought I already was

KAYLA

It's a Car-co-nut

ASHLEY

Car-coon

CASSIE

I have to tell you about the flying truck

HOLLY

You can't distract us that easily. Car-nary

ASHLEY

Car-nana

KAYLA

Car-ñata

CASSIE

How did you do that with the n?

ASHLEY

Stay out of this. We're on a roll. Car-terfly

HOLLY

Car-dsu

. . . . .

Acknowledgments

I've had two Akitas. They served as models for Jupiter. Both grew from twenty-pound puppies of fur and fun to intimidating giants who outweighed me, but were still mostly fur and fun. Many a bird built a nest from the fluff those lovely dogs shed when we went for walks. They were brave defenders of their territory, cowards in a thunder storm, and completely undisciplined. And I miss them.

Thanks to my sisters for giving me a lifetime of material. The sisters in the story are not my sisters, but they are sisters all the same. They will tell you the harsh truth and tell you the soft lie. They'll criticize you to your face and always have your back. They're the only ones who really understand when you complain about your parents.

My personal telescope is similar to Cassie's, but I purchased it through a conventional source and not from the widow of an eccentric astronomer. The battle with mosquitoes while trying to stargaze is real. I have yet to find an effective defense.

Special thanks to astrophotographer Robert Gendler, who kindly allowed the use of his gorgeous photo of the Ring Nebula in the cover art. It hovers in the background over the landscape. You can see the brilliant reds bleeding through the title. Its presence is subtle; but I know it's there, and now you do, too.

Meet the Author

Meet the Author

Like her character Cassie Windom, DANITH McPHERSON spends many nights under the stars with her telescope. In keeping with her Scottish heritage, she is a kiltmaker and proudly wears McPherson tartan. Her writing includes science fiction, fantasy and mysteries. Her short story "Roar at the Heart of the World" was selected for *The Year's Best Fantasy and Horror, Seventh Annual Collection.*

Find out more at https://danithmcpherson.com/

Check out her posts on facebook at Danith McPherson

amazon.com/author/danith

goodreads.com/danith

Leave a Review

If you enjoyed *Averted Vision*, please leave a review on Amazon and Goodreads through the links below. Like most authors, I depend on reviews to help readers find my stories. Thank you for reading!

Amazon

Goodreads

NOT HER FIRST MURDER
A Cassie Windom Mystery

On a trip to an island with strangers, Cassie hopes to connect with a memory that shaped her life. Instead she discovers a dead body.

Well, it's not her first murder.

Cassie struggles to solve a puzzle of missing pieces: a stolen necklace, a teen who vanished years ago, and the dangly private parts missing from a scandalous sculpture of a human torso.

Her best source of assistance is Dale, a high school student who knows Wolf Haunt Island, a place with a notorious reputation—and several social media sites. But Dale has his own secrets to keep and three dates for the dance.

Scan to order from Amazon

Join the unlikely duo as they romp through their second mystery together.

Scan to order from Barnes and Noble